AF557801

THE FUTURE
in the PAST

Also by Romila Thapar

Gazing Eastwards: Of Buddhist Monks and Revolutionaries in China

Indian Cultures as Heritage: Contemporary Pasts

On Nationalism

The Public Intellectual in India

The Past as Present: Forging Contemporary Identities through History

The Past Before Us: Historical Traditions of Early North India

The Aryan: Recasting Constructs, Three Essays

Somanatha: The Many Voices of History

Early India: From the Origins to AD *1300*

Cultural Pasts: Essays in Early Indian History

History and Beyond

Śakuntala: Texts, Readings, Histories

Cultural Transaction and Early India: Tradition and Patronage, Two Lectures

Interpreting Early India

The Mauryas Revisited

From Lineage to State: Social Formations of the Mid-First Millennium B. C. in the Ganges Valley

Voices of Dissent: An Essay

Ancient Indian Social History: Some Interpretations

The Past and Prejudice

Ancient India, Medieval India

A History of India: Volume 1

Aśoka and the Decline of the Mauryas

THE FUTURE *in the* PAST

ESSAYS & REFLECTIONS

ROMILA THAPAR

ALEPH

ALEPH BOOK COMPANY
An independent publishing firm
promoted by ***Rupa Publications India***

First published in India in 2023
by Aleph Book Company
7/16 Ansari Road, Daryaganj
New Delhi 110 002

ISBN: 978-93-95853-14-9

3 5 7 9 10 8 6 4 2

Printed in India

CONTENTS

VI: EDUCATION

PREFACE

The study of history has undergone immense change and has to be conveyed to the general reader. That is the impulse that made me decide to publish this book. History is no longer the comfortable, colonial, laid-back nineteenth century history that read as a string of narratives emerging from the 'great men syndrome' of kings and battles and territories lost and won. It has matured and extended itself into a discipline explaining and analysing a far more extensive past than had been earlier imagined; and equally importantly it presents to us the many interfaces of all that went into the making of events, and of cultures. Over the past several decades, I wrote many essays for *Seminar* magazine that had to do with various aspects of history, and it is these essays, suitably updated and revised, that are published here.

In the summer of 1959 my brother, Romesh Thapar, and his wife, Raj, were thinking of possible pertinent publications that would have relevance to the many discussions that were being held on the form and future of India. They were thinking of a publication that could be a starting point for discussion and debate on contemporary happenings. Slowly the idea of *Seminar* began to gel. It was thought of as a monthly, focussing on one theme or question of immediate interest. The format involved a knowledgeable person in a particular subject who would write a 'poser' presenting various facets of the theme and these were projected as provoking half a dozen persons with expertise to present aspects of the theme but from diverse perspectives, each focussing on one. It would work somewhat like the seminars that were taking place in real time and place. Each issue every month would then summarize a range of thinking on a particular theme or the question.

For many of us who were seeking a space to express our aspirations or our angst, centred on the times we were living in, *Seminar* provided just that space. We did not hesitate to express themes and explore them. We were after all in the process of thinking about the forms and the futures of Indian society, newly independent from colonial rule, and playing the role at that moment, of the elder sibling among many independent colonized societies mutating into independent nation-states. Our future as a secular democracy was in our hands and it was necessary that we speak out clearly. The early issues of *Seminar* were closely linked to such thoughts.

It was in a sense the uncertainty of our thinking which led to considering that perhaps it was more appropriate to explore ideas than to insist on the validity of formulations which were in any case being questioned. The exploration of ideas was to take the form of a regular publication, somewhat in the nature of a commentary on facets of the continuing present, approaching it from various perspectives. Therefore, it was to be a regular monthly publication in the format of a seminar with a selected theme each month, comprising essays from a few specialists or commentators on the subject, approaching it from various perspectives, and the collection resulting in informed opinion: the idea of *Seminar* was born.

Diversity of views was something new even if the diversity was to some extent directed by the choice of theme and authors. Some feared that this would result in an aimless potpourri. The insistence on diversity was troublesome to a few potential participants seeking single answers. Others, although sympathetic to the idea, feared that the publication would not succeed since a sufficiently informed opinion among Indian academics, journalists, and writers was not available to sustain such a publication. Indian writers, it was said, were notorious for not meeting deadlines and the envisaged publication would be difficult to coordinate.

The birth of the first issue was momentous. I was then teaching at the University of London and was home for the summer vacation. I was enthused by the discussion on whether the chosen theme—The Party in Power—was the most appropriate, and if the six contributors were the most qualified to explore the theme. This was crucial as it would establish the difference between *Seminar* and other serious magazines such as *Economic Weekly*, soon to morph into the *Economic and Political Weekly*. As it turned out, the initial choice set the sights to a high level of analyses and discussion.

There followed some weeks of anxiety. Would those who had agreed to write honour the agreement in time for the first issue to be published on 1 September 1959? I was at the time vacationing in Delhi and received messages from Romesh to meet the Delhi-based contributors and remind them of the deadline. This was daunting for me since it required my setting aside my diffidence in meeting people, and especially meeting those who were potentially major players on the Indian intellectual scene. It was the first time that was I venturing into conversations about the current situation in India with those that I held in awe. I found it exhilarating in its own way.

I started writing articles for *Seminar* in the early 1960s when I returned to India. We all recognized that historical subjects needed to be weaned away from colonial interpretations and analysed afresh in the manner in which many historical subjects the world over were being analysed. The purpose of history was going beyond narratives about the past to explanations of the past. Various issues surfaced and some had a connection with the themes I was researching as a historian or that I had been thinking about as a free Indian citizen and not as a colonial subject. My attempt was to see these themes in historical perspective, a perspective that was new in many cases. This also uncovered aspects that were not obvious to the general reader. I felt the need to do this. As happened, this activity clarified some of the fog in my own mind.

It was not inappropriate for a historian, who professionally writes about the past, to be commenting on the present. The past is a continuous process in which some of it may fall by the wayside, but some may also continue into the present albeit even if occasionally in disguise. Continuing into the present, means a possible contribution to the future. Continuation is often seen as those practices that do not change, or others that take on new forms, and yet others that evolve entirely new forms and are inducted into the existing scene. There can be a slower pace of change over many centuries, there can be a deliberate reinvention of what are thought to be ancient traditions, and there are still others that contradict such traditions or at least modify them.

Reading the articles that I wrote over the last fifty years, I am struck by how topical the issues remain. Have we therefore stood still, or have we only inched forward, or am I missing the wood for the trees? These topics are significant in today's India as some are still hovering over us, some remind us that we have not achieved what we set out to seventy-five years ago, and some show us the changes, although we may not recognize them—or for that matter where they are unpalatable, we may try not to recognize them.

I have revised the essays where necessary—the additions are by no means elaborate. They retain the thoughts and questions still pertinent, at least in the broader view if not the specific.

My thanks to David Davidar and Aienla Ozukum of Aleph Book Company for reading the essays so meticulously and suggesting changes that have made the essays more accessible to readers.

I would like to gift this collection of essays that originated with *Seminar* to the memory of the founders of *Seminar*, the late Romesh and Raj Thapar, and in the spirit of continuity from the past, also offer it to those who have manfully kept it going this half a century: their daughter, Malvika Singh, and her husband, Tejbir Singh.

I

HISTORY

1

IN DEFENCE OF HISTORY*

To comprehend the present and move towards the future requires an understanding of the past: an understanding that is sensitive, analytical, and open to critical enquiry. This was the turn taken by professional Indian historians writing in the decades since Independence and is now regarded as legitimate historical writing. Their studies were not only fine examples of historical enquiry but were also pointers to new ways of extending historical methods. They widened and sharpened the intellectual foundations of the discipline of history and enriched the understanding of the Indian nation. These studies either, directly or indirectly, have been attacked by the agencies of certain governments, thereby making a mockery of history. It is because of this assault on history that some of us have to speak in defence of the discipline of history.

INDIAN HISTORY AS WRITTEN BY professional historians in the 1960s and 1970s moved from being largely a body of information on dynasties and a recital of their 'glorious deeds' to a broad-

*An earlier version of this essay was first published in 2003. This essay was written during the rule of NDA-I when the NCERT school textbooks in history were heavily attacked by the then government as being anti-Indian, anti-national, and anti-Hindu, none of which was in any way correct. It was an attempt to negate the historian's history and replace it with fantasies of the past as imagined by Hindutva.

NDA-I, or the second Vajpayee ministry, came to power on 18 March 1998. A number of political parties joined this coalition government. NDA-I lasted for thirteen months, until October 1999, when the All India Anna Dravida Munnetra Kazhagam, led by J. Jayalalithaa, withdrew its support.

based study of social, economic, and political forms. In this there was a focus on religious movements, on patterns of the economy, and on cultural articulations. The multiple cultures of India were explored in terms of how they contributed to the making of Indian civilization. Therefore, many aspects of this multiplicity and its varying cultures—from that of forest dwellers, jhum cultivators, pastoralists, peasants, artisans, to that of merchants, aristocracies and specialists of ritual and belief—all found a place in the mosaic that was gradually being constructed. Identities were not singular but plural and the most meaningful studies were of situations where identities overlapped.

In recent years, Indian history has moved towards what some have described as almost a historical renaissance. The writing of Indian historians, ranging over many opinions and interpretations, were read and studied in the world of historical scholarship, not only in India but wherever there was an interest in comparative history. Historical interpretations at this time and in many parts of the world used methods of historical analyses that were derived from a range of theories that attempted to explain and interpret the past.

These included Marxism of various kinds, schools of interdisciplinary research such as the French Annales school, varieties of structuralism, and others. Lively debates on the Marxist interpretation of history, for example, led to the rejection of the Asiatic Mode of Production as proposed by Marx, and instead focused on testing whether other modes of production of Marxist history applied. There was no uniform reading among Marxists, leading to many stimulating debates on social and economic history. The ideas of historians other than Marxists, such as Marc Bloch, Fernand Braudel, and Henri Pirenne were included in these discussions. The intention was not to apply theories without questioning them, but to use comparative history to ask searching questions. If those who are currently busy attacking every serious historical interpretation took the trouble to read historiography—

the history of historical writing—they might begin to understand what history is all about.

Some of the more obvious examples of these debates relate to varying themes of historical interest. The changing history of caste in Indian society was being studied in detail to ascertain social change and explain social disparities. It was also being viewed in a comparative sense with other systems of social organization, such as the patterns of social hierarchy viewed as that of masters and slaves as in the Greco-Roman world, or of feudal lords and serfs of the medieval world or of the more easily recognizable class-oriented societies of recent centuries. Historians were asking the same questions that the Buddha had asked when told about Greek society: why do some societies have caste and others have a two-fold division of master and slave? These were questions that were not concerned primarily with making value judgements about caste but with trying to comprehend it as a system of organizing society.

The debate on whether or not there was feudalism in India has caught the attention not only of Indian historians but also of many medieval historians in other countries. The categories of feudalism are no longer restricted to a single definition of a feudal mode of production, for many permutations and combinations are recognized and these give new forms to the concept of feudalism.

The historical investigation of the range of ideas that went into shaping Indian nationalism became a testing ground for assessing forms of nationalism in societies other than the Indian. The ideology of nationalism was enquired into and the enquiries ranged from its role in intellectual history to its impact on lesser-known local and popular movements.

New themes came under the purview of historical investigation. Gender history focused on women, not merely as additional players but as primary players and their role in the genesis of some social forms began to be studied. Systems of knowledge came to be examined in terms of their influence on society and their function rather than restricting their history to merely repeating the obvious—that these were great advances in knowledge. The formation and definition of a range of Indian cultures came to include the formulations of culture from communities other than elite groups and this widened the base of social history. It also influenced the extensive study of new religious movements, their beliefs and rituals, and their audiences. An interest in the history of the environment suggested fresh hypotheses about the rise and decline of urban centres or the impact of hydraulic changes or deforestation on settlements of various kinds.

This intellectual efflorescence was suddenly sought to be terminated by the authorities in power. A blight began about ten years ago, culminating in the present enforced clampdown on the process of exploring ideas. This has reached the point where the attempt is to denigrate the independent intellectual and to undermine a historical understanding of our society and its past. It has taken a variety of forms. Sometimes it has taken the form of political actions, later it resorted to intervening in and closing institutions connected to academic research, and most recently it has taken to censoring books and textbooks, to reducing the curriculum to a ridiculous minimum of objective type questions, of deleting large portions of history of the medieval period, and giving historical study a questionable twist to favour only the garbled history of the majority community. Each action is orchestrated to a single aim.

The political action that initiated this blight was the tearing down of the Babri Masjid in 1992. This was an attempt to insist that a single culture and a single identity—a Hindu identity, defined not by Hindus in general but by those Hindus indulging in the destruction of the masjid—defines Indian culture. It was a violent, aggressive act of destruction claiming to glorify Hinduism but was a far cry from representing civilized Hindu values. Implicit in this act of destruction was the theory that it drew its legitimacy from history, that it was avenging the destruction of the temple at Somanatha by Mahmud of Ghazni and thereby setting right a wrong of history.

This fallacious idea that the past can be changed through destroying the surviving present-day heritage from the past was, of course, a blatant attack on history: for the axiom of history is that the past cannot be changed, but that if we intelligently understand the past, then the present and the future can be envisaged in a more positive manner. The destruction of an item in the heritage of our society, paralleled in the case of the Taliban destroying the images of the Buddha at Bamiyan, is the subordination of past history to present politics. The claim that the past can be annulled is actually a crass attempt to redefine people, their culture, and their history. The effort was and is to create a nation moulded not by all-inclusive national aspirations as of the earlier anti-colonial kind, but instead by a narrow, perverted nationalism identified with a particular version of a single religion. This makes it easier to impose an ideology of the sort that facilitates political mobilization and access to power. History is being made a handmaiden to this process.

Once the process comes into being, it encourages an appeal to what is projected as a collective memory. Collective memories are not innate and are constructed. As we all know from parallel political movements that have used history in this fashion, such as in Europe in the 1930s, the notion of a collective memory encourages simplistic explanations, single agendas even for explanations of happenings in the past, and preferably a replacing of historical fact with mythology. Collective memory can be ahistorical or even anti-historical and is therefore a convenient tool for spreading fallacies.

The Hindutva approach to history ignores all other histories and schools of interpretation. They are all dismissed as Marxist or equivalent. They are then replaced with a reconstruction of the past, based on dubious evidence and arguments, and which differs from the accepted mainstream history. Hindutva history derives its legitimacy from nineteenth-century colonial history. The periodization of Indian history maintained by James Mill divides Indian history into the Hindu, Muslim, and British periods. Mill's argument and that of many other colonial historians was that the Hindus and Muslims formed two distinct nations and that they were perpetually in conflict.

This has been taken over by the Hindutva ideology in which the enmity of Hindu and Muslim is foundational. It is argued that Hindu civilization suffered because of Muslim rulers who victimized the Hindus. This view is propagated despite the fact that some of the most creative forms of Hinduism such as Bhakti—the religion of devotional worship, that is now the most widely practised form of Hinduism—evolved in South India but became prevalent in North India during the period of Muslim rule. That Mill has been challenged by Indian historians and his views discarded makes not the slightest difference to the Hindutva insistence on supporting the two-nation theory.

A major contention is that Hindus were forcibly converted to Islam. This view is based on the claims of the court chroniclers of various sultanates. Some may well have been conversions under pressure. Others such as well-placed families, as for instance of some Rajputs, more frequently converted for reasons of social and political expediency. But the majority of conversions were by caste—jati—and these would have been voluntary and in the expectation that Islam held out a better deal of social equality than Hinduism.

There was of course no guarantee that the expectation would be met, not even where a caste hierarchy was meant to be terminated with conversion. But what is of interest is that where a caste converted, it generally retained its rules of marriage, custom, and some rituals and continued to have occupational relationships with Hindu castes. When weavers in some North Indian towns such as Chanderi converted to Islam, they continued their earlier relationship with Hindu textile merchants. Prior to their conversion they were anyway regarded as low caste and the traders maintained a social distance, and this distance remained.

The issue of conversion that was once a matter of historical debate is now being used politically to threaten Muslims and Christians. Historians have shown repeatedly that conversions did not create a monolithic, uniform community. Those that followed Islam had immense variations not only between the Arabs and the Turks or between the Sunni and Shia, but also between what might be called mixed Islamic sects such as the Khojas, Bohras, Navayath, and Mappilas. These variations enriched the culture of each community and endowed them with varying identities of language, region, and custom—identities that frequently intersected with those of other groups in the area. In trying to understand the history of communities, whether Hindu, Muslim, or any other, there are many distinctive forms that give multiple identities to such groups. These have evolved from a long process of social negotiation, some of it contentious and some of it convivial. These identities cannot be negated as in the Hindutva interpretations that sweep them all into a single religion-defined communal entity.

Another aspect of the relations between Hindus and Muslims in the ideology of Hindutva focuses on the Muslim destruction of temples in the past. This is not denied by historians but attempts are made to try and place such actions in historical perspective and count the numbers without exaggerating them. This was not the only activity of Muslim rulers and temple destruction has to be juxtaposed with other undertakings that were not destructive. This is also related to the question of what we chose to recall from the past and reiterate, and what we chose to forget. Destroying a temple was a demonstration of power on the part of invaders, irrespective of whether they were Muslim or Hindu. We chose to forget that there were Hindu kings who destroyed temples, either wilfully as did Harshadeva of Kashmir to acquire the wealth of the temples in a period of fiscal crisis or as part of a campaign as in the case of the victorious Paramara raja destroying temples built by the defeated Chaulukya.

My purpose in drawing attention to this is not to add up the scores, but to argue that temple destruction was not merely an act of religious hostility. Temples were certainly places of ritual space and had a religious identity. But royal temples were also statements of power and were surrogate political institutions representing royalty. They were depositories of wealth and centres of finance, they maintained social demarcations through allowing some castes to enter the temple but excluding others, and they were the cultural nucleus of at least the elite groups of a region. Temple destruction and its aftermath therefore calls for historical explanations of a wide-ranging kind. It cannot be made the justification for destroying or threatening to destroy mosques and churches in the present day.

In order to assert the superiority and antiquity of the Hindu community as the indigenous and earliest inhabitants of India, the theory of Aryan identity is being revived but in a curious way. The Orientalist and philologist Max Müller had argued in the nineteenth century that the Aryans were the foundation of Indian civilization and that they came from Central Asia. The first part of Max Müller's argument has been adopted by Hindutva ideologues and the second part has been stood on its head. The Aryans are said to be the foundation of Indian civilization but at the same time they are said to be indigenous. They are now being equated with the authors of the Indus civilization, even though the Indus civilization was pre-Aryan and distinct from the Aryan. It was a mercantile culture focusing on its many cities and artisanal production and trade, and using a pictorial script, whereas the Vedic corpus depicts a cattle-keeping society unfamiliar with both urban culture and literacy. The Vedic corpus is rich in its depiction of an agropastoral culture, but this is in no way the same as the urban sophistication of the Indus cities.

The American theosophist Henry Olcott associated with

Madame Blavatsky, founder of the Theosophical Society, was the first to argue in the nineteenth century, as do the Hindutva ideologues now, that the Aryans of India were not only indigenous but were the fountainhead of world civilization, and that all the achievements of human society had their origins in India and travelled out from India. Vedic Sanskrit was the mother language of all languages and this reverses the argument of Sanskrit being descended from Indo-European. The thesis of indigenous Aryans also dismisses the argument of Jyotiba Phule and the Dalits that the Aryans were alien upper castes who oppressed the lower castes of Indian society. Caste Hindus, according to the Hindutva theory, have a lineal descent from the Aryans. This descent is also sought to be established by arguing that the authors of the Rig Veda were the builders of the Harappan cities. Further that only the Hindus can legitimately call themselves indigenous for Muslims and Christians are foreigners since they practise religions that originated outside India. Both the foundational theories of history according to Hindutva, namely, that the Hindus and Muslims were two separate nations, and that the Aryans were indigenous to India, are taken from foreign historians writing on India—James Mill and Henry Olcott.

The intention of Hindutva history is to support the vision of its founding fathers—Vinayak Damodar Savarkar and Madhav Sadashivrao Golwalkar—and to project the beginnings of Indian history with the indigenous Aryans. This contradicts the archaeological and the linguistic evidence of the Indo-Aryan speakers—but then who cares for evidence when a political message becomes the primary function of history. This theory ignores all the other societies, some of which were speaking Dravidian and Munda languages, of which there are traces in Vedic Sanskrit. It ignores the widely accepted argument among historians today that the concept of Aryan is not an exclusive racial identity, but the social evolution of a group speaking Indo-Aryan incorporating linguistic, cultural, and ritual features, brought in by migrants from across the Indo-Iranian borderlands.

Desperate attempts are being made to prove that the Vedic people and the Harappans were identical. The linguistic evidence is ignored, particularly the presence of Dravidian and Munda groups of languages, and only Sanskrit receives attention. The reading of archaeological evidence is forced to the point of supporting the equation of Harappan with Vedic, even if Harappan onagers have to be identified as the horses of the Vedic ashvamedha. Contrary to the evidence so far excavated, there is an insistence that the origins of the Indus civilization be located on the banks of what some identify as the Sarasvati River. This would allow it to be called the Sarasvati civilization, further evoking a Vedic presence. But neither the identity of the ancient Sarasvati with any known river nor the beginning of the Harappa culture on its banks has been confirmed. Yet this wishful thinking is being passed off as fact.

A history having been invented, the next question is how it is to be implemented? It is being implemented at two levels. One is the level of projecting this kind of history through research institutions and the other is through the school curriculum. It has taken on the dimensions of a campaign with the full involvement of the Education Ministry and all its agencies.

Research centres have now been staffed with those who have an ideological commitment to Hindutva history. The council and supervisory positions in the Indian Council for Historical Research (ICHR) in Delhi and their research projects are also oriented to the same kind of history. This makes it necessary for such institutions to include non-historians as experts, since they will accept the orders of the ministry in writing the history that the government wants.

Whereas earlier the ICHR used to finance a variety of historical organizations, attempts are now being made to exclude those that support secular history which is dismissed by the ICHR as being left-wing history. The Indian Institute of Advanced Study (IIAS) in Shimla now has research projects that focus on ancient Hindu civilization and more particularly Vedic culture with a particular orientation with other aspects of history receiving far less attention.

These interventions by the ministry have been politicized by statements to the effect that earlier these institutions were under the control of left-wing academics so now it is the turn of the right-wing academics. If the debate is formulated in terms of leftist and rightist historians then each time the party in power changes, the curriculum and the syllabus will also have to change. History is not a shuttlecock that can be thrown back and forth in accordance with the views of governments. It also means that since procedures are not being observed, not only the curriculum but also the research programmes will change. And this is precisely what has happened.

Excuse after excuse was made to prevent the publication of certain volumes of documents already in the press, as part of the project entitled, 'Towards Freedom'. It was first said that they had not been properly edited, then that there were no indexes, and now they have to be cleared by yet another committee although they have already been cleared. A source quoted from the ICHR states that the real reason was to prevent the publication of documents which apparently showed that a Hindu right-wing organization was collaborating with the British.

Procedures of functioning as they have been laid down and followed earlier should continue to be followed. There is also a need for respecting the professional training in a discipline and ensuring that professionally trained people are appointed to the agencies that determine education. Is it just a coincidence that in educational institutions including the NCERT, recent appointments are said to be of those partial to the RSS if not party cadres?

The other action relating to institutions is of course even more high-handed. It takes the form of arbitrarily shutting down institutions of research or threats to do so as and when the government wishes. Recently the BJP in Madhya Pradesh has attacked the scientific programmes of Eklavya, an educational NGO that produces school-level books on the sciences and social sciences. If these threats become a pattern, it will be disastrous for research and for a secular investment in Indian society.

Shutting down an institution is a sign of extreme insecurity on the part of those who do so. By way of contrast, even though the ICHR is now manned by those who are sympathetic to Hindutva history, the rest of us as historians are not demanding the closing of the council but are trying to point out that it should include historians reflecting a wider range of views. Given that there are attempts to substitute mainstream history with propaganda, it is all the more necessary to have independent bodies to counteract the hegemony of the propaganda.

To argue that Marxist historians when placed in charge of institutions bring about a hijacking of history to left-wing ideology is a view resulting from an unfamiliarity with Indian historical research of recent years. The most wide-ranging debate on pre-modern Indian history has been the debate on whether or not there had been feudalism in India. The polymath D. D. Kosambi's understanding of feudalism deviated from the model of the strictly Marxist feudal mode of production. Many of us were inspired by Kosambi's work, yet the histories we have written don't necessarily follow only his line of thought.

The major critiques of the feudal mode were initiated by Marxist historians and were later added to by those who were not Marxists in their orientation. What resulted from this debate has been the exploration of many areas of Indian history in terms of the nature of the state, polity, economy, and religion that have given us immense insights into our past.

The confrontation among historians today is not between leftist and rightist historians, nor over establishing a Marxist view of history, as is crudely stated by some, but over the right to debate interpretations of history. There cannot be a single, definitive, official history. Such a definition of history is restricted to those for whom being a historian is merely an end to getting a government job. If some of us feel that Hindutva history is less history and more mythology, we should have the right to say so without being called 'intellectual terrorists' and being threatened with arrest and being put down. In the final analysis, history is an intellectual enterprise and does have an intellectual dimension in its understanding of the past, however much Hindutva ideology may try and prevent that.

Basic to the Hindutva interpretation of history is the attempt to give a single definition to Indian culture, the roots of which are said to lie in Vedic foundations. This annuls the notion of a multicultural society. It destroys the sensitive and variant relations that have existed throughout Indian history between dominant cultures and subordinate cultures and between the focus of a central culture and that of regional cultures. This sensitivity is particularly important today in forging cultural identities that are subcontinental but at the same time incorporate the articulations of the region. These are the demands of a federal or near federal polity.

Let me illustrate this. If the new school curriculum is to consist of what has been recommended by the ministry, children are now going to be taught Vedic Maths, Sanskrit, the glories of Vedic culture, yoga and consciousness, and a mish-mash of subjects under the rubric of social studies. This may be well motivated—although I doubt that—but it is inadequate for any exploration of knowledge or of coping with the complexities of our times and our aspirations. Where would a young person go looking for good jobs if all that he or she knows anything about is Vedic culture. Vedic culture is fine in its own place, but it is not a substitute for modern knowledge of various kinds.

These changes have not been subjected to the normal rules of the ministry, hitherto observed by other governments. So, the Central Advisory Board of Education (CABE), which is required to meet to discuss and pass any modifications of the curriculum, has not been called, and therefore the new curriculum framework has not been passed by it, as required. Thus, the changes take on the character of being illegitimate if the rules of the ministry are still tenable. Nevertheless, the ministry and its agencies are going ahead and paying no attention to procedures. Perhaps this is their definition of an effective government. The Supreme Court passed a stay order but that was some time back and by now it seems not to matter to the ministry that its changes have not been approved by any independent body. Professional bodies are now treated as of no consequence.

Let's look at this curriculum in the context of literacy and education. The highest literacy percentages today are in Kerala, Himachal Pradesh, and Mizoram—all sustaining very different societies. To what extent should the difference be taken into consideration when drawing up a syllabus? Growing up in Kerala or in Himachal Pradesh have very different requirements and some of these have to be conceded.

Kerala has a culture of wet rice cultivation with lineally organized homesteads, of horticulture in the production of pepper and spices, fisheries and maritime trade and a diversity of religious groups of various religions. Himachal Pradesh has none of these. Its villages are nucleated, pastoralism is common and the crops and their cultivation are different. Himachal Pradesh has religious sects largely drawing on Puranic Hinduism and to a smaller extent populations of Sikhs, Buddhists, and Muslims. Kerala has a variant on these and has large populations of Muslims and Christians going back to early times. The language of Kerala, Malayalam, is entirely different from the Punjabi, Dogri, and Tibetan of Himachal Pradesh. Some basic educational demands therefore will also be different and such differences have to be woven into the curriculum.

But what they do have in common are the aspirations that result from education. Schooling and curriculum would need to have some relationship with the local context and ethos, with employment openings and some regional concerns. The question would be how best these can be introduced without denying the importance of national concerns. Educational curriculum has to be such that regional concerns are recognized as an intrinsic part of those that are of national interest. This would ultimately be more viable than forcing everyone to conform to a top-down pattern.

If we agree that we are a society of many cultures then the presence of the many should be registered. This can only be done through centres of research with a regional orientation. This does not mean only the histories of the current dominant communities or castes in a region but a discussion of the interface of the cultures of a region. The danger today is that in an effort to restrict history to that of the upper caste Hindu—as seems to be the game plan of the central government—the richness of the many other cultures will be eliminated. This makes it necessary to have state councils of historical research where the regional variation can be articulated and at the same time can interface with the national. This should be a more considered approach than just a history of local heroes and legends. It also makes it necessary for the curriculum to be worked out in association with the State Council of Educational Research and Training (SCERT).

In replacing history with social studies we thought that perhaps some of these ideas reflecting the presence of varying cultures would find a place in the syllabus. But the syllabus has no sensitivity to the varying requirements of different parts of the country. The new social studies syllabus is a package consisting of some history, economics, civics, and geography. For all its modern-sounding jargon, the history syllabus derives from a nineteenth-century colonially oriented outline of history. It is a body of information rather than a method of critical enquiry about the past. It is substantially a listing of dynastic history and moves away from the kind of history that has in the last half century advanced our understanding of the past. It is essentially therefore an out-of-date syllabus.

There is no evidence that any academic discussion on history or on the pedagogy of writing textbooks preceded the drawing up of the syllabus or the writing of the new textbooks. And it is all being done clandestinely in a cloak and dagger fashion. There is a refusal to reveal the names of the authors of the new textbooks or of any historians that may have been consulted—perhaps no historians were consulted. This is a contrast to the complete transparency that was observed when the previous NCERT textbooks were being drafted and a number of known historians were involved in discussing their content and there were consultations with teachers teaching history in schools. The minister has stated that the heads of various religious organizations would vet the history textbooks, although we are not told who they are. This predicts the kind of narratives we can expect in the textbooks and again challenges the discipline of history.

The treatment of the syllabus and the changes now brought in speak volumes about the attitude towards and meaning of education to the current ministry in charge of education. There is a constant repetition of the aim being to equip students to face challenges with confidence but no mention of familiarizing students with systems of knowledge and enquiry. The syllabus to this day remains a heavily North Indian centred one with bits added on indiscriminately from a few other areas. The original syllabus had fifteen units on ancient India and three on medieval India. This met with considerable criticism, so virtually overnight the three were increased to twenty-two. Those of us who have worked on syllabuses are amazed that such massive changes can be introduced so quickly, and one wonders whether the exercise is being taken at all seriously.

What then should we think of as the process of ensuring a transition of knowledge that is independent and draws on critical enquiry. It would seem that no dialogue is possible with government agencies. We have therefore to think of alternate strategies.

At one level one would have to work towards establishing councils of historical research and local archives in state capitals and large cities in the various states so that regional histories can be treated in a seriously professional manner and not be reduced to being dependent on the patronage of those in power. Historical records are no longer limited to files in state archives. Over the last century the sources of history have been extended to include a vast range of material that tells us about our past. The range, apart from official documents, includes archaeology, linguistics, inscriptions, coins, monuments, documents of professional groups and of private families, and the oral tradition.

This range means that statements about the past have to draw from a multiplicity of records and if they contradict each other this may be the source of a new illumination about authorship and audience. All these records have to be preserved—not just the state archives and gazetteers. This can only be done by state councils, properly organized and financed and carrying out research into and preserving historical material. And it should be the function of these councils to act in dialogue with those responsible for drawing up the history syllabus and curriculum for schools.

At another level it would be required of independent historians to be more involved in the teaching of history in schools—at least in terms of drawing up an alternate and viable syllabus to that of the NCERT, based on both professional expertise and pedagogy. This would not be an innovation as there are groups that have been doing just this and in some cases their textbooks have been used very effectively in state schools as well as private schools. The example of the Eklavya group comes to mind. Their work will have to be continued.

Civil society will now have to take the initiative in planning educational centres. The availability of more than a single textbook would provide a challenge to those that are anxious to restrict the writing of textbooks to a single source and thereby control knowledge. If such textbooks, different from those produced by the NCERT are reliable, friendly to young readers, and cheaply available, such an alternative system might be an excellent outcome of the present crisis. Given the high return on textbook publishing, there might even be a competition among publishers to acquire rights to publishing such books.

A significant difference between pre-modern and modern history is that now we construct history by analysing the past, and asking why and how events happened, and by making casual connections that are based on logic and reasoning. Questioning the data is crucial. Since history was not a distinct discipline in pre-modern times there are no theories of history to explain the past. The same holds for India. There are narratives claiming to be describing past events and persons, but no theory of explanation. However, there are ways of representing the past that have patterns, such as in the epics, Puranas, inscriptions, biographies, and chronicles. As in every other culture, theories explaining the past evolved in modern times. Such theories have also to be understood as aids to analysing the past. Theory cannot be applied literally or in an identical way to all cultures. Obviously, there are degrees of difference because of varying contexts. These can help in formulating a range of questions to be put to the data. All histories that claimed to be interpreted in terms of Marxist/Weberian/Foucauldian, or whatever theory, may have a broad overall framework in the questions considered, but will differ in interpreting that data. In some ways the most serious challenge is the closing down of discussion since it is an attempt to close the mind. This is not a matter that concerns history alone, as it is equally important to all human sciences—be it the humanities, the social sciences, or other sciences. This is a frontal attack on knowledge and as professionals engaged in the furtherance of knowledge, it seems to me that we have no choice but to oppose it. The world has moved on since the colonialism of the nineteenth century and we have come to value independent thinking. There are enough historians in this country that will continue to write independently. There will be enough historical concerns growing out of the multiple cultural aspects of our society to ensure that the Indian mind is never closed.

2

THE PERENNIAL ARYANS*

The history of the second half of the first millennium had earlier been problematic because of a lack of diverse evidence and because of attempts to trace concepts such as race, language identities, and nationalism back to this period. These are modern concepts and have to be examined as such, even if attempts are made to take them back in time.

WHEN THE THEORY OF THE Aryan race was first thought up in nineteenth-century Europe, its inventors did not know that it would lead to a holocaust in Europe and to riots in South Asia. If Aryanism was for Germany the nationalistic denial of barbarism among the German tribes who opposed Rome, in South Asia too it has become foundational to a nationalistic identity. The theory of the Aryan race is not limited to some facets of Indian nationalism. It has also been used in the debate on the Sinhala identity, where some Sinhala groups claiming to be of Aryan origin demarcated themselves from the Tamils. Degrees of Aryanness in contemporary Sinhalas has been talked of. The issue is not merely one of degrees of racial purity, but, as in the Indian situation, also hinges on the question of who were the first inhabitants of the land who might be associated with the introduction of civilization. That these questions in themselves are no longer relevant seldom strikes those who pose them

In all such movements there is little problem in discarding attempts at factual history and replacing it with mythology which

*An earlier version of this essay was first published in 1992.

is important to the self-perception of a narrow nationalism arising from a particular social group. The search is for an identity in modern times but its parameters are imposed by the past. This is then justified as the rewriting of history from a national perspective. In fact, it is really the inoculation of a particularly vicious racist ideology into the understanding of history. And when this is done at the level of school textbooks, it becomes all the more pernicious.

In references to nationalism, it is necessary to distinguish between the Indian nation in the broad sense where all Indians were regarded as equal citizens and the intention was to make them participants in social well-being, and the more narrowly defined nationalism of a section of society, where such a section is seen as more equal than others and certainly more privileged because it constitutes the majority. When nationalism draws on ideas such as Hindutva or Hindu nationalism, then it seeks to justify itself through a partisan history. The winds of change—what is referred to as the rewriting of history—which have been introduced into textbooks by the BJP governments are not motivated by historical accuracy. Rather, they are an attempt to find historical bases for its own ideology. I would like to discuss two of these changes, namely, that the Aryans were indigenous to India and that Chandragupta Maurya and Chanakya were instrumental in creating a nationalist ethos in ancient India.

It is as well to remember that the term Aryan applies only to a language: it refers to, and is a shortened version of, Aryan-speaking-peoples. People cannot be identified racially as Aryan since there is no such racial category. But the word 'race' is loosely and incorrectly used in general parlance. Hence the frequency of expressions such as 'the Indian race' or 'the Hindu race' which, strictly speaking, are meaningless. The Aryan race was an invention of the European imagination and it has now been discarded in the West, except among a variety of white racist groups supporting terrorism. There is also no such thing as 'a pure race' for people have been constantly intermingling.

People can only be identified as Aryan-speaking and, since the same language can be spoken by people belonging to different racial groups, depending on the historical context. Language cannot be equated with race. For example, it would be grossly wrong for historians in AD 4000 to assume that since all North Americans in AD 1900 spoke English, therefore they must have all belonged to the same race. Historical situations involving more than one group identified as races speaking the same language have been frequent in the early past as well. Given the diversity of origin of the peoples of the Indian subcontinent and the numerous migrations and movements in this and the larger geographical area from 6000 BC onwards, it would be incorrect to assume that if they spoke languages of the same language family, they must have been racially of the same stock. This axiom that language cannot be equated with race was stated even by Max Müller, although sometimes confused by him, but was also ignored in popular theories in the nineteenth century. Therefore, to state that the Aryans were indigenous to India makes little sense. The label 'Arya' is used by both the early Indians and the early Iranians who called themselves Arya and Airiia. This distinction was on both using an Aryan language

Who then were the Aryans? Aryan, which is a language, referred to technically as Indo-Aryan or Old Indo-Aryan, is known to us in India in its earliest form as the language of the Vedas: the earlier Rig Veda and the later Sama, Yajur, and Atharva Vedas. Old Indo-Aryan has as its ancestral language Indo-European. It also has similarities with Old Avestan and Old Iranian and philological parallels with fragments from Northern Syrian inscriptions and some European languages. The earliest evidence for compositions in Old Indo-Aryan comes from the Rig Veda and the geographical background of this text relates to Afghanistan and the Punjab and particularly the area which is now in Pakistan—the Sapta Sindhu. Compositions by speakers of Indian and Iranian Aryan languages are concentrated in north-eastern Iran and north-western India with a tiny presence in a few scattered sources in the eastern Mediterranean area.

The language of the Rig Veda has affinities to Old Avestan, closer than the language of the later Vedas. This earlier link with Avestan indicates a possible movement from north-east Iran to India by Aryan speakers. The geographical background to the later Vedas is that of the western and middle Ganga plain and the language of these texts indicates a greater borrowing from non-Aryan languages associated with this area. The language therefore changed and evolved over the centuries as it was used by a variety of ethnic peoples, some of whom, or whose forefathers, originally spoke other languages.

Vedic Sanskrit provides evidence of dialect variations which can be used to trace the geographical movement of the speakers of Old Indo-Aryan, to assist in trying to work out a chronology for the composition of the Vedas and to assess the importance of non-Aryan language elements in them. The geographical migration is from the north-west into the Ganga plain. The generally accepted chronology is that the Rig Vedic hymns were composed over a period extending from about 1500 to 1000 BC, with some hymns of a slightly later period. The other three Vedas are dated to approximately 800 to 500 BC or thereabouts. Some references to what have been interpreted as configurations of astronomy were used to suggest dates of about 4000 BC for these hymns, but there is now little general acceptance among scholars for this argument. Planetary positions could have been observed in earlier times and such observations been handed down as part of an oral tradition. So, these do not constitute proof of the chronology of the Vedic hymns.

Some non-Aryan languages were current in northern India where the Aryan language spread. These have been listed in broad categories as Proto-Dravidian, Austro-Asiatic, and Tibeto-Burman. Archaeological evidence points to settlements and cultures in northern India prior to 1500 BC. These cultures are likely to have been speakers of any of the non-Aryan languages.

Vedic compositions make it clear that they were speakers of other languages among whom the Aryan speakers settled and the former could not always use the Aryan language correctly and were therefore treated as alien by the Aryan-speakers. Terms such as mridhra-vac and mleccha referred to those who spoke Indo-Aryan incorrectly. Given the present evidence, the use of the Aryan language in India does not predate the Rig Veda. Indo-Aryan has elements of non-Aryan spoken in India, and such elements are absent in Iranian Aryan.

There are characteristics of non-Aryan languages, such as retroflex consonants, even in Rig Vedic Sanskrit. The notion of what was the correct language would also undergo change. The language of the Harappans, when the script has been deciphered, will mark a major breakthrough in the history of language in northern India. The script remains undeciphered so far. Attempts to read it as Proto-Dravidian have been more systematic than those reading it as Indo-Aryan. The reconstructions of Sanskrit which have been suggested deviate from the known rules of Sanskrit grammar. However, the language of the Harappans remains an open question.

The linguistic evidence of Vedic Sanskrit supports the coming into India of Aryan speakers most likely from Iran and Central Asia but does not support the notion that India was the homeland of the Aryan-speaking people. Attempts have therefore been made to use a different set of evidence and to try and identify one of the many archaeological cultures in India as 'Aryan'. However, material remains which constitute archaeological cultures cannot provide the identity of the language used by the authors of the cultures in the absence of a script. At most a comparison can be made between the material remains found in excavations and the description of material culture from the texts, in an effort to analyse the nature of given societies.

But even this has little to do with defining and identifying the language or languages used by the people whose settlements have been excavated. There is therefore little point turning to archaeology for evidence of the Aryans, barring a comparison of material culture, yet attempts are made to do this. Because references are made to the supposed archaeological evidence, it would be as well to briefly review the archaeological picture in northern India at that time.

The geographical gaze of the Harappans was westwards since they were providing articles of trade—pepper and lapis lazuli—to the Mesopotamians, taking the route via the Gulf. There was maritime contact between the Indus civilization and Mesopotamia during the Harappan period in the third millennium BC. However, the languages of Mesopotamia were not of the Indo-European group. It is only later, between 1800 and 1500 BC, that there is evidence of a small, temporary scatter of languages of the Indo-European family suddenly appearing in Turkey and Mesopotamia.

The Indus civilization came as far the Ganga–Yamuna Doab and northern Maharashtra. The overlap with Harappan sites is limited to the Punjab extending to the Doab. The migration of the Indo-Aryans, so vividly described in the Shatapatha Brahmana, was in the opposite direction, namely eastwards from the Doab to the middle Ganga plain. It is difficult to equate the Harappan civilization with descriptions in the Vedic compositions since they each represent entirely different cultures. Urban centres were the focus of Harappan life, and familiar with writing and trade. The culture was prior to the discovery of iron and evidence for the use of the horse is sparse if at all. Vedic culture, on the other hand, is not urban but is pastoral and agricultural, has no knowledge of writing and extensive trading, knows the use of iron, and the horse has a central role both in function and ritual.

Some Harappan traits did continue into later periods since there are a few sites with overlapping levels of late Harappan and post-Harappan cultures. Some of these traits could have been picked up by the Aryan-speakers. There is evidence of the

Gandhara Grave culture in Punjab and Haryana possibly having contacts with trans-Indus areas. Possibly small migrant groups were arriving in the north-west and merging with the local population. However, the evidence of the Gandhara Grave culture does not spread into the middle Ganga plain.

In Haryana and the western Ganga plain, there was an earlier Ochre Colour Pottery culture going back to about 1500 BC. Elements of the Chalcolithic cultures using Black-and-Red Ware also surface. Only some varieties of these post-Harappan cultures, identifiable by their pottery, are found beyond the Indus. Yet this would be expected if 'the Aryans' were a people and indigenous to India with some diffusion to Iran, and if the attempt was to find archaeological correlates for the affinities between Old Indo-Aryan and Old Iranian.

If there is no evidence of a diffusion outward there is also no evidence of a large-scale invasion from West Asia via the north-west into the Indian subcontinent. The idea of such an invasion followed from a mention in the Rig Veda of the destruction of purs (walled settlements) which was interpreted as alluding to the destruction of the Harappan cities by 'the Aryans'. However, it is now generally accepted that the decline of the Harappan cities was due to environmental changes of various kinds and a possible break in trading activities, and not to any invasion.

The likely picture is that there were small groups of Aryan-speaking migrants from across the northern mountains who mingled with various populations and cultures in the north-west of India. And gradually over the centuries the language which evolved, Old Indo-Aryan, spread from Punjab and Afghanistan to the Indo-Gangetic watershed and the Ganga valley.

And what do Indian sources have to say on the subject? The imposition of the Aryan theory of race on ancient Indian history began with the reading of the Rig Veda in which mention is made of the arya. The Rig Veda distinguishes between the two varnas—the arya and the dasa. The difference is substantially cultural—a difference in customs, religious practices, and perhaps language and a possible physical difference in that some dasas are said to have dark skin and snub noses although the latter reading cannot be taken as evidence of a racial difference. Nor does this imply, as is popularly believed, that the arya was invariably tall, fair, long-nosed, and blue-eyed.

The term arya is more frequently used with reference to those who are familiar with Sanskrit, occupy an honoured or respectable status, are generous in giving dana (gifts) and are given a high varna status. This did not stop the good Brahmana from accepting donations from the dasa and performing rituals for them. Like all cattle-herding societies, the clans of the Rig Veda were given to endless skirmishes and cattle raids, a few of which were visualized as battles. These were not always between the arya and the dasa, as is popularly supposed, but were also among and between the clans occupying an honoured status.

Some of these clans may have been given the status but in other texts are said to be of uncertain origin. Thus the Purus, ancestral to the protagonists of the war in the Mahabharata, are described as descended from an asura rakshasa (quite clearly not an 'Aryan') and, not surprisingly, speak a faulty Sanskrit (mridhra-vac). To argue then that the Rig Veda in differentiating between the arya and the dasa varna is basically describing two separate racial entities is merely to impose a nineteenth-century European concept of race onto the Rig Veda.

What spread from the north-west in the Ganga valley was not a body of racially pure 'Aryans', but rather the use of the language, Old Indo-Aryan. This is likely to have been through its adoption by local people and its function in ritual. Why it was so adopted raises a number of major questions for the historian. Answers may lie in the language being associated with various technologies which provided it with an edge in the north Indian environment. Those through whom the language arrived in a new area and those who, living in such an area, started using it, were speakers of divergent languages. The process of bilingualism may have been one reason for the changes in Old Indo-Aryan.

Elements of non-Aryan were incorporated in Vedic Sanskrit because it was being used in the vicinity of non-Aryan speakers and by initially non-Aryan speakers themselves. The language therefore underwent change when it came to be used by a variety of people. Such changes can be traced in the vocabulary and syntax which draw on other languages. The incorporation of new features in the language points to a parallel intermixing of peoples and ways of life. The authors of sections of the Vedas and of the Mahabharata and Ramayana were members of the upper castes and, in theory, observed the rules of varna.

However, varna roles, which are erroneously believed to have preserved racial purity, were happily broken. There is the example of Veda Vyasa or Krishna Dvaipayana, the redactor of the Mahabharata: he was the son of the Brahmana Parashara and a low caste fisherwoman, Satyavati. There is no way in which he could pass for an 'Aryan' if a racial meaning is given to the term. And there are other such examples. As far as being of 'the Aryan race', such persons were by now too mixed through marriage unions of various kinds to be anything other than the result of local interbreeding.

The question then is, why is it so necessary to insist that 'the Aryans' as a broader category originated from India? More so when seen that historically there have been multiple migrations from neighbouring geographical regions into India from the earliest historical times. In part it is an attempt to argue that what are perceived as the roots of Indian and European culture originated in India, and India is therefore the cradle of what used to be called the Indo-European culture; forgetting of course that the research of this century has indicated that the Indo-European or 'Aryan' component is no longer the foundation of civilization in either India or Europe but is a linguistic manifestation in the evolution of early history. At another level it is an attempt to project a unified, continuous Indian identity where Aryanism, encapsulated in the culture of the Vedas and the upper castes, is not only at the root of Indian history, but moulds history and is projected as the major cultural expression of India. Furthermore, that what are described as 'Aryan' beliefs and values, are eternal. This definition of 'Aryan' draws neither from Indian history nor from linguistics or for that matter, the modern study of culture.

The equation of language and race in Europe in the nineteenth century was important to claiming racial purity for the European aristocracy and to build up anti-Semitism. In the Indian context it was equally important for claiming racial purity for the upper castes. Caste society was explained earlier as a system of racial segregation where the separateness of each caste was maintained over the centuries by controlling marriage through caste rules. Thus even into modern times those castes which were familiar with Sanskrit learning—inevitably the upper castes—could claim racial purity. Implicit in this theory therefore is the superiority of upper castes and the edging out of lower castes as contributors to the Indian mainstream. This is not a revival of past national glory but an attempt to maintain social inequality through recourse to 'history'.

Empirical evidence as we have it today supports neither the theory of Aryan race, nor that of the invasion of India by 'the Aryans', nor for that matter the theory of the indigenous Indian origin of 'the Aryans'. This is not of interest only to historians. The theory of the Aryans being a people has been seen as fundamental to the understanding of the identity of modern Indians and the question of identity is central to the change in Indian society from caste to class. The upholding of a false theory is dangerous. The next step can be to move from the indigenous origin of 'the Aryan' to proposing the notion of an 'Aryan nation'.

Nationalism cannot be taken back to the Mauryan period. Nationalism is a historically specific condition and the kind of nationalism that one is familiar with in the last two centuries has to do with industrialization and imperialism, both in Europe and in what were the colonies. It was this nationalism in India that emphasized an independent rule by Indians and the equality of Indian citizenship. To say that Chandragupta Maurya and Chanakya were nationalists because they stood up against the foreign (i.e., Greek-Hellenistic) invaders in the north-west and that there was a consciousness of an all-India entity called Jambudvipa or Bharatavarsha is not history.

Chandragupta Maurya or Chanakya are not known to have organized Indian kings against Alexander and the Greeks. The young Chandragupta's ambition was to capture the throne of the Nanda king at Pataliputra and he appears to have been less interested in the Greeks. Towards the end of his reign, he made an amicable treaty with the Greek Seleucus Nicator ruling in Iran. As for Chanakya's fight against foreign forces, a Sanskrit play of later date, the *Mudrarakshasa*, presents a picture of sordid intrigue on the part of Chanakya in which the Greeks and Persians are merely listed as among the many allies of the Nanda king. They do not even arouse a comment from Chanakya. It does seem interesting that Chanakya should now be projected as the conscience keeper of Indian nationalism, given that he had so little use for political morality!

As regards the consciousness of the unity of India, the precise connotation of the terms used for India need to be clarified. The terms used by West Asians—the Hindush of the Persian kings, the Indoi of the Greeks, the Indica of Latin writers and the al-Hind of the Arabs—were all terms derived from the name of the Indus, the Sindhu, which they saw as the great divide, and the terms used referred to the land on the other side. It was not a geographically exact definition but very broadly so, and what came to be included in it depended on current knowledge of the area on the part of the writers.

For the Persians it was only the north-west. The Greek and Latin sources expand their descriptions of India as and when they become familiar with new areas of Indian geography; hence the limited knowledge of Ktesias, the enhanced knowledge of Megasthenes and the much more detailed information of the geographer Ptolemy and the historian Pliny. For the Arabs, al-Hind was initially the trans-Indus region and only gradually came to include other areas, when the geography of the subcontinent became better known. Although the authors use the same name for the large territory which approximated the Indian subcontinent, nevertheless none of them speak of the Indians in all these areas constituting a single nation. 'Indian' is not a term of national identity in these texts but is essentially a term of proximate geographical placement.

The Indian concepts of Jambudvipa and Bharatavarsha were again not exact geographical concepts but were cosmological notions. Jambudvipa, used as early as the Mauryan period, appears to have included more than the Indian subcontinent. Bharatavarsha, references to which are much later, was one of its nine divisions. Bharatavarsha in turn was divided into nine areas each one an island separated by enclosing seas. Clearly there was not even an attempt at geographical exactitude. The identification of various regions with Bharatavarsha is more recent. The Mauryan empire may have included almost the whole of the subcontinent but it lasted as such for little more than a century and rapidly broke up into smaller kingdoms and states. This does not support the sublime nature of national culture as projected by the Rashtriya Swayamsevak Sangh (RSS).

If Indian patriotism is to be strengthened then attention must turn to the problems of the present and the alleviation of these in a manner which will make Indians take a pride in our society. Teaching spurious history to the next generation of young Indians is not the way to go about it.

3

WHICH OF US ARE ARYANS?*

'The Aryan question' as it was called earlier was relatively simple inasmuch as the search was for the existence of the Aryans by combing through the Vedic texts. It has now become more complicated with issues of trying to discover the identity of contemporary non-Aryans as well, and the nature of the interface between them and the Arya speakers.

THE THEORY OF AN ARYAN race arose out of European preoccupations and preconceptions and was applied to the early Indian past as part of the colonial interpretation of Indian history. It does not have its roots in Indian views of the past. Nevertheless, it has been accepted and has become an axiom of the historical interpretation of some situations in the Indian past. Whereas scholars largely working on the European past have questioned and discarded this theory, we in India hold fast to it, and those who attempt alternate interpretations of the sources are few and far between.

The European search for its identity gained momentum in the eighteenth century. This was in part the result of a groping towards the concept of the nation-state that made it imperative that there be individual identities for the various states, although stemming if need be from a common origin. In looking at the past, the roots of European civilization were taken back to what was regarded as the miracle of Greek culture. Nationalist thinking tends to search for origins in antiquity and the age of the civilization with which it claims links is pushed back.

*An earlier version of this essay was first published in 1989.

The discovery of the Orient had been commented upon at the popular level through the writings of European travellers, merchants, and missionaries. Gradually, classical scholarship, the views garnered through the writings of earlier Greek and Latin authors, was added to this and it conjured up the Orient as the epitome of luxury and of mythical beings and activities. In the colonial age the interest shifted to those who were using the origins of languages and their comparative study—philology—as a method of arriving at the common ancestry or the roots of European culture, a mood which was best captured in the Romantic movement in German literature. Thus when, at the end of the eighteenth century, the British philologist William Jones declared that there was a similarity in the structure and vocabulary of Sanskrit and Greek (an idea which had been floated even earlier), it fell on fertile ground and became the basis for a large number of theories regarding the origins of European and Indian culture.

In the nineteenth century, therefore, the Indologist (a term used originally for non-Indians studying India) came into his own. Using comparative philology as the method for obtaining the data, a common original language, Indo-European, was proposed as the source for a group of related languages that included Sanskrit, Old Iranian, Greek, Latin, Celtic, and some other European languages. Comparative philology became important to the reconstruction of the Indian past. Having arrived at a common language it did not take long for the language to be seen as the expression of a common race, the Aryan race. Given the newly propagated 'race science' in nineteenth-century Europe, language was regarded as major evidence of race.

The equation of language with race is not particular to the Indo-European and Aryan situation. It has been extended to other regions as well, such as the equation initially made between Bantu speakers and the supposed Bantu race in Africa. There is, of course, no basis for such an equation. There is no support for the argument that those who speak an Indo-European language must belong to the same Aryan race. It is equally difficult to define, with even a remote degree of precision, what the Aryan race might be. In the latter part of the nineteenth century, the fallacy of equating language with race was recognized, and despite statements to the effect that the two cannot be equated, the idea had caught the imagination of people and could not be dislodged. Even some scholars such as Max Müller who were well aware of the difference occasionally confused the two.

In the mid-nineteenth century, the French writer Joseph-Arthur de Gobineau expanded on the idea of the Aryan race which he identified with the European aristocracy. His influential book *Essay on the Inequality of Human Races* had natural appeal, particularly to the aristocracy that was in decline in Europe, and also to groups gradually replacing this aristocracy but wanting nevertheless to be regarded as having a special status. Gobineau argued that the fairer races were pre-eminent because they were instrumental in creating and spreading culture largely through the conquest of others. But conquest, because it required settling in new areas, led to the mixing of races and hence to decline. This theory was to have disastrous consequences in Germany in the twentieth century.

Some comparative philologists and those working on the early Sanskrit texts, such as the Vedas, read the word arya as having a racial connotation. For example, Max Müller's discussions encouraged the idea of a superior Aryan race subduing the inferior indigenes and settling in India. Although at a later stage he argued that race and language were separate, it was by then too late to make the distinction, for the theory of the Aryan race was becoming the established explanation for much of the reconstruction of early Indian history.

Language groups were now equated with race and there were references to not only the Aryan but also the Dravidian and the Austro-Asiatic races, based on the various languages spoken in different regions. Even the origin of caste society was sometimes explained as an attempt at racial segregation where, ideally, each caste constituted a different race and racial purity was maintained by forbidding intermarriage. Thus, the argument could be stretched to maintain that the upper castes, and especially the Brahmanas, were lineal descendants of the Aryans.

It was, however, in the reconstruction of early Indian history that the theory of Aryan race had its biggest impact. It was argued that the foundation of Indian civilization was laid by the coming of the Aryans. This took the form of an invasion of the north-western part of the Indian subcontinent to begin with and the subjugation of the existing populations often described as Dravidian, because of the presence of Dravidian languages in the southern region. The Aryans were seen as conquering northern India and pushing the Dravidians into the peninsula and the south, leaving pockets of the Austro-Asiatic and some Dravidian speakers in central India. Cultural history involved the spread and establishment of the Aryan race and culture over the subcontinent.

The term arya is more frequently used in the Vedic and Buddhist texts to refer to one who is respected and regarded as an honoured person. It referred to those who spoke Sanskrit and observed the varna regulations. But in the nineteenth-century reading of the Rig Veda, the counterposing of the arya with the dasa was interpreted as a racial demarcation. The dasa, it was argued, is differentiated, among other characteristics, by physical differences as well. So the term arya was used to refer to those of the Aryan race and the dasa to those of the indigenous races. The pre-eminence of the aryas was explained by reference to their being the conquerors. The term varna, which literally means colour, but which was probably used in a symbolic sense, as is suggested by the colours of the castes listed in other texts, as white, yellow, red, and black, was nevertheless taken literally by some to refer to differences in skin colour and this, in turn, was sought to support the argument that caste was a form of racial segregation.

Society was depicted by those who were sympathetic to Indian culture as living in idyllic village communities characterized by harmony and a lack of aggression. Such descriptions, frequently found in the writings of Max Müller, were also extended by him to contemporary nineteenth-century India. Part of the reason for this depiction of ideal communities was that such village communities were seen as similar to the village communities from which the peoples of Europe had originated. The Indian present was seen as reflecting the features of Europe in its infancy.

The history of early India therefore became a channel for propagating European views on the origins of peoples and cultures more generally. Thus even the culture of non-European societies was conditioned by the prevailing debates in Europe. This was in part an aspect of Orientalism where the use of knowledge as a form of power was implicit. The recreation of a colony's culture and image of itself in terms of the Orientalist paradigms was a mechanism of control by the colonial power, as has been suggested by Edward Said in his study of Orientalism. Thus, for Lord Curzon the furtherance of such scholarship and knowledge was what he called the necessary furniture of empire.

The interpretation did not have to be reductionist in terms of the colonial framework but it tended to conform to its essentials and there is little attempt at any critique of this framework among earlier Orientalist scholars. Much of the detailed scholarship on early India, which was a legitimate means of discovering many aspects of the past, came from those who were employed as officers by the East India Company either in India or in England, such as William Jones, James Mill, H. T. Colebrooke, H. H. Wilson, and James Prinsep, and later, by officers of Her Majesty's Imperial Government such as Alexander Cunningham and Vincent Smith. As such, therefore, they were unlikely to question the interpretations supporting colonial policy.

Even when nationalist historians in India began to question some of the colonial paradigms, the theory of the Aryan race was not among these. It could be argued that since many Indian historians who had been influenced by the ideology of nationalism came from the upper castes (Brahmanas, Kshatriyas, and Kayasthas) and from the middle class, the theory of the Aryan race appealed to them as it supported their claims to social superiority. It also suggested that Sanskritic Indian culture sprang from the same roots as that of the colonizing power. According to the philosopher and reformer Keshab Chandra Sen, the coming of the British to India was symbolic of the meeting of parted cousins.

Even those who were opposed to what they regarded as upper-caste interpretations of the past also accepted the theory, but turned it to their own use. Thus, thinkers such as Jyotiba Phule in Maharashtra, and others who were members of the non-Brahmana movements in South India, maintained that the lower castes were the original inhabitants of India and that the upper castes, descended from the incoming Aryans, were foreigners. Once again it was assumed that the speakers of a particular language constituted a different race from the speakers of another language. Phule's interpretation introduced the relevance of caste as well. Despite the denial of the equation of language with race by scholars, this equation was firmly embedded in both European and Indian views of the Indian past.

The questioning of the theory of the Aryan race has arisen both from new evidence and from new methods of analysing the evidence. The new evidence comes from archaeology and linguistics and the new method is demonstrated in the manner in which caste has been studied in recent years.

The major new discovery in archaeology relates to the Indus civilization. The chronology of this civilization, the third to early second millennium BC, would place it earlier than the Vedic texts that are generally dated from the mid-second to the mid-first millennium BC. If the texts are dated earlier, as some would like to do, then they would coincide with this civilization. But the societies reconstructed from archaeology and from the texts are strikingly different from each other. Therefore, the texts cannot be taken as descriptions of the excavated civilization. The Indus civilization was urban, with planned cities built on elevations commanding the plains, it communicated by written signs that have not as yet been deciphered, it had a copper-bronze technology, it was unfamiliar with the horse, and had extensive trading contacts not only with the Oxus region and the borderlands, but also with the Gulf and with Mesopotamia. The Vedic texts depict a society which is pastoral and agrarian but is unfamiliar with urban centres and commerce, knows no script, appears to have used a copper and then an iron technology, gave considerable functional and ritual importance to the horse and the chariot, and its contacts were largely confined to north-eastern Iran and perhaps the Oxus plain, before the migration eastwards into the Ganga plain.

What is equally important is that if there was an Aryan invasion it would be reflected in the archaeological evidence, either in the decline of cities or in large-scale devastation at a later time. Some decades ago, the British archaeologist Mortimer Wheeler maintained that the Indus cities declined because of Aryan invasions, which he summed up in his phrase, 'Indra stands accused'. But the more extensive and detailed evidence now available points in an altogether different direction. The theory of invasion has long since been discounted. The decline of cities is no longer attributed to a single cause, since their decline was not simultaneous, those of Gujarat declining somewhat later.

Further, the evidence points to environmental changes. Massive flooding at Mohenjo-daro is a possibility, as are changing river courses of the Hakra and the Sutlej, deforestation due to agriculture and brickmaking resulting in desiccation, and a decline in agricultural production on which the cities were dependent. It is likely that with further analysis the decline of these cities will relate more directly to changes in the political and economic structure as well. There is virtually no evidence for any large-scale invasion in the north-western part of the subcontinent during the second millennium BC.

If Central Asia and eastern Iran were areas occupied by people speaking Indo-European languages, as is generally held, then contacts seem extremely limited given the evidence so far in the Punjab, Haryana, and the Ganga–Yamuna Doab, that is, the area where the earliest part of the Vedas were composed. It is equally difficult to argue that the Aryans originated in India and spread to West Asia as this is not supported by archaeological evidence nor by mention in the Vedic texts. Distinctive archaeological cultures subsequent to the Indus civilization, were located in northern Rajasthan, Punjab, Haryana, and eastern UP, and not much beyond the Indus to the west.

The linguistic evidence does, however, cross borders. There was an affinity in language between the speakers of Vedic Sanskrit and Avestan in Iran, an affinity that was recognized many decades ago. It is possible, therefore, that small groups of migrants from Iran were proximate to people settled on the borders of north-western India and through a process of mutual exchange evolved into a variety of communities, among which the speakers of Indo-Aryan were dominant. Such communities can only be identified by speech, using the literature that survives and, therefore, in referring to them the correct form would be not Aryan, but Aryan-speakers, meaning, 'speakers of Indo-Aryan'.

There is a close affinity between the culture and the cognate languages of the Avesta and Old Iranian. Mitra and Varuna occur in both texts, as do deva and asura/daiva and ahura (in Old Iranian), but the meaning is reversed as in some other cases as well. The Sapta Sindhu region of the Indus is referred to as Hapta-Hendhu, and the Haraxvati River in south-east Afghanistan would be rendered in Sanskrit as Sarasvati, since the 's' sound changes into 'h' in Old Iranian. The relationship of the societies that produced the Avesta and the Rig Veda was clearly close and needs to be investigated in detail. The dates would tally approximately. Further west in northern Syria there is the evidence of a treaty between the Hittites and the Mitannis, dated to about 1380 BC, which mentions the gods that carry names similar to those of some Rig Vedic gods. Another text has turns of phrase in training horses that are reminiscent of Indo-Aryan. These pockets of similar languages would date to the late second millennium BC. There are no archaeological connections between them and the territory where the Vedas were composed, so it is thought that those using the language may have originated in the Oxus plain (the Bactria–Margiana Archaeological Complex), and migrated from there. The presence of an Aryan type of language is momentary. Aryan in the region occupied by the Hittites and the Mitannis did not evolve into a dominant language.

The debate on the language that might have been spoken by the people of the Indus civilization introduces the evidence of linguistics. The debate as it stands currently is substantially between those who support a possible Dravidian language being used by the Harappans, and those who are in favour of its being an Indo-Aryan language. None of the actual readings in either of these languages has met with acceptance among the scholars. If the script remained a pictographic script with little indication of marked evolution and change, it is also possible, as has been suggested, that there was more than a single language spoken but using a common pictographic script.

Recent linguistic analyses of Vedic Sanskrit suggest a rather different picture from the one that prevailed earlier. Non-Aryan vocabulary and syntax are being recognized in the earliest of the Vedas, the Rig Veda, and elements of this increase in the later Vedas. For example, the word langala for plough is non-Aryan and it is also known from archaeological evidence that plough agriculture goes back to the period just prior to the Indus civilization. The non-Aryan presence in Vedic Sanskrit could suggest symbiotic relations between speakers of Aryan and non-Aryan languages, possibly even some bilingualism.

That Sanskrit itself, in the course of a few centuries, underwent change is well established. The existence of etymological works in relation to Vedic Sanskrit—contemporary with the Vedic corpus—

indicate that the language was changing noticeably. The grammar of Panini, generally dated to the fourth century BC, is another indicator since he distinguishes between what is now referred to as Vedic and Classical Sanskrit. Such changes can be explained by the evolution of the language in use and by non-Sanskrit speakers using the language. Thus, even in the process of its spread, Sanskrit as a language was constantly adapting itself to local linguistic forms. This is a normal procedure in the history of a language, more so in languages of significance.

Studies of caste formation have come a long way from the simplistic notions of caste being separate racial entities. The origin of caste in the theory of the four varnas, as expounded in the Vedic corpus, appear to have been symbolic explanations of status differentiation to begin with. It is unlikely that a social system as complex as a caste society began with a simple four-fold division of society into Brahmanas, Kshatriyas, Vaishyas, and Shudras with the untouchables added on as a fifth category. Possibly the varna system, reflecting social stratification, was nevertheless an idealization of a stratification. Caste looked at as jatis suggests other avenues and emphases in caste society.

Jatis evolve from the intermeshing of a variety of factors such as rules of endogamy and exogamy, location, environment, technology, occupation, access to resources, differences in the patterns of social observances, and the ideology of ritual purity. A caste society consists of hereditary groups so recruitment is by birth; these groups are arranged hierarchically which is actually or notionally associated with occupation among other factors; the hierarchy is important particularly to permissible marriage circles and to rules regarding the inheritance of property, particularly in relation to women; and they are often viewed as performing services for each other. The social historian, therefore, has to trace these factors over time and in relation to historical changes. History provides evidence of the importance of kinship patterns and occupation to caste identities, as well as evidence of the transition from what has been called 'jana to jati' (generally translated as tribe to caste, but perhaps better translated as clan to caste).

Another important aspect is the adaptation to a culture, which has sometimes been called a Sanskritic culture, but would include more than just the language. It would consist of the norms and rituals associated with life cycle rites such as birth, marriage, and death. These were generally not uniform across caste in earlier times, although we today tend to think that the upper caste norms applied universally. What is regarded as 'Sanskritic' changes over time, for although on some occasions the Sanskritic assimilates the local non-Sanskritic culture, sometimes the process is reversed and there is more of the non-Sanskritic in the 'Sanskritic' although the veneer of the Sanskritic may be retained. This is particularly apparent in rituals. Some rituals have become relatively uniform and practised across castes, but many are specific to particular castes. Similarly, practices also change over time and the definition of what constitutes correct behaviour for a particular caste may be reversed from earlier periods. Thus the Vedic corpus makes clear that the good Brahmana could consume the flesh of a sacrificed animal even if bovine, and, as part of certain sacrificial rituals, he was required to drink the juice of the soma plant, which if not an intoxicant appears to have been a hallucinogen. Yet, in a later period, from the point of view of the Brahmana, it was regarded as heretical to eat meat and consume intoxicants even on ritual occasions. Cultural habits constantly change and explaining the change is as important as recording the change if one wishes to understand the change. This is again an area where social history and anthropology can provide helpful explanations. Historically, the interesting question is when and why did the prohibition on eating beef become the requirement of an upper-caste Hindu.

The assertion of the purity of race among upper castes, tracing ancestry back to early times, often came apart given the fact that physically some castes have greater regional affinities than pan-Indian. Nor is this surprising for there was some conversion into castes at local levels with aspirations to higher status and the fitting of these castes into a hierarchy. Regional variations, even in the broader structure of caste, do make it difficult if not impossible to maintain that there was a dissemination of the pure race that retained its purity and its status through time. Today, the concept of race as defined in the nineteenth century has been discarded among scientists and scholars. Identities are based on other factors and claims to race are no longer tenable, although the word continues to be used in popular parlance.

The theory of an Aryan race, therefore, is not supported by historical evidence. What the historian is concerned with is not the spread of a race but the spread of a language and some of the related culture. We know from many examples all over the world and from many periods of history that it was perfectly feasible for people of different racial origins, brought together through migration, trade, conquest, or persecution, to find themselves ultimately using the same language. Thus, the historian of early India has to explain how the two Indo-Aryan-based languages, Prakrit and Sanskrit, became current in northern India from the first millennium BC. Those who spoke these languages were the Indo-Aryan speakers and could well have been from a multiplicity of racial stocks. The important question is why the language was adopted by elite groups in northern India. In the absence of widespread and evident conquest other factors have to be considered. Was the language associated with a superior technology, such as the use of iron and of horses and chariots, which would have attracted elite levels of society? Did those who spoke the language introduce new calendrical knowledge that would have had an impact on the agrarian cycle?

The Vedic corpus emphasizes the importance of the destruction of the enemy and many hymns and rituals are in praise of the destroyer or are the means towards the ultimate triumph over the enemy. The identity of the enemy is, however, not certain in every case. There are occasions when the enemy is referred to as the dasas or the dasyus, but there are equally many occasions if not more when the enemy is of another clan but of the same culture. Such internecine raids among clans are characteristic of cattle-keeping societies as also of those in the process of clearing and settling land for agriculture, as was the case among the people referred to in the Vedic corpus. Competition over access to resources was intense and did at times benefit from marriage alliances and the intermingling of various groups. Thus, some of the most pre-eminent among these clans, such as that of the Purus who were ancestral to the protagonists of the Mahabharata war, are described in the Vedas as being descended from an asura rakshasa and speaking a faulty Sanskrit. Yet the Purus are regarded by some as pure Aryans in modern times!

The empirical evidence, as we have it today, from archaeology, linguistics, various literary sources, and more recently from genetics, does not support the theory of the Aryan race. But this is not merely a matter of interest to the historian. This theory has been used by many others and has come to be seen as significant to the understanding of the identity of modern Indians. It is here that its greatest danger lies: the upholding of a theory supposedly explaining our origins, when the theory is in fact false. The question of identity is particularly important to the process of change from caste to class. The theory was eagerly appropriated by those who were in this condition of mutation over the last hundred years.

This is, of course, not peculiar to Indian society, for such theories of racial origins and identities have been known to other societies undergoing similar mutations. It has been plausibly argued that the uncertainty of social change and the expansion of the middle class in early twentieth-century Germany was one of the root causes of the rise of fascism carrying with it the Aryan myth. This experience, so close to us in time, should make it obvious that theories of origins and identities have to be handled very carefully else they may explode in a manner which can devastate a society. The historian in these situations has to be alert to the way in which historical ideas can be used or abused in the name of history.

4

WHY DID ANCIENT INDIA'S MATRIARCHY DISAPPEAR?*

SEEING THE PAST IN A long duration but as creating the present, a relevant question remains as to whether there was once matriarchy in India and did it disappear? This is what I am touching on in this essay. Probably yes, as it was in many societies that have slowly moved to patriarchy to a lesser or greater degree. One cannot make a pronouncement in the singular and apply it uniformly to the entire subcontinent. There are regional differences. Even within a region there sometimes are strong variations among different social groups. What we need to accept is that although matriarchy/matriliny only remains in small pockets, often tucked away, its imprints have not been wiped out. We occasionally meet them in unexpected places. Nor do we have to argue that there was a linear evolution of matriarchy from earlier societies mutating into or adopting patriarchy, as was the popular view a century ago. Kinship patterns at the base of matriarchy/matriliny and patriarchy can coexist or can vary or one of them can fade giving way to other. History does not provide an answer but there is much in the material and textual remains from the past that makes such questions relevant. The variations in kinship pattern are often explained as due to conquest by foreigners or imitation of a different pattern, but the question remains as to why it was adopted—local considerations, a society flexible in adjusting to

*An earlier version of this essay was first published in 1963. It is a prelude to later discussions.

change against well-established norms, the demography of gender, or patterns like the relations between polyandry and the status of women can be among the causes.

Kinship as a lens through which to view early societies made an impact on social history as well. The question asked and is still inconclusively answered is whether early societies were matriarchal/matrilineal and then changed to patriarchy, or have societies always been either one or the other.* There has been much discussion on this in relation to the earliest Indian societies.

Women could have authority over the extended family or the small community. This may have had an element of matriarchy but did not involve women as rulers and it is unclear whether descent was traced through women. These two features are characteristics of matriarchy as a socio-political system. It can be extended to the context of moral authority as well. The attention to matriarchy is less because it is associated with early history and evidence of its having existed and preceded patriarchy is uncertain.

It has been argued that in the hunter–gatherer societies of prehistoric times, women took care of the settlement and the children, and were responsible for gathering wild crops and plants for food. They tended to become the decision-makers in terms of where to settle and how to distribute the food. Since food was crucial those who distributed it would come to have power. In addition to gathering uncultivated food the hunting of animals for food become equally if not more important. This is thought to have been a male occupation. Gradually therefore the authority of the women in society was curbed and that of the men increased.

The use of the term matrilineal is more frequent these days

*The terms matrilineal and patriarchal refer primarily to differences in lineage and inheritance. In the case of the first, these factors operate through the female members of the family and in the case of the second, through the male. What were originally described as matriarchal societies in India were not in fact the female counterpart of patriarchal societies. Hence the abandoning of the term matriarchy and the preference for matrilineal.

and refers to tracing descent through the female line, and to power being directed through the activities of women. Elements of this may lie in customs such as bride price as a form of marriage where the groom has to give substantial gifts to the family of the bride before being accepted. There are vague references to what seems to be bride price in some of the stories in the epics.

It is sometimes held that the worship of the mother-goddess in a society is a pointer to matriarchy. If that is so then there is evidence of female figurines in the Harappan culture. Whether these were deities and had a ritual of worship is uncertain, although arguments have been made to support this idea. Female deities in the Vedic texts are not of major importance especially when compared to male deities. It would have been a religion geared to patriarchy and would also be supported by other facets of such a society.

The Brahmanical religious sects were strongly patriarchal and were in confrontation with Shramanic sects mainly Buddhist and Jaina. The Brahmanical sects gave little freedom to women in the form of personal choice and social activity. The code of social behaviour as set out in the Dharmashastras and enjoined on Hindu society made it clear that women had virtually no freedom as they were to be controlled by their father, husband, and son, in the three phases of their life as daughter, wife, and mother.

The Shramana sects were much more liberal in the freedom they allowed women. There was an initial controversy about whether women could become nuns. But soon after, this was allowed, although permission from the husband was required of married women. Shramana texts present a picture of women being active in social life.

In the Hindu case there is a curious contradiction where the woman has little freedom as she has to observe Shastric norms, nevertheless the same society observes an intense and almost desperate worship of the female goddess. The deity is all powerful and is adorned by all the symbols of power. The worshipper is abject in his worship of her. Yet this is not referred to as a matrilineal society but one that is asserting patriarchy.

In subsequent history there are variations in degrees of freedom for women. But despite some concessions in special cases the essentials of matriarchy did not exist. The governance and administration of a political entity was not in the hands of women although occasionally women did succeed to the throne, with hesitant control. Lineages recording power going through matrilineal descent were rare. The history of certain Upanishadic teachers identified by their mother's name was known but not common. Such markers of identities were not the norm. Women do occasionally comment on the morality of ascetics but moral authority was rarely in the purview of women. Property was equally rarely owned solely by women. However some did have a minimal ownership of property because they are known to have made donations to religious institutions, as for example in the construction of stupas. In medieval times royal women or wives of the wealthy donated wealth to temples and some religious buildings. This was charity and not strictly a secular ownership of property. The women had no control over the use that this wealth was put to.

Women at the two ends of the social spectrum possibly had a freer life, but for different reasons. Those of the elite were symbols of status where freedom was in any case more for effect than for actual function. Those at the very lowest occupation where they either laboured themselves or assisted their husbands in their work, such women were also relatively more free except when the mores of the upper castes reached down and their freedom was curtailed. For example, what did rules such as forbidding women to touch the plough or the wheel of the potter do to their self-esteem? Women laboured in various occupations but had no control over the result of the labour. It was the women of the middle castes who loyally followed the rules laid down for all women.

It is thought by some that there was a time, many centuries

back, when matrilineal societies were the accepted initial social pattern in the Indian subcontinent. This was in the days before the coming of the Aryans who brought with them a patriarchal culture. Vestiges of the matrilineal system have remained and are met with more frequently in peninsular India or the Northeast, where the impact of Aryan culture is thought to have been less.

Initially, the arrival of the Aryans soon after 1500 BC perpetuated the system of clan societies in northern India. Despite the patriarchal form, the fact that the clans were nomadic pastoralist, moving from place to place with their herds of cattle ensured an equal status for women as is suggested in the early hymns of the Rig Veda. But as the Aryans moved into the Ganga plain, cleared the forests, settled in village communities and changed from being pastoralists to agriculturalists, the patriarchal element was asserted. The unit of Aryan society was now the patriarchal family, with authority invested in the eldest male, and lineage being traced through the males in the family. This was coupled with the fact that property was inherited by the sons and not the daughters. The increase in the status of the male led to a proportionate decline in the status of the female.

First Divisions

The Aryan distancing from existing social norms is clear from the initial division between Aryan and non-Aryan. A carefully formulated theory of dividing society into castes followed. The Aryans were included among the twice-born castes and the non-Aryans were the Shudras and, later, some were the untouchables. Such a total refusal to allow for assimilation, albeit theoretical, prevented the possibility of the earlier kinship system modifying Aryan patriarchal society. In the working out of the social and legal framework, Aryan orthodoxy supported the privileged position of the male.

Aryan orthodoxy did not however dominate every level of

society. It had its effective following amongst those who were grouped in the three upper castes. The Shudras and the outcastes were outside the social pale and evolved their own norms of social behaviour, in spite of the fact that they formed a larger percentage of the total population than any of the other castes. In addition, they also formed, from an early period, the majority of the pastoralists and peasants. Shudra society would have retained far more of the pre-Aryan tradition than upper-caste society. This accounts in part for the fact that women in peasant society have a better status within their own society than the women of upper-caste society, both in the rural areas and in towns.

An additional but equally important reason is that the peasant woman has to participate fully in the work of her husband and is therefore an economic asset. This in a small family automatically raises her status and prestige. Not surprisingly, therefore, agitation for the improvement of the status of women was generally restricted to the urban areas and to the artisan sub-castes.

The centre of Aryan orthodoxy was the Ganga plain—the modern states of Uttar Pradesh and Bihar. Here arose the earliest monarchies strongly rooted in Vedic thought and ritual.* On the periphery of this region—in the Himalayan foothills, Punjab, and Rajasthan—were the oligarchic republics where the general atmosphere was far more liberal than in the monarchies. It was in these areas that some of the 'protest' movements, such as Buddhism, became popular, since they were opposed to the orthodox ordering of the cultural pattern. In the Ganga plain the urban classes supported these movements. The Buddha took the unorthodox step of permitting the establishing of an order of nuns, thereby conceding the point that a woman could opt out of society if she so chose.

---

*A society which stresses ritual has to maintain exacting laws of purity. Menstruation amongst women automatically excludes them from participation in the ritual and this in turn results in their being treated as inferior.

The Options

This was to become one of the two 'classic' options available to a woman should she wish to express her individuality. Dedication to religion was acclaimed, provided she had taken the permission of her husband or her father and her dedication followed an established form. The scurrilous attacks on Mirabai who refused to worship in the established Brahmanical manner is a case in point. The second option was that of becoming a courtesan or, at a more basic level, a prostitute/sex worker. Dedication to religion was on occasion a sublimation. The devadasis of the South Indian temples combined the options with great success. There was one important aspect of the second option: society did not snigger at the courtesan. She was often an educated and accomplished woman whose contacts were limited to the upper classes, and as such had the respect of the rest.

The 'intellectual' woman was a rarity. The name of Gargi is mentioned time and again to prove that advanced learning was available to women, but Gargi was an exception. She was the daughter of a Vedic sage and known for her impressive participation in philosophical discourse. She figures in the Upanishads. Her debate with Yajnavalkya is often referred to. The Law Books of the early Christian era make it very clear that the pursuit of knowledge was not to be encouraged amongst women.

Rigid Restrictions

By the time of the Gupta period, in the middle of the first millennium AD, women had a minimal number of rights and an overwhelming number of obligations. The movement of upper-class women came to be increasingly restricted in subsequent centuries. The establishment of the joint family emphasized the patriarchal character of the family. Pre-puberty marriages became normal. Even though the marriage was not consummated, the fact of an adolescent girl being a married woman imposed many restrictions on her behaviour. Pre-puberty marriages may have been psychologically successful, but they detracted from a woman's self-assertion. The stigma attached to widow remarriage was introduced. Whereas the early Aryans had regarded it as normal, levirate being a known practice, it was now regarded with disfavour.

The system of putting women behind a veil heightened their seclusion, particularly amongst the upper castes. The higher the caste status of a woman, the more restricted were her actions. This unnatural isolation of women produced two reactions. At one level women were romanticized and were made the object of a chivalrous code of behaviour. At another level there was an outburst of erotica, both in the composition of poems and in temple sculpture.*

These were also the centuries which were to see the break-up of kingdoms into small feudal states, frequently at war. Societies which stress warfare often have a masculine cast. Women were exalted when their sons became heroes or their husbands performed heroic feats. A woman, even against her own instinct, was expected to encourage her son or her husband into battle. The epitome of all this was the demand that women become satis on the death of their husbands.

The Champions

This is not to suggest that women did not have their champions. Apart from the Buddhists and the members of earlier heterodox sects, there were always groups (in various parts of the subcontinent) which were in favour of enlarging the activities of women in society. Most of these groups came from the artisan classes both

*It was during this period that the cult of Radha and Krishna swept across northern India. The passionate love of the two was the excuse for some of the most beautiful though highly erotic poetry in Sanskrit.

in the towns and the villages. The socio-religious reformers, for instance, who opposed the priestly monopoly of worship and religious expression, encouraged women to participate in their gatherings. The Tamil devotional cult arising from the artisan groups and the rural population of Tamil Nadu included women hymnodists and preachers, such as Andal. The Tantric sects of the medieval period were opposed to the orthodoxy and were regarded by the latter as social aberrations, Yet, they were the ones who popularized the worship of feminine deities, accorded women a place of great importance in their cult and, perhaps, influenced by the Buddhist nuns, introduced an order of female ascetics. These sects maintained a tension in society whereby the status of women (amongst other social inequities) was never entirely forgotten.

Alien Social Forces

The coming of the Turks and Afghans in the thirteenth century is said to have intensified the existing situation. Inevitably new persons in authority and of a different culture would strengthen the opposition to them from the existing orthodox society. The Turks and Afghans were strongly patriarchal as also had been the other invaders of northern India, coming from Central Asia—the Scythians and the Huns. Legally, however, Muslim women had a better status. They were permitted a religious education (not that this stressed anything but their subservience), divorce and remarriage, and rights of inheritance. The latter were the only real privileges, though the application of these in the woman's favour is a debatable point.

The challenge of an initially alien social force, as was Islamic society, put the existing orthodoxy on the defensive. But now, again, the Bhakti movements in their social aspects continued some of the tradition of the earlier sects in being non-caste movements and in demanding a more liberal attitude towards the role of women. Unfortunately, the protest of these movements remained ineffective in the long run. The biggest barrier was caste. The structure of caste being what it was prevented the mobilization of ideas in a form which would cut across caste and enable a protest movement to acquire political status: this was necessary before any reform could be implemented within society. Caste was intertwined with professions and had been so since its very inception. It therefore required a major economic change before any impact could be made on the caste structure. Thus the pattern of tradition and opposition ostensibly continued until the nineteenth century.

However, some small mobility occurred with the introduction of the migrant Arabs and Turks settling in India. In many ways caste was strengthened by the fact that Islamic society inducted some of that existing caste hierarchy into its own functioning. Foremost among these was that those castes that were earlier outside caste society, and therefore regarded as inferior, remained in a low status even on conversion to Islam. This is linked to the contemporary problems of the Pasmanda Muslims still being treated as Dalit.

The nineteenth century was a watershed between medieval and modern India. The British had begun to acquire territory in India in the eighteenth century and by the early nineteenth century the idea of empire had taken root. Together with the British came the impact of an entirely alien culture, the culture of Protestant Europe. The Indian reaction to this impact was, to begin with, the traditional one. A number of socio-religious reform movements emerged, most of which were the inheritors of the earlier protest movements. On the question of the status of women, there were two groups, the Revivalists and the Reformers.

The Revivalists, looking back to a utopian past, agitated for a return to those conditions. Their argument was that if women could have had equal status with men in the early Aryan period, why should they be denied that status in the nineteenth century? But they failed to realize (as did many people who later argued on the same lines) that the condition of society had changed fundamentally and that the social relationships which emerged from a clan-based tribal society could not be identical with an agrarian, feudal society. The plea of the Revivalists was linked with a general hankering for the past which was characteristic of many sections of society in the nineteenth century. They were not in favour of women's rights per se. To some extent the male ego was also involved, since it wished to bestow emancipation on women.

The Reformers

The Reformers, who were more influenced by the philosophic liberalism of eighteenth and nineteenth-century Europe, objected to the subordinate position of women because they believed in the equality of the sexes and individual liberty. They believed that a society was not healthy if women were kept in a state of subjugation. The most vocal of the Reformers was Raja Rammohun Roy, who founded the Brahmo Samaj in 1828 as an organizational body to propagate his ideas. He attacked social customs such as sati and female infanticide and supported the social reforms of Lord Bentinck viewed as a more concerned governor-general. What was even more important was that he demanded a change in the inheritance laws to include women's rights to inheritance.

The movement of 1857 initiated India into the modern period. It was an attempt of the old ruling order to oust the British from the subcontinent, but it failed. It resulted however in India being directly governed by the British government and being more closely associated with the British economy which led to the introduction of limited industrialization. This was the technological change which was to bring new elements into the Indian social structure, not least amongst them being the rise of a new professional middle class. The movement for the emancipation of Indian women was associated with the activities of the middle class.

Marriage Reform

Pre-puberty marriage was the first item which came in for attack. This was formulated in the debate over the age of consent. What with caste rules and the joint family system, marriage had become entirely a social obligation and the margin of choice even within this system was eliminated by the instituting of child marriages. Such marriages were a way of confining girls and leaving them with only one option. In 1880, after much agitation, the age of consent was raised to ten years in the case of girls. It took another thirty-one years before it could be raised to twelve.

The debate was taken up by men such as the social reformer Mahadev Govind Ranade who attacked both child marriage and the ban on the remarriage of widows. The stricture on the latter had applied even to child widows. Ranade also realized that if the pattern of a woman's life was to be made more humane, then the issue must be fought on a national level and not in isolated local groups. To this end, a National Social Conference was called in 1887; the aims of the agitation were made more specific and the movement given an organizational foundation.

Raising the age of consent introduced a related problem: the education of women. If girls could not marry before adolescence, then they must be educated in the meanwhile. In addition, faith in education was growing since it provided an entry into the middle class, caste no longer being the sole criterion in improving social status. It was inconceivable therefore that education could be denied to any section of middle-class society, even women. Swami Vivekananda felt that women should be educated so that they would understand the purpose of improving the status of women and would be encouraged to participate in the movement. The Arya Samaj, founded in 1875 by Dayananda Sarasvati, despite its revivalist character made 'education for women' one of its slogans. Dayananda insisted that girls should be at school until the age of sixteen and that they should receive a general humanities education and not merely be taught domestic science. Sir Sayyad Ahmed Khan was equally forceful in advocating more educational facilities for women.

Educational facilities meant the existence of schools and there was a great shortage of these for girls. The Brahmo Samaj and the Arya Samaj had started some and there were also the Christian mission schools. But the latter were regarded as somewhat suspect by Hindu caste society since it was feared that the girls would be converted to Christianity, or at least made familiar with liberal, egalitarian ideas which were not always in keeping with their home tradition. The government was slow in providing schools for girls, perhaps because the idea of educating women on a large scale was revolutionary even in Europe.

It was not until the end of the nineteenth century that activities relating to women's education moved faster. This was largely due to the realization that educated women could find employment and the economic independence of women would bring about social equality. This trend of thinking led to the founding of the SNDT Women's University in 1916 by the educator and social reformer Dhondo Keshav Karve. In the first year there were only six students, but gradually the numbers grew until it became a centre for women who wanted university education.

The Political Movement

The last quarter of the nineteenth century brought a tremendous momentum into Indian middle-class life; it saw the birth of the political movement for national independence. The formation of the Indian National Congress in 1885 with its initially limited demand for Indian representation in government was to lead eventually to the demand for total independence. Inevitably the women's movement came to be linked with this broader movement. Annie Besant expressed in unequivocal terms the demand for the emancipation of women in India. It was essential that women have an intelligent understanding of what the men were fighting for in the national movement and, in order to acquire this understanding, they had to participate as well.

The Link

The first session of the Indian National Social Conference in 1887 was a stormy and controversial one. It was recognized that social reform and political reform could no longer be kept separate, but controversy arose over the methods to be adopted. Some favoured legislative reform, others the rousing of public opinion. The controversy was identical with the larger one within the national movement. The founding of the Women's Indian Association in 1917 by Annie Besant and others made it clear that the emancipation of women had now ceased to be the eccentric ideology of a few reformers, and had become a part of the larger struggle for political independence. In a sense, the active role which Sarojini Naidu played both in the Women's Association and the National Congress symbolized the link between the two forces.

The All India Women's Conference (AIWC) founded by Margaret Cousins held its first session in 1926 and became the forum for women's rights. It not only sympathized with and encouraged the participation of women in the political movement, but it had a more militant nature as well. It supported adult literacy amongst women, and fought for better conditions of work in professions such as nursing and teaching where women were employed in large numbers. There was also a demand for legislation which would ensure minimum welfare facilities such as an adequate basic wage, the right to join trade unions, equal pay for equal work, maternity benefits, etc. The movement had now been strengthened by the existence of a large number of women working in the urban areas in factories and industry. A few years later, the AIWC voiced the demand for female franchise.

Political activity, whether at the level of going to prison or picketing liquor shops, despite having to listen to the jibes of male passers-by, or at the level of policy decisions in the national movement, liberated women. It gave them a confidence in themselves and a self-reliance which they had not known before. In addition, political activity led to the removal (or at any rate the overlooking) of many of the restrictions which had been placed on women. Women were accepted as political comrades. Some were elected to the legislative assemblies and other constitutional bodies which provided yet another outlet. In fact, politics became a very respectable profession for women. Under the leadership of Mahatma Gandhi, large numbers of women joined the Non-cooperation Movement in 1921 and the Civil Disobedience Movement in 1930.

Effects of War

A national crisis such as a war also tends to break social restrictions. The mobilization of Indian men in World War II led to vacancies in the professions which were partially filled by women. The working woman was becoming a far more familiar feature of the urban landscape. Increasing urbanization and industrialization led to the gradual breaking up of a basic institution of Indian life—the joint family. Economic mobility led to sons leaving the joint family and establishing their own nuclear families in the urban areas. In these small families the status of women improved. In cases where the woman also worked in order to supplement the income, she almost became the pivot of the family.

Legislation in favour of women working in industry brought an element of greater reality into the women's movement, since the conditions of work were often inhuman. 1947 brought political independence to the Indian subcontinent, but for the women's movement the fight continued. The Constitution of independent India declared equal status for women. Yet there were many details which remain to be worked out. The question of inheritance was finally settled in 1955–56 with the passing of a bill to the effect that daughters also had a claim to inherited property. This bill was associated with another by which marriage was made monogamous in Hindu society and divorce was permitted. All three features contradict traditional norms and attitudes.

Demands of the Future

But legislation alone does not change social opinion. The association of the women's movement with the political movement made things considerably easier for Indian women, The bitterness and the tragedies of the British suffragettes' movement, for instance, were eliminated. In a sense, the fight for emancipation has only just begun in India. Social mores and traditional behaviour are being openly challenged. There is no camouflage of an anti-colonial movement to blur the issues. That men and women will have equal status in the society of the future is inevitable. It is a question of now or later. The inevitability does not lie in imitating early Aryan tribalism, but in the demands of the society of the future, which should be based on a perceptive understanding of the needs of men and women and of their mutual adjustment.

An appeal to the past cannot detract from the fact that the Indian woman has had an inferior position over the last two thousand or more years in the articulate and advanced levels of Indian society. And this is true of most 'civilized' societies elsewhere in the world. The irony of it is that the real emancipation of women—the possible individual expression of a woman at every level of her being—is more often to be found in societies which we in our infinite wisdom have called savage and primitive.

If more women today have come closer to being liberated it is not because of women having had a superior status in ancient India, but because women have to struggle to be free and are still struggling.

5

IN HISTORY: SATI*

The action of becoming a sati is an example of an activity taken as traditional, an aspect of the assertion of patriarchy. Was its continuation restricted to the continuation of a ritual, or was it a continuing of a mechanism to ensure the subordination of women irrespective of how murderous such continuity may be? Has it been effectively terminated or do elements of the attitude continue? Was this ritual incumbent on all the women in society or only on particular sections of it? If it was the latter then what has been the specific need for it to be continued, even after its context and meaning have drastically changed?

IN THE PAST, AN UPPER-CASTE woman would become a sati—a woman in an auspicious condition, through a ritual that required her self-immolation as a widow on the funeral pyre of her husband. (The colonial usage of 'committing' sati makes little sense and should be discontinued and be replaced by 'becoming a sati'.) The performance of this ritual has become rare in our times but the ethos in which it was enveloped has not been discontinued. The last recorded sati was Roop Kanwar in Rajasthan in 1987. The ritual may not be performed now, nevertheless its glorification in some sections of society continues through the deification of the sati and her being worshipped or in films that focus on it as a ritual significant to our past. This is despite the fact that it has been controversial throughout Indian history. In writing about

*An earlier version of this essay was first published in 1988.

sati one is discussing what is hopefully a ritual of past times but the implied question in this discussion is whether current attitudes towards the meaning of such a ritual have really been discarded, or is there still a lurking admiration for the idea among some sections of Hindu society.

P. V. Kane in his monumental work, *History of Dharmasastra*, starts his brief chapter on sati with what can only be described now as a quotable quote. He states: 'This subject is now of academic interest in India since for over a hundred years (i.e., from 1829) self-immolation of widows has been prohibited by law in British India and has been declared to be a crime.'

What is of significance today is not just the now rare incidence of widows becoming satis, but the attempt to justify a custom at an earlier historical juncture, a justification which involves more than merely a custom, since it also symbolizes an attitude towards women as well as a view of what is regarded as 'tradition'. The occurrence has died down but we still have to understand why it was regarded by many upper-caste Hindus as an acceptable part of their tradition. It is rooted in an attitude which maintains that women are inferior and like animals can be ritually sacrificed to benefit the man. There is today an official prohibition on immolating the living wife together with the dead body of her husband, nevertheless there are those who do not question this act. It is defended as being a recognized symbol of Hindu values especially those concerning the idealized relationship between husband and wife, the assumption being that it was required in theory of all Hindu women. Another prevalent view is that it was necessitated by the 'Muslim invasions' when upper-caste Hindu women resorted to it to defend their honour from Muslim marauders, a view which was propagated in the nineteenth century to justify both sati and jauhar. Neither of these is supported by historical evidence. The defence of sati today is a deliberate attempt at justifying an act for reasons quite other than the preservation of Hindu values and the assumptions which had accompanied the practice of sati require investigation. Does a woman have to immolate herself to acquire honour?

It is easy enough to take the stand that those who do not accept sati as part of the Hindu tradition are westernized Indians deracinated from the mainsprings of the Hindu ethos, and therefore unable to understand either the Rajput concept of honour or to appreciate the idealized relationship between a Hindu husband and wife, such that it is sought to be perpetuated to eternity through sati; or to see that sati is a pure act of the ultimate in sacrifice (even if such an act is reduced to a public spectacle with a variety of entrepreneurs literally cashing in on it). Such arguments deny a discussion on the subject and the latter is necessary if we are to attempt an understanding of our traditions. Traditions in any case often arise out of contemporary needs but seek legitimation from the past. Therefore the past has to be brought into play where such legitimation is sought. It is not just the ritual but the reasons for its continuance.

There is no simple explanation for the origin of the custom of burning widows on the pyres of their dead husbands. It is said to be a symbol of aristocratic status associated with many early societies such as those of the Greeks and the Scythians. There is however no other society where it was practised by variant social groups for different reasons at various points in time, and where the controversy over whether or not it should be practised was so clearly articulated over many centuries. Because of this, in India it underwent changes of meaning as well as degrees of acceptance.

Its origin is generally traced to the subordination of women in patriarchal society and this seems to be the form it takes in more recent times. One may well ask whether subordination has to take such an extreme form? In searching for origins, it might be as well to consider other situations which prevailed in India. The notion of bride price, for example, can suggest in some situations the purchase of a woman, the logical termination of which may have been the requirement of her dying together with her husband, although this is not typical of bride price. But perhaps a more acceptable explanation may relate to societies changing their systems of kinship and inheritance. In some circumstances the wife would be an alien in the early stages of change. Marriage meant the introduction of another kinship group into the family. The children would have split loyalties towards maternal and paternal kin. Only after the death of one parent would they be fully integrated into the family of the surviving one as successors and inheritors. Significantly the children are not mentioned in connection with this ritual. Burning the widow would eliminate any claim that she or her kinsmen might make on inheriting the dead husband's property, whether moveable or immoveable.

Control over female sexuality would be a further reason. The practice may have originated among societies in flux and become customary among those holding property such as the families of chiefs and Kshatriyas. Once it was established as a custom associated with the Kshatriyas it would continue to be so among those claiming Kshatriya status as well.

The earliest hint comes from the Rig Veda of the second millennium BC although the text does not provide evidence of the act. The Vedic texts on the contrary endorse the system of niyoga or levirate where a widow is permitted to marry her husband's brother if she has not borne a son to her husband. Levirate in patrilineal clans is often intended to consolidate property. In the Rig Veda the act was only a mimetic ceremony. The widow lay on her husband's funeral pyre before it was lit but was raised from it by a male relative of her dead husband. Attempts were made, probably in the sixteenth century, to seek Vedic sanction for the act by changing the word agre, to 'go forth', into agneh, 'to the fire', in the specific verse. But since the widow is not meant to immolate herself this change could be spurious. The Vedic act, referring to families of high status, may encapsulate the termination of an earlier practice or the symbolic death of the wife.

The act of immolation in India is first described in Greek texts of the first century BC quoting from earlier accounts referring to incidents of the fourth century. Widows are burnt on the funeral pyres of their dead husbands among the Katheae (Kshatriya/Khattiya) in the Punjab. Unable to explain this practice the author remarks that it was an attempt to prevent wives from poisoning their husbands! According to the same sources bride price was the prevalent custom in the Punjab. If bride price was a factor, then one would expect it to encourage the legitimacy of sati in other parts of India as well where the Kshatriya ethos combined with this form of marriage. Bride price incidentally is objected to in the early Dharmashastras as being degrading whereas the giving of a dowry is favoured.

The Mahabharata has references to some widows becoming satis such as Madri the wife of Pandu or some of the wives of Krishna. Curiously the custom is not generally observed among other Pandavas or by the wives of those Kauravas who died in the battle at Kurukshetra. It was obviously not required of all Kshatriyas. It has been argued that these references to sati are late interpolations. Madri however was from the Punjab. Her clan, that of the Madras, are said to have had liberal attitudes to women. Would they have endorsed sati? Krishna's marriage to Rukmani was said to be unorthodox as he had abducted her. Kidnapping and the paying of bride price were ranked as low among the eight forms of marriage listed in the Dharmashastras.

The Dharmashastras seem to hold contradictory views on sati. The *Manu Dharmashastra,* dating to the turn of the Christian era, requires the widow to live a chaste life and if she has no son then alone is she permitted to obtain one through niyoga. The later *Vishnu Dharmashastra* allows an option to the widow: she can either be celibate and live like an ascetic or else can become a sati. Medhatithi, the major commentator on Manu, writing in about the tenth century AD is strongly opposed to widows becoming satis. He argues that the practice is adharma and ashastriya, against the laws of dharma and not conceded by the shastras. He maintains that it amounts to suicide which is forbidden and that each person must live their allotted span of life. He even urges that in some situations a widow should be permitted to remarry. Medhatithi's position was not unique and the discussion was controversial and continued to be so over the centuries. That Medhadithi felt it necessary to comment forcefully on sati whereas Manu does not even refer to it, indicates its wider prevalence during the later period. Nevertheless there are also inscriptions from these times which record widows from royal families donating property to religious beneficiaries.

This change is reflected in other sources as well. More precisely dateable evidence comes from inscriptions. An inscription of AD 510 at Eran in central India refers to the wife of Goparaja who immolated herself when her husband died in battle. The practice was by now well-known in this area. Similar inscriptions from Rajasthan and Nepal date to the seventh and eighth centuries AD. This evidence predates even the emergence of Islam let alone its arrival in India. It cannot therefore be said that the rise in women being burnt on their husbands' funeral pyres was due to the invasions of the Turks and Afghans. The increase in the memorials do not indicate this symbolically nor mention it.

Banabhatta writing the *Harshacharita* in the seventh century AD does not condemn the mother of King Harshavardhana for becoming a sati, perhaps because the book was an official biography. But in his other work, the *Kadambari*, he objects strongly to the practice and lists many women of high status who did not become satis. The *Hitopadesha*, a collection of stories dating probably to the first millennium AD, glorifies the act of becoming a sati with the theory that it ensures for the wife and the husband an eternity of living together after death. The act is described in various texts as sahamarana (dying together), sahagamana (going together), and anuvarohana (ascending the pyre).

Inscriptions from the peninsula refer to women becoming satis when their husbands died in battles fought between and among Hindu rulers such as the Chaulukyas, Yadavas, and Hoysalas, in the period from the tenth to the fourteenth centuries AD. Many of these inscriptions are located in Maharashtra and Karnataka. The peak period of sati in these areas was pre-Islamic in that Muslim invasions were not the cause. However, when faced by Turkish armies from the end of the thirteenth century, the earlier ritual could have continued. The other interesting feature is that most of these inscriptions refer either to families of Kshatriya status or those seeking such a status. One oft-quoted inscription of the eleventh century refers to a Shudra woman whose husband died in battle against the Ganga ruler and who, in spite of the opposition from her parents, became a sati. Her husband held a high military position under Chola control. Her insistence may have been occasioned, among other things, by the wish to establish status. The custom it would seem was prevalent at this time among those who held high administrative and military positions generally associated with kshatriyas. Therefore, it is likely that members of lower castes holding similar positions emulated the style of the Kshatriyas.

Another indication of the existence of satis are the sati memorial stones. These have been recorded and studied in some detail only in recent years. The location, numbers, chronology, and the statements, both inscriptional and visual, of the hero-stones and the associated sati-stones have provided new insights into the history of these areas. Some of these areas were subject to raids by kingdoms in the vicinity, contesting this territory. The sati-stones generally occur in the same locality as the hero-stones which commemorated death in the course of a heroic act of either defending the village or a herd of cattle or of killing predatory wild animals and so on. Sometimes the sati-stone and the hero-stone are on the same slab. The sati-stone has a standard set of symbols: the sun and the moon indicating eternity; an upright, open right arm and hand, bent at the elbow and clearly showing bangles intact (a woman's bangles being broken when she is widowed, the bangles being intact would be an indication of her continuing marital status); a lime held in the hand to ward off evil. On occasion a sati is indicated by a single standing female figure or a couple, where generally the right arm of the woman has the same features as above.

Sati-stones like hero-stones occur more often not in fertile agricultural mainlands but in ecologically marginal areas, where local conflicts and skirmishes would be frequent. Possibly in marginal areas, the process of transition from tribe to jati may have required an underlining of the new norms which would have implications for the inheritance and status of women. Tribal chiefs are also memorialized in hero-stones and this was part of the process of Kshatriyaization, assimilation into the Sanskritic tradition. Doubtless by now, sati would also have played a part in the adoption of a Kshatriya lifestyle.

Inscriptional and archaeological evidence suggest that the greater occurrence of immolation seems to date to the late first and the early second millennium AD. This was a time of new areas being opened up to settlement by caste-based society and encroachments on a larger scale into tribal areas. New castes emerged in this background of a changing economy, some with antecedents in the earlier pre-caste society. In the competition for status, various observances of upper caste society became current. Why the immolation of widows was introduced requires explanation. Apart from other things it may relate to a deliberate subordination of women who had earlier had an important role. As a ritual it was the most traumatic in underlining the subordination of women. Or, it could have been a reaction against the many growing socio-religious movements some of which disapproved of caste differentiations and supported the continuing participation of women in social roles whether as wives or widows, and which movements may not have been regarded with favour by the upper castes. The immolation of widows may have been seen as a method of demarcating status.

It is interesting that there is little reference to the deification of the woman at this time. The incentive to becoming a sati is accompanied by a listing of rewards for the woman. She will dwell in heaven for as many years as there are hairs on the human body and will dwell with her husband served by apsaras. In some Kannada texts the wife is said to be jealous of the apsaras and therefore insistent on dying with her husband! Her act will purify not only her husband but also her parents and of course herself of all sins. The inclusion of her parents was a shrewd move appealing to her filial emotions. The ultimate threat is that if she does not burn she will be reborn as a woman in many successive births. This is a strong comment indicating the unhappiness of being a woman in a patriarchal society. The package of rewards is based quite clearly on the Kshatriya view of the after-life. Only the hero went to Indraloka (or to Shivaloka as in the Kerala tradition), and lived eternally in heaven. The other view of the after-life, as developed in the theory of karma and sansara, action and rebirth, did not necessarily apply to the hero. Heaven for the hero is a paradise land. The notion of sati therefore is tied to the heroic ideal of the Kshatriya and it is not surprising that upto this point in history it is not permitted to other castes and specifically not to Brahmana women as is stated in the Padma Purana. But this was soon to change. In the early second millennium AD, the *Mitakshara*, a legal text treating of family law, argued that all women be permitted to become satis and that niyoga be prohibited.

A very different point of view emerges from another category of people and texts. The followers of the Shakta sects were opposed to it even from the religious point of view. The *Mahanirvana Tantra* states, 'A wife should not be burnt with her dead husband. Every woman is the embodiment of the goddess. That woman who in her delusion ascends the funeral pyre of her husband shall go to hell.' This contradiction of the Kshatriya ethic has its own interest as a statement of opposition, particularly as it comes from those who were initially regarded as being of lesser status but constituting the larger percentage of people. Possibly this kind of opposition nurtured the compensatory notion of a sati being converted into a goddess, a notion which seems to have gained currency in the later second millennium AD. Madri in the Mahabharata, for instance, is not deified. Women have an important role in Shakta ritual.

As the idea developed it was said that the goddess entered the body of the woman when she resolved to become a sati. Deification was a compensation for suicide and acted as an incentive as well as an attempt to take the act onto another plane, where mundane considerations would not apply. But the deification was not individualized, for the women are not worshipped as goddesses in their own name but as part of the generalized sati goddess. There was less emphasis now on the continuity of living with the husband after death in heaven. Was this due to non-Kshatriya women, especially Brahmanas, being encouraged to become satis?

It is also worth remembering that Buddhist texts did not support sati and widows were instead welcomed as nuns if they so chose, and had been given permission. Some of the votive inscriptions at Buddhist stupas record donations by widows. The later Jaina texts conceded that in special circumstances a Jaina muni could die by slow starvation. This concession prevented the Jainas from opposing other forms of suicide. However, judging by the large number of Jaina widows who became nuns, it is evident that although some might have become satis, this was not the prevailing custom.

It has been stated that there was an epidemic of satis in South India at the time when the Vijayanagara kingdom was collapsing. In 1420, Niccolò de Conti visited Vijayanagara well before its peak period in the early sixteenth century and left an account which survives only through a series of translations. He describes the ritual of self-immolation and adds that three thousand wives and concubines of the king of Vijayanagara had pledged to burn themselves on the death of the king. We have only Conti's word for the pledge and there is no other evidence to prove that it was carried out. Nor did the neighbouring Muslim Bahmani kingdom have to do with such a pledge since the princess of Vijayanagara had been married with great pomp and splendour to the Bahmani sultan. Portuguese travellers Duarte Barbosa and Fernao Nuniz visiting in the early sixteenth century also refer to the ritual but again in general terms.

There was a spate of European traders after the Portuguese established settlements on the coast. These visitors found the custom new and strange and described it at length. This perhaps gives the impression that it was more prevalent in Vijayanagara than elsewhere. There is in fact little evidence to suggest that there was a substantial increase to epidemic proportions in self-immolation in the south at the time of the collapse of the Vijayanagara kingdom in the late sixteenth century.

State intervention to try and control incidents of widow immolation begins during the time of the sultans and the Mughals. They could not prohibit it but indirectly attempted to reduce the numbers by insisting that it should not be forced on the woman. We are told that those wishing to become satis had to obtain a special licence from the governors of the Mughal provinces. If this was actually so it might have acted as a deterrent. That the need for permission became part of the procedure seems evident from incidents occurring even among Indian communities living outside India. As Fernand Braudel noted in *The Wheels of Commerce*: 'In 1723, the widow of an Indian merchant in Moscow asked permission to be burned alive alongside her husband on his funeral pyre. Her request was refused. At once the Indian traders disgusted by this act, decided to leave Russia, taking their wealth with them. Faced with this threat the authorities gave in. The incident was repeated in 1767.'

That families of wealthy traders took to this practice in the eighteenth century was doubtless due to their close proximity to political power and Kshatriya practice. This was particularly the case in regions such as Rajasthan where many kingdoms derived substantial revenue from commerce. Possibly this association with commercial groups encouraged the emergence of the sati temples. Sati memorials in the past were simple memorial stones, but the more recent temples are vast enterprises such as the one at Jhunjhunu, where the Marwari talent for finance has combined with Rajput notions of honour, to the material benefit of both. There is a continuing link between sati temples and the Marwari community elsewhere too. The appropriation of the custom by other upper castes was known in the eighteenth century, although there was no uniformity of attitude towards it within the caste or even within the extended family. Thus whereas one Peshwa was opposed to it, the wife of another became a sati in 1772.

The practice of immolating widows took a turn in a new direction from the seventeenth century in eastern India. The overwhelming incidence was among the Brahmanas of this area and particularly in Bengal. The major cause for this unprecedented rise in widow immolation, particularly in the early nineteenth century, has been attributed to the legal system relating to inheritance. In areas where the Dayabhaga system prevailed, as in eastern India, women were entitled to a share in the inheritance of immovable property on the death of their husbands. Sati became a means of removing one among the claimants to inheritance. It is interesting that during the second millennium AD when Brahmana widows were permitted to become satis, this was also the time when Brahmana property holders increased both in numbers as well as in the size of their holdings owing to the land grants which they received from royalty. Thus what was in origin a custom associated with Kshatriya notions of heroism and honour was now converted into a convenient way of eliminating an inheritor. It has been suggested that the largest occurrence was among Kulin Brahmana families, for the ratio of male to female seems to have been severely out of balance, requiring that the Kulin marry many wives, from several families. The effect of this on the ritual of widow immolation was self-evident.

The movement for the abolition of widow self-immolation

was hesitatingly taken up by the British Indian government and was supported by Rammohun Roy. Eventually in 1829, a law was passed prohibiting the practice in territories held by the British Indian government. The figures given for registered cases of sati in the early nineteenth century in the Bengal Presidency are quite staggering. In 1815, there were 378 cases. In 1818, the figure rose to 839 and, in 1828, there were 463 cases. These figures make an interesting parallel to those of dowry deaths in recent years, when young brides were said to have accidentally caught fire in the kitchen and died, this action being actually resorted to by her in-laws because of the dowry being smaller than anticipated by them. If widow immolation is to be seen as significant to Hindu values, then it would seem that Hindu culture has a propensity to burn its women. A magistrate of Hooghly describes the practice in 1818 as a religious act but also a choice entertainment for the neighbourhood. In areas where the Dayabhaga system of inheritance, directly affecting women, did not prevail, and there was also an absence of Kulin custom, the figures are substantially lower. The Madras Presidency in 1818 registers about 170 cases and the Bombay Presidency over the period from 1819–1827 about 50. Here it was largely among the families of chiefs and rajas.

This sharp variation in figures suggests that the appalling frequency of widow immolation was for various reasons endemic to Bengal at this time and its occurrence cannot be attributed only to the disjuncture in society caused by British colonial domination. Given the wide popularity of Shakta and Tantric sects in eastern India it is possible that the deliberate subordination of upper caste widows was also a reaction to the more equitable status of women in these sects. The Shakta sects which, more than most, emphasized the androgynous both in belief and deity, were opposed to the self-immolation of widows.

Viewed over time, the justification for widows becoming satis moved from the initial explanation that it was the faithful wife following her husband into death to one which included the idea of the sati becoming a goddess. In some cases, the faithful wife followed her husband irrespective of how he died, as in the case of Madri. Here the question of honour was not centrally involved as Pandu if anything died an ignoble death, unable to contain his lust for Madri.

The memorial stones suggest a different situation, where the husband dies a hero's death and the self-immolation of the wife is also memorialized. It is possible that immolation could have been enforced as a requirement to enhance the glory of the hero's death. The question of honour becomes central to the explanation where there is the possible violation of the wife by the enemy. The third situation relates to that of the elimination of a competitor for inheritance where both faithfulness and deification are emphasized. These situations relate to families of the upper castes and of high status and wealth. The act is supported by some persons of the upper castes, condemned by others of the same castes, but prohibited among those whose beliefs and values are said to have prevailed to a larger extent among the lower castes and persons of lesser status. The degree to which the motives conformed to the explanation given or arose from other factors needs to be analysed.

This is not to deny that on rare occasions it may have been an act of genuine grief and the desire to follow a husband into death. That the act of immolation is a form of sacrifice seems to be a more recent interpretation. The widow's life was not an offering or bali, for the motivation of the act in theory is that she continues to live after death with her husband in heaven. Furthermore, it can only be an act of self-sacrifice if it is not enforced.

It is argued that sati involves the question of Rajput honour and is deeply ingrained in all Rajputs. It is surely rather dishonourable that a society's honour should be dependent on women having to immolate themselves. The frequency of female infanticide in these areas makes one suspect that it was less a matter of honour and more a matter of other concerns. The custom has not been limited to Rajputs alone in the past, as has been claimed by various recently organized Rajput associations.

It is also quoted as a symbol of an idealized husband–wife relationship. If so, it has an unbalanced manifestation for, as has often been remarked, there is never any question of the husband immolating himself on the pyre of his wife. Nor is the immolation of the widow invariably voluntary. The widows of Bengal had to be tied to the pyre and kept down by bamboo staffs and there is little certainty that recent acts of immolation were also not enforced.

When it is stated that sati is a revival or continuation of a tradition, the particular tradition and the particular social group professing it needs to be ascertained. An attempt is being made to transfer a ritual associated with a small segment of upper-caste society to the entire society with the claim that it is the rite of the Hindu community. It was never regarded as universally applicable to all Hindus and even its limited applicability has always been controversial. Neither among Kshatriyas nor among Brahmanas was there a universal adherence to the custom. When it is taken up arbitrarily by some members of castes other than the Kshatriyas it is in the context of demonstrating status, or is linked to property inheritance. Thus, in spite of the disapproval of the act in their own religious texts, it was nevertheless observed on occasion by the wives of certain Sikh chiefs and of Maharaja Ranjit Singh. The justification incorrectly sought from Hindu dharma is an attempt to legitimize it, so that it can be treated as universally applicable.

To argue that the abolition of sati is a deliberately anti-Hindu act is to replay the debate of the nineteenth century where Rammohun Roy had maintained correctly that it does not carry the sanction of the Vedas and Mrityunjay Vidyalanka maintained that it was not enjoined by the shastras. If status has to be demonstrated today there are other ways of doing it than by burning wives.

That sati is being claimed as a Rajput ritual links it to the present-day concerns of the Rajputs. They were earlier the dominant caste both in terms of social status and access to economic resources not only in Rajasthan but in many parts of northern India. That dominance is now being eroded by new political groups. The Rajputs therefore seek to demonstrate their solidarity and status through other kinds of actions. One mechanism is to choose a ritual which is controversial and insist on supporting it. This is also one way of testing strength.

The choice of sati ties in with what is seen as a major threat to traditional authority, the changing role and status of women. The questioning of the earlier subordinate status of women is perceived as a loss of face for a male-dominated society. This reflects a social crisis but nevertheless the reason why it results in the burning of widows cannot be explained merely by the existence of a social crisis. Apart from this, by demonstrating solidarity on an issue such as sati there is a covert attempt to mobilize Rajputs and to undermine the perceived changes. This is in turn linked to political faction fights where those claiming to belong to Rajput castes can use this issue either way to consolidate their factions.

The notion of sati has moved a long way from questions of honour, the faithfulness of the wife, and the deification of the widow. The particular social groups supporting sati have changed over time and this change has had to do with the role, function, and rights of women in social relations, property relations, and rituals. Some social crises may have enhanced the idea of sati but significantly this idea was also endorsed by upper castes in situations where those of lesser standing argued for a better status for women. The extension of the symbolism of sati from the faithful wife to the goddess was not unrelated to the purposes of the social group endorsing the act. What is being objected to now by many is not merely the act of suicide, or when it is as in most cases enforced, the act of murder, but also the context of the act. This endorses an inconsequential existence for a woman and her subordination to the vulgarity of a public spectacle and to the manipulation of those claiming to be acting in defence of traditional values.

Sporadic references for or against the ritual do not tell us much. If sati is to be properly understood it would require a tracking down of information on widow self-immolation involving a number of sources, pertaining to a range of social groups and with reference to various regions at different points in time. Only when we examine the juxtaposition of kinship, property relations, rights of inheritance, the approach to sexuality, the ethic of the hero, attitudes to deity, and adjustments to social change in the context of our history, will we begin perhaps to understand why and how women were encouraged, or forced to, become satis.

II

CONTEMPORARY TIMES

6

RELIGION, CULTURE, AND NATION*

The infusion of a religion into politics changes, alters to various degrees, both the ideologies in politics as well the social application of religious ideas. This is currently demonstrated in the relationship of Hinduism to Hindutva.

NATIONAL CULTURE AND DEMOCRACY ARE said to be characteristic of the nation-state. Nationalism, among other things, situates that which is viewed as the national culture. Democracy can at one level be a mechanism for representing those that make up the nation-state, but it can also descend to becoming a numbers game in which politics is conditioned by a mechanical calculation of the number of voters. The assertion of the latter aspect of democracy is more easily visible. The definition of the majority usually takes the form of the assertion of a particular identity which can be religious or ethnic or linguistic and where the larger identity covers over and tries to erase the variations within the group irrespective of their more parochial affiliations, or else it can cut across all these in a general definition of the coming of nationalism.

Mobilization takes place through an assertion of this identity and a single religious identity is the qualifier. It is claimed that were this identity to come into being as the sole identity of the nation, there would be a true democracy based on equal rights for all—refraining from mentioning that 'all' here signifies only those that claimed that identity. Democracy then becomes a manipulation of votes in which not only are vote banks central but even changes

*An earlier version of this essay was first published in 1990.

such as the lowering of the age limit are due less to concerns about making the young responsible citizens and more to arithmetical calculations linked to voting patterns. Sentiments of various kinds are invoked and ratha yatras become vote yatras. In such situations the concept of a national culture takes on dimensions much larger than before, since it has to give a context to one or more majoritarian nationalisms.

The creation of a national culture in the colonial past was anti-colonial in its political message, but in its more narrowly cultural message it was inevitably defined in accordance with the views of the middle class. This led to its construction being influenced by both upper-caste culture and the 'discoveries' and interpretations of Orientalist research. The self-perception of the middle class was in terms of its own social origins, those of landowners, Brahmanas, scribal castes and those from families of well-established mercantile castes. The surnames of those who enter the lists of professionals in colonial times provides an index since most are the names of job or occupation or of geographical location. The transfer of power was at one level from colonial rule to upper castes. The secular ideal becomes important as and when the transfer of power draws near.

The problem of identity in the nation-state had by then assumed importance with the two-nation theory articulated in the demand for Pakistan and a majoritarian Hindu state, cutting across the main nationalist ideals. There was perhaps a subconscious concern that there might be a need to accommodate a variety of cultures, lest they each begin to demand independent states. The liberal values of the nationalist struggle required the inclusion of the culture of the lower castes, but this was never given serious thought and was more often than not included in the nebulous category of 'folk culture'. Even in areas such as Maharashtra and Tamil Nadu, where lower caste and scheduled caste movements had been prominently articulated during the struggle for independence, the subsequent situation endorsed a variant cultural idiom.

The need for a national culture was underlined and this

remained essentially a middle-class culture and largely 'Hindu'. The insistence on a single culture breeds its own opposition and groups fissioning off are characteristic of the ferment within the smooth exterior of the nation.

The fact of the plurality of Indian cultural expression whether of caste, language, religion, or class, whether popular or elite, and together with its implications, were not worked out. Plurality was seen as the coexistence of diverse cultures rather than their intermeshing. Since the Hindu religion was not projected as a clearly defined entity in historical terms as were the Semitic religions, there was greater mixing in the area of religion and culture. Themes which had played the role of cultural idioms were slowly confined to a narrowly defined religious expression, a process which was intensified after independence. There was neither a sufficient widening out of the themes through discussion nor presentation in experimental forms.

The most obvious example of this is the narrative of Rama, which has been treated in a variety of divergent ways by various social groups in the subcontinent in the past but which is now virtually seen only as a single religious concept. We seldom stop to think of what Rama may mean to the upland populations of north-eastern India for instance, so convinced are we that the numerical majority of Hindus and particularly those of the Hindi heartland can be the only arbiters of national culture. There are other narratives of a similar kind from other traditions which meet with the same result in a nationalizing process. To speak of various versions has been problematic.

This has a bearing on how we see the notion of tradition today. Tradition is not something which is handed down in its pristine form through generations. It is that which is chosen from the past, imbued with a meaning which derives from the present, or can even be an invention of the present which is legitimized by an association with the past. A conscious comprehension of tradition does not imply a severance with the tradition of the past but it does require a distancing from it.

To be steeped in tradition is frequently to be steeped in what one believes, or would like to believe, is the tradition. The appropriation of tradition also becomes a matter of political importance. This perhaps is where the rational, secular approach to the Indian past and the Indian present has ignored tradition, or at any rate has not come to terms with having to define tradition differently in order that those who have already done so be denied the political mileage which they obtain from such claims.

Seen in this context the BJP–VHP–RSS–Bajrang Dal politics with its claim to speaking in the tongues of religion and culture becomes a major political and cultural crisis for the Indian nation-state. The Sangh Parivar a few decades ago invented a tradition in focusing on one issue, that of the Babri Masjid–Ram Janmabhoomi dispute. It originally claimed the historicity of Rama and his birthplace, and when this was questioned, it argued on the basis of faith and disallowed history. Today it has shifted its ground and is trying to use archaeology to prove the existence of a temple dedicated to Rama, destroyed and replaced by the Babri Masjid. It is back again claiming historicity but on contested evidence. In other words, it conforms to creating what is passed off as tradition and is given a historical basis which again is created in the present and does not reflect the actual past. It relates to the imagined past. It tries to keep up with the professional construction of the historically attested past, by introducing garbled versions of new sources, as for instance in archaeological data.

Even if such a temple existed, that is not the point at issue. To insist on the destruction of the mosque and its replacement by a temple is merely to return to the politics of the medieval past as well as an attempt to maintain that history can be unravelled and reknit. Earlier periods of history in many parts of the world witnessed the quick-change act of churches and mosques and temples being converted and reconverted from one to the other—the most impressive examples being Cordova and Istanbul. In other cases, the destruction of the monument was an act of politics. Similarly, the issue at Ayodhya was also political and the demand for the destruction of the mosque was a return to the politics of an earlier period of history, which period cannot be brought to life and changed, nor can the acts of that time be avenged, for such vengeance has first to be proved necessary and if carried out can only spell disaster for present times. Such a stand is essentially a mobilization for political representation in the present period on the basis of religious affiliation. Such mobilization further forecloses the need to consider the plurality of cultures in India, our national culture will be defined by one group alone as is currently happening. In the official defining of a national identity, pluralities come under attack.

The concept of a Hindu Rashtra is projected as the national aim. It seeks to bind everyone by discarding those cultural elements which are not in conformity with its definition of what constitutes a nation and national culture. Uniformities, however, breed their own dissenters. The experience of Pakistan since 1947 is a clear pointer. In India, too, not all protesting groups are inspired by a communal ideology. Often the protests arise from a different construction of identity or the desire for such.

The urge towards political domination by those who proclaim this ideology is strengthened by taking an extreme position and then insisting that others should comply with the demands of the BJP. It is the practice of brinkmanship where the issue is forced to a critical point and even a compromise at this point is a bigger gain than from a campaign which is conducted along democratic lines. This further requires a hysterical momentum which is achieved by mounting deadlines, emphasizing threats, and making an all-out effort to draw in large numbers as supporters.

Such an effort has no qualms in propagating lies, as for example attributing incorrect statements to past leaders or maintaining that the temple at Somnath was built on a graveyard or that the government has paid a sum of ₹50 lakh to the imam of Jama

Masjid in Delhi as yet again an appeasement of the Muslims. The repetition of the lie makes it into a truth for their followers. The ratha yatra carried overtones of a dig-vijaya and it only remained for Advani to have ridden a white horse or posed as Kalkin, the avatara yet to come.

In a curiously inverted kind of way, the Sangh Parivar movement has a 'minority' character and is reminiscent in form and spirit of separatist movements such as we have in its initial phase of public proclamation witnessed in the last few decades. It used the symbols of separatism and the question therefore arises as to what was and is the nature of its separatism.

Perhaps the BJP saw itself at that time as a minority within the large mass of what is called the majority community. The confrontation has therefore to be seen at two levels: one is with the non-Hindu religious communities, and the other is within the Hindu community, a label which includes the whole hierarchy of 'Hindu' castes. Its militancy and aggressiveness come not only from the nature of the political backing which it commands but also from the fervour of the young armed with weapons. This is where the role of Hindutva as ideology is significant.

Rusty swords and trishulas should not be underestimated, nor the possible switch to more lethal arms, should the movement be thwarted. Looting and killing in the name of Rama does not seem to strike a discordant note among them. Those that die in police firing become martyrs. Where aggression fails, the movement becomes coercive. The militant hysteria is fanned now by the playing of cassette tapes exhorting Hindus to violence and the showing of films whose message is the same and more recently in public speeches of politicians and heads of religious institutions. That these are having the desired effect is clear from the increase in communal rioting. This hysteria is necessary to militancy. The parallel with the tapes of the speeches of Bhindranwale heard all over the Punjab comes to mind.

Earlier the focus was on a demand—the destruction of a mosque and its replacement by a temple—a demand which is basically a test of political strength although it is couched in religious and cultural terms. In fact, it involved power, status, and territory. The demand has now been met by the BJP. This was merely the initial demand and it is a foregone conclusion that more would follow. There is a deliberate use of symbols, such as the name of the Bajrang Dal, and the enforced use of the greeting of Jai Siya Ram which has become almost a password. It is reported that a lucrative souvenir business has sprung up with the selling of postcards showing the capturing of the mosque, photographs of those who died in police firing, and a general commercialization of these events. The carrying of the ashes of the 'martyrs' in processions is a rather unfortunate part of the general build-up, unfortunate because it is so out of character with what is the normal ritual of the ashes of the dead. This is passed off as tradition but it is an invention of recent politics.

Such activities would come as a surprise to the genuine Rama bhakt. The latter is unconcerned with the historicity of incarnations, the validity of birthplaces and sacred spots, which he will happily accept as a matter of faith and which he may also reject as a matter of faith. There is little of the devotion to a deity or the sharing of divine grace which was associated with bhakti, for the ethos of bhakti has given way to the ethos of danda—coercive authority. The mechanism of coercion has drawn in even the media, and is accompanied by an advertising skill that many ad agencies would envy. The hidden separatism which conditions the demands of the BJP is not just for the setting up of a separate nation-state, but also for the setting up of a separate state of mind.

Separation requires an enemy against which it can define itself and the enemy is generally within the nation and constituted of other groups. The enemy is basically those who identify or are said to identify in parallel forms, namely, the religious minorities who go under the label of Muslim, Sikh, and Christian. The use of the word 'minority' hides the strength of such groups by giving them a negative connotation. The attack is directed towards the largest of the 'minorities' so that the reduction to silence of this group will have a salutary effect on the rest.

Also the largest is the most visible. The strength sought by minorities through communalizing their identity plays into the hands of majority communalism. As long as such 'minorities' also insist on seeing themselves identified only as religious communities, their weakness in the face of the larger religious community will remain. If the minorities were to emphasize other identities, other than religion, such a change would weaken the 'majority' communalism. The enemy would be obscured. And without a clearly defined enemy, the thrust of communalism would get diluted.

This is not to suggest that confronting communalism should not also come from within the community to whom the appeal of communalism is addressed. To make such an appeal relatively ineffective would require more than just the countering of communal rhetoric: it would require the kind of social change which reduces dependence on communal fantasies and the manipulation of such fantasies by political parties.

The enemy within includes others such as the Dalits and those referred to as 'tribals'. The latter are, for the moment, viewed as too distanced culturally, and are therefore better handled by being acculturated to middle-class Hinduism: hence the active Hindu missionary efforts among the 'tribals'. The Dalits and the lower castes are sought to be incorporated but only at the level of token association, such as getting a Dalit to lay the foundation stone of a temple. In effect, militant Hinduism has little use for the Dalit except, literally, for providing a vote.

Lower castes similarly have to maintain an uneasy balance. Caste articulations can change. The leadership of the BJP and much of its support came previously from the upper and middle level castes. Their articulation at the time when the Mandal Commission Report was sought to be put into practice made it clear that they would not accept a sharing of the cake. There is among them little sensitivity to the views and perceptions of the lower castes, the Dalits, and the tribals in the construction of Hindutva. The latter groups would have to find other means of incorporating their perceptions into what is often described as the 'national mainstream'.

By converting the debate into pro- or anti-Mandal Commission at the end of the last century the historical significance of the moment was missed, when there could have been a powerful demand for the reordering of national priorities so as to bring about a substantial change in the ordering of Indian society. The present dissonance in the fragments of Indian society followed and is likely to continue.

Today there are erstwhile upper castes anxious to be included in the category of Other Backward Classes (OBC) so as to obtain the benefits given to this category in education and government employment by applying the Mandal Commission Report.

7

CONTINUOUS BEGINNINGS*

A historical moment is never a static condition. It is constantly moving from the past into the present, anticipating the future. Such movements are mutations that help us to recognize change, and we learn to relate each movement to its context.

CULTURAL SURVIVALS IN INDIA PROVIDE a perspective on Indian history which is unusual and valuable. The survivals are not fossilized and the impact of what are generally regarded as important factors in cultural change such as the environment, economy, the intrusion of alien cultures and ideology that come to be internalized, can therefore be seen as contemporary processes which take on the quality almost of flashbacks in history. These early forms of culture and society as they undergo change provide insights into the past, some of which are suggestive of the genesis of social forms. I would like to relate these ideas to the need for looking more critically at the process of change in the past, confining myself however to the early period of Indian history. I would at the same time like to emphasize that many of the questions raised with reference to the more remote past remain pertinent to some of the less evident but nonetheless significant aspects of contemporary India.

In the study of the many sub-periods within the broad boundaries of the ancient period, fundamental questions arise, providing scope for wide-ranging discussion. For a better definition of these sub-periods, and in the interest of historical clarity, a considerable refinement of concepts and theories becomes

*An earlier version of this essay was first published in 1984.

necessary. Many of the crucial terms used in the definitions have been applied to such diverse social forms that they cease to have a specific meaning and tend to mask the diversities.

This sharpening of focus becomes particularly necessary with the growing interest in social and economic history. It will also help in understanding the process or historical mutation over time. Although there is now a rich literature describing segments of the period, the explanation of change from one to the next and the linkages between these require a fuller consideration. A creatively critical discussion is called for on the terms used to translate categories mentioned in the sources since much of the interpretation depends on such discussion.

The nineteenth century was the age of the grand edifices of historical explanation and theoretical construction. While some of these edifices still stand firm, others are tottering. Even those which still stand often require repair and renovation, sometimes of a structural kind, in the light of new knowledge and fresh theories. The refining of concepts and theories therefore becomes a necessary part of the historical exercise and is particularly incumbent on those who, as conscientious historians, build their explanations on the basis of theoretical frameworks.

Among the early sub-periods, Vedic society has been described as a tribal one. The term 'tribal', which we have all used in the past, has rightly come in for some questioning. In its precise meaning it refers to a community of people claiming descent from a common ancestor. Marriage alliances have to follow an order. It is easier to organize this if groups of people are identified by status which would mean varna i.e., social rank and control over resources. In its application, however, it has been used to cover a variety of social and economic forms, not to mention racial and biological identities; and this tends to confuse the original meaning. Even as a convention it has lost much of its precision. The more recently preferred term, lineage, narrows the focus, as also does the use of the term clan. Although the economic range remains, lineage does emphasize succession and descent with the implication that these are decisive in determining social status and control over economic resources. It also helps differentiate between chiefship where lineage dominates and kingship, which as a different category, evokes a larger number of impersonal sanctions and a greater centralization of authority within an extended family. A clan relates its kinship connections but is a larger unit than an extended family and may therefore be governed by endogamy—marrying within the group—or exogamy—marrying outside the group.

The concept of vamsa (succession) carries a meaning similar to lineage and is central to Vedic society with its emphasis on succession even as a simulated lineage. Thus vamsa is used to mean lineage or descent group among the Rajanyas and Kshatriyas but is also used in the list of Upanisadic teachers where succession does not appear to be by birth but by the passing on of a tradition of knowledge. Lineage also becomes important in the structure of each varna defined by permitted rules of marriage and kinship and by ranking it in order of status, the control over resources being implicit. The emergence of the four varnas is the marking of status, but within its smaller groups, is closely allied to the essentials of a lineage-based society.

In a stratified society the reinforcing of status is necessary. But where there is no recognized private property in land, and no effective state, such reinforcing has to be done by sanctions which often take a ritual or religious form. In the absence of taxation as a system of control in the Vedic period, sacrificial ritual functioned as the occasion for renewing the status of the yajamana (he who orders the sacrifice, the patron).

Apart from its religious and social role, sacrificial ritual also had an economic function. It was the occasion when wealth which had been channelled to the yajamana was distributed by him in the form of gifts to the Brahmana priests which strengthened their social rank and ensured them wealth. The ritual served to restrict the distribution of wealth to the Brahmanas and the Kshatriyas but at the same time prevented a substantial accumulation of wealth by either, for whatever came in the form of gifts and prestations from the vish, the lesser clans, to the Kshatriyas the ruling clans, was largely consumed in the ritual and the remainder gifted to the Brahmanas. Generosity being important to the office of the chief, wealth was not hoarded.

The display, consuming, and distribution of wealth at the major rituals such as the rajasuya and the ashvamedha was in turn a stimulus to production, for the ritual was also seen as a communication with and sanction from the supernatural. Embedded in the sacrificial ritual therefore were important facets of the economy. This may be a partial explanation of why a major change to the state system and a peasant economy occurred initially in the mid-first millennium BC not in the western Ganga plain but in the adjoining area of the middle Ganga plain. This change was occasioned not only by an increase in economic production and a greater social disparity but also by the fact that the prestation economy associated with the lineage-based society and the activity of gift-giving became more and more marginal in the latter region and in some areas was altogether absent.

The term 'peasant economy' is frowned upon by some scholars as an imprecise concept. However, it is of some use as a measurement of change. The label of 'peasant' has been applied to a variety of categories, some of which are dissimilar. The use of a single word as a portmanteau description confuses the categories and therefore a differentiation is necessary. The anthropologist Eric R. Wolf defines peasants as: 'Rural cultivators whose surpluses are transferred to a dominant group of rulers that uses the surpluses both to underwrite its own standard of living and to distribute the remainder to groups in society that do not farm but must be fed for their specific goods and services in turn.'

This definition seems to me inadequate, for the important point is not merely the existence of a surplus but the mechanism by which it is transferred and it is to this that I would relate the emergence of a peasant economy. That the recognition of an incipient peasant economy in various parts of India is significant to the study of social history hardly needs stressing, since concomitant with this is also the establishing of particular kinds of state systems, variant forms of jatis, and new religious and cultural idioms in the area.

For the early period of Indian history, the term peasant has been used to translate both the Rig Vedic vish as well as the gahapati or grihapati (head of a household) of later texts. But some distinction is called for. The Vedic vish was primarily a member of a clan although this did not preclude him from being a cultivator as well. The transferring of surpluses, in this case the voluntary prestations of the vish to the Kshatriya, points to a stratified rather than an egalitarian society and the simile of the Kshatriya eating the vish like the deer eating the grain would indicate greater pressures for larger prestations.

But the transfer was not through an enforced system of taxation. In the absence of private ownership of land, the relationship of the vish to the Kshatriya would have been less contrapuntal with little need of an enforced collection of the surplus. The context of Vedic references to bali, bhaga, and shulka (the terms used in later periods for taxes) suggest that they were voluntary and random although the randomness gradually changed to required prestations particularly at sacrificial rituals.

However, the three major prerequisites governing a system of taxation—a contracted amount collected at stipulated periods by persons designated as tax collectors—are absent in the Vedic texts. The recognition of these prerequisites in the post-Vedic period and the collection of taxes from the cultivators by the state would seem decisive in registering the change from cultivators to peasants in which the existence of an economy based on peasant agriculture becomes clear.

The introduction of taxation presupposes the impersonal authority of the state and some degree of alienation of the cultivator from the authority to whom the surplus is given, unlike the lineage-based society where prestations are more personalized. Taxation reduced the quantity of prestations and became the more substantial part of what was taken from the peasant, but prestations were not terminated. The sanction of the religious ritual becomes more marginal and that of the state more central, the change occurring gradually over time.

The formation of the state is therefore tied into this change. For the cultivator, land becomes property or a legal entity and the pressures on cultivation have to do not only with subsistence but also with a provision for ensuring a surplus. This highlights the difference between appropriation in the earlier system and exploitation in the latter.

The Vedic vish was more a generalized term in which herding, cultivation, and minimal crafts adequate to a household were included. Such groups were germane to the later peasant household. In effect, because the relationship with the dominant Kshatriyas was based on gifts and prestations rather than on laws, these cultivators would seem part of a lineage society in which their subservience to a dominant group arose more out of the exigencies of kinship or the ordering of clans than out of exploited labour, although the latter can be seen to increase in time.

The gradual mutation which took place becomes evident from the frequent references in the Pali sources to the gahapati. The existence of the gahapati focuses more sharply on the presence of what might be called a peasant economy. But to translate gahapati as peasant is to provide a mere slice of its total meaning. Derived from grhapati, the head of the household, the term gahapati includes a range of meanings such as the wealthy Mahashala Brahmanas addressed as gahapatis by the Buddha, who had received as donations extensive tax-free arable land as well as those who paid taxes to the wealthy landowners who cultivated their large farms with the help of slaves and hired labourers (dasa-bhritaka).

Those at the lower end of the scale who either owned small plots of land or were professional ploughmen are more often referred to as the kassakas. The *Arthashastra* mentions tenants as upavasa and also refers to another category—the Shudra cultivators settled by the state on cultivable or waste land on a different system of tenure from the above; as also the range of cultivators employed on the state farms supervised by the overseers of agriculture, the sitadhyaksha.

Gahapati, therefore, is perhaps better translated as the landowner of some substance who would generally pay taxes to the state except when the land which he owned was a religious benefice. The ownership of land and the payment of taxes demarcates this period as one in which a peasant-based economy is evident. Traces of the lineage-based society continued in the marking of status by varna and the performance, although by now of marginal economic significance, of the sacrificial rituals.

That the gahapati was not even just a landowner but more a man of means is supported by the fact that it was from the ranks of the gahapatis that there emerged the setthis or financiers. The two terms are often associated in the literature and this is further attested in the votive inscriptions recording donations to the sangha in central India and the western and eastern Deccan from the late first millennium BC. Gahapati fathers have setthi sons as well as the other way round. It would seem that gahapati status was acquired through the practice of any respectable profession which provided a decent income, although the most frequent references are to land-ownership and commerce.

This is not to suggest that trade originated with the land-owning groups but rather that the large-scale commercialization of exchange was tied to the emergence of the wealthy gahapati. In examining the origins of trade, it is necessary to define more clearly the nature of the exchange involved. Broadly, there are some recognizable forms of exchange which can either develop into commercialized exchange or supplement it. There is evidence of luxury goods exchanged by ruling groups as a part of gift exchange. Marriage alliances between Kshatriya families involved an exchange of gifts. Thus, when Bharata visits his maternal Kekeya kinsmen, he returns with gifts. This is not an exchange based on need but is a channel through which status and kinship is confirmed. It may in addition lead to other forms of exchange.

The major royal sacrifices required tributes and gifts and the rajasuya of Yudhishthira provides an interesting inventory of valued items. The more ordinary sacrificial rituals involved the giving of gifts such as cattle, horses, gold, dasis, and chariots by the yajamana to the priests. These gifts became part of a distribution and exchange of wealth which in lineage-based societies formed the salient part of the wealth of those who ruled, whereas in the change to an economy based on peasant agriculture, they were merely a part of the wealth accumulated by the ruling families and the more wealthy gahapatis.

Less spectacular but more essential was another form of exchange, that of raw materials and commodities brought by itinerant groups such as smiths and pastoralists. It has been argued that the itinerant metalsmiths formed a network of connections between villages. Metal, particularly iron, was also a major item of regular trade. The role of pastoralists in trading circuits is now coming in for considerable attention particularly with reference to those groups which had a regular pattern of transhumance. Exchange through sources of itinerant professionals was probably the starting point of the beat of pedlars which is a continuing feature of one level of exchange in India.

Yet another category is what might be called exchange between one settlement and the next. This is a useful basis for plotting the gradual diffusion of an item as, for example, the better-quality varieties of pottery in archaeological evidence. Such an exchange provides evidence not only on local trade but also on the geographical reach of intra-regional contacts. Some of these settlements may then have come to play the role of local markets, the equivalent perhaps of what the Pali texts refer to as the nigama. These in turn are likely to have been the nuclei of urban growth as in the case of Rajagriha and Shravasti.

Distinct from all these is the familiar picture of trade which dominates the scene in the post-Mauryan period. This is the commercial exchange between two or more centres processing and producing commodities specifically destined for trade. The organization of this more complex form involved a hierarchy of producers and traders some of whom were sedentary while others were carriers of the items traded but of a different order from pedlars and pastoralists. The picture of commercialized exchange emerges from Buddhist texts and by the time of the *Arthashastra*, it is regarded as a legitimate source of revenue for the state. The question then arose of the degree of state interference and control which would be conducive to increasing the finances of the state.

The major artefact in this trade (other than the commodities) was coined metallic money, providing evidence of the degree of complexity and the extent of such trade and trading circuits. These early coins in some instances were issued by the nigama and in other cases may have been issued by local authorities or possibly by ruling families. In the post-Mauryan period, dynastic issues gained currency, a clear pointer to the importance of commercialized exchange. However, even in this period local issues remained in circulation suggesting multiple levels of exchange.

With such commercialized exchange, the control of trade routes becomes a significant factor in political policy and military annexations. Recent analyses of the Central Asian Silk Route involving a variety of levels of exchange from gift exchange to sophisticated emporia, in the context of political relations between tribal groups and established centres of political power, suggest ways in which the complicated question of trade, often treated as a uniform monolith by historians of ancient India, may be investigated. The Roman or Eastern Mediterranean trade with India at the turn of the Christian era, as is clear from both commodities and the function of money, also spans a similar range. Diverse forms of exchange within a larger trading system suggest the coexistence of various economic levels within that system and sharpen the social contours of the groups involved. The same can be said of the maritime trade of Indian traders with Southeast Asia and Arab traders with Western India.

The analysis of trade also requires locating those involved in these exchanges in the social hierarchy of the time. In the production of goods for exchange, artisans, whether individuals or in guilds, related to merchants and financiers in forms as diverse as the various categories of cultivators to landowners. The role of the shilpin (artisan) and the shreni (guild) is quite distinct from the setthi. Their presence registers a change in the nature of the trade as also does the differentiation between categories of professionals such as the vanija, the setthi, and the sarthavaha.

Clearly, there is a sea change when commercialized exchange becomes active. The investment required for an elaborate trade can only be provided by a well-endowed social group which can invest its surplus in risk-taking ventures. The obvious category was the gahapati who could fall back on cultivating land if the venture failed. That it turned out to be highly successful is clear from the fact that not only did the setthis emerge from the ranks of the gahapatis, but, by the post-Mauryan period, had an independent identity as financiers and gradually were on a par with the gahapatis.

The wealth of the setthis became in turn an avenue to power, for some of them were known to be financiers of kings and obtained in return rights to collect revenue, perhaps the prototype of what was later to become the regular form of emoluments to administrative officers. On the manifestations of trade, Buddhist and Jaina sources together with epigraphic and archaeological evidence provide a useful counterpoint to the Dharmashastra literature of this period. An inscription from Pehoa (Haryana) was issued by a group of Brahmanas who state that they made their wealth through trading in horses imported from Central Asia, and who became so wealthy that they made substantial donations to various temples.

The link between agriculture and commerce is important for understanding the changes in the subsequent period. The opulence of those involved in commerce was poured into the adornment of religious monuments, monasteries, and images and later into temples, and also in the conspicuous consumption which is associated with the wealthier town-dwellers of these times. This tends to obscure the agrarian scene where one notices less of mahashala landowners and large estates and more of those with smaller holdings.

Small plots of land could be purchased and donated to religious beneficiaries and it seems unlikely, as has been argued, that such sales were restricted to religious donations. Small-holdings together with the alienation of land could point to some degree of impoverishment among peasants. The inclusion of debt bondage (ahitaka and atmavikreta), as a regular if not frequent category of slavery, as well as the increasing references to vishti (forced labour or a labour tax), suggest a different rural scene from that of the preceding period. That oppressive taxation had become a recognized evil is explicitly mentioned in various texts.

This mutation was endemic to the evident change in the post-Gupta period. Where trade flourished, the resources of the urban centres and the trade routes buoyed up the system; but this period points to a declining trade in many areas. Internal commercialized trade requires the ballast of agrarian settlements and where lineage-based societies could be converted into economies, the agrarian support to trade would be strengthened.

Earlier networks of exchange had permitted an easier coexistence with lineage-based societies. Their resources, generally raw materials such as timber and gemstones, could, as items of exchange, be easily tapped by traders through barter and direct exchange without disturbing the social structure to any appreciable degree. On the other hand, because of the requirement of land and labour, state systems more heavily dependent on a peasant economy had to absorb these societies and convert them into peasant economies in order to extract the benefits.

Where trade declined or where new states were established, the need to develop the agrarian economy became urgent. The granting of land appears to have been the mechanism adopted for changing the agrarian situation. The reasons for this change in the post-Gupta period need more detailed investigation particularly at a regional level. In the very useful work done so far substantial data has surfaced. What is now required is a sifting and classifying of the data to provide more precise answers and to evoke fresh questions.* It is curious that there is little resort in this period to

---

*Much of the argument in the debate on the economy of India in the late first and second millennium AD has been of a generalized form. Perhaps what is required at this stage is a comparative regional view which could better cope with the areas of investigation which call for analysis. Initially, a few selected regions could be analysed in depth for both the urban and the agrarian aspects of the economy but a start could be made with the agrarian. A tabulation of the data might sharpen the focus. Grants in a region could be classified in accordance with the type of grantee and the nature of the grant. Categories could be defined such as grants of wasteland or cultivated land, grants converting lineage-based societies into peasant economies where the grant would be made to the lineage chief, or grants of state-owned lands already cultivated where cultivators were transferred along with the land, and other such categories where data is available. The chronological order and quantum of each would be useful information. Proprietor rights could also be part of this tabulation.

At another level, the analyses of the titles of grantees and changes therein might provide clues. The question of whether the peasantry was free hinges not only on the technical and legal definitions but also requires a discussion of the actual status of the peasant. Rights, obligations, and dues of the grantees vis-a-vis the peasants would need to be tabulated in detail. These would provide some indications of the essentials of the prevailing system.

A worm's eye view of agriculture also needs to be investigated since some aspects of the debate involve questions relating to soil fertility and control over water resources. Some of these questions could be better answered through inter-disciplinary research if historians were to work jointly with specialists in soil analysis and hydrology. The expertise of a wide range of agricultural scientists has entered into debates on the archaeological evidence relating to agriculture but curiously it has not been invited by the economic historians into their domain.

the policy recommended by the *Arthashastra* and other texts of establishing colonies of cultivators on land of the state so as to extend agriculture and thereby increase the revenue. This was to come later. Was the state unable to do so because it lacked the administrative infrastructure or was it because it did not have the power to implement such a policy? Instead, the state increased the grants of land to religious beneficiaries and later to administrative officers in lieu of a salary. Thus helping to extend cultivated land. This points to a need for an evaluation of the nature of the states of this period with the possibility that their formation and structure were different from the previous ones.

Was this type of state attempting to restore the economy to an extent greater than the previous ones which appear to have been more concerned with revenue-collecting functions, judging by the model advocated by Kautilya? Did the system of granting land predominate (perhaps initially) in areas where lineage-based societies were prevalent so as to facilitate their conversion to a peasant economy where lineage could also be used for economic control and to a varna and jati network? The identification with

---

Now that the study of these subjects has become so specialized, this reluctance as well as the absence of field studies is to be regretted. Considering that the data from survivals of various forms would be much richer for medieval history than for the ancient period one can only hope that a trend in this direction will become more extensive in the various regions. An increase in data of the technical kind can assist the quality of theoretical analysis. Questions more specific to the history of agriculture relate to investigating cultivation techniques, crop patterns, crop rotation, irrigation systems, and water cesses, the percentage of arable land available in an area which would condition decisions about starting new settlements or intensifying existing agriculture, variations in the system of fallow for particular crops, the site of holdings in relation to the quality of the soil and the crop, the subsistence level of the peasant, labour input and land and crops and other similar questions. Many of these questions would involve extrapolating back from revenue records as well as considerable fieldwork in the area under study, in order to sharpen the questions and gain insights into possibilities for an earlier period. It is not for nothing that R. H. Tawney is believed to have said that the first essential of research into agrarian history is a stout pair of boots.

varna status would have acted as a bridge to a peasant economy and prevented a rupture with the lineage system. Elements of lineage have often continued even in some areas where peasant agriculture became the norm.

Religious benefices were on the pattern of earlier grants and were not strictly an innovation except that now grants were made increasingly to Brahmanas and ostensibly in return for legitimizing the dynasty and for acquiring religious merit. These were the stated reasons for the grant but were not sufficient reasons. Grants of this nature, as has been pointed out, were a channel of acculturation. They could also be used as foci of political loyalty.

If the grants were made initially from state-owned lands, they amounted to a renouncing of revenue. If the state was unable to administer the extension of agriculture, then was the system of grants also introduced to encourage settlements in new areas where the grant was of wasteland, or alternatively of cultivated lands to stabilize the peasantry and induce increased production? Given the fact that slaves were not used in any quantitative degree in agricultural production at this time, was the system of grants an attempt at converting the peasantry into a stable productive force through various mechanisms of subordination and a chain of intermediaries?

Interestingly, the term gahapati drops out of currency for the system had changed and terms incorporating raja, samanta, and bhogin became frequent. The recipients of land grants had the right to receive a range of taxes and dues previously collected by the state and were given administrative powers as well. This permitted them to act as a 'backup' administration where the grant was in settled areas and to introduce the system where new settlements were being established. It may in origin have been a fiscal measure but in effect became the means of controlling the peasantry.

The apparent increase in debt bondage and the fear of peasant migration would point to this being one of the functions of the large-scale grants. That the possibility of peasant migration to alleviate discontent was being slowly stifled is suggested by the fact of peasants taking to revolt as well, from the early second millennium onwards. A rise in brigandage may well have been a possibility for this period. A qualitative change occurs when the state begins to grant villages or substantial acreages of land already under cultivation: a change which reflects both on the economy and on the nature of the state.

The need to fetter the peasantry would seem an evident departure from the earlier system and this in turn introduced a change in the relationship between the cultivator and the land now riveted in legalities and liabilities, with tax or rent no longer being the sole criterion of a peasant economy. The cultivator of this period found himself in a different situation from the same of earlier times. The term 'peasant' therefore cannot have a blanket usage or meaning since the variations within it and its changing context have to be distinguished.

The secular grantees were part of a hierarchical system in which they mirrored the court at the local level. This is evident from their attempts to imitate the courtly style as depicted in the art and literature of the time. Grants of land to the Brahmanas as the major religious grantees rehabilitated them to a position of authority and (their anguished invocation of Kalki as a millennial figure became less urgent).

A new religious ideology evolving in the mid-first millennium AD gained popularity focussing on the image and the temple and asserting an assimilative quality involving the cults and rituals of Puranic Hinduism and the genesis of the Bhakti tradition. Ideological assimilation is called for when there is a need to knit together socially diverse groups. It is also crucial when there is an increase in the distancing between such groups as well as the power of some over others and the economic disparity between them.

The significance of these new cults and sects may lie in part in the focus on loyalty to a deity which has a parallel to their loyalty to an overlord. But it would be worth examining the rudiments of each sect in its regional dimension, its groping towards a jati status, and the use of an ostensibly cultural and religious idiom to express a new social identity. Were these also mechanisms of legitimizing territorial identities drawn on sacred geography and pilgrimage routes with the temple as the focal point?

The egalitarian emphasis of the devotees in the eyes of the deity has rightly been viewed as the assertion of those lower down the social scale in favour of a more egalitarian society. But its significance grows when the social background to this belief is one of increasing disparity. Movements of dissent which had religious forms were often gradually accommodated and their radical content slowly diluted. The move away from community participation in a ritual to a personalized and private worship encourages the notion of individual freedom even if it is only at the ideological level.

In the justifiable emphasis on social and economic history there has been too frequently a neglect among historians of the analysis of ideology. To study ideology without its historical context is to practise historical hydroponics, for ideas and beliefs strike roots in the humus of historical reality. To restrict the study of a society to its narrowly social and economic forms alone is to see it in a limited two-dimensional profile. The interaction of society and ideology takes a varied pattern and to insist always on the primacy of the one over the other is to deny the richness of a full-bodied historical explanation.

Ideas are sometimes analysed as a response to social pressures and needs. This is particularly pertinent for those dealing with social history. Some of the more important literature is suffused with a theoretical representation of society even in symbolic or ideational forms. Meanings very often do not stem from just the vocabulary but require familiarity with the cultural context of the word. Examples of this would be the levels of meaning in words such as varna and jati as they travel through texts such as the Dharmashastras. The ideological layers in the latter as codes of behaviour have to be peeled in order to obtain a better comprehension of their ordering of society.

Central to any concern with ideology in the ancient past is the critique of religious thought (as distinct from religious practice or organization). Some analyses of the Upanishads, for instance, can provide an interesting example of this. One of the major strands of Upanishadic thought is said to be a secret doctrine known only to a few Kshatriyas who teach it to select, trusted Brahmanas. Even the most learned among the latter, the Mahashala, are described as going to Kshatriyas for instruction. The doctrine involves the idea of the soul, the atman, and its ultimate merging with the Brahman as well as metempsychosis of the transmigration of the soul; in fact, a fundamental doctrine of this age which was to have far-reaching consequences on Indian society.

That it should have been secret and originally associated with the Kshatriyas raises many questions, some of which have been discussed by scholars. It is true that the Brahmanas and the Kshatriyas were both members of the leisured classes in Vedic society and could therefore indulge in idealistic philosophy and discourse on the niceties of life after death. But this is only a partial answer and much more remains to be explained. Was the ritual of sacrifice so deeply imprinted on the Brahmana mind, and so necessary to the profession at this point, that it required non-Brahmanas to introduce alternatives to salvation, other than the sacrificial ritual? The adoption of meditation and theories of transmigration had the advantage of releasing the Kshatriyas from the pressures of a prestation economy and permitting them to accumulate wealth, power, and leisure.

Alternatively, was the accumulation of those already present in the fringe areas described as the mlecchadesha (impure lands) in Vedic texts, areas where the sacrificial rituals for various reasons had become less important? Thus Janaka of Mithila, Ashvapati Kaikeya, and Ajatashatru of Kashi could reflect on alternative ways to salvation. This also places a different emphasis on the function of the Kshatriya who had now ceased to be primarily a cattle-raiding warrior chief.

These are not the only kinds of connections relevant to a history of the period. Upper and lower social categories or even classes treated as monolithic belie social reality. The tensions within these should also be noticed where the evidence suggests this. The competition for status between Brahmanas and Kshatriyas, and the separation of their functions, as well as their mutual dependence, is symbolized in the sacrificial ritual which becomes a key articulation of the relationship. The new belief was the reversal of the sacrificial ritual in that it required neither priests nor deities but only self-discipline and meditation. At another level, the transmigrating of the soul through the natural elements and plants to its ultimate rebirth carries an echo of shamanism which may have remained popular outside priestly ritual.

There is in the new belief the first element of a shift from the clan to the individual inasmuch as the sacrificial ritual involved the clan but meditation and self-discipline, perhaps in opposition to the clan, involved only the individual. It symbolizes the breaking away of the individual from the clan. It also introduces an element of anomie which becomes more apparent in the later development of these beliefs by various sects. These reflections were seminal to what became a major direction of a minority in Indian thought and action, the opting out of the individual from society, and where renunciation is a method of self-discovery but can also carry a message of dissent.

That the new ideas were attributed to the Kshatriyas and yet included in a Brahmanical text was probably because for the Brahmanas to author a doctrine openly questioning the sacrificial ritual would, at this stage, have been an anomaly. That the doctrine stimulated philosophical discussion would in itself have required that it be recorded. But its inclusion may also partially have been motivated by the fact that when the doctrine was appropriated by heterodox teachers such as the Buddha, it could be claimed that even the roots of heterodoxy stemmed from the Vedic tradition.

This was to become yet another technique by which orthodox theory in subsequent centuries sought to disguise ideas contradicting its own position. The Buddha not only democratized the doctrine but also nurtured the idea of karma and samsara and related it, among other things, to social iniquities. But his negation of the soul (atman) introduces a contradiction of the doctrine as visualized in the Upanishads. Such theoretical contradictions were current at that time. The positing of a thesis and an anti-thesis became a characteristic feature of philosophical debate and was reflected both in empirical disciplines such as grammar as well as in more abstract analysis.

The relating of ideology to historical reality can result not only in new ways of examining an historical situation and be used to extend or modify the analysis from other sources but can also help in confirming the reality as derived from other sources. It might also stir the still waters of contemporary interpretations of early Indian thought.

Such a study, incorporating elements or deconstruction, would sharpen the awareness of concepts and theoretical frameworks. Historical explanation then becomes an enterprise in which the nuances and refinements of concepts and theories are a constant necessity, not only because of the availability of fresh evidence from new sources but also because of greater precision in our understanding of the categories which we use to analyse these sources. It is a bi-focal situation where the frame of reference provided by the analysis of ideology remains the distant view while the historian's use of a theoretical explanation of the data indicates the nearer reading.

8

HISTORICAL REALITIES*

The writing of history imprinted with the communal ideology became more and more apparent in the late twentieth century coinciding interestingly with professional historical writing coming closer to the social sciences and extending its reach to introducing new methods of analysis and new sources of data into the study of history and communal history. This essay discusses communal history and how it creates a distance between history researched by the trained historian and the popular history propagated by others.

A CRITIQUE OF COMMUNALISM IN the context of India is often mistaken for a critique of religion. It therefore needs to be emphasized that communalism is the political exploitation of a religious ideology. It is a phenomenon of recent times, when communities are identified by religion and this identification is brought into play as a major political articulation. Communal ideology defines groups in society as religious communities and it is believed that this definition wipes out concerns with status or class.

It is often argued that the roots of communalism go back in history: but, in fact, history is brought in as an attempt to provide justification from the past. The ideal communal society is posited as having existed in the past. Equally important to the communal ideology is the insistence that the total separation of religious communities also has its roots in the past, and the denial that social systems cut across religious identities.

---

*An earlier version of this essay was first published in 1987.

This projection owes a great deal to the initial periodization of Indian history by James Mill, who, using the model of the three-age periodization current for European history, imposed it on India in his *The History of British India* published in 1817. But he changed the labels thinking his labels were more apposite to changes in India. But in fact they imported an untenable history into India. He referred to the Hindu, Muslim, and British periods, a legacy of the British interpretation of Indian history, which Indian historians have recently discarded after showing that they are quite inapplicable.

Historians influenced by secular nationalism reverted to the traditional European labels which they believed were more neutral and renamed the periods of Indian history as Ancient, Medieval, and Modern, but the criterion of change remained that of the religion of the dominant dynasties and rulers. In spite of the recent historical research on subjects which have nothing to do with the content of these labels, for the non-historian, the persistence of Hindu and Muslim periods continues.

For Hindu communalists, the presumed superiority of the Hindu was based initially on the work of European Orientalists who had argued that the origins of the Hindu community go back to the Aryan race and the speakers of the Indo-Aryan language. The Aryan theory of race was a central problem in the ideology of European nationalism in the nineteenth century. It was taken up and applied to Indian sources on the basis of Vedic Sanskrit being Indo-Aryan and therefore a part of the Indo-European language family and the racial structure was adopted to explain the differences between Aryan and non-Aryan speakers in India.

The Aryans were seen as the superior race of conquerors and it was they who were responsible for organizing social distinctions in the form of caste stratification. This theory underlined upper-caste superiority and was therefore very acceptable to upper-caste ideologues. Those who accepted the racial affinities of language groups also flirted with the idea that the Indian upper castes were of the same racial stock as some European aristocracy which was believed to be Aryan. In spite of the extensive research which has negated the Aryan theory of race, it still has protagonists among the Indian middle class and the identification of 'the Aryans' with various archaeological cultures remains an historical perennial.

The 'Hindu period' is also seen as the golden age, when Hinduism was in the ascendant politically. By contrast, the 'Muslim period' is seen as an age of decline, since the dynasties were not Hindu. The fact that some of the features, which today would be regarded as characteristic of Hinduism, evolved during this period is conveniently ignored.

For the Muslim communalist, the reverse situation is projected. Pre-Islamic Indian history is unimportant and irrelevant. History begins in India with the establishment of Islam. This, of course, creates immense problems for historians who wish to toe the official line in a theocratic state such as Pakistan. They can record and describe pre-Islamic history but can rarely make judgements on the quality of society.

Even with the coming of Islam, where the 'Muslim period' is seen as the golden age, the attempt is to trace historical roots back to the early history of Islam. *Five Thousand Years of Pakistan* by Mortimer Wheeler was an attempt at giving historical legitimacy to the new state but, for the theocracy of the new state, posed an uncomfortable proximity to a non-Islamic past.

The question becomes even more difficult for Sikh communalists and others of similar ilk, who will have to consider roots in more recent times, and the subordination of earlier history will pose many problems. If the history of the Punjab is to begin with the birth of Guru Nanak, as some would like to suggest there is considerable evident history which will have to be wished away.

The ideology of Hindu communalism argues that the Hindus form the 'majority community' in India and are therefore the inheritors of the past and claimants to dominance in the present. It is also maintained that religious tolerance and non-violence in relation to religion are characteristic of this community. A particular 'tradition' is regarded as the Hindu tradition and this underlies the comprehension of culture and social values. The Hindu communal ideology also seeks to redefine Hinduism for its followers. These kinds of attitudes are not limited to Hindu communalism, but occur in other religious communalisms as well.

The term 'majority community' for the Hindus has come to be accepted even by those who do not subscribe to the communal ideology. But it requires a little historical exploration. As I have explained elsewhere in this book, the term 'Hindu' is an invention of the Arabs, and refers to the inhabitants living in the land beyond the Indus as viewed from West Asia. A few centuries later it came to refer to those inhabitants of this area who professed religions with a sizeable following other than Islam. It is in origin a geographical term and a religious connotation was extended to it.

The reason for this appears to be the fact that those who identified with the various sects which went into the making of the 'Hindu' had no common term by which they identified themselves. This was so because the sense of a monolithic *religious* community cutting across caste, region, and language was absent. The nearest perhaps was the notion of the common identity of those who observed the 'varnashrama-dharma', the norms of caste society and the life stages of the Hindu; but this excluded the larger number and, in any case, emphasized the segregation and segmentation of caste society, rather than the all-inclusive sense of community.

The rigid exclusion of 'unclean' Shudras and untouchables was very different from the present-day political wooing of these groups by the upper castes. It would be worth examining whether the appropriation of the Islamic label 'Hindu' by the Hindus in order to identify themselves, for which there is evidence from the period of the coming of the Europeans was not the first occasion when a sense of the Hindu community began to take root.

The Hindus and Muslims in their early interaction viewed each other as the Other: the Hindu view of the Muslims was expressed not by using the label Muslim but in the preference for ethnic, geographical, and cultural labels given to them when they were referred to as 'Turushkas', 'Yavanas', and 'Mlecchas'. The Hindus did not appear to have seen themselves as a unified community, but rather preferred the identity of castes, sects, and regions. This hypothesis can be confirmed or otherwise by an analysis of the self-perception of such groups in the literature of the second millennium AD in the regional languages.

Some groups did manage to cut across this segmentation. The Brahmanas of the subcontinent, for instance, were identified through language and ritual as well even though the use of these in various ways led to multiple gradations within their ranks. Political exchange required a certain recognition of the office of kingship across geographical barriers. The renouncer and the wandering ascetic were frequently familiar figures on the edges of many landscapes, although language often determined their effective boundaries. Above all, it was the recognition of a social system encapsulated in caste or jati which was what required the creation of a larger identity, and one which included a variety of castes or sects pertaining to various religious affiliations.

The notion of a Hindu community as it is defined today became necessary when there was a competition for political power and access to economic resources between various groups in a colonial situation. There was need to change from a segmented identity to a community which cut across caste, sect, and region. This social need also required a reformulation of Hinduism which was attempted in various socio-religious reform movements of the nineteenth century.

To establish the *implicit* antiquity of the community as also its demarcating characteristics which made it different from other communities, it was argued that among its essential features was a spirit of tolerance and non-violence. These values were picked up from ethical philosophy but were posited as being descriptive of the reality of social relations.

However, historical facts suggest otherwise. If we read the edicts of the Emperor Ashoka, a constant refrain is the plea for tolerance and particularly tolerance among the various religious sects, often summarized in the phrase 'Brahmanas and Shramanas', where the enmity between the two was proverbial. If tolerance and coexistence prevailed, then there would not have been this repeated plea.

Somewhat later in time, there are references to the persecution of Buddhists, particularly by Shaiva sects referred to by Kalhana in the *Rajatarangini*. Still later, in the late first millennium and early second millennium AD, there is evidence of the persecution of Jainas in the peninsula and, again, particularly by Shaiva sects. Jaina monastic centres were appropriated, Jaina temples were desecrated and images removed, and Jaina monks not only ridiculed but impaled and beheaded.

This intolerance has been ignored for a variety of reasons. It is generally dismissed more as sectarian rivalry rather than religious intolerance. It is argued that the Hindu community did not commit such acts but only one sect among its many. But, for the situations where this intolerance and persecution prevailed, it was of a substantial kind.

If some Shaivas sects were intolerant, the Vaishnavas were perhaps a little less so. Vaishnavism was an assimilating religion via the various avataras and less confrontational, so that other groups tended to get absorbed in a process of acculturation and this came to be viewed as the Hindu way of coping with sects in opposition. What was absent in the persecution was the equivalent of jihads and inquisitions. However, the absence of extreme behaviour does not cleanse the record, for the latter shows the presence of a potential if not actual extremism.

Communal ideologies claim to base themselves on an appeal to tradition. But tradition, as is well known, is not a given package of ideas and practices. Traditions are invented or are put together through a selection of items from the past and the selection is deliberate and frequently relates to the social underpinnings of the group involved. Each of the communal ideologies is careful to pick items from the religious beliefs and practices applicable to its community. And the traditions therefore are socially segregated as well.

In the case of Hindu communalism, upper caste beliefs and practices are seen as more attractive and obviously appeal to those who have been excluded socially in the past and regarded as outside the social pale. Thus, rituals of Brahmanism are at a premium and are looked upon as the core of tradition. The ban on beef eating and the insistence on cow protection become important issues. These were now regarded as manifestations of the upper caste. This of course contradicts what is said in earlier sources—texts such as the Upanishads. Needless to say the diet of beef among the lower castes was not mentioned in spite of its continuing to be acceptable. In such situations, communalism attempts to imitate upper caste mores and gives the illusion of upward mobility to the socially inferior group now being reunited with the community. It acts as a kind of all-purpose Sanskritization. Nevertheless, the actual differences of economic and social status remain. These are not done away with because this is not the purpose of communalism. The pose may be egalitarian, but the reality remains conservative.

It is sometimes argued that within the context of a religious community, if people are declared equal, then communalism has a democratic component. But in the insistence on the return to the practice of what are seen as religious laws, there is a return to conservatism and an anti-democratic system. It is as well to remember that sacred laws, whether they be the precepts of the Dharmashastras or of the shariat, were promulgated to support and further a hierarchical society and are therefore by their very nature opposed to democratic rights.

Communal ideologies, because they use religion for political purposes in the context of a changing and modernizing society, also attempt to refashion the religion. This is evident in recent trends in Hindu communalism. By way of an example, there is a search now for historicity which did not exist in earlier times and the Rama and Krishna janmabhoomi movements are clear indications of this.

Possibly this is influenced again by the socio-reform movements of the nineteenth century, when, in imitation of the Semitic model, there was an attempt to postulate a founder or teacher for the religion, to emphasize a single sacred book (often either the Gita or the Upanishads), to suggest or invent some kind of congregational worship, and to introduce the notion of conversion to Hinduism. The search for historicity makes it necessary to locate the central figure in space and time and the question of a precise location for a janmabhoomi becomes important.

Yet, the great strength of Vaishnavism in the past was precisely its ahistoricity where the historical fact of the existence of Rama or Krishna was irrelevant to the beliefs and practices of the devotee. This is what made a number of the Hindu sects unique in the religious experience of civilization and gave to them a distinctively different character—a character which is now being negated.

In this current refashioning of the Hindu religion, there is an attempt to dictate to all Hindus what their religion should be. As such, it cuts away from the major strength of the Hindu sects of the past which included an entire range of belief and practice, from atheism to animism. The narrowing of this identity can only detract from the quality of the religious experience.

The claim to places being historically associated with the biography of the avataras has also to be seen as an attempt to claim valuable property and to control vast resources provided by the offerings of pilgrims and the estates of temples. The claims to such locations are now made because the Hindus see themselves as powerful. But do we pause to give the same rights to Buddhists, Jainas, and animists to claim those of their sacred sites which were forcibly taken over by various Hindu sects? Comparable to this has been the recent move to revivify disused mosques. The ones chosen are either those with a property potential or else those with a potential to being locations of a political nucleus. This move is again intended to test an assertion of power. Religious buildings, whether temples or mosques, when desanctified for many decades if not centuries, and brought under the protection of the Archaeological Survey of India, become part of an historical heritage and are not therefore negotiable for being used as sacred spaces again. Such buildings should not be surreptitiously brought into religious use.

In the historical process which we are undergoing at this time, relating to industrialization, modernization, the building of a nation-state, and other similar experiences, there is a premium on the annulling of segmented, segregated groups and the restructuring of society with larger identities. It is not secularism which brings about the communalization of our society, but the deliberate choice of a religious identity which can be used in the game of numbers related to democratic representation and by which groups aspiring to power can manipulate the system.

The choice before us is not limited to the defining of the larger community only by a religious identity. We can choose to organize our society along different lines where concepts such as a majority community and minority communities, each with their attendant rights, is seen as a divisive process which merely allows a change of persons in power but does nothing to ensure the well-being of society. Communalism does not bring about social and economic change at essential levels since this is not part of its programme. It is fundamentally a hunt for power, moralizing by resort to religion.

If a demonstration of this is required, we do not have to look far. Our northern neighbour, Pakistan, was created in the matrix of Muslim communalism and it was believed that a religious identity was sufficient to build a nation. Not only did the breaking away of Bangladesh upset this calculation, but the strife within Pakistan and the incipient nationalisms of Baluchistan and Sind have demonstrated the ineffectiveness of religious identity backed by a religious community providing the basis for a secure nation.

That communalist ideologies attract a following again has to do with a particular historical situation. Nationalism of the anti-colonial variety which provided the ideological magnet in the earlier half of this century is now seen as irrelevant in India. There is therefore a search for a new ideology.

This is a particular requirement among those sections of society, such as the urban middle classes, who have experienced some degree of affluence but who have in the process had to change their lifestyle or move away from or give a different form to what they were taught to accept as traditional values, and who are facing increasing competition to retain their place in the sun. In such a condition of insecurity and loss of ideology, there is a turning towards a replacement. The notion of a religious community defined by this group provides it with the necessary ambition to reach for power and covers this striving with a garb of pious sentiment and religiosity.

In earlier times, when societies were hierarchically organized and privilege was the hallmark of the few, customary law prevailed in the segmented groups and the state safeguarded customary law. But communities are in any case not sacrosanct and heritable. They are created and they change over time. Today, with the demand for the equality of all before the law and the equal access of everyone to rights, customary law can no longer prevail. This particularly affects the rights of women in marriage and inheritance and to property. Conventional religious laws insist on a subordinate status for women which is now entirely unacceptable.

We already have claims to many different personal laws and more can be created if various communalisms so require it. But in the perpetration of such laws we violate basic human rights. Equal rights does imply a uniformity of laws and this in turn implies at least a different concept of society. Given the nature of the society we aspire to, it would be tragic if we were strangled in the entrails of communalist ideologies playing with the politics of power, and were to become vulnerable to the fascism of religious fundamentalism.

9

THE POLITICS OF RELIGIOUS COMMUNITIES*

Politics at the time of Independence was largely non-communal. Communal politics grew in the subsequent decades, and is now amongst us, nourishing fear, as if it were a monster out of Jurassic Park. Part of the problem has been the constant association of 1947 with communal politics, rather than with the far more important move towards becoming a nation-state.

AT THE TIME OF PARTITION in 1947, there was a popular belief that the division of the country would end the communal tension as those in favour of a separate Muslim state would migrate to Pakistan. This in part accounts for the slogan voiced these days that all Muslims are the progeny of Pakistan and should go there. Such an attitude arises from an erroneous understanding of what the partition of India was about and, more than that, a failure to comprehend the complexities of a multireligious society. That the solution to communal conflict did not lie in religion-based states was evident from the rapidity with which East Pakistan broke away as Bangladesh and by the frequency of violent confrontations between variously defined groups in Pakistan. The fact that in every case the involvement is of members belonging to the same religious community, Islam, does not reduce the tension or the violence.

The notion of the religious community being the unit of modern political functioning has its roots in the nineteenth

*An earlier version of this essay was first published in 1990.

century. Not only did the British perceive Indian society in terms of the two—Hindu and Muslim nations, as is evident also from Indological scholarship on the subject, but this perception was later projected into political representation as well with the notion of separate electorates defined by religion. The acceptance of separate electorates by Indians was an indication of the social and political disparity being by then perceived as a religious one.

For colonial governing there were two main communities. The larger, which they referred to as the majority community, was an amorphous mass to which they applied the label of Hindu (and this included Buddhists, Jainas, and Sikhs and a variety of lower caste and tribal religions), and the others, the minority communities, were the more easily defined Muslims and Christians. Included among minorities were what later came to be called the Scheduled Castes and Scheduled Tribes, a nomenclature derived from constitutional usage. The term minority community at that time referred generally to the Muslims. Today it includes others such as the Sikhs.

Societies define themselves by their own perception of what they think constitute social units. In India the notion of religious communities as demographic units was reinforced and graded into majority and minority communities by colonial authority. It is debatable whether what constitutes the Hindu community today was in fact a consciously recognized all-India community in the Indian subcontinent in pre-modern times. It has been argued that the very nature of 'Hinduism' in the past, its flexibility, and the identity of belief and ritual with various castes and sects, precluded the idea of a single, closed community characteristic of Semitic religions. There were in pre-modem times a conglomerate of communities, identified by language, beliefs, caste, and ritual, distinctly separate or overlapping in one or the other of these features but rarely presenting a uniform, univerzalising form. What is often mistaken for uniformity, namely Brahmanical culture, was only the culture of one of the elites.

In the attempt to make inter-caste functioning more cohesive and mould social groups into larger entities, the notion of religious communities has been an acceptable alternative over the last century. The opposition to substituting caste by religious community has been a source of major ideological conflict both within the national movement and since. This is not to suggest that one should return to caste identities, but rather to understand that the notion of the religious community is not embedded in the foundations of Indian civilization.

The posing of secularism against communalism did not at one level face the issue squarely. It was, and is, not enough to negate the emphasis of religious identity in public life; it is equally necessary to encourage other alternative identities. These can also be sought from more analytical studies of the past where the nuances and sensitivities of a variety of inter-community relationships need to be investigated and understood. There was also a lulling of the fears aroused in the 1940s by communalism with the adoption of a constitution in the subsequent decade where secularism was given importance not by the constant reiterating of the mantra of secularism, particularly at the level of the state, without vigilantly ensuring that it was being put into practice, but by assuming it to be essential.

The centrality of communalism in our lives today, is now being more widely discussed than before largely because of the political success of the BJP. Yet for some of us who have been stating for some years that communalism is on the rise and who have been dismissed as alarmists in the past, this is not surprising. It has, however, required a political demonstration for there to be a recognition of a change which goes beyond politics. The BJP also represents the ideological right wing in politics. This combination is perhaps the more startling, although not unexpected. It was earlier debated whether the BJP will continue to support the demands of extreme Hindu nationalism, or whether the taste of power will require a degree of distancing from it. The silence and inaction of members of the BJP with official status in response to calls of violence against the minority communities points to the debate having being decided in favour of violent solutions.

What is more disturbing is the increasing communalization of Indian society where various confrontational religious identities of the Hindu right openly supporting resistance are now no longer objected to, and where religious identities are deliberately reiterated as political and social solutions, irrespective of whether such a reiteration is relevant or not. The seminal period of these communalisms is not the present, for they each have roots in the immediate past. More evident on the social and political landscape are the various shakhas, senas, parishads, sammelans, leagues, jamats, and various other organizations—most of which have had at the core an aggressive, narrow, political concern which is articulated in religious terms.

The state, during the last few years, has lent itself to the politics of these groups in attempts to manipulate them, instead of exposing them. Slogans on city walls and messages on WhatsApp and on social media carry the statements of these groups. Where the more aggressive among them go further and appropriate state space, the state has pretended apathy, where apathy means connivance. The Congress has taken a 'holier-than-thou' attitude in its public opposition to communalism, but it failed to explain what it was doing in the past during riots in Delhi, Meerut, Bidar, Bhagalpur, and other places, when it was in control of the state machinery and was unable to protect citizens. When the representatives of the state, who are supposed to be impartial protectors of the citizens, become participants in the riots, or take definitive positions, then either the state has to take action against them or else it is to be understood that they have the backing of the state.

The growth of communalism is not merely the result of governments which at best have been unable to contain it and at worst have tried to use it to remain in power. As an ideology, communalism has a wider appeal and it is also other situations that have given it encouragement. Communalism has to be seen for what it is: an intermeshing of ideology and power, where groups aspiring to power use a particular religious ideology to subvert a social order and replace it with an order that is based on sharp differentiations between those who accept the ideology and those who do not. It also places power in the hands of the authors of that ideology. This combination of a religious ideology and power enables such groups to define social practice and law apart from symbols and belief, all of which condition the ensuing social order.

In a multireligious society attempts are sometimes made to introduce ascendancy through other channels, such as claims to racial superiority as among those who claim to be Aryans, or civilizational continuity which is deliberately defined largely in terms of ritual and belief, eliminating or ignoring other aspects which go into the making of a civilization and thereby also marginalizing those who do not observe that particular ritual and belief. Such channels are diversionary for the centrality of action remains the intertwining of the particular religious ideology and power.

The major springs of communal support are from those who are in some ways disembodied from their earlier social moorings: the growing middle class of those whose standard of living materially has risen and who see themselves as having to modernize without being fully aware of the implications of this process; who see modernization as westernization and therefore an implicit contradiction between what they have been taught to think of as 'traditional' and what they believe is modern and who therefore think they are establishing a 'traditional' identity by supporting the new religious movements. In the same way they imitate and adopt the outer trappings of Western modes and assume that this makes them 'modern'.

The insistence on a dichotomy between 'traditional' and 'modern' confuses the understanding of tradition, which is, in effect, a continual process of selecting from the past, both consciously and subconsciously. Part of the flotsam and jetsam which gets carried into the communal stream are the erstwhile princelings and faux aristocracy who have lost both status and power and seek to find a new status as purveyors of a disappearing world. The leadership of some fundamentalist groups and communal organizations includes smugglers and drug peddlers, the kind of clientele which has also found its way into political parties. Where the religious 'cause' is highlighted, it becomes an attempt at whitewashing other activities. This in turn encourages the criminal elements already present on the political scene, who can be relied upon to start a communal riot as and when required.

Aspirations to wealth and status, whether among lower caste artisans, some of whom have improved professional prospects with new openings or among the middle class moving into new professions, bring with them intense competition and consequent insecurity. Apprehensive of how to remain on top, as it were, of these changing prospects, it often becomes necessary to search for either a prescription or a scapegoat. The prescription seems to lie in talismans, in what is depicted even in the most elitist advertisements—the wearing of mauli threads and moonga rings to avert the evil eye; the scapegoat is often found in the members of the other community who are seen as competitors. Communal roots are common where the target is Muslims. The destruction of Christian churches or burning alive of Christians have also been resorted to.

Added to this is the aspiration to political power. Secularism in India has been converted into a system by which a particular party could draw on the votes of a particular minority community, and of the outcastes. Democracy is seen as a numbers game. Mobilization is therefore crucial and draws on religious communities. The resort to mobilization happened not so long ago through the making of bricks and the shila pujas linked to the Ayodhya agitation, and processions as the backdrop to riots that were an assertion of power; these combined both religious and political mobilization in a manner which has so far been unprecedented. Should this become the vehicle for political mobilization then the future is frightening.

If the initial appeal of communal ideology is apparent among the prosperous middle class, it does not rest there, for the politicization of religion requires mobilization on a large scale. Unlike the RSS whose leading figures initially tended to be Brahmanas, the Vishva Hindu Parishad draws on a wider group for leadership extending to what would earlier have been regarded as middle castes and to professional classes. Its missionary programme of converting Dalits and tribals to Hinduism (in spite of 'conversion' being alien to Hinduism) will serve a double purpose should it succeed: it will increase the numbers of those who can be called Hindus and it will reduce the numbers involved in the policy of reservation.

This policy as applied in education and in employment for Scheduled Castes and Scheduled Tribes has been a source of considerable resentment on the part of caste Hindus who regard it as a threat to their opportunities for upward mobility. Built into this kind of communalism therefore is the implicit factor of keeping the Dalits oppressed, for even if the policy of reservation is dropped, any concessions made to Dalits will be resented. The fear of the lower castes breaking away from the status defined for them by the upper castes and attaining a better status is endemic to caste society. It has been mentioned as a threat to society even in the past in what may be called the crisis of the Kaliyuga. On repeated occasions from the first millennium AD onwards there have been descriptions of the evils of the Kali Yuga where the rise of the lower castes is seen as evidence of the world being turned upside down.

Equally implicit in communalism is the place of women, which, drawing from the conservative interpretation of ancient texts and social codes, such as the Dharmashastras and the shariat, forecloses possibilities of independent action. The religious ideology in communalism has to be defined for contemporary times and in its representation of the universal values of ancient times, it requires that women be subordinated. Such subordination, often characteristic of those in power, provided the illusion of complete authority.

The reality could often be very different in other segments of society, but these realities find no place in communal ideology. Whether it is the endorsement of the ritual death of a sati or the denial of maintenance to a divorced Muslim woman, the underlying statement is that of subordination. That a woman must know her place and stay within its bounds is also seen as the solution to the problem of the independent woman staking new claims of status on a society in the process of change.

The projection of the past in terms of communal history, namely that the history of India, is to be seen as the glory of the ancient period when Hinduism was in the ascendant and its decline during the medieval period when that place was taken by Islam, continues to be the simplistic view of Hindu communal groups. The variation is that Muslim communalists see the period of Islamic dominance as the period of glory and Sikh communalists perceive their relations with the Mughal state entirely in terms of the religious confrontation between Muslim and Sikh. The appeal to history for legitimation by communal groups is in effect a red herring. The issue is not that of the historical correctness of the claim, for the claims being made are in fact political and relate to the society of today. But by reiterating a communal history, justification is sought for trying to undo the past by communal actions in the present. A communal interpretation of the past, even where clearly untenable, is useful for whipping up hysteria in mobilizing a community.

If, however, history is to be brought into the controversy, then communal interpretations of history have to come to terms with many facts which are now conveniently ignored. It has to be conceded that there has been intolerance and persecution of religious sects not just under Muslim rulers but also under Hindu rulers and by powerful Hindu groups even in pre-Islamic times. The evidence of Shaivite persecution of Buddhists and Jainas is conveniently ignored, even though it involved some killing of monks and the desecration of religious sites. The very notion of untouchability is an extreme form of intolerance and persecution. Will the Hindus of today first come to terms with their own intolerance and victimization of the Other before rushing to set right the intolerance of others from the past?

The bulk of the conversions to Islam were not by force of arms but under the influence of various religious teachers. These conversions were frequently by jati where an entire professional group would convert. This raises questions about the nature of Hindu society and what might have encouraged conversions. Relations between groups in society, even if identified by religious practice and belief, are never simplistically black or white. The evidence on such relations in the past and the analysis of this evidence by present-day historians suggests a very different interpretation from that which was current fifty years ago. But in spite of historians constantly reiterating this change, the old theories still hold in the popular mind.

The refusal to recognize that historical analyses have changed our image of the past stems from the refusal on the part of the mediators of knowledge (both the educational system and the media) to first read and then pronounce. It is far easier to go on mouthing old ideas even if these are unacceptable to current historians. The old cliche of Muslim rulers being bigots to a greater or lesser degree continues to be repeated despite the work which has been done on their policies, suggesting a far more historically complex context for such policies. This is not a question, for instance, of Hindus being more aware of Aurangzeb but of Aurangzeb being consistently depicted only in one form.

The media is not innocent about fostering communalism. The fashion for glitter and tinsel as news and the underlining of the need for media hype has resulted in an obsession with instant stories focusing on the view of anybody and anything as long as it can be presented as spectacular news. Thoughtful commentaries are dismissed as too academic for the press and TV channels, with a few exceptions and have been largely concerned only with projecting the lowest common denominator both in politics and in 'culture'. It is therefore not surprising that the definition of culture lies in the assumption that Indian society consists in the main of caste Hindus transmuting into a middle class. The success stories of TV channels are serials portraying narratives linked for example to Vaishnava worship projected as part of the national culture of India. At least if the aesthetic qualities of the original are portrayed it might mitigate the religious propaganda.

The fostering of communalism in some cases requires the issuing of fatwas and hukumnamas. Alternatively, riots are made the excuse to damage if not destroy the religious sites of those one is rioting against and this ensures a continuing hostility and problems of rebuilding. Frequently such sites or others which become the focus of dispute are in the centre of urban areas and therefore, as property, extremely valuable. The acquisition or control of such sites becomes an economic asset as well. But communalism can also spread in a far more subtle manner in the gradual building up of hostile feelings against other communities which results in the expression of sub-conscious discrimination. It is strange that inspite of the large numbers of educated Muslims, few seem to reach the upper echelons of government. A creeping discrimination against Sikhs was noticeable after the 1984 anti-Sikh riots.

There is of course in addition the involvement of the Indian diaspora with communalism. The Vishva Hindu Parishad and other Hindu organizations with the same agenda receive extensive support, financial and otherwise, from Indians settled in the United States, Canada, and Britain, as indeed do Sikh communal organizations from equivalent bodies in these countries. Centres of the VHP in Britain have received hefty monetary donations from official British agencies on the grounds that the VHP is a purely cultural organization. Muslim communal organizations are said to receive support from the wealthy in West Asia as well.

Financial support is not, however, the only encouragement to such organizations. The question of identity is crucial to Indians in the diaspora, for in the world of Europe and North America they are the minority groups in an alien culture. Yet they have to come to terms with this insecure situation and their solution is the attempt to assert their identity by recourse to mobilization on the basis of a religious idiom. Their minority character in foreign lands isolates them and they frequently seek unity in religious organizations, trying to combine a Western lifestyle with 'traditional' religion. Such groups become the role model for upwardly mobile middle-class Indians who, with economic improvement, are in any case able to maintain close contacts with segments of their families who have settled abroad.

The existence of the diaspora has implications for the growth of communalism in India and commitments are contracted. The obvious form this takes is comments from groups and organizations and even governments outside India. When Muslims outside India and governments of Islamic states condemn riots in India where Muslims are killed, this is objected to in India as outside interference. As long as Indian society continues to define itself only in terms of religious communities, members of such communities living outside India will comment on the situation in India. And perhaps there will be more than comment. For example, one of the ceremonies imitating the Ram Janmabhoomi movement, a sammelan was held in London, and bricks intended for Ayodhya were worshipped by local citizens, both white and those of Indian origin. Such activities, particularly by the former, are seen not as interference but as welcome endorsement.

The Ram Janmabhoomi issue was something of a time bomb. Are there other similar time bombs still ticking which will explode in the years to come? Such explosions can only be diffused if the government takes a firm stand on those ticking and does not make concessions to communal politics. This it has failed to do. The VHP's next campaign to agitate for the destruction of the mosques at Mathura and Varanasi is under way.

All this made it possible for a community to organize itself, gain some political leverage, and to claim prime urban sites in the name of religion. Should the Muslims, Sikhs, Christians, Jainas, and Neo-Buddhists all get into the act, there will be pandemonium in both urban centres and at archaeological sites, not to mention those which are also places of tourist interest. Some such activities take the form of groups attempting to reclaim for worship monuments that have been desanctified and which are under the protection of the Archaeological Survey. The acquisition of the Ram Janmabhoomi will be quoted as precedent on future occasions, and the outcome can only be violence worse than what has been witnessed so far. The protection ceases to be exercised when the Archaeological Survey of India acts under orders of the government or its allies and allows the monument to be desecrated or destroyed.

If the redressal of believed wrongs of the past become the right of religious communities, then temples located at the sites sacred to other religions will also have to be destroyed although, with the predominance of Hindu communalism other religious communities might hesitate to make such a demand. What, for instance, is to happen to the temple at the supposed Krishna Janmabhoomi which is built at the site of Katra in Mathura and which, according to one authority, was the site of a Buddhist religious complex and could therefore be claimed by the Buddhists? There are a few other Hindu temples that were originally Buddhist chaityas. How far back in history will we have to go in order to satisfy the politics of religious communities?

It is not election results alone which will condition the future of communalism in India. If the reasons for the rise of communalism are understood, then it becomes clear that it is not religious sentiment which is at stake, but the exploitation of this sentiment at a moment in time when there is a closeness to political control by the BJP, but there is apprehension that this may be thwarted. The apprehension has to be reduced and the easy slipping into religious identities as social units has to be questioned.

Alternative identities will hopefully emerge with the growing strength of lower caste and Dalit movements as also with the demands of the Adivasis/Scheduled Tribes for greater representation and statehood. There are already movements in this direction which tend to be overshadowed by the immanence of communal violence. These sacred sites supporting a different kind of belief will also have to be protected. What Hindu communalism fails to recognize is that at the end of the road there is not going to be a dominance of the majority community because inspite of its supposed uniformity at present, given that the real objective is the acquisition of power, it too will split into contending groups.

The fundamental change which is taking place in the form of Hinduism, which has been variously described as New Hinduism or, as I would prefer to call it, Syndicated Hinduism, will eliminate the very flexibility which allowed it as the sanatana dharma to survive. From a religious form that had the openness of thought as in the Upanishads, it is now being reduced to the worship of bricks. Its aggressive militancy belies its earlier claims to tolerance and non-violence. When reference is made to ostracizing non-believers, then the divorce from earlier Hinduism is complete. Part of the reason for the communalization of politics lies in the importance it was given in 1947. Instead of emphasizing the centrality of independence as India emerged from the status of a colony in the British empire and was transformed into a free democratic, secular nation-state, we kept on discussing the partition of the ex-colony into two communally defined nations. Despite Nehru's attempts to focus on the secular nation-state and its future, it was communal politics that was brought back repeatedly. Today we are steeped in communal politics and in attacking the minorities.

To support a religion as the articulation of religious sentiments, beliefs, and practices is not under question. The objection is to the manipulation of such identities for the purposes of political mobilization, where the manipulation requires violence and aggression and destruction in order to succeed. In this latter sense religious communities fostering religious nationalism are imagined communities and it is therefore possible to change them. In the search for identities as an alternative to the notion of the religious community for purposes of political mobilization, liberalization in all such communities will have to proceed at the same pace. Minority insecurity underlies their conservatism and hesitancy to change. Civil codes and criminal laws will have to be common, but fully debated before becoming laws.

There is a difference between the communalism of the majority and that of the minorities. The former is often born of an aggressive assertion of power. The latter is born of fear and a sense of powerlessness in the face of the majority. In a society which sees itself as a conglomerate of religious communities, the onus for removing this fear lies with the majority community. Enhanced communalism can make communalism the only form of political dialogue. In each case communalism suppresses the aspirations of other groups as indeed of dissident groups within the community since it is based on the fundamental assumption that its constituents are superior to the rest—be it a Pakistan, a Khalistan, or a Hindu Rashtra—and the believers are defined by those who have created the communal ideology. Its removal therefore becomes a necessity.

But such qualifications do not mitigate the existence of either the majority or the minority communalisms, for neither is justified. The fight is not only against the dominance of Hindu communalism asserting itself amidst a range of minority communities, but also the need within each community to marginalize the communal elements. This would be imperative if there is to be an alternative to the politics of religious communities.

III

EPICS

10

THE RAMAYANA SYNDROME*

One of the ways of ascertaining historical change is to examine how a familiar narrative is rendered differently at various points in time and in varying historical contexts. The narrative of Rama—Ramakatha—is one of these. Every locality used to have virtually its own version, varying from stories with little religious content to those that were primarily religious. This was before the television version of Ramanand Sagar† took over and audiences switched to watching only this version or similar ones as is the current practice. How did the narrative change and how did a change enter the perceptions of present-day audiences are questions worth thinking about.

IN THE OPINIONS THAT WERE gathered by newspapers when the serial on the Ramayana closed, various comments were made. It was stated that its popularity resulted from its being a part of the collective unconscious, that among adults it evoked memories of childhood stories and among children it paralleled the exploits of the hero Superman, that it was an embodiment of higher values and laid out the quest for dharma in a simple narrative form; that it projected the ideal woman in Sita; that it appeased the apprehensions and insecurities of a society transiting to modernity; that it gave visual form to the spiritual fountainhead of Hinduism.

*An earlier version of this essay was first published in 1989.

†Ramanand Sagar produced a TV serial based on the narrative as given in the Valmiki Ramayana and the Tulsidas *Ramacharitmanas*. The episodes were telecast in 1987. The serial was a phenomenal success.

Those that were unhappy with the rendering complained of the absence of poetry and meaning. It was also described as a folk genre, a small town Ramlila that managed to hit the big lights through projection on television.

Only a few seemed concerned about the long-term effects of such a serial. Were we perhaps then witnessing an attempt to project what the new culture should be, as we experience it today—an attempt to expunge diversities and present a homogenized view of what the Ramayana was and is? Can this be seen as part of an increasing trend in current times of treating the state as the arch patron of culture, of state patronage requiring a uniform culture with the state determining its manifestations, whether it be the festivals, the media or other presentations? The state defines culture, finances culture, is the final arbiter and, as the patron, bestows recognition on those whom it regards as creative and worthy. Private initiative cannot compete with the financial outlay which the state can provide and there is not enough public initiative to sustain alternate avenues to support innovatory forms. This has become a major difference between the localized, decentralized culture of half a century ago and the uniform, centralized, sanitized culture that is projected as Indian culture today. The required official stamp of a dictated Hinduism after the censoring of some turns in the story that make it more imaginative has further reduced the creativity of the narrative. The state prefers to endorse a uniform, homogenized culture for such a culture is simple to identify and easy to control. To concede that a nation's culture may be constituted of a variety of cultural systems would require that the functionaries of the state be sensitive to these multiple cultural systems and respond to their political implications. Where culture is taken over by the state as its major patron, there the politics of culture is inevitably heightened. It is therefore often easier for the state as patron to adopt a particular cultural stream as the mainstream: a cultural hegemony which frequently coincides with the culture of the dominant social group in the state.

Some would see this new extension of patronage by the state as legitimate, for the state is now expected to provide for everything. But others would see this as a threat to creativity. The relationship between the patron and the one who creates what is recognized as a cultural item, is delicate, where, although the patron controls finance and recognition, the patron is at best merely the agency for the act of creativity. In earlier times, acts of creativity had an audience but could do without a patron, although the more elaborate arts and literature required a patron. That creativity today is far more dependent on patronage, requires the patron to be particularly careful about the representation of culture, particularly where culture is being represented through the authoritative state-controlled media. I would like to illustrate this by reference to the Ramayana.

The Ramayana does not belong to any one moment in history for it has its own history which lies embedded in the many versions which were woven around the theme at different times and places, even within its own history in the Indian subcontinent leave alone its extensive writing in the cultures of Southeast Asia. The Indian epics were never frozen as were the compositions of Homer when they changed from an oral to a literate form. Professional reciters, kathakaras, recited the written versions with their own commentary and frequently adjusted the story to contemporary norms. The appropriation of the story by a multiplicity of groups meant a multiplicity of versions through which the social aspirations and ideological concerns of each group were articulated. The story in these versions included significant variations which changed the conceptualization of character, event, and meaning.

The oral versions are quite open to mutation of various kinds and at varying levels. Even within the literate tradition there are substantial differences. The now non-existent original Ramakatha is thought to be the core of the Valmiki version. This version was likely changed by the Bhargava Brahmana redactors who introduced the concept of Rama being an avatara of Vishnu, thus transforming the epic into sacred literature, a transformation which was resorted to in the past as a means of capturing popular literature for didactic purposes. Parallel to this, as we have seen, was the Buddhist rendering in some of the *Jatakas*, where in the *Dasaratha Jataka* the kinship relationship between Rama and Sita was different as compared to other versions. This change in the kinship pattern is reflected in Buddhist origin myths and carries its own distinctive meaning.

A Jaina version, the *Paumacharyam*, claims to be the authentic version of the story and maintains unequivocally that the Brahmana version is a false one. The treatment of Ravana in this text is much more sympathetic, Lanka is as important if not more so than Ayodhya and the events are coloured by Jaina ethics. Thus Dasaratha and Rama end up as Jaina munis and Sita gets herself to a nunnery. The earliest Tamil version by Kampan changes the treatment of Ravana who is here the tragic hero rather than the villainous demon. The religious importance of the story increased in the early second millennium AD with the spread of the Ramanandin sect who worshipped Vishnu in his incarnation as Rama. The most popular sacred literature in the Awadhi Hindi-speaking region in the sixteenth century was Tulsidas's *Ramcharitamanas*.

Even within the literate tradition the significance of these variations is not ignored. The differences highlight the varying perceptions of ethical behaviour, whether it be the ideal of the Kshatriya in the Brahmanical version, or the ideal of the Jaina ascetic in the *Paumacharyam*; of historicity, where the Jaina version claims it, but the Brahmanical ignores it; of the depiction of Ravana as the personification of evil or as a tragic hero; of the embodiment of women where the role of Sita varies. These were not simply variations in the story to add flavour to the narrative. They were deliberate attempts at taking up a well-known theme and using it to present a new point of view arising out of ideological and social differences of perspective.

These were acts of deliberate innovation, where the creator of the form felt free to experiment with the story even after the story had been given a sacred character by Brahmana authors. These variants were not hidden in some obscure treatise. They took the form of popular narratives, recited and written in Pali and Prakrit later in the regional languages and therefore available to large numbers of people. If we are to be aware of at least this strand of our cultural tradition then the debate and the dialectic embedded in these various versions should be more openly discussed.

What would happen if today an attempt were made to project on TV the version of the *Dasaratha Jataka* with its unique take on the relationship between Rama and Sita? It is likely that no TV channel would allow it, arguing that it would hurt the religious sensibilities of the majority community. Even if an attempt were to be made to put it not on the media, but only as a play, the self-appointed guardians of Hinduism would prevent its being staged. The assault on a theatre in Bombay and the beating up of the playwright, where a play was to be performed on the interlocking theme of Rama and Sita and Romeo and Juliet, is an indication of what would happen. Unfortunately, public protest has been too ineffectual to counteract such attitudes. But if the state claims to be the major patron of culture, such incidents require at least a statement from the patron.

If the state has taken on the role of the main patron of culture and if it should then withdraw from innovations in creativity on the grounds that it will hurt the sentiments of a particular 'religious community', culture will tend to be reduced to the lowest common denominator. The interface between religion, politics, and culture becomes a central issue in this situation. Religious sects in India, even those with Semitic origins, are characterized by a relative absence of the equivalent of the fiat from the Vatican. Who then speaks for that nebulous mass which is referred to as a 'religious community'? Those that force the issue on the state taking action on cultural or intellectual items are not the religious functionaries of a community, but the political spokesmen of some groups claiming to represent a religious community.

Thus the government of Maharashtra was prevented from reprinting a chapter of Dr Ambedkar's book because it questions the authenticity of the Brahmanical version of the Ramayana among other things. It may not even be a question of objecting to the suppression of the views of Ambedkar per se, but of allowing variant readings of a cultural tradition. Or a Syed Shahabuddin and his group demanded the banning of Salman Rushdie's book *The Satanic Verses*, and again the government acceded to this demand. Predictably the next step will be that the government would anticipate a demand from some Christian groups to ban *The Last Temptation of Christ*, and yet again the film would be banned. Are we then to be left with laundered strips of culture because the state as patron cannot distinguish between religious sensibilities and cultural articulation?

Our politics are being increasingly conditioned by appeals to the sentiments of various religious communities resulting in a politicizing of religion. But at the same time, we insist that religion is sacrosanct and cannot therefore be treated as a political ideology in spite of its having become a political ideology in association with communalism. How long will we continue to use this political blackmail, namely the threat that something will hurt the religious sensibilities of a community, in order to keep religion as a convenient ploy with which to play politics? This is all the more objectionable in a society which has traditionally been open to intellectual and cultural discourse even where it is conducted through religious texts.

A statement which is repeated ad nauseum is that of tolerance being a value characteristic of Indian civilization. There has been little attempt to analyse the nature of this tolerance. It assumes a segmented society in which each caste functions in accordance with its own dharma and the totality is juxtaposed and coexists. Intolerance was effective within each caste but by and large other castes were left alone to do and believe as they pleased. There was intolerance even before the coming of Islam, when people were killed, and their religious structures damaged, but as I have noted previously, intolerance never took on the dimensions and scale of a Catholic Inquisition. Polemics were, in fact, an essential part of ideology and belief. Now that we are moving away from a segmented society, we have to consciously acquire a concern for tolerance. We can retain tolerance only if we refrain from rushing to censorship of all kinds.

Tolerance does not grow with banning what is thought to be unpalatable; it grows with arguing and talking about it; that which is unpalatable anyway gets discarded. The banning or not of a book should at least be preceded by a minimal debate. There was no attempt to discuss what had actually been said in *The Satanic Verses* and the issues involved. Those who demanded the ban blatantly stated that they had not read the book. Presumably those who rushed to ban it had not read it either. The rush to demand the banning of the book was shrewd as it also pre-empted any discussion, even among Muslims, on the issues raised in the book. Such a discussion might have revealed differences of opinion, differences proving that not every Indian Muslim is an Islamic fundamentalist. And such discussions are imperative even for those who have a strong religious identity of any kind, if, as a society, we are to break the siege of communalism.

Let me return to the Ramayana and its different versions. The authorship changed from bards to Brahmanas to monks to local storytellers. Change in authorship and social setting introduced new features. Even those which are regarded as intrinsic to the story, such as the birth of Sita from the furrow, and the ten heads of Ravana, were, at one point, innovations. So too were other events, as for example, the notion of the shadow Sita—in a version that narrates that the real Sita was not the one kidnapped by Ravana but an illusory or shadow Sita, for the real Sita returned to Rama after the agni-pariksha. This innovation has been explained as deriving from the Advaita Vedanta philosophy and the doctrine of maya/illusion. Possibly a more immediate reason was the influence of the Shakti cults, where woman was viewed as an embodiment of power and the indignity of a fire ordeal to prove her chastity would not have been easily accepted. This episode might even reflect the debate on sati which was prevalent at the time, since the self-immolation of a widow was supposed to lead to reunion with her husband and the sati was regarded as a symbol of chastity.

The gradual diffusion of the story influenced the folk genres and the result was something very different from the literary tradition of upper-caste culture. One of the major areas of difference focused on the various depictions of Sita. In many folk versions (some in Kannada) Sita is the daughter of Ravana (as she is in versions from Southeast Asia). This carries a very different meaning for the abduction by Ravana. In one tribal version, the fire ordeal is performed not by Sita or a shadow Sita but by another woman substituted for the purpose, a tribal woman. This speaks volumes for the way in which a tribal society perceives its relationship with the mainstream culture.

Tamil-speaking societies derive their version from Kampan or from a variety of local forms, which were earlier recited but during this century have come to be published and are now read. A recent discussion on this genre focusses on the *Catakantaravana-katai*, or the story of the ten-headed Ravana. Here it is Sita who, with Rama as her charioteer, goes into battle against Ravana. In single combat she is the one who kills Ravana. Clearly the imprint of the powerful, assertive goddess figure overrides the more accommodating and gentler image of the Sanskrit and Hindi texts. These are not marginal traditions for they are central to the societies from which they emerge. If it is claimed that Indian culture as being propagated by the state is representative of the Indian people, and not just of a small segment of Indian society, then these variants must also find a place.

The question then is that of whose version of the story are we propagating? What was shown on TV and has now become the received version was a mix of the Valmiki and Tulsidas versions. The choice of these versions must have a reason: perhaps because they are best known among Hindi speakers and therefore familiar to North Indian Vaishnavas? Epics are not religious documents in origin. But some versions of an epic story can be transformed into religious statements and this was certainly the case with the later version of the Valmiki Ramayana and even more so with the *Ramacharitamanas*.

The TV version was not a folk genre. It borrowed from the films of the 1940s, the 'mythologicals' and it borrowed from the popular local Ramlilas. The latter are again prevalent in the Hindi-speaking region, for in other parts of the country, Dussehra and Diwali have other major connotations and rituals. But what was absent from the TV version was the incorporation of the folkways and the comedy of the Ramlilas. Local issues and local commentary gave a flavour and vibrancy to these performances. The street Ramlilas had a tremendous vibrancy. An episode from the text would be recited, followed by an explanation of it or a commentary on it by the bard reciting it. This often meant a comment on contemporary events as well as parallels, providing a kind of clarification. These latter could sometimes be so effective that it is thought that they may have quietly slid into the narrative—and become an aid to understanding the text, that doubtless went back to early, unfamiliar times.

If the literary version in Sanskrit attempted to freeze the rendering of earlier centuries, the TV version could now have the same effect on future Ramalilas. It may even have led, as it seems to have done, to the closing down of live performances, the preference being to watching a version on TV. Yet these multiple and conflicting versions have a legitimacy since they are statements of a social condition and a historical moment. Received versions deny the legitimacy of others as also the idea that a society does not have a single culture but is a collation of cultural systems.

Culture is not an object. It is among other things a way of conducting social relationships expressed in various idioms. State patronage and direction of culture tends to look for a single 'national culture'. It tends to take on the perspective of the dominant group and the culture of this group is projected as the mainstream national culture. Cultural hegemony requires the marginalizing and ironing out of other cultural expressions. Those who complain against this hegemony and argue that to treat Ramanand Sagar's version as the received version is to display a poverty in understanding Indian culture are described as deracinated, westernized Indians, out of touch with the culture of the masses. They are dismissed as 'elitists' seeking to dictate cultural norms, forgetting of course that in the system described, choice is anyway restricted and the so-called 'elitists' are, in fact, supporting a more extensive choice. What is also surprising in this context is that no comment is made on some of the more glaring examples of deracination and elitism seeking to influence cultural choices, namely, the advertisements which precede and follow the sponsored programmes on TV and elsewhere.

The enthusiasm of the masses has been repeatedly invoked in claiming the Ramanand Sagar version as an expression of national culture. Which masses are we invoking? Those below the poverty line in rural areas who are unable to come within watching distance of a TV set? Or are we referring to the urban underclass who have access to a neighbour's set? Even if it is the latter, one wonders what they made of the commentary spoken by Ashok Kumar, who, like the bard of olden times introduces parallels with contemporary life. When the four young princes of Ayodhya are sent at a tender age to the gurukul for training and their mothers are saddened by their departure, Ashok Kumar introduces the parallel of young children today going to boarding school—hardly an experience with which the masses would be familiar.

When supernatural weapons swirl and zig-zag across the screen, the commentator compares them to the weapons of *Star*

Wars—perhaps a subtle appeal to the wishful thought that Indian civilization once might have had space weapons, but certainly an endorsement of such weaponry. The depiction of the demons who threaten the noble rishis and whom Rama and Lakshmana are fetched in order to destroy them are so evidently the physical type associated with 'tribal peoples' that the message of their being alien and evil hardly needs stating in words. If the TV version is fulfilling the role of the storyteller in the life of the young child then what are the nuances which it portrays? Comics, drawing on these stories and the TV version, are part of an urban child's fantasy. It might be educative for us to ask for the reaction of urban children in schools, or even not so, to the presentations in the Amar Chitra Katha. The versions which had a universal appeal also had a different kind of message. Are we really talking about an appeal to the masses or are we talking about the middle class and other aspirants to the same status?

Tulsidas's *Ramacharitamanas* did have an appeal for caste Hindus. As a good Brahmana, Tulsidas complained of the upsetting of caste hierarchies and the rise of the low castes to positions and status (as also good Brahmanas had complained in earlier times). A return to a Rama-rajya would set society on the right course since caste hierarchies would be re-imposed. Each man functions according to his allotted caste and then all is right with the world. The notion of Rama-rajya does have a widespread appeal. It is a generalized millennarian dream which envisages the well-being of all. It does not go into the question of social inequities. To romanticize hierarchy is one way of supporting it and the message means different things to those at the upper levels and to those down below. The appeal to the latter is the religious message. The religious wrapping in the past tended to hide the political message. If religion is reduced to a vote-catching mechanism then the political message is neither democratic nor secular.

The religious message of the Tulsidas version is stated in no uncertain terms. Tulsidas repeats again and again that the only thing of supreme importance is Rama-bhakti—unqualified devotion to Rama as the incarnation of Vishnu and to which his text is dedicated. Clearly this rendering of the Ramayana theme has to be differentiated from the many others which either identify with other religions and ideologies or else are genuine folk genres where such identities are subordinated or are at any rate less sectarian. The very specific identity of the Tulsidas version cannot be extended to include the picking up of the earlier narrative and its alteration in other religious traditions (including incidentally Islamic features in Indonesian and Malay versions).

There have been statements by the public, commenting on the serial, in defence of the right of the Hindus to see their religious literature on state-sponsored TV. It is said that the majority of Indians are Hindus and therefore a public broadcasting system and television has a duty to bow to the tastes and preferences of the majority. This is a statement which may be seen as impinging on the government's policy towards programmes on the audio-visual media and would require a response from the government. If the media had been autonomous, as has often been urged by various government-appointed committees, then the onus would not be on the government. But since the media in large measure are supportive of government policies, the government should be answerable for what is said in programmes that support it and the influence of these programmes on public opinion and issues, not to mention concepts of culture. If the state is anxious to be the patron par excellence, one assumes that it is aware of what it is patronizing.

Of course, the Ramanand Sagar version has popular appeal. It is the world of Indian middle-class fantasy, in which problems arise but are miraculously solved. Its presentation through spectacular sets, glittering costumes, and ham acting, matches up to these fantasies. And we all need fantasies.

One's anxieties about the Ramayana syndrome arise from other causes: that the fantasy of one social group should not be projected as the fantasy of the entire society, for the essence of cultural renewal is the freedom to innovate and to use changing idioms even for themes regarded as traditional or sacred—as indeed was done in the past; that culture be treated not as a single, homogenized, national package, but as free, intersecting cultural systems reflecting the assumptions of all the constituents of Indian society; and lastly, the question of whether the state realizes that behind every fantasy there lies a reality and the fantasies of some can be in conflict with those of others. Is the state aware of the reality behind this particular fantasy?

11

THE EPIC OF THE BHARATAS*

It might be worth exploring the possibility of locating a sense of history in the Mahabharata and explaining why it is called itihasa—thus it was—whereas the Ramayana is called a kavya—a poem. This does not lie so much in the character of the narrative as in society being at the cusp of change from chiefships to small kingdoms.

THE MAHABHARATA CALLS ITSELF ITIHASAM-PURATANAM—THUS indeed it was in times past. This is not a Rankean statement and there are no definitive claims to historicity of persons and events in the narrative. However, there is a hint that some of the narrative may have been an attempt to cull from the remembered tradition that which may have happened, even if what is culled is disordered in the retelling. The Ramayana, however, is most often described as a kavya, in fact the adikavya, suggesting a small distinction between the two.

There have been many commentaries in Sanskrit on the epics from the eleventh century to the seventeenth century examining their meaning and intention. An analysis of these could tell us about how the epic was perceived in periods prior to ours. One wonders, for instance, whether historicity as we understand it today was of concern to the authors and to the audience of past times. Undoubtedly among the more attractive features of the epic, although historically tantalizing, are its many enigmas. Some

*An earlier version of this essay was first published in 2010.

however suggest the occasional facet of the historical past. The attempt in this essay is to point to these and indicate the problems they raise.

Epic as a genre uses narrative to represent situations from the past. It looks back nostalgically from the point in time when it is being composed and given form which is its present. The nostalgia is for a past age of heroes and the clans to which they belonged. This slowly gave way to the present where the heroes are less important in a society governed by kings and the code of castes. The nature of authority is more focused and therefore different in kingship, and the determining of status and social attitudes by reference to caste, gradually becomes predictable.

Given that it spans more than one kind of society, re-examining the concepts we use in interpreting the epic becomes essential. Some are inflected by the translations we use. The context of the epic was that of clan societies and small-scale kingdoms. It is as well to remember that the term 'raja' did not in origin mean a king, but referred simply to 'the one who shines', an appropriate title for a chief. As such it is likely to have been continued when the system changed to kingship. To translate samrat as 'imperial monarch' is to impose a later meaning on an earlier term. A more accurate meaning might refer to the one 'who has authority over many'. The context of the term can illumine its meaning.

Part of the transition from clan to kingdom also lay in the evolving form that was being given to varna and jati. The structure of clan societies did not require that they follow the rules of the Dharmashastras but a king ruling a kingdom had to uphold caste. There were of course exceptions such as Ashoka who does not mention caste in his edicts, but this may have been due to his heterodox thinking.

The transition is vividly etched in the different nuances of how the clans functioned. The Vrishnis in Dwaraka in western India with their eighteen kulas, extended families/clans conform to a distinctive way of functioning reminiscent of oligarchies and chiefships. The Kauravas and the Pandavas battling for territory in the Doab and the western Ganga plain still observe the rules of clan ethics and codes of kin relationships but are seen to be slowly succumbing to the rules of kingship and the codes of caste, the pattern emerging in the easterly region of Magadha.

Authorship of the Mahabharata is attributed to Krishna Dvaipayana Vyasa, a Brahmana of uncertain antecedents, born of the sage Parashara and a fisherwoman, and of whom it is said that he sired Dhritarashtra and Pandu. Authorship and fatherhood are coalesced and in effect Vyasa is narrating the lives of his own sons and grandsons. They in turn have no blood connection with the lineage of the Bharatas although they are constantly referred to as 'bull of the Bharatas'. The blood connection actually ended with Bhishma, unless of course his being called pitamaha—the paternal grandfather—is taken literally, despite his vow, but in which case the story would have been different.

Genealogies can be accurate over a few generations. But as sources they are also available to those who wish to fabricate connections and latch on to a respectable ancestry. This fragment of the lineage has an equally ambiguous end since the lineage continues through Parikshit, who is stillborn but revived by Krishna. Possibly the invented connection was necessary, since in the Vedic corpus the epithets used for the ancestor Puru are not the most complimentary: his speech is said to be mridhra-vach, impure, and he has an asura-rakshasa ancestry.

The epic recitation had two beginnings a generation apart. It was first recited at the snake sacrifice of the Kshatriya raja, Janamejaya (the son of Parikshit) by the Brahmana Vaishampayana. A generation later it is recited at a sattra, a sacrificial ritual usually intended for and performed by Brahmanas, although the recitation this time is by the bard Ugrashravas. A Brahmana recites it to the Kshatriyas and a non-Brahmana to the Brahmana, an inversion which is curious. The epic, as we know it, was in origin the bard's memorization of what he had heard from the Brahmana's recital, and there is an insistence that both renderings are exactly as composed by Vyasa. One is immediately suspicious about changes and interpolations. The interleaving of Brahmana and bard as authors or the likelihood of bardic origins is not unknown.

The dasharajna, the battle of the ten rajas described in the Rig Veda has been viewed by some modern scholars as the seminal event for the war at Kurukshetra. Some of the clans from the Vedic corpus such as the Bharatas, Purus, Yadus, and Kuru–Panchalas reappear in the Mahabharata as lineage ancestors of the epic protagonists, but not necessarily in the same situations. Panini in the fourth century BC refers indirectly to grammatical constructions associated with words such as mahabharata, yudhishthira, arjuna, and vasudeva.

Epic personalities have parallels in the Buddhist *Jataka* stories where persons with the same names occur in events that are often dissimilar to the epics. The secreting away of Krishna as a baby, his hostility as a young man to his uncle Kamsa at Mathura, and the migration of his clan to Dwaraka are part of the narrative of his clan, the Andhaka-Venhu/Vrishni. Its end came through a drunken massacre, a story repeated in the Vaishnava texts. Neither Krishna nor his clan is particularly attractive in these stories.

But as a contrast to this, stories of the descendants of Yudhishthira ruling the Kuru realm from Indraprastha, and advised by the minister Vidura-pandita, are characterized by what is called Kuru righteousness, particularly noted for its practice of virtue. Whether these variant versions were taken from the epic or contributed to the making of the epic remains a debated subject. The ideological underpinning also differs.

The stories are not identical but may go back to a common source. The boxing-in of stories as in the epic is also a technique of adding to a narrative by attaching yet another story. Subsequently, when they were given an ideological gloss, they served the needs of Buddhist ethics and later of Jaina versions, or the sectarian beliefs of Vaishnava Bhagavatism, each in disagreement with the other. The diversity of these initial fragments seems to be echoed in the varied regional versions and recensions of the epic, a process that continued through the centuries. This multiplicity makes it necessary sometimes to identify the version one is referring to.

The composition was doubtless in the nature of a slow accretion as is characteristic of the early epic genre virtually anywhere. Nevertheless at some point it was brought together. Tradition has it that a small text, the Jaya, became larger, the Bharata, and the larger became still larger, the Mahabharata. It is, therefore, virtually impossible to calculate a precise date for the events and to define an 'epic period' in ancient history as was once done.

This would also be one reason for the difficulty in identifying a particular archaeological site as the archaeological equivalent of a location in the epic. Excavations have been conducted at locations that are called Hastinapur and Indraprastha. These could be ancient sites although we know that place names also travel especially with migrant populations. Distances on the ground do not always tally with the text. In today's identifications these two places were a considerable journey away from the battlefield. Equating a site with a text can raise problems of reconciling material culture with evocations of poetic licence. Will we ever find the fantasy palace of the Pandavas built by Asura Maya even if we believe it existed and dig up the whole of Indraprastha? Homer's epic met with similar problems after the extensive excavations at Troy and other sites.

The epic maintains that the war at Kurukshetra took place on the cusp of the Kaliyuga. This has been dated as equivalent to 3102 BC. Dates calculated on the basis of the genealogical lists of Kshatriya lineages in the Puranas generally work out to between 1200-1000 BC. The archaeological evidence of a heavy silt deposit at the site of Hastinapur which has been linked to the epic reference to a flood after the war points to a date of circa 800 BC. Mention of Yavanas, Shakas, Hunas would be interpolations in the late BCS and early centuries AD.

V. S. Sukthankar, to whom the critical edition of the epic owes much, argued that its composition ranged from 400 BC to AD 400. More recently scholars have suggested that the oral epic was put together as a text in about 150 BC and that this may have taken a century or so. Attempts have been made to correlate readings in astronomy with references to planetary configurations in the epic. These differ and would relate not to the text as a whole but to particular segments carrying the reference. Diversity in dates also makes it problematic to attribute authorship to a single author. The meaning of Vyasa is, interestingly, one who edits and arranges.

To add to the complexity, it has been argued that the epic had two intentions. The earliest narrative was constructed out of fragmentary stories of the heroic: tales of combat, marriages, games of dice, exile in the forest—and were probably formulaic on occasion. The same process has been noticed in the Homeric epics. Exile is a marvellous background for the bard as it can be stretched with add-ons heightening the reach of the imagination. Heroic exploits can be enlarged with every recitation, whether the hero is wandering across the 'wine-dark seas' of the Mediterranean as in the *Odyssey* or in the tangled forests of northern India as in the Mahabharata. Exile to the forest in India reinforced the dichotomy of grama—settlement—and aranya—forest—central to cultural perceptions.

It was probably the immense popularity of the epic, both as a linear narrative of the heroic as well as in the embroidered intricacies of the stories, that led to the second intention and reformulation—its conversion into a Bhagavata text. Sukthankar argued that this was done by the Bhrigu Brahmanas who also 'Bhriguised' the Ramayana. Both Krishna and Rama became avataras of Vishnu and this changed the character of the epic. It is worth noting that on the second occasion of its recitation the bard was required to proclaim the descent of the Bhrigu lineage, perhaps to legitimize the Bhrigus and their appropriation of the epic.

The Bhrigus were often linked to the Angiras Brahmanas, associated with the Atharva Veda and, among other things, were regarded as the practitioners of sorcery and magic. Neither group was the most highly respected among learned Brahmanas. The Bhrigus were called Brahma-kshatra when they married Kshatriya women. Their learning extended into knowledge and custom beyond the conventional and in addition they were said to know niti and dharma.

The question could be asked that if the Bhrigus were not pre-eminent Brahmanas why were they permitted to reformulate the epic? Epic origins lay in popular compositions not in divine revelation; therefore they were not as sacred as the Vedas. The Bhrigus may have wished to convert the epic into a Bhagavata sectarian text, if they were associated with early Bhagavatism. The didactic section was the palatable way of teaching the various Brahmanical dharmas. The Mahabharata can be viewed as a civilizational text not because it reflects the propagation of a particular view of these dharmas but because, among other things, it speaks to the debate on social ethics, especially between the Brahmanical perspective and those that question it—a debate that has continued over many centuries.

The Bhagavata religion was not identical with the Vedic even if the Mahabharata is referred to as the fifth Veda—as indeed was the itihasa-purana itself and many other bodies of knowledge. The Bhrigu Brahmanas may have had associations with pre-Vedic and non-Vedic ideas as has been suggested. In one Upanishad the Bhrigu-Angirasas are linked to the itihasa-purana. This would, up to a point, make them appropriate editors of texts pertaining to the past. Nevertheless, the controversy on 'Bhriguisation' continues.

Why the Bhagavata reformulation was necessary needs an explanation. Perhaps the realization that the Buddhist gloss on popular stories was a successful way of propagating sectarian belief may have encouraged Bhagavatas to do the same. Buddhism was subordinating the worship of clan deities to the higher ideal of the ethic of dharma as defined by the Buddha. Bhagavatism required the worship of Vishnu as the supreme deity and the varna dharma was its social ethic, both of which incidentally reinforced the requirements of kingship. This subsequent addition has left a heavy imprint on the Mahabharata and the epic genre of the text has tended to be subordinated. It is to this genre that I would like to give more space.

The first few books narrate the epic of the Kauravas and the Pandavas and take the story, together with whatever is tagged onto the narrative, to the point where war is imminent. The description of person and event veers towards the functioning of a clan-based society. It conforms in the main to the pattern of a segmentary system of lineages functioning as segments of an extensive network. The Puranas a little later called it the Chandravamsha, the lunar lineage. Identity is through being born into a clan, kinship controls behavioural relations and social functions, governance is through an assembly of the heads of families and status is relatively egalitarian within the clan.

Agro-pastoralism is the major source of income with an emphasis on cattle herding and the occasional cattle-raid described more than once in the epic. The Vedas also refer to the Kuru-Panchala clans going out in 'the dewy season' to raid cattle. The more spectacular sacrificial rituals asserting the political authority of the patron, such as the rajasuya performed by Yudhishthira, are occasions for gathering-in tribute and exchanging gifts. These are largely in the form of the produce of hunting and herding, of weaving textiles, of mining gold and gems, and maintaining domestic slaves—mainly women. Agricultural activity is of course a necessity but tends to be low-key. Dependence on agriculture increases in the later parts of the text. Items of wealth placed as stakes in the game of dice are similar but of larger amounts. Ultimately Yudhishthira stakes the town, the territory and eventually himself.

The listing of wealth is in substantial if not exaggerated terms. Such occasions have been thought to be rituals but also gift-giving ceremonies, characteristic functions of heads of clans. On special occasions, the chief collects, consumes, distributes and, if need be, even destroys what remains of his wealth. The rajasuya was one such occasion with inevitable consequences. The intention is to assert status which in turn leads to a competition among clan chiefs each trying to outdo the previous one. Therefore gift-giving is not a one-way process. It assumes that the holding of these ceremonies turn by turn ensures the circulation of whatever is produced. It also prevents a chief acquiring excessive power through accumulating enormous wealth. Should this happen conflict may be unavoidable. The items brought to the yajna come as gifts and tribute and not as tax.

The clans were described as Kshatriyas, with status dependent not on caste but on the hierarchy among the clans. Identity came from the clan. Hence the emphasis on genealogies, all of which may or may not have been taken literally, the social forms reflected in their structure also being significant. Breaks in the genealogy can be indicators of change.

That the rules of caste were not strictly observed would explain why three disparate systems of marriage are adopted over two consecutive generations in the family of Pandu. In Pandu's marriage to Madri it would seem that a bride price was involved, even if not in material goods, making it an asura marriage according to the Dharmashastras. The fraternal polyandry of the five Pandavas marrying Draupadi is outside any Dharmashastras scheme and is discussed at some length in the epic before it is accepted. Draupadi questioning Yudhishthira's right to stake her in the dicing match is not the kind of statement that matches the patriarchal values advised for wifely behaviour in the social codes. The three women who command the narrative are Draupadi who poses the question of the legality of Yudhishthira's right over her, Kunti who chooses the deities she wants as surrogate husbands, and Gandhari who insists on being permanently blindfolded after her marriage to a blind husband.

The third variant form was that of Arjuna's marriage to Subhadra (cross cousin) which is a rakshasa form according to the

Dharmashastras yet the lineage continues through their stillborn but revived grandson, Parikshit. Such flexible social practices suggest societies where alien custom could be incorporated to accommodate a new situation.

Krishna's clan, the Andhaka-Vrishni, had a lower status than the Kurus. Political functioning among them lay in the sangha—assembly—where the senior kinsmen of the eighteen kulas sat to take decisions. In kingdoms, the assembly was reduced to an advisory body whose views were not binding on the king. The concentration of power required in kingship perhaps accounts in part for the hostility of the Vrishni clans towards Magadha. The kingdom of Magadha was a challenge to the gana-sanghas, the clans of the middle Ganga plain. Eventually the clan confederacy of Vaishali was destroyed through devious means resulting in the consolidation of kingship as a polity.

Beyond the clans was the non-caste 'Other', treated by the heroes as virtually bereft of human value, as is apparent at various points of the narrative. These were the people of the forest such as the Nishada and the Shabara, the excluded and impure mleccha and therefore dispensable. The episode that has been commented on is that of Eklavya, who being a Nishada, had to give his thumb as a fee to the Brahmana guru thus terminating his skill as an archer. But equally traumatic is the reference to how a Nishada woman and her five sons were left in the house of lac, which was set on fire to mislead the Kauravas about the presence of the Pandavas. As a comment on clan society this requires explanation, unless it can be argued that such episodes were introduced later when the mleccha were treated as less than human.

The narrative of the battle at Kurukshetra forms a substantial section of the epic. As a time-marker it touches many dimensions. It marks the end of clan societies. Krishna's comment is telling: Sarvam kshatram kshayam gatam—It is the destruction of all the Kshatriyas. It is said that the end of the war marked the end of the Dwapara Yuga—the third of the four ages—and the start of the new and final Kali Yuga. The theory of the four yugas is referred to in various texts of the post-Mauryan period and was probably not in the early epic. It seems to have been a later reflection on a substantial historical change expressed literally as the coming of a new age. As with exile, war is another occasion for the bard-poet to show his skill, so the narrative extends over many parvans (books) of the epic. Despite references to formations of standing armies familiar from warfare in later periods, the battle was essentially heroic warfare and often single combat—thus allowing for some of the dubious manoeuvres attributed to the advice given by Krishna.

That the war was pushed by Draupadi's demand for revenge is an epic-heroic feature. So too was the fact that the initial succession was contested by the absence of unchallenged primogeniture, both brothers being physically disabled. It was probably in origin a clan conflict involving those that had claims on the territory and their friends or enemies. Enlarged into a massive eighteen-day event it was said to have involved clans from all over. That this was an exaggeration is suggested by Arjuna arguing the futility of war prior to the event, and Yudhishthira doing so after the event. Validating violence becomes a necessity, and even the simile of the battle being a yajna, ritual of sacrifice, is used as it was in later times as well.

Although the Bhagavad Gita in the narrative is placed just before the start of the war, its teaching seems more appropriate to the society that emerged after the war and the contested definition of dharma. Arjuna, dismayed by the thought that he would have to kill his close kinsmen, questions the ethics of such an act. The killing of kinsmen seems to have been more heinous in a society where kinship was a primary identity than in a society where kin ties were subsumed in caste. Krishna speaking from the perspective of a caste society explains to Arjuna that as a Kshatriya it is his svadharma—the social obligation of one's caste—to fight against evil even if it means killing kinsmen. Is the moral dilemma being subordinated to caste duty?

As has been pointed out in recent studies, the urgency of this discourse most likely had to do with the current debates on dharma and ahimsa provoked by Buddhist and Jaina teaching and by the alternative ideal of kingship propagated by Ashoka. In the latter, the social ethic is not dependent on caste but on the quality of human behaviour as encapsulated in dhamma. This may have been the context to Yudhishthira questioning the Kshatriya model. Judging by inscriptional evidence, support for Buddhism and Jainism at all levels of society was extensive in the post-Mauryan period and there would doubtless have been at least ideological confrontations with the code of the dharma-shastras. Is the Shanti Parvan of the Mahabharata therefore a polemic in the debate with the heterodoxy? Yet there is also the play on Yudhishthira being the son of the deity Dharma which would have enhanced his sensitivity to the question of ethics.

The later part of the epic, sometimes described as the didactic sections, although these were scattered briefly elsewhere as well, begins effectively after the end of the war and consists substantially of the much-quoted Shanti Parvan and Anushasana Parvan. These are important in themselves but in some ways represent a discourse outside the epic. To discuss the epic largely on the basis of these sections as is sometimes done is to do it an injustice.

Yudhishthira, appalled by the violence of the war, is reluctant to assume kingship and wishes to retreat to the forest. Bhishma wounded in the war and lying on his bed of arrows, persuades Yudhishthira not to renounce kingship and instead to govern as an established king in a kingdom. His long peroration on various categories of dharma and even on situations where it fails is significant in these political transitions. Kingship as a political form is viewed implicitly as superior to what came before or which continued as an alternate system. The discourse by Bhishma is almost certainly a later interpolation of the time when the gana-rajyas, chiefships and oligarchies had declined—but not disappeared—and in many places had been replaced by kingdoms.

The discussions on rajadharma—the code for kingship and administration—on punishment, on times of distress, run parallel to themes in texts such as Kautilya's *Arthashastra* and the *Manu Dharmashastra*, not to mention the continuing memory of the Mauryan state. Kautilya's list of what constitutes a state system, assumes a kingdom ruled by a king with decision-making powers, through an administration manned by non-kinsmen, located in a capital city to which the revenue comes via taxes, and where the kingdom is identified by demarcated territory, defended by a regular standing army and where other kings are allies. These are features more familiar from the later books.

The didactic sections were in a sense looking back at the epic past, but were legitimizing the coming change to kingdoms. The change was not linear and determined. It was somewhat meandering with various offshoots and in some cases earlier forms may have continued as we know that they did historically until much later. But that such a change was represented in the eventual version seems apparent. What I am suggesting is not a dichotomy between clan-society and the kingdom, nor a textbook version of each, but the difference in societies with more of one than the other.

This essay is only one passing historical perspective of the Mahabharata. Even from historians alone there are many more. And beyond them the perspectives multiply still further. The narrative of the epic is sequential, set in a frame of linear chronology, nevertheless there are substratum layers of structures, order, legitimation, and claims that seem extraneous to the narrative but are insightful. What is perhaps being indicated in all this is that historicity should not be sought for only in person and event for it may lie at a deeper level.

In the interface of the two kinds of societies that I have sketched, partially sequential and partially concurrent, there lies what might be seen as a historical tradition—the tradition of a later society remembering and reconstructing what it believes to be the earlier one, where the reconstruction becomes the perceived past. Perhaps it is because of this that the Mahabharata can call itself itihasam puratanam.

12

BACK IN TIME[*]

There are many ways in which the past can be used. One of these is to legitimize the present. An example of this is the attempt to give a date to the two epics—Mahabharata and Ramayana. The difference of opinion lies in either giving a date within a short bracket of time or else conceding that there were many interpolations over extended time. Since the subject is now being linked to cultural identities, it is inevitably widely debated.

THE ARGUMENTS ON THE CHRONOLOGY and authenticity of the epics as historical narratives have been current in scholarly circles for the last many decades. The lack of any further incisive analysis at this point at the scholarly level demonstrates a certain paucity in our understanding of epic traditions and in our handling of the historical method. But there is probably more to it than that. It indicates a point of uncertainty where both a questioning of and clinging to what is regarded as the social and cultural tradition becomes enmeshed with social and political change. Attitudes to the tradition then become a pivot for mobilization on other matters: a process which has been repeated throughout history but which has become more pointed in recent times.

Ancient traditions and what are believed to be cultural roots hold a central place in cultural nationalism. During the nineteenth and early twentieth centuries, Indian scholarship was as much a party to the interconnection of contemporary politics and the study of ancient traditions as scholarship anywhere else. But

*An earlier version of this essay was first published in 1976.

cultural nationalism has many historical phases and one wonders if the present interest in the epics is not in some ways parallel to the interest in the *Nibelungenlied* in nineteenth-century Europe. The 'ancient tradition' poses at least two difficult problems for its inheritors. One is the need to identify with it. The other is either to disprove its historical authenticity and dismiss it as, therefore, valueless or else to constantly verify its authenticity by testing it with the most recent and, what are thought to be, the most scientific methods available. The recent debate suggests that it is in this last situation that we find ourselves.

For those of us professionally involved in these matters, the dating of the Mahabharata and the Ramayana and the problem of their historical authenticity are hardy perennials which crop up at every all-India conference and which have come to be treated with a certain indifference. The indifference stems from the fact that there has not been in the recent past any strikingly new interpretation on this specific subject calling for prolonged discussion or suggesting new perspectives to the problem that alter existing views. It is a sad commentary on the state of investigation of these problems that it is substantially the old evidence which is being juggled back and forth in attempts to suggest a range of dates. The present controversy has brought all the old guns to the fore—the technique of trying to read astronomical data in the texts and use these to work out the dates, as also the computation of the genealogies listed in the epics and the Puranas as a basis for chronological reconstructions. The only relatively new method of investigation is the comparison with archaeological data, whatever is recent, and there is little conclusive evidence. It might be worthwhile to look a little more closely at these methods and see why the results are not taking us forward.

Some participants in the debate base their chronological conclusions on what they believe to be references, veiled or direct, to the position of the stars and constellations which they take as readings for astronomical data. The most popular of these are the readings suggested at the time of the death of Bhishma in some versions of the Mahabharata. The interrelation of constellations is then calculated back in time for many hundreds of years until a correlation with the supposed evidence of the text can be made. These arguments tend to be highly esoteric and the debate is restricted to a few persons conversant with the language of astronomy and astrology. I say 'supposed evidence' not in any derogatory sense but, literally, since in cases where the references to astronomical data are veiled, the interpretation of these statements as symbolic of such data is, after all, a personal matter and usually is doubted by those wanting precise evidence. It is true that ancient texts are often highly symbolic in content. The cross-check in the interpretation of symbols is that the meaning/interpretation must have a link to the culture. If on one occasion rikshas (bears) refers to the seven bears/Ursa Major constellation, it must do so on all occasions where it is mentioned in that context. The interpretation of symbols having by now become methodologically fairly systematic, this should be the first step in claiming the viability of certain symbols as astronomical data. Such a step is still not always taken as conclusive evidence.

Where the reference to astronomical readings is not veiled but direct, as where mention is made of the position of the nakshatras (lunar mansions), it is possible that these references could be interpolations of later editors wishing to give antiquity to the events described. Such references vary from edition to edition, from region to region and some are absent in the critical edition of the Mahabharata, which is now accepted as the standard text. For any valid use of such data there would have to be a collection of all such references to astronomical readings and a general acceptance of the interpretation of these readings, followed by a careful scrutiny to exclude those which are evidently late interpolations, as well as a correlation of the remaining readings with the known knowledge of astronomy and mathematics for the period to which the text is being ascribed. The understanding of astronomy is one thing, its application to history is quite another.

Others, mathematically inclined, but less rigorous than the astronomers, have tried to compute the dates of these texts from the genealogical lists which the texts provide. The argument runs that if a mean average can be taken for the life span of each generation, then by counting the generations a chronology can be worked out for the events described in the texts associated with particular generations. Much time and energy have gone into calculating the average life span of a generation in India, particularly with reference to royal families. For the dynasties of the medieval period, fairly precise data is available from court chronicles, and royal inscriptions which were used as primary data. The average length of reign of rulers was computed. Other sources on regnal years of dynasties were also consulted. The figures ranged from fourteen years to twenty-two. Depending on the figures one accepted, it was thought possible to work out the life span of epic genealogies.

The way in which this system works is as follows: we are told that a king, Udayin, believed to be a contemporary of the Buddha, reigned approximately twenty-four generations after the end of the Mahabharata war. Assuming that the Buddha died in 468 or 483 BC, Udayin's reign can be placed at around 500 BC. Taking an average of fourteen years per generation we arrive at the date of 836 BC for the war, as indeed has been suggested. But we could as well take twenty-two years per generation as the time span in which case we would arrive at a different date of 1028 BC. The choice in either case is arbitrary since there is no reason for choosing fourteen in preference to twenty-two. And, if we accept, as some scholars do, 544 BC as the date for the death of the Buddha, we would arrive at a still earlier date for the war. If we accept a date closer to 400 BC as has been suggested then the date of the Buddha's nirvana would also be later. Since there is no certainty that the number of generations listed is precise, the calculations stand on shaky ground.

Others compute the generations from the start of the Kali Yuga which is sometimes dated to 3102 BC, but in some sources, it is also said to be associated with the Mahabharata war. So that is not of much help either. Not only is the acceptance of a particular figure for a generation highly subjective, but the figure itself is open to question. Little thought was given to the fact that habits of nutrition change over a period of a thousand or two thousand or (who knows) maybe even three thousand years and these habits together with general ecological changes affect longevity and average life-expectancy. Or, for that matter, that the chieftains of clans or the heroes and kings of early states would be living in a different social system from the rajas of kingdoms or the sultans of Delhi and that this might affect not only life expectancy but also the rate of turnover of those in political ascendancy.

Nor has there been concern with examining the role of genealogies in history and society, on which there is now a large body of literature both from historians working on the genealogies of early West Asia and from anthropologists concerned with the function of genealogy as a social tradition in many parts of the world. If this literature is studied, it will soon become apparent that attempting to compute precise chronology on the basis of genealogies is not a simple calculation based on counting generations or regnal years. Genealogies merely record which persons (and to that extent the events associated with them) came before and which after. Time-reckoning is approximate. Further, they serve an essentially social function as, for example, to allow more recent upstarts to attach themselves to an ancient lineage in order to acquire social status; or to prove the claim of a particular family to rights over land. At most, some information on the system of succession and the geographical location of a lineage can with difficulty be milked out of a genealogical record.

The genealogists had little compunction about either conflating the number of generations or of reducing them should they be desirous of fitting the lineage into a politically expedient pattern.

The variants in the genealogies listing the lineage of Rama or of the Pandavas and Kauravas are almost as many as there are texts. The purpose of the genealogy has much more to do with the time when it was compiled than with the early ancestors whom it claims to be listing. And ancient Indian genealogical material is no exception to this.

In the last half century or so, the attempted chronology for the Indian epics has turned to archaeology as a possible source of information. This has resulted from the exploration and excavation of modern sites bearing place-names or associations occurring in the epics, the classic example being Hastinapur, the city associated with the Kauravas or more recently the site of Indraprastha, linked to the Purus. The situation is analogous with the excavation of Troy to prove the Homeric epics. (The discussion is virtually limited to the Mahabharata since the important sites associated with the Ramayana have yet to be excavated, although one of the arguments for archaeology linked to the Ramayana is based on this premise). If the contribution of an archaeological culture is found to roughly coincide with the geographical locale of the epic, a correlation is suggested. However, even this can be deceptive since the geographical reach of the epic can undoubtedly expand as the geographical knowledge of its editors and interpolators increases from century to century. Thus, the geographical locale of the epic can only refer to the time of the most recent redaction of the text. Nevertheless, it has been argued that the archaeological culture called the Painted Grey Ware, distributed in the main over Punjab, Haryana, north-western Rajasthan, and western Uttar Pradesh, and dating to the late second and early first millennium BC, may be associated with the Mahabharata since this is broadly the core of the geographical area to which the text relates. On the assumption of this association and the genealogical exercise to which reference has been made above, the date of 836 BC for the war has been suggested.

To calculate such pinpointed chronology from archaeological evidence is almost to deny the validity of the evidence. One of the joys of using archaeological evidence for those of us who are non-mathematically inclined is precisely that it shifts the focus from the historian's obsession with chronology to the wider implications of the society under consideration. Thus, apart from the geographical correlation, the more important investigation is whether the material culture excavated from the site/sites conforms to that described in the epic. Such an analysis which would be of immense value is almost impossible at the moment since few of the more important sites associated with the epics have as yet been excavated horizontally and sufficiently to reveal the larger canvas of the culture at any given point in time. Since the excavations are vertical, the evidence on material culture is limited. The comparative data from the epics also need to be more systematically collated.

It is here that we come up against the core of the problem. Only a few isolated attempts have been made to examine the social contexts of the epics. In the main, the texts are taken as 'a given' and whoever wishes to prove a point about the past delves into the epics and picks out his evidence. Yet, the compilation of an epic is a study in itself. It is a collection of bardic poetry describing heroic exploits, folk tales, narrative episodes, fragments of genealogies, gobbets of customary law, myths, segments of religious cults, ethical theories, and even philosophical speculation. The time-dimension of all these various nuggets ranges over many centuries and refers to a variety of social forms and situations. The epic unlike the myth is assumed to contain some trace of an historical kernel. But this does not mean that all the events are historically accurate or that even the historically proven event is accurately described in the epic. Epic literature based on bardic fragments is by definition a collection of many social traditions, generally referring back to the twilight period of tribal societies and the dawn of early kingdoms. The bard evokes nostalgia for the heroic age and imbues it with a utopian gloss to which future generations look back with envy. This contributes to the richness of the text.

Epic literature is therefore difficult to date precisely: events merge into events and narrative slowly gets welded with commentary. The Mahabharata is a clear example of this as has been shown by scholars who have discussed the many accretions and interpolations over equally many centuries. The purpose of such accretions was both to bring the epic up-to-date with contemporary changes as well as to use it as a channel for new ideas and new ethics. The Ramayana carries fewer traces of the early epic tradition and is evidently of the more developed literary form of court poetry, hence its description as a kavya. Although even in this text the composition is not uniform in style and time.

Any archaeological correlation therefore would be complicated, to say the least, as it would require the sorting out of the stratification of the text, before such a correlation could be attempted. At most, some period of occupation of a particular site could be connected with textual references. To try and identify an entire epic with an archaeological culture is virtually to attempt the impossible. What archaeology can be used for is the correlation of items of material culture with literary descriptions from the epics and this would indicate the technology, perhaps the socio-economic background, and possibly an approximate time-context for that particular episode.

Some preliminary work on this kind of identification was done by the Sanskrit scholar and archaeologist Hasmukh Sankalia with reference to the Ramayana and the material culture of northern India. Those who claim that the Painted Grey Ware culture is the archaeological counterpart to the Mahabharata show no understanding of the stratification of the text and the archaeological identification therefore carries little conviction. (Quite apart from the fact that if this identification is accepted then those who take as literal the descriptions of the wealth and splendour of the court at Hastinapur are in for a rude shock since the archaeological evidence indicates a rather simple, pastoral-cum-agricultural, pre-urban society.)

The concern for dating the central event in the epic can become an exercise in futility, since the reflections of the epic can change with each new skin the epic acquires over time. A question posed a few decades ago still has considerable relevance, namely, was there only a single Bharata war or was there an earlier one whose memory alone lingered and that the one referred to in the present text is a more recent conflict which got accreted on to an earlier epic? There are a number of inexplicable discrepancies such as that the two protagonists, the Pandavas and the Kauravas, are not related by blood to the lineage whose rights over land and government they are claiming to inherit. The kinship link with the lineage is based on a series of fictions. A strange situation, indeed, for a society where kinship links were fundamental.

There has also been much discussion on the question of why the two epics have survived in India and have been accepted as a part of the tradition in other parts of Asia, whereas in Greece the *Iliad* and the *Odyssey* have virtually disappeared, in England *Beowulf* is known only to scholars and much the same happened to the *Nibelungenlied* in Germany—but for the fact that it was revived as part of cultural nationalism.

It has been suggested that the ethical values of the texts and the negation of the finality of death were among the reasons for this survival. These reasons would apply to any epic literature since its creation links it to situations of changing values and epics try to comment on these in an ethical strain. The didactic thread is always present though possibly more emphasized in the Indian epics. Bardic poetry, since it sets out to immortalize the exploits of the hero is, in a sense, a negation of death as a finality. Bhishma's lengthy discourse on life and death as he lay dying on the battlefield, which is what is often quoted in support of the argument, is more likely extraneous to the original epic and was introduced by later redactors who were manipulating the epic for other functions.

There are, of course, more obvious reasons for the lively continuity of the epic in India. In epic literature, generally, the distinction between gods and heroes is clearly demarcated. The gods participate in key events but strictly as gods. The heroes may be close to the gods but are essentially heroes. In the Indian epics, some of the heroes are converted into incarnations of gods. Some may have a divine parent, but Rama and Krishna are claimed to be incarnations of Vishnu. The literature which began as a secular folk tradition is at some point converted into sacred literature. In some other parts of the world the new religion, Christianity, dispelled the earlier gods; in India one of the new religions, Vaishnavism, devoid of any notion of paganism, introduced the idea of incarnations of Vishnu and used the epics for proselytization. Conversion was not the usual transference of devotion from one deity to another, but was the subsuming of a cult or a deity into Vaishnavism. This was a specific and characteristic feature in the construction of Hinduism.

Apart from this, social groups moving up the social scale and acquiring Kshatriya status sought and were given, connection with the two traditional genealogies, the solar and the lunar lineages, each of which form the genealogical core of the Ramayana and the Mahabharata respectively. Newly arrived elites therefore helped popularize the epics, which they projected as the story of the ancestors with whom they had claimed connections. A perusal of the late first millennium AD inscriptions from various parts of India makes this link very clear.

The diffusion of the epics as part of the Sanskrit tradition was carried by traders and by settlers in new areas both in the Indian subcontinent and in Asia, with monks and priests strengthening the impact. Where it became the literature of those in power it was also accepted by others. But it would be as well to remember that it is not the Valmiki Ramayana or the Mahabharata ascribed to Vyasa that is being discussed in a pan-Indian or pan-Asian context. It is the local version of what has been made of the bare bones of the story and which is of greater significance, and these variations on the original theme need to be analysed.

The Buddhist version of the story in India, for instance, as related in the *Dasaratha Jataka*, changes the kinship pattern and refers to Rama and Sita as brother and sister. This reflects the original myths of the early Buddhist tradition where sibling ancestors are regarded as the purest. From the Buddhist perspective this gave the story the highest status and legitimacy among origin myths.

Changes in the story occur in greater or lesser degree in all the different versions of the epics. It would be more worthwhile to try and understand how and why these stories were incorporated into the tradition of a culture or society and the function which they performed as media of ideologies (both religious and secular), values and social concerns, than merely to reiterate ad infinitum, the pan-Asian reach of the stories.

It would seem, therefore, that the necessary groundwork on the epic tradition still awaits completion before we can enter meaningfully into a discussion on its historical authenticity, let alone the date of the events described. This will require not only a sifting of the strata and 'skins' of the epics and an analysis of the changing function and purpose of the literature from age to age and region to region, but also a rigorous questioning of the methodology of analysis. The controversy emerges partially out of the wish to determine the accuracy of the tradition, but more one suspects out of the fear of attack on the bastion of tradition as well as the desire to prove it right. The controversy has focussed on statement and counterstatement rather than examining the methods used to arrive at the statements. Such a focus always carries the danger that what is being sought to be proved right is not the actual tradition, but what we today would like to interpret as the tradition.

IV

RENUNCIATION AND DISSENT

13

RENUNCIATION, DISSENT, AND SATYAGRAHA*

So strong has been the wish to project early India as registering social harmony and a tolerance of all ideas that it has seldom been conceded that dissent is an important aspect of pre-modern Indian thought. Yet there were major dissenting views expressed by a variety of social groups. Some of these ideas were raised again and were reincarnated in a different political context in modern times.

THE THEME OF THIS ESSAY was and still remains a subject of general interest. Although the degree of interest may have declined a few generations ago, the theme has returned and is now of critical importance to the present. I am referring to the right of the citizen to dissent—as part of the right to free speech. The right to dissent has come to be recognized as such in modern times, but its actual practice goes back many centuries.

However much we may wish it, Indian society—as every other society—has not been a seamless harmonious unity, with little or no contradiction. As with others, we too had our share of intolerance and violence, along with a clash of ideas. Dissenting voices were many. They had a much wider articulation in the past than we choose to recognize today.

Let me begin by briefly clarifying what I mean by dissent. It is in essence the disagreement that a person or persons may

*An earlier version of this essay was first published in 2020.

have with others, or more publicly with some of the institutions that govern our pattern of life. Institutions have a long history but the right to question their functioning is recent. Earlier only the elite had this right but today it extends—in theory at least—to all citizens. In earlier times the right was often argued over, but did not become a public issue. Implicit in having these rights is the exercising of dissent where thought appropriate. This has an historical continuity even if its forms have changed.

In historical terms, the political relationship of earlier times was encapsulated as that of the lord and the subject. This has given way to a new construction in the form of the relationship between the citizen and the state. This historical change coincided with the emergence of industrialization and capitalism through the evolving of the middle class controlling the new technology, and was expressed in the new identities that came with the emergence of nationalism.

This phase marks an alteration in governance. In many cases, theoretically secular democracies replaced kingship, and representatives from all sections of society had rights, in theory, of equal status. This helped to integrate the secular, the democratic, and the national. In a true democracy the right to dissent and the demand for social justice are core concepts. Since it includes all citizens, its inclusiveness requires it to be secular.

Since satyagraha was so integral a form of nationalism, let me say a few words about nationalism. In India, its initial and overwhelming form was anti-colonial nationalism, common to most erstwhile colonies. This implied the assertion of the free citizen ready to challenge political orthodoxies of various kinds. The construction of this identity recognizes that it is new, nevertheless it seeks legitimacy from the past. So history becomes crucial. As was common to most colonies, the colonial reading of the colony's earlier history that contributed to formulating its identity was from the perspective of the colonizer. The colonial writing of Indian history led to the emergence of a legitimate anti-colonial nationalism, but also to two less legitimate forms—those of religious nationalisms. Less legitimate because nationalism ideally endorses a single all-inclusive identity whereas religious nationalism endorses a single selected identity that is not all-inclusive and excludes all but the one.

The colonial comprehension of India was founded on the two-nation theory. As has been mentioned earlier in the book, James Mill argued in 1817 that India and therefore Indian history was essentially that of two nations—the Hindu and the Muslim—and that the two had been permanently hostile to each other. Colonial scholarship based itself on this idea and its implications. This theory was also loyally followed by both religious nationalisms—Muslim and Hindu. The concept of the Islamic state and of the Hindu Rashtra, the latter based on the Hindutva version of history, are each rooted in the colonial understanding of Indian history. Each of the two excluded the other and each distanced itself from anti-colonial nationalism.

Anti-colonial nationalism however, saw India as a nation of citizens who, irrespective of origins and with substantially a similar identity, were all of equal status and were coming together in the demand for independence. It was all-inclusive and secular in its demand for a democratic nation-state. It envisaged no primary or exclusive citizens as in the two so-called religious nationalisms. Nationalism, if defined by a single identity, becomes majoritarianism.

Unlike religious nationalisms, anti-colonial nationalism did not exclude dissent, neither in its own evolution nor in opposing colonial authority. This was one of the differences separating anti-colonial nationalism from religious nationalisms. Anti-colonial nationalism incorporated various forms of opposition to colonial rule from passive resistance to militancy. The most striking of these was the satyagraha of Gandhi. It seems to me that it echoes some of the earlier historical concepts of dissent that surface at various times in Indian history. But my argument is less concerned with

Gandhi's use of these ideas in constructing satyagraha, and more with how they have been appropriated by the public. What explains the overwhelming response to Gandhi's satyagraha?

I would like to begin on a personal note by speaking about how my interest was aroused. There was one occasion a lifetime ago, when I very briefly met Gandhi and exchanged half a sentence on a simple matter. In a curious way it came to symbolize for me the need to go beyond the obvious, to search for what I like to call the context of thought and action.

I was in school in Pune in the early 1940s. Gandhi, when not in jail, would hold prayer meetings that we, as young budding nationalists, made a point to attend. One evening I took my autograph album to the meeting and with much trepidation requested Gandhi to sign in it. He signed in the book and when handing it back to me asked why I was wearing a salwar-kameez of mill-made cloth, adding that I should only wear khadi. I readily agreed and assured him that I would do so. But what did khadi mean other than it being a kind of textile, and in some way associated with Gandhi's ideas? This question remained unanswered until many years later when, searching for the context, I began to comprehend the meaning of satyagraha—and not just the concept but how it became relevant to anti-colonial nationalism. Even more important for me was how and why did it resonate with the many who participated in the national movement. Without this resonance it would have remained just a slogan.

The events of the 1940s, the Quit India movement, and the mutiny in the Royal Indian Navy had their own message. Independence was imminent and the future was enveloped in debate. How would a colony be transformed into a secular democracy? What was going to be our identity as Indians, as free citizens? We would have a new relationship with the state—a state of our making. The Constitution was in a sense the covenant between the citizen and the state, recording the rights and obligations of each. Hovering over all these questions were those concerning the methods that we had used to attain independence. It was said that what marked our movement as distinctive was the concept of satyagraha.

Over the years, I have asked myself why this concept became such a bedrock specifically in Indian anti-colonial nationalism. Predictably, it failed to find any place in the two religious nationalisms—the Hindu and the Muslim. These religious nationalisms converted the two religions into political agencies—the Muslim League supporting an Islamic state and the Hindutva version of Hinduism becoming the base for a Hindu Rashtra. In the politics of these, the chickens of the colonial interpretation of Indian history and culture came home to roost.

To understand the context, I would like to go back a little in time and briefly trace the flow of some ideas that I regard as foundational to Indian civilization. These have had a noticeable presence in Indian society for two millennia. Since religion has become central to politics, I would like to look at the way in which we in modern times have given shape to our religions and how this differs from the past.

In the last two centuries, Indian religions have been reconstructed largely along the lines suggested by colonial scholarship. This was seldom seriously challenged and therefore came to be accepted. The focus has been on belief, ritual and texts, with little space for analysing the reach of religion into society. What social forms did it create or endorse and how might these have differed from what was there before?

When a religious teaching acquires a following, it establishes institutions that are initially places of worship—chaityas, viharas, mandirs, masjids, gurdwaras, churches. Monuments are not just architectural features. They exercise control over those that use them as places of worship, and as institutions of socialization, bonding society to religious norms. At this point ideological support or opposition becomes a matter of asserting domination. This can be met by acceptance from some and dissent and disagreement from others, sometimes becoming protest.

Religions in India were generally not viewed as monolithic, and especially not so in their practice. Religion was articulated more often in the form of a range of juxtaposed sects, some marginally linked with existing ones, others distant. In pre-modern times the religion of a person was identified more often by sect or caste and less frequently by an overarching label of Hindu or Muslim. Even in the last century we saw the birth of a new deity in Santoshi Ma and a new sect following Sai Baba.

However, colonial perceptions of Indian religions projected a different form. Religious sects that seemed similar were bonded together under a few distinctive labels. Thus the label of Hinduism included, apart from Vaishnavas, Shaivas, and Shaktas, almost all others—such as Buddhists, Jainas, Charvakas, Sikhs. These latter actually originated from an opposition to Hindu belief and worship. Even as late as the sixteenth century AD the Buddhists, Jainas, and Charvakas were regarded as alien by the Brahmanas. Madhusudan Sarasvati lists them and also the Turushkas—the name used for those that initially came from Central Asia and were Muslim—and describes them as nastika and mleccha. They were dismissed as non-believers because even if they worshipped Allah they did not believe in the Vedic and Puranic deities.

Within the label of Hindu, as defined by colonial scholarship then, some sects contradicted each other's teaching and practice. The implications of this were ignored and uniformity was insisted on. The nineteenth century middle class interest in religion was largely confined to its own social boundaries, virtually unconcerned with the religions of what we now call Scheduled Castes (SCs), Scheduled Tribes (STs), and Other Backward Classes (OBCs). Interest in the religion of these avarnas, those outside caste, was casual and of little importance in the definition of Hinduism or Islam or any other religion.

Not recognizing the role of sects, each religion was treated as monolithic and uniform. Nor was it recognized that every religion has adherents, but it also has dissidents who question its belief and practice. Serious contradictions have been resolved at times only by changes in the code and creed. Despite this, religious hostility was practised, but generally between the sects, as for example, between the Vaishnava Bairagis and the Shaiva Dashnamis. Even now dissenting opinions can evolve into marginal sects that can find an almost unnoticed place in the spectrum of religious sects.

Sects shape the nature of Indian religions. Each religion is a collective of sects some of whom are proximate to the orthodoxy and some are far removed. Belief can be flexible and accommodating. Adherence to code and creed links religion to society in which caste plays a major role. This is true for all religions in India. For the larger number of people in the past, the sect was a legitimate religious identity. Hence the easy mixing of religious observances among a range of sects in earlier times, when all religious festivals were open to everyone, barring of course the Dalits. This is perhaps what allows Hindus to worship at Sufi shrines if they choose to. This form militates against a unified, monolithic, overarching religious structure. Caste and region had a presence in the making of a religion. Orthodoxy tended to gravitate to the core with dissenting groups at the periphery. Some degree of dissent was therefore always present.

Dissent takes various forms. In philosophical argument dissenting opinions are necessary if theories are to be tested and advanced. The presence of dissent was acknowledged and in more sophisticated discussions it had an assigned place in the argument. The recommended procedure, perhaps akin to some legal procedures, and to the dialectical method, was simple. The argument has first to state as fully and correctly as possible the views of the opponent—the purvapaksha. Then follow the views of the proponent—the pratipaksha. After this comes the debate and a possible resolution or siddhanta. This would have been the pattern in the many debates between the Buddhists and the Brahmanas referred to in texts.

The presence of dissent in religion is equally clear. Mention is made since early times of dharma, but of two parallel and distinctive streams, that of the Brahmanas and that of the Shramanas. Modern scholars have given the collective name of Shramanism to the heterodox sects of the Buddhists, Jainas, Ajivikas, and some even include the Charvakas. These were the dissident sects whose teaching was in disagreement with Vedic Brahmanism and later Puranic Hinduism. They denied the Vedic deities, the divine revelation of the texts, and the ritual of sacrifice. Brahmana texts refer to the Shramanas as the nastikas, the non-believers.

The Shramana dharmas gave substantial attention to social ethics. This was expressed in their absolute commitment to ahimsa (non-violence) to karuna (compassion) and to working towards the social good. Social ethics were not absent in Brahmanism but became increasingly ambivalent with the influence of caste laws.

For the first few centuries of the Christian era, Buddhist and Jaina sects had a well-respected social presence and received royal and elite patronage. This however changed when in the post-Gupta period Brahmanism came to dominate the political scene. By medieval times, Buddhism had been exiled from India but had become a powerful religion in Asia. Jainism was limited to western India and parts of the peninsula. By colonial times almost all non-Muslim sects were labelled as Hindu, even those that were not, such as the Shramanas and some avarna and Adivasi religions. The geographical identity mutated into a religious identity.

The dissenting ideas of the Shramanas were expressed in part by their beliefs and practices that did not coincide with Brahmanism, and their pattern of life being alternate to that of established society. Monasteries enabled the alternate way of life. They flourished on handsome royal donations, on grants from merchant donors and support from lay followers.

Shramanas as renouncers should not be confused with ascetics. The true ascetic performs his funeral rituals as a prelude to declaring himself dead to family and social connections and goes away to live in solitude. He seeks wisdom through meditation and searches for release from rebirth. It is a moot point whether Gandhi can properly be called an ascetic. That he was influenced by the philosophy of the renouncers would perhaps seem more accurate, and that is what I would like to argue.

Let me try and explain what I mean by the renouncers. Two dharmas are mentioned as visible on the Indian landscape, starting from about the mid-millennium BC, and are referred to as those of the Brahmanas and the Shramanas. This gave rise to major debates. The Greek visitor to Mauryan India at that time, Megasthenes, refers to the two as the Brachmanes and the Sarmanes. The edicts of the Mauryan emperor Ashoka have many references to bahmanam-samanam, a compound term in Prakrit for the sects. The grammarian of Sanskrit, Patanjali, when referring to dharma mentions only these two, and compares their relationship to that between the snake and the mongoose. These were the dominant two with multiple sects not conforming strictly to either.

The early Puranas demonstrate the antagonism between the two in their hostile remarks on the Shramanas. In the eleventh century AD, Al-Biruni describes the Brahmana religion at length and also mentions those that oppose it as the Sammaniyas. The second millennium AD witnessed the rise of a series of sects—the Bhakti sants of diverse Vaishnava and Shaiva and other persuasions. Many Sufi schools were also established and were active. Some supported the rulers and some opposed the mullahs and qazis. There was noticeable interface with the beliefs and ideas of Bhakti sants. Their followers were a mix across the range of sects, at shrines, khanqahs, and dargahs. The initial arrival of the Sufis was in the borderlands of the north-west and from here they gradually spread across the subcontinent.

Dissent did not lead only to the founding of renunciatory orders; it extended to discussing religion as an agency of social norms. The dissent of the renouncers took diverse forms some of which were continued by the Bhakti sants. The views of Kabir,

Dadu, Ravidas, and others underlined social ethics and questioned caste. We tend to set this aspect aside in our single-minded focus on religion alone. Historically therefore, there was a continuing multiplicity in religious beliefs with some sects clearly dissenting from established views.

Renunciation therefore became a parallel stream to the orthodox, ritual-based patterns of religions. Religious institutions mushroomed through the patronage of the elite. There were flourishing agraharas and mathas as well as temples richly endowed and established from the late first millennium AD and continuing throughout the second. The Sufi khanqahs were equally impressive. Bhakti and Sufi teachers were the source of much of popular religion. Folk literature and the poems and myths on local deities drawing from all religious traditions, are evidence of this. Renunciation and dissent take on something of a continuing counter-culture from earlier times.

The sects of the renouncers could and sometimes did question the Dharmashastra rules, so they were open to all. The alternate society did not arise out of a violent social revolution but it envisaged social change as coming from a process of osmosis. It was essentially a way of stating and legitimizing dissent by persuading people to its ways of thinking, with an emphasis on social ethics and freedom to choose whom to worship. This freedom also imbued renouncers with a degree of moral authority in the eyes of people at large. Social equality and justice were demands that were not readily supported by established religions except occasionally in theory. The act of renunciation became an expression of dissent.

Foremost in the ethical code of most renunciatory sects was negating violence of any kind. The concept of ahimsa as physical violence is variously discussed and continues to be discussed. Is non-violence tied to bodily needs that might discourage violence? What was consumed as food therefore, was important to some, for whom the diet had to be vegetarian. Fasting was a form of bodily purification and control. But undertaking a fast even to death for personal reasons was not the same as a fast in support of social protest.

The articulation of protest took diverse forms in different cultures and societies. Unlike in China where peasant revolts of a violent kind were known, in India, peasant protest in earlier times resorted to migrating to a neighbouring kingdom. We are told that kings feared such migrations since they resulted in a loss of revenue.

Urban protests took different forms. One of these was included in the repertoire of Gandhi. It was known by various names, one among which was dharna. Its success lay in its being undertaken by a particular body of people—the charan and bhat. These were bards, regarded as repositories of knowledge that was crucial to legitimizing the power of the ruler. This is another instance of people investing authority not in an officially designated person but someone viewed as respected and integral to society. Today, with social change, they do not perform their earlier functions, but recognizing their role provides a glimpse of how societies operated not so long ago.

Some activities of these bards were essential to power. Authority needs legitimation. The bards maintained the genealogies of the rulers, and occasionally of the important functionaries, through which they became the keepers of the history of the dynasty. They legitimized the dynasty through a claim to its history. The status of those in authority was asserted by the charan through alluding to the believed historical evidence of clan and caste. The charans themselves had a low social status but since early times they had been treated as inviolate, and were called upon to arbitrate in disputes.

Authority is of various kinds. In some situations, moral authority takes precedence over the political. It goes with the belief that a particular kind of person being what he is and does, has moral authority. The charan had it. He would take up the protest of the people once he was convinced of its being justified.

To support the protest, he would position himself at the threshold of the royal residence, and go on a hunger strike until there was a resolution of the conflict, or alternatively the nearness of his death by voluntary starvation.

The effectiveness of the fast was dependent on the person fasting being someone who commanded moral authority, and was respected by both rulers and subjects. His power was intangible, but based on this respect. His protest was legitimate if it focused on a demand for justice. If the charan lost his life owing to the fast, the ruler was doomed.

Thus the moral threat posed by the fast was feared suggesting thereby that dissent could have moral reasons as well. The dual purpose of the fast as dissent and as a moral evaluation, was not unknown in earlier forms of registering protest. The fast subsumed the protest and diverted it from becoming violent.

Can one see in this some parallels to the use of the fast by Gandhi. The British Raj may not have admitted it publicly but each of Gandhi's fasts was a matter of anxiety to their political control, he being the leading national figure. The title of mahatma in turn recognized his moral authority with the people. The fast was a protest against injustice but also carried a grave threat should it have taken its toll. This was understood by all.

But let me turn to the implications of this activity. Dissent of various degrees was at the core of the renunciatory tradition. Can we then ask whether Gandhi's satyagraha drew to some degree, from this tradition, either consciously or subconsciously? More central to my argument is that this feature probably encouraged the massive public response to satyagraha. Is there a link between the essence of Shramana renunciation and the resonance of the people to Gandhi's satyagraha?

His understanding of the concept drew from the authors he read and wrote about who have been much discussed: Leo Tolstoy, David Thoreau, and John Ruskin in particular. He had lengthy conversations with Raichandbhai on the Jaina religion, as he would also have done with his mother and others in Gujarat. He read many texts of the Hindu sects. My concern is more with trying to understand what it was that struck a public chord in this particular form of protest.

His reading of the texts associated with Hinduism was of a different genre, as for example, his careful reading of the Gita and the attraction of brahmacharya. Could the prevalence of alternative cultural patterns from the past have nudged him into an instinctive response? The imprint may have been less apparent than we have realized? Did the form of and justification for satyagraha reach out to a stronger tradition of expressing dissent? Some have argued that it was the ideal of brahmacharya that he was emulating. But this was not born out of dissent; on the contrary, it was acceptable to orthodoxy and focused not on the social ethic but the individual. Satyagraha was primarily a political statement.

Parallels with renouncers are more noticeable in the making of the practitioner, the satyagrahi. To be effective, a period of training was preferred although there were exceptions. There is some mention of taking vows or consenting to observe certain rules. Once accepted, the discipline of living in the ashrama was reasonably strict. Satyagraha was not a monastic order, nevertheless it had its own rules, relationships, and identity.

To assert a greater moral force, it was preferable that the satyagrahi be celibate, although this was not insisted upon. Protest included the non-violent Swadeshi movement—the boycott of foreign goods, especially cloth, was linked to weakening industrialization in Britain. This was part of civil disobedience with its much broader concerns. Objections to mill-made cloth and the wearing of khadi was not intended as a Luddite movement but as registering another form of dissent and explaining why it was necessary.

Some symbols of renunciation also surface. Underlying satyagraha lay the force of moral authority—soul force—of the person calling for civil disobedience. This in a sense echoed what also gave authority to renouncers of various kinds, and in diverse ways. That Gandhi was named a 'mahatma', an honour that interestingly he did not reject, was partially recognition of his moral authority.

A fundamental requirement of satyagraha, as also in the Shramana religions, was to refrain from using violence. Violence destroys moral authority. Ahimsa faced two kinds of opposition: that of the colonial power and its continued violence against nationalist protestors; and that of Indians in authority, some of whom doubted its effectiveness in directing protest.

The commitment to non-violence and truth also underlined the idea of tolerance. All religions were to be equally respected. This came from satyagraha not having its own singular religious identity, although one of the religions was perhaps more equal than others. However, there was a moral right to break the law if it caused widespread suffering. But who had the right to judge? Did being called a mahatma strengthen Gandhi assuming this right? The dilemma becomes more acute if one accepts what one may call the contingent ahimsa of the Gita, that where evil prevails it can be fought with violence. Yet the satyagrahi tried to persuade the other to his view in non-violent ways, and through a system where the means and the ends are not contradictory.

A more complicated issue was present when satyagraha was practised in the larger social context. This involved the equality of all castes including the outcastes. Did the equal status of all castes as frequently maintained among dissenting sects apply to both the varna and avarna members of society or only to the former? How was the hierarchy to be countered in practice? Gandhi tried, but to little effect. Many maintain that the actions of one's previous life determine one's birth in this life. But if actions are evaluated according to the Dharmashastra codes then the codes would have to be discarded if the hierarchy is to be annulled. Few argued for this.

The Shramana sects claimed that the monasteries did not observe caste. On a wider social scale, it was some of the Bhakti sants who also opposed caste, particularly those who came from the lowest castes. For Gandhi, if the varna castes began doing the demeaning jobs allotted to the avarnas, the stigma might go. But caste by now had many other ramifications as well. Unlike the renouncer, the satyagrahi could not necessarily discard caste identity.

The appeal of satyagraha is evident from the large numbers that responded when the call was given for civil disobedience. We have to ask what went into the making of this form of defiance. Could there have been an echo of the persistence of dissent that still surfaced when injustice was experienced? It galvanized national sentiment, but it also diverted this sentiment away from violent revolution when it came to channelling it into protest. This was true to type as such movements, even in the past, had steered away from violent revolution. In the colonial situation satyagraha forced both the protestors and the authority against whom they were protesting—be it over salt, or cloth, or the freedom of a people—to give the protest visibility. It underlined a claim to status by the colonized by fore-fronting moral authority against colonial power. This was outside the experience of the colonizer.

Admittedly Gandhi, in his readings, lists little that goes back to the texts of the Shramanas. His formal interest in such sources seems marginal, especially compared to his intensive study of the Bhagavad Gita. However, that satyagraha could envelop dissent rather than violent protest suggests that these ideas did have a presence, however inaudible. Given the complexities of thought, society and politics in the first half of the twentieth century in India, it would seem that a major player on the scene may have held on to the truth of some forms of dissent from the Indian past, and used them almost instinctively to recreate a new form of dissent.

One could ask whether Gandhi's endorsement of the Gita was a seeming contradiction of the insistence on non-violence in satyagraha. The translation he chose to read frequently—apart from the Gujarati—was curiously the English translation by Edwin Arnold, *The Song Celestial*, published in 1885. The potential of the Gita *to* be the single sacred book of Hinduism, the equivalent of the Bible and the Quran, was being discussed at the time.

The Gita and the segments added to it are thought to date to around the turn of the Christian era. There were regular commentaries on it over the centuries. It surfaced in a big way in the nineteenth century in the colonial search for the single sacred text of all Hindus. It rode the European Orientalist wave that was searching for wisdom from the East. The Theosophists adopted it as their central text and gave it wide diffusion. Inevitably, many Indians wrote on it as a representative text. Some saw it as an allegory and this excluded questions of historicity. W. B. Yeats, T. S. Eliot, and Christopher Isherwood, all flirted with its ideas. Its appropriation by many nationalists was possibly because it could be used to endorse even violent political action as the duty of those fighting for rightful demands and justice. If colonial rule was evil then violence against it was justified.

What is perhaps curious in this thinking is that the question of violence and political action should have drawn so heavily on the Gita. A more challenging text is the twelfth book of the Shanti Parvan of the Mahabharata that unambiguously focuses on this subject. This segment of the epic is dated generally to the post-Mauryan period. Subsequent to the battle at Kurukshetra, Yudhishthira was expected to take up the kingship, but he initially refused to do so, preferring to retire to the forest. His objection to ruling was that kingship involves many levels of violence and he was averse to these.

He asked how any war could be called dharmic when it is the duty of some, such as the Kshatriya, to kill others. Bhishma, lying on a bed of arrows after the battle at Kurukshetra, justified such killing as the ruler needing to defend the realm. This conversation is a fine example of dissent explored through debate. Yudhishthira eventually agreed—although it would seem with a very heavy heart.

Those for whom ahimsa was absolute would obviously oppose ahimsa as contingent. Yudhishthira has a moral and ethical objection to violence. This debate reflected the discussions on violence at this time, perhaps enhanced by the views of Emperor Ashoka in support of ahimsa, as has been argued by various scholars. Was the centrality of ahimsa in this conversation a concession to Shramanic thought? Unlike Nehru, Gandhi had a perfunctory interest in Buddhism. Nor was he particularly interested in a sequential study of the past. History was perhaps less of a subject of great intellectual interest for him, his concentration being more on other categories of texts.

That there were occasions of violent and intolerant actions in our past is undeniable. That there were also legitimate traditions of non-violent dissent is also undeniable. The forms of the latter changed in conformity with a changing society and we have to recognize the forms and how they were used and when. Gandhi created new forms of dissent. Yudhishthira's statements on political violence seem to argue that when religious ideas and their implications become agencies of political mobilization, their fundamental purpose changes, as indeed it does. That which is political tends to determine thoughts and actions. The continuation of the right to dissent, to disagree, to debate, can be seen in the varied manner in which it has been formulated. Satyagraha has been one effective form in recent times.

In many ways the right to dissent has been highlighted by the coming of the nation-state in our history. It calls for a new relationship involving the rights of the citizen and the obligations of the state. It remains open to the citizen immersed in the ideology of secular democratic nationalism to articulate this new relationship by reiterating the right to dissent. And it needs the state to acknowledge the validity of this right.

14

SYNDICATED MOKSHA?*

My attempt to provide a historical perspective on the evolution of the Hindu religion began decades ago. This was not a single linear projection. My concern was to view its current form, and to differentiate it from Hindutva which has a different intention.

THE TERM HINDUISM AS WE understand it today to describe a *particular religion* is modern, as also is the concept which it presupposes, both resulting from a series of choices made from a range of belief, ritual, and practice which were collated into the creation of this religion. Unlike the Abrahamic religions (with which the comparison is often made), which began with a structure around historically attested persons at a point in time, and evolved largely in relation to and within that structure, Hinduism (and I use the word here in its contemporary meaning) has been largely a reaction to historical situations. The attempt to delineate a structure relates to each such situation. Comparisons with Semitic religions are inappropriate since these have been catalysts in the search for a structure among contemporary 'Hindus'.

Whereas linear religions such as Islam and Christianity and Buddhism can be seen to change in a historical dimension both in terms of reacting to their original structure and the interaction with the constituents of historical circumstances, such changes are more easily seen in individual 'Hindu' sects rather than in 'Hinduism' as a whole. This may be a reason for the general reluctance of

*An earlier version of this essay was first published in 1985.

scholars of 'Hinduism' to relate the manifestations of 'Hinduism' to the historical contexts and to changes in society.

The study of what is regarded as Hindu philosophy and texts and beliefs has been so emphasized as almost to ignore those who are the practitioners of these tenets, beliefs, rituals, and ideas. Furthermore, the view has generally been from above, since the texts were earlier composed in Sanskrit and their interpreters were Brahmanas. But, precisely because 'Hinduism' is not a linear religion, it becomes necessary to look at the situation further down the social scale where the majority of its practitioners are located. The religious practices of the latter may differ from those at the upper levels of society to a degree considerably greater than that of a uniform, centralized, monolithic religion.

Academic discussions on Hinduism tend to stay close to Hindu philosophy and theory. But the manifestation of contemporary, resurgent, active movements, largely galvanized for political ends, provides a rather different focus to such discussions. It is with the projection of present-day popular ideas of Hinduism and of its past that this essay forms a comment. The new Hinduism, which is being currently propagated by the sanghs, parishads, and samajs, is an attempt to restructure indigenous religions as a monolithic, uniform religion, rather paralleling some of the features of Semitic religions. This seems to be a fundamental departure from the essentials of what may be called 'Hindu' religions. Its form is not only in many ways alien to the earlier culture of India but equally disturbing is the uniformity which it seeks to impose on the variety of 'Hindu' religions.

My attempt here is to look at some of the significant directions taken by various 'Hindu' sects which have an historical dimension and try and relate these to social change. The study of what is regarded as 'Hindu' philosophy and thought has its own importance but is not of central concern to this essay. The manifestation of religion in the daily routine of life draws more heavily on social sources than on the philosophical.

Religions such as Buddhism or Islam or Christianity do diversify into sects but this diversification retains a particular reference point—the historical founder and the teachings as interpreted at various historic moments embodied generally in a sacred text. The area of discourse among the sects in these religions is tied to the dogma, tenets, and theology as enunciated in the beginning. They see themselves as part of the historical process of the unfolding of the single religion even though they may have broken away from the mainstream.

'Hindu' sects generally had a distinct and independent origin related to their particular founder or cult. Only at a later stage, and if required, were attempts made to try and assimilate some of these sects into the dominant sects through the amalgamation of new deities as manifestations of the older ones and by incorporating some of their mythology, ritual, and custom. Subordinate sects sought to improve that status by a similar incorporation from the dominant sects if they were in a position to do so.

What has survived over the centuries is not a single monolithic religion but a diversity of religious sects which we today have put together under a uniform name. The collation of these religious groups is defined as 'Hinduism' even though the religious reference points of such groups might be quite distinct. There was a time when Hinduism was a convenient general label among some scholars for studying the different indigenous religious expressions. This was when it was claimed that anything from atheism to animism could legitimately be regarded as part of Hinduism. Today, the new Hindus would look upon atheists and animists with suspicion if not contempt. The term Hinduism is now being used in a different sense.

Hinduism as defined in contemporary parlance is a collation of beliefs, rites, and practices consciously selected from those of the past, interpreted in a contemporary idiom in the last couple of centuries and the selection conditioned by historical circumstances.

This is not to suggest that religions with a linear growth are superior to what may apparently be an ahistorical religion, but rather to emphasize the difference between the two.

In a strict sense, a reference to 'Hinduism' would require a more precise definition of the particular variety referred to—Brahmanism, Brahmo Samaj, Arya Samaj, Shaiva Siddhanta, Bhakti, Tantricism, or whatever. Present-day 'Hinduism', therefore, cannot be seen as an evolved form with a linear growth historically from Harappan through Vedic, Puranic, and Bhakti forms, although sects may carry elements of these in varying degrees. In this it differs from Buddhism, Jainism, Islam, and Christianity.

Its origin has no distinct point in time, the Vedas being regarded as the foundation until the discovery of the Indus civilization in the 1920s when its origin was then pushed back and taken to a much earlier date. It had no historically attested founder from whom the teaching originated as is acknowledged by all Hindus. Nor does it have a single sacred text which is pre-eminent because it comprises the teaching of the founder. This gives it an element of ahistoricity. However, this also makes it easier to reinterpret if not to recreate a fresh version of the religion as and when required.

Many of these features, absent in the religion as a whole, do however exist among the diverse sects which are sought to be included under the umbrella label of 'Hinduism' which makes them historical entities. But then, not all these sects would accept certain rites, beliefs, and practices as essential. Animal sacrifice and libations of alcohol would be essential to some but anathema to others among the sects which the census labels as 'Hindu'. The yardstick of the Semitic religions which has been the conscious and subconscious challenger in the modern recreation of 'Hinduism' would seem most inappropriate to an understanding of what existed before.

Historically, we know little for certain about the Harappan religion except for a possible fertility cult involving the worship of phallic symbols, a fire cult, perhaps a sacrificial ritual, all suggestive of an authoritative priesthood. The decipherment of the script will hopefully tell us more. The Vedic texts perhaps incorporate elements of this religion but emphasize the central role of the sacrificial ritual or yajna and include a gamut of deities. A substantial element of shamanism can also be noticed. The Vedic texts and the Dharmashastras are said to constitute the norms for Brahmanism and the religious practices for the upper castes.

Brahmanism is differentiated from the subsequent religious groups by the use of the term Shramanism for the latter. The Buddhist and Jaina texts, the inscriptions of Ashoka, the description of India by Megasthenes, and the accounts of the Chinese pilgrims in the first millennium AD all refer to two main religious categories: the Brahmanas and the Shramanas.

The identity of the former is clear. The latter were those who were often in opposition to Brahmanism such as the Buddhists, Jainas, Ajivikas, and a number of other sects associated with both renunciatory orders and a lay following, who explored areas of belief and practice different from the Vedas and Dharmashastras. The Brahmanas referred to them as nastikas—non-believers, because they challenged the fundamental beliefs of Vedic Brahmanism. They often preached a system of universal ethics which spanned castes and communities. This differed from the tendency to segment religious practice by caste which was characteristic of Brahmanism. The segmenting of believers into sects is, of course, common even among other more linear religions, but the breaking away still retains some historical imprint that carries a trace of its previous history.

Brahmanism was free of this. The differentiating of Brahmanistic practice for a particular caste makes it an essentially different kind of segmentation. It was this segmentation which some Shramanic religions opposed in their attempt to universalize their religious teaching. The hostility between Brahmanism and Shramanism was so acute that the grammarian Patanjali, as has been mentioned earlier, when speaking of natural enemies and innate hostility, refers to this characteristic as present between Brahmanas and Shramanas and compares it to that between the snake and the mongoose and the cat and the mouse. This indigenous view of the dichotomous religions of India is referred to even at the beginning of the second millennium AD in Arab sources which speak of the Brahima and the Samaniya. It is a logical, rational categorization since the two systems of religion, if they can be called that, were distinctively different. The absence of the single, all-purposive, and commanding deity led Émile Durkheim to insist that Buddhism cannot be described as a religion, because it does not support the existence of deity.

Brahmanism did maintain its identity and survived the centuries with fewer fundamental changes, particularly after the decline of Buddhism. This was in part because it was well-endowed with grants of land and items of wealth through extensive royal patronage, which in turn reinforced its claim to social superiority and enabled it further to emphasize its distance from other castes and their practices.

The extensive use of Sanskrit as the language of rituals and learning gave Brahmanism access to high political office and proximity to the royal courts. This again supported its exclusive status. The use of a single language—Sanskrit—gave it a pan-Indian character, the wide geographical spread of which provided both mobility as well as a strengthening of its social identity. But, of course, it was a segregated religion open only to the upper caste elite.

The Hinduism that emerged as the more widespread religion differed from Vedic Brahmanism. The deities changed from Mitra and Varuna to the later Indra and Agni. In the contestation with the Shramana religion, these again changed to Shiva and Vishnu, and later the concept of Shakta. The ritual of worship was no longer focused on the enormous sacrificial altar, but was now the more individual worship of icons—objects that had no place in the Vedas. But this was the same period when icons of the Buddha, and Mahavira among Jainas, had come into worship. Icons have to be housed, so the earliest temples were small rooms where the icons were placed and which became the sanctum of the larger temple. Housing a symbol and later an icon in a small hall of worship was known to the Shramanic religion. The performance of rituals was not prescribed as were the grand Vedic yajnas: they could now be performed by the single worshipper in any space. The sacred space in the temple was parallel to the Buddhist chaitya hall. Not surprisingly, when this new form of Hinduism, labelled Puranic Hinduism, became common, Buddhist chaitya halls were sometimes converted into Hindu temples, their Buddhist association being wiped out.

The texts of this form of Hinduism were partly the epics—Mahabharata and Ramayana—suitably reformulated to focus on dominant persons and events, and with references to deities and sectarian loyalties. The Puranas grew in numbers, each dedicated to a particular deity, and were added to as the number of deities grew. Origin myths may have attempted to present the deities as historical figures but their divinity could not be set aside. They were not in themselves historical founders. The spread of Hinduism also required that it incorporate the local worship of animals and others as locally practised. The avatars of Vishnu suggest such incorporations. Other forms were also resorted to such as the log in the myth of Jaganath of Puri, or the hero stone in the making of Vitthala of Pandharpur. The ability of Puranic Hinduism to induct any myth or icon it wished to is most impressive. It was one of the reasons for its success in the post-Gupta period, when Jainism was geographically confined and Buddhism was slowly exiled.

This was the prelude to the third massive mutation in Hinduism that resulted in the evolution of Bhakti Hinduism. It moved further away from Vedic Brahmanism which became more confined to its original community of Brahmanas. The religions that are labelled as Bhakti opened up Hinduism to a wider of spectrum of people, especially in terms of caste and was more reflective of the plurality and diversity of societies in India.

The Bhakti tradition of the first millennium AD is sometimes traced to the Bhagavad Gita and its message, which text although historically post-Buddhist, was interpolated into the earlier Mahabharata. The Gita moved away from the centrality of the sacrificial ritual and instead emphasized worship through devotion to the deity and the selfless action projected as the need to act in accordance with one's dharma. Dharma now became the key concept. Given the discussion in the Gita there may well have been a debate on the connotation of dharma/dhamma between the Brahmanas and the Shramanas. The question is whether the shift was because of the impact of the Shramana religion that Brahmanism had now to contend with in post Vedic times i.e., the period from the Mauryas to the Guptas.

This shift of emphasis provided the root in later times for the emergence of a number of Bhakti cults—Shaivite, Vaishnavite, Shakta, and others—which flourished from the mid-first millennium AD and provided the contours to much that is viewed as 'Hinduism'. The Shiva Bhakti of the Pashupatas, or the teaching of the Alvars and Nayanmars of the Tamil-speaking area, the Shaiva-Siddhanta and the Lingayatas, Jnaneshvara, Vallabhacharya, Mira, Chaitanya, Shankaradeva, Basava, Vemana, Lalla, Tulsidas, and Tukaram are often bunched together as part of the Bhakti stream. Where deities are introduced in Bhakti sects there are distinct differences in their teachings and their emphases. The absence of a recognized deity in some contrast with the focus on deity in others.

In fact, there are variations among them which are significant and need emphasizing. Some among these and similar teachers accepted the earlier style of worship and practice, others were hostile to the Brahmanas and did not accept the Vedic tradition; some were non-caste and objected to caste distinctions and untouchability, whereas for others such distinctions were normal. A few felt that asceticism and renunciation were not a path to salvation whereas others were committed to these. Kabir and Nanak infused Sufi ideas into their teaching. The choice of deity and form of worship was as the devotee wished. This choice was open to anyone irrespective of the religion they may have identified with prior to their accepting bhakti. There are notable Krishna-bhakts among some erstwhile Muslim devotees such as Ras Khan and others and these take pride in proclaiming themselves as such.

The major differences among them are rarely discussed and commented upon in modern popular writing which is anxiously searching for similarities in the tradition. Some of the sects that were opposed to caste-based belief and worship discouraged their members from going to temples or on pilgrimages and observing the essentials of the upper-caste dharma. That these dissimilarities were to be expected and were in a sense their strength is seldom argued.

The Bhakti sects were in some ways the inheritors of the Shramanic tradition. They arose at various times over a span of a thousand years in various parts of the subcontinent. They were specific in time, place, and teaching but were limited by the language which they used. They did not evolve out of some original teaching or spread through conversion; rather, they arose as and when historical conditions were conducive to their growth often intermeshed with the need for particular castes to articulate their aspirations. Hence, the variation in belief and practice and the lack of consciousness of an identity of religion across a subcontinental plane. Similarities were present in some cases but even these did not lead to treating it as participation in a single religious movement. Formal Buddhism declined in India replaced in many ways by Bhakti sects, but became a major religion in much of Asia.

With the growth of some Bhakti cults, the worship of the image of the deity gained popularity, possibly influenced by the emphasis by now on the icon in Buddhism and Jainism. Whereas the Greek Megasthenes visiting in the fourth century BC does not refer to images at all, the later Chinese and Arab accounts of the later first century AD make icons a major feature of the indigenous religions.

This was also the period which saw the currency of the Shakta sects and Tantric rituals. Recorded by some as the resurgence of an indigenous belief associated with subordinate social groups (gradually becoming powerful), it was clearly popular at every level of society including the royal courts. The attempt in recent decades to sweep it under the carpet or to give a respectable 'gloss' to its rituals is largely because of the embarrassment these might cause to middle-class Indians heavily influenced by Christian puritanism and somewhat titillated in imagining erroneously that Tantric rituals consist essentially of erotic activities. That there has been little effort to investigate and understand such cults derives also from the attempt to define 'Hinduism' as Brahmanism or from upper-caste rituals and such cults were alien to traditional Brahmanism, until these were adapted to or incorporated into Brahmanical religion.

Another noticeable manifestation of indigenous religion is what has recently been euphemistically called 'folk Hinduism'—the religion of the Dalits, tribals, and other groups at the lower end of the social scale. This is characterized by a predominance of the worship of goddesses and spirits represented symbolically and often aniconically and with rituals performed by non-Brahman priests for a variety of reasons, not least among them being that since the offerings and libations consisted of meat and alcohol, they would be regarded as polluting by Brahmans. Needless to say, such groups would not be able to afford the costly donations required of a Brahmanical yajna. For the upper-caste 'Hindus' these groups were (and often still are) regarded as 'mlecchas' or impure and certainly not a part of their own religious identity (however insistently the Registrar General of the census or politicians may try to include them as such!).

The sects included in the honeycomb of what has been called 'Hinduism' were multiple and ranged from animistic spirit cults to others based on subtle philosophic concepts. They were oriented towards the tribe, the caste, and the profession. The social identity of each strongly imprinted on its religious observances.

This may in part explain why the word dharma became central to any understanding of this indigenous religion. It referred to the duties regarded as sacred which had to be performed in accordance with one's varna, jati, and sect and which differed according to each of these. The constituents of dharma conformed to ritual duties, social obligations, and the norms of family and caste behaviour as stipulated in the Dharmashastras. It has been argued that there is an absence of theology as also of any ecclesiastical authority, both of which again point to the difference between these religions and the Semitic. A major concern was with ritual purity. The performance of sacred duty heavily enmeshed in social obligations was so important that absolute individual freedom only lay in renunciation.

But the significance of dharma was that it demarcated sharply between the upper castes—the dvija or twice born—for whom it was the core of the religion and the rest of society who were often regarded as neither requiring nor practising any dharma: they were adharma in every sense of the word. The attempt today in trying to redefine Hinduism is the implicit attempt to hold up the dharma of the Dharmashastras as essential to this religion, even for those traditionally regarded as adharma.

'Hindu' missionary organizations, taking their cue from Christian missionaries, are active among the Adivasis, Dalits, and economically backward communities, converting them to a 'Hinduism' as defined by the upper-caste movements of the last two centuries. What is important to such missionaries is that these communities declare their support for the dharma, often defined by whatever may have been the choice of Hinduism. That this 'conversion' does little or nothing to change their status as Adivasis, Dalits, and so on, and that they continue to be looked down upon by upper-caste 'Hindus,' is of course of little consequence.

The origin of the word 'Hindu' is geographical, as has been noted earlier, and related to those living in the Indian subcontinent. The Sindhu (Indus) River was referred to as the Indos in Greek and the Indus in Latin and as Hendu in ancient Iranian. The Arabs and others referred to the subcontinent as Al-Hind, so named after the river. Thus the inhabitants of Al-Hind were called the Hindi or the Hindu. The term Hindu was originally used to refer to all those who lived in Al-Hind. Later, it referred to those that were not Muslim. In terms of religious definition, reference is made in Achaemenid Persian sources to various Hindu religions, the earlier texts mentioning forty-two and the later ones listing at least five. Some descriptions suggest Brahmanism and others include a variety of sects.

'Hindu' became a term of administrative convenience when the rulers of Arab, Turkish, Afghan, and Mughal origin—all Muslims, had to differentiate between 'the believers' and the rest. Hindu therefore referred to the rest. In Sanskrit texts all those that came from the west, Arabs included, were called Yavanas; those that came from Central Asia—the early Kushans to the later Turks—were called Turushka. Although these terms were applied to Muslims, their significance lay in geographical and ethnic identity.

The first step towards the crystallization of what we today call Hinduism was born in the consciousness of being the amorphous, undefined, subordinate Other. In a sense, this was a reversal of roles. Earlier, the term mleccha had been used by the upper-caste Hindus to refer to the impure, amorphous rest. For the upper-caste man, the Muslims were of the same category as the low castes including untouchables and all were barred from entering the sanctum of the temple and the home. Now the upper castes were clubbed together with those beyond the social pale as 'Hindu'—undoubtedly a trauma for the upper castes.

This perhaps accounts in part for the extremely exaggerated statements made by upper-caste Hindus today that Hindus in the last one thousand years have been through the most severe persecution faced by any religion. Such statements can only come from those who conveniently forget that the last one thousand years in the history of Hinduism has witnessed the establishment of the powerful Shankaracharya mathas, ashramas, and similar institutions attempting to provide an ecclesiastical structure to strengthen conservatism; the powerful Dashnami and Bairagi religious orders; the popular cults of Nathpanthis; the extremely significant sects of the major Bhakti teachers such as Tukaram, Namdeo, Vallabhacharya, Chaitanya, Dadu, and Kabir, not to mention Nanak; and, more recently, the very influential Brahmo Samaj and Arya Samaj.

In fact, many of the facets which are regarded today as essential to popular 'Hinduism' come from this period. The establishment of the sects which accompanied these developments often derived from wealthy patronage which accounted for the noticeable prosperity of the temples and institutions associated with these sects. Where then is the severe persecution? The last thousand years have seen the most assertive thrust of the major 'Hindu' sects.

If by persecution is meant the conversion of Hindus to Islam or Christianity, then it should be kept in mind that the majority of the conversions were from the lower castes and this is more a reflection on 'Hindu' society than on persecution. When the destroying of temples and the breaking of idols by Muslims is mentioned, and quite correctly, it should at the same time be stated that there were also some Muslim rulers—not excluding Aurangzeb—who gave substantial donations to Hindu sects and to individual Brahmans. There was obviously more than just religious bigotry or religious tolerance involved in these actions.

Nor should it be forgotten that the temple as a source of wealth was exploited even by 'Hindu' rulers. Those who refer to Mahmud of Ghazni's destruction of Hindu temples and the carrying away of their wealth generally prefer to ignore the statement of Kalhana in the *Rajatarangini* that Harshadeva, an eleventh-century king of Kashmir, and therefore a close contemporary of Mahmud, defiled and looted temples when he required funds for the state treasury. He appointed a special officer, with the ironic title of devotapatanayaka—the officer for uprooting the gods—whose function was to seize the images and the wealth of temples. Given the opulence of most temples, such evidence may be forthcoming from other areas as well. The wealth stored in them required some to be walled in and defended almost like fortresses.

The European adoption of the term 'Hindu' gave it further currency as also the attempts of Catholic and Protestant Christian missionaries to convert the Hindu/Gentoo to Christianity. The pressure to convert, initially disassociated with European commercial activity, changed with the coming of British colonial power when, by the early nineteenth century, missionary activities were either surreptitiously or overtly, according to context, encouraged by the colonial authority. The impact both of missionary activity and Christian colonial power resulted in considerable soul searching on the part of those Indians who were close to this new historical experience.

One result was the emergence of yet another variation in the themes constituting Hinduism. A number of sects emerged such as the Brahmo Samaj, Ramakrishna Mission, Prarthana Samaj, Arya Samaj, Theosophical Society, Divine Life Society, Swaminarayan movement, et al., which gave greater currency to the term 'Hinduism'. Some of these were influenced by Christianity and Islam and some reacted against them; but even the latter were not immune from their imprint.

Embedded in many of these movements was the challenge from Christian missionaries. This was not merely at the level of conversions and religious debates. A more subtle form was the use made by Christian missions of the school, college, and educational institutions. Many who were attracted to these new 'Hindu' groups had at some point of their lives experienced Christian education. In the organization of the educational institutions of the Arya Samaj, for example, the Christian missionary model plays an important role. Such movements attracted the middle-class seeking cultural self-assertion and was to that degree a parallel to many such movements in the country. Added to this was the contribution of Orientalist scholars who interpreted the religious texts from their own viewpoint which furthered the notion of 'Hinduism'. The impact of Orientalism in creating the image of Indian, and particularly 'Hindu' culture, as projected in the nineteenth century, was considerable, and religion was a major part of that image.

Those among these groups influenced by Christianity attempted to defend, redefine, and create 'Hinduism' on the model of the Christian religion. They sought the equivalent of a monotheistic God, a book, a prophet, or a founder and congregational worship with an institutional organization supporting it. The consciousness was again of creating as a reaction to being 'the Other'; once again by a Semitic religion. The monotheistic God was sought in the abstract notion of Brahma—the universal soul with which, according to the Upanishads, the individual soul or atma seeks union and moksha; or else with the interpretation of the term deva or deity, which in early English translations was rendered as God, suggesting a monotheistic God.

The focus on a single deity among many others is not strictly speaking monotheism, although attempts have been made by modern commentators to argue this. Unlike many of the earlier sects which were associated with a particular deity, some of these groups claimed to transcend deity and reach out to the Absolute, the Infinite, the Abstract. This was an attempt to transcend segmentary interests in an effort to attain a universalistic identity, but in social customs and ritual, caste distinctions were maintained between high and low.

The teaching of such sects drew on what they regarded as the core of the tradition: the atma–Brahma relationship, the theory of action and rebirth (karma and samsara) and salvation lying in the union of the individual soul uniting with the All-soul. The book was either the Bhagavad Gita or the Vedic texts, especially the Upanishads. The prophet being altogether alien could at best be substituted by the teacher figure of Krishna in the Gita. But Krishna was neither a prophet nor the son of God.

Congregational worship became the channel for propagating these versions of Hinduism. The discarding of the icon by both the Brahmo Samaj and Arya Samaj was like an allergic reaction. It was seen as a pollution of the original religion but, more likely, it was the jibe of idol worship which brought about this reaction.

Much of the sacred literature had been orally preserved and served a variety of social and religious ends. Some texts, secular in origin, were sacralized, such as the Mahabharata and Ramayana. Interpolations could be added as and when required, as for example, the Gita. This is a different attitude from the Semitic to the centrality of the book or, for that matter, from that of the Sikhs to the single sacred text that symbolizes duty.

These new sects were in part the inheritors of the older tradition combining social aspirations with religious expression and establishing new sects. But at the same time, they were trying to create a different kind of religion and gave currency to the term 'Hinduism'. It was used to connote the juxtaposition of the sects suggesting a coherence of the many.

Traditional flexibility in juxtaposing sects as an idiom of social change as well as the basic concepts of religious expression now became problematic. In the absence of a single 'jealous' God, demanding complete and undiluted loyalty from the worshipper, there were instead multiple deities some of which survived over time while others faded out.

Thus, the major Vedic deities, Mitra and Varuna, followed by Indra and Agni declined with the rise of the Shaiva and Vaishnava sects in the first millennium AD. Shiva and Vishnu have remained major deities supported by a variety of sects although not always in agreement with what the deities represent for them. This has not prevented the creation of fresh deities as has been witnessed even in the twentieth century, with the popular worship in parts of northern India of the goddess Santoshi Ma.

The attitude to deity would in part explain the argument that it is not theology which is necessarily important in Hinduism but the mode of worship. The yajna was a carefully orchestrated performance of ritual with the meticulous ordering of every detail down to the correct pronunciation of the words constituting the mantram. Worship as part of Bhakti was different. The emphasis on oblation and sacrifice now transformed itself into devotion to the deity, sometimes even taken to the extreme of ritual suicide.

The deity was conceptualized in a variety of ways—abstract, aniconic, an image, an image elaborately sculpted and housed in an equally elaborate temple; and devotion could also be expressed in various ways. There was no requirement of uniformity in methods of worship in who performed the ritual. There was little ecclesiastical order involved and no centralized church.

The question of conversion therefore was marginal. In its absence, sects grew through segmenting off or through assimilating other cults or amalgamating similar sects. The religious sect was also an avenue to caste mobility. Origin myths of middle and lower castes often maintain that the caste was originally of higher status but a lapse in the ritual or an unwitting active pollution led to a loss of status.

Imitation of higher-caste norms of the dropping of caste obligations would normally not be permitted unless justified by the creation of a new religious sect. The latter would initially be regarded with hostility by the conservative but if it became socially and economically powerful it could be accommodated.

The absence of conversion accounted for the absence of the distinction between the true follower and the infidel or pagan. Yet, distinctions of another kind were more relevant and sharply maintained, particularly in sects with a substantially upper-caste following. These primarily excluded all those who are outside the social pale or the mlecchas, such as untouchables, tribals, foreigners, those observing the social mores of the foreigners and even upper castes who did not conform to dharma regulations. They were regarded as polluting because they performed neither the ritual duties not the social duties required by the dharma.

It is often stated that one is born Hindu, i.e., into a particular caste with an identity of a sect whose regulations are to be observed, and one cannot therefore be converted to Hinduism. In fact, conversion came to be discussed subsequent to the nineteenth century, sects making it the occasion of some debate. Previously it was maintained that each sect had its own regulations, applications, and duties which often drew both on religious antecedents and social requirements. Gradually, if a sect acquired a large following cutting across castes, it tended to become a caste in itself. It would perhaps be more correct to speak of the Hindu religions (in the plural) rather than of 'Hinduism' (in the singular). Some would argue that the correct description of the latter would be Sanatan Dharma, sanatan meaning eternal. The use of this label for the specific religious identity of Hinduism is modern.

That was one category of renunciatory orders which did include sects recruited from any caste. Some of these orders restricted themselves to recruiting only Brahmanas but, in the main, most of them recruited from a variety of castes. Although theoretically the latter were open to all, needless to say members of the first four if not the upper varnas were preferred. Open recruitment was possible because renouncers were expected to discard all social obligations and were regarded as being outside the rules of dharma. Renunciatory sects were generally not expected to maintain a caste identity.

Joining such an order was also in some cases the only legitimate form of dissent from social obligations. The multiplicity of renouncers in India has therefore to be viewed not merely as inspired by otherworldly aspirations but also with the nature of the links between social forms and dissent.

The Shramanic religions were similar to these sects in that they did recruit members from a range of castes although, as was the case also with Indian Islam, Indian Christianity, and Sikhism, converts often retained their original caste identity, especially where connections of marriage were to be decided. Among the renouncers of the non-Shramanic persuasion, the Dasnami order founded by Shankaracharya and the Vaishnava Bairagis were among the better known.

Sects battened on patronage, whether royal or other. Even the renunciatory orders were not averse to accepting wealth which ensured them material comforts as is evident from the many establishments of such orders scattered across the Indian landscape both in the past as well as now.

In addition to economic wealth, these institutions had access to political power and the intertwining of politics and religion was obvious. The real texture of Indian social history in the second millennium AD has been bypassed by the obsessive concern with Hindu–Muslim relations to the exclusion of the more pertinent investigation of how politics and religion at the level of the sects interacted.

Caste identities, economic wealth, and access to power also contributed to providing the edge to sectarian rivalries and conflicts. Initially, in areas where Shaiva sects were establishing themselves, there was a persecution of Buddhists and Jainas. Such actions go back to Mihirakula and Shashanka who in the northern India of the mid-first millennium AD are remembered for their destruction of Buddhist monasteries and the killing of monks. Early in the second millennium AD, Karnataka witnessed the destruction of Jaina temples and images by Shaivite groups and the sixteenth century records a similar series of events in Kakatiya territory.

Sanskrit commentaries dating to the sixteenth century on the Dharmashastras and on philosophical schools reiterate the earlier two-fold religious divide into the believer in deities and the non-believers—nastika and astika. The believers follow the teachings of Brahmanism in its various forms. The nastikas consist of the earlier Shramana religious sects and that of the Turushkas/Muslims. If some Muslims kept the Hindus at a distance, some Hindus felt the same way about the Muslims.

The rewriting of texts to correct the prevailing perspective from Jaina to Vaishnava was a less gruesome form of religious intolerance. Once the Buddhists and Jainas were virtually out of the way, hostility among the 'Hindu' sects was not unknown, even between ascetic groups as is evident from the battles between the Dasnamis and the Bairagis over the question of precedence at the Kumbh Mela.

Such antagonism was not that of the 'Hindu' against another religion but that of a particular sect expressing its hostility towards others. Tolerance and non-violence therefore have to be seen at the level of sectarian aggression. It is true that there were no Inquisitions. This was partly because dissent was channelled out into a separate sect which, if it became a renunciatory order, lost much of its social sting. In addition, there was no centralized church whose supremacy was endangered. However, social subordination, justified by theories of pollution, replaced to some degree the inequities of an authoritarian church.

Religious violence is not alien to 'Hinduism' despite the nineteenth century assertion that the 'Hindus' are by instinct and religion a non-violent people. One suspects that the genesis of the idea was in the requirements of nationalism stressing the superiority of Indian culture of which non-violence was treated as a component.

Non-violence as a central tenet of behaviour and morality was first developed in the Shramanic tradition, that of Buddhism and Jainism. These were religions which not only were allowed to decline but were persecuted in some parts of the country. One is often struck by how different the message of the Gita would have been and how very much closer to non-violence if Gautama Buddha had been the charioteer of Arjuna instead of Krishna. Mahatma Gandhi's concern with ahimsa is more correctly traced to the Jaina imprint on the culture of Kathiawar.

Not that the Shramanic tradition prevented violence, but at least it was the central issue in the ethics of Buddhism and Jainism and was emphasized to a far greater degree than in the ethics of most 'Hindu' sects. Sporadic killing apart, even the violence involved in the regular burning of Hindu brides in the city of Delhi in our time in order to get more wealth through a dowry does not elicit any threat against the perpetrators of such violence from the spokesmen of 'Hinduism' or even Hindutva.

Sectarian institutions acted as networks across geographical areas, but their reach was limited except in the case of the major institutions such as those of the Dasnamis, the Bairagis, or the Nathpanthis. Bhakti as a religious manifestation was predominant throughout the subcontinent by the seventeenth century; yet, curiously, there was little attempt to link these movements to forge a single religion. This was partly because each tradition used a different language which imposed geographical limits and also because there was no ecclesiastical organization to integrate this development.

The medieval Radha–Krishna cult began gradually to take on a wider geographical identity with the expansion of Hindi and the encouraging of pilgrimages in the second millennium AD. The closest to ecclesiastical organizations were the institutions associated with the Shankaracharya movement but these were concerned basically with Brahmanism. The Bhakti communities saw themselves as self-sufficient, with religious forms closely tied to local requirements.

The emergence of Bhakti has been linked to what have been described as the feudalizing tendencies of the time and parallels have been drawn between the loyalty of the peasant to the feudal lord being comparable to the devotion of worshippers to the deity. The Bhakti emphasis on salvation through devotion to a deity and through the idea of karma and samsara was a convenient ideology for keeping subordinate groups under control. It was argued that they might suffer in this life, but by observing the dharma they would benefit in their next birth. The onus of responsibility was therefore on the individual and not on society. The emphasis on individual salvation gave the individual an importance which was absent in real life and therefore served to keep him quiescent.

Interestingly, this explanation of karma is not acceptable to lower-caste groups who while supporting the notion of rebirth do not accept that they were born low because of misdemeanours in a previous birth. Common as is the belief in karma and samsara among many sects, it did not however preclude the growth at a popular level of the concepts of heaven and hell as is evident in the widespread references to svarga and naraka, going back to early times.

The segregation of social communities in worship and religious belief and the absence of an overarching ecclesiastical structure demanding conformity was characteristic of the Hindu religions. Attempts at such structures were made by the founders of certain sects, the most prominent being Shankaracharya when orders were established and institutions founded across the subcontinent (the pithas). In part, these were in imitation of the Buddhist sangha and the recognition of the strength of an institutional base but identity was limited to this movement.

But such movements were rooted in caste differentiations unlike the Buddhists who in theory did not restrict the availability of their religion to any caste. The 'Hindu' institutions therefore came largely to cater to the upper castes and legislated (on the occasions when they did) for these castes. The lower castes were not important to such institutions which were not concerned with the beliefs, rituals, and practices of such castes so long as they remained in a subordinate status.

The segregation of social communities and the relatively distinct religious identity of these led to the possibility of each group leading a comparatively separate existence. The clash could only come in the competition for patronage. This might partially explain the notion of tolerance with which the nineteenth century invested indigenous Indian religions. However, sectarian rivalries did exist, sometimes taking a violent form, thereby projecting a different picture of the past.

Nor did this lack of tolerance grow with the coming of Islam. Curiously, although some Islamic popular belief was internalized, particularly among sects identified with the socially less privileged, there was little overt interest in Islamic theology on the part of Hindu groups, except in a marginal way, by some scholars maintaining that certain aspects of philosophy in the second millennium AD might be traced to Islamic influence. There are few major studies of Islam in Sanskrit or in the regional languages until much later. References to the Muslims were either to Turushkas/Turks in the early sources, which was the correct ethnic identity of the earlier north Indian rulers, or more generally they were described as mlecchas. This was a term used across religion for those not following aspects of the sects and were not identified by caste.

Similarly, the more learned among Muslim authors such as Abu'l Fazl merely give résumés of Brahmanism when they come to the details of some of the Hindu religions which they speak of, since this was socially the most prestigious of them all. There is little detail of the other sects except in a very generalized way. Abu'l Fazl refers to the strife among the various indigenous religions which he attributes to diversity in language as well as the resistance of Hindus to discuss their religions with foreigners!

The confrontation of Islam and Hinduism is often posed as two monolithic religions, face-to-face. In fact, for Islam the Indian experience must have been extremely bewildering, since there was no recognizable ecclesiastical authority or structure among the Hindus as a whole to which Islam could address itself. It faced a large variety of belief systems of which the most noticeable common feature to Islam was idol worship—but even this was by no means uniform. Hence, the frequency with which references are made preferentially to castes, ethnic communities and occupations, rather than religions—Rajputs, Jats, Zamindars, etc.—in the context of the indigenous religions and only on a very generalized scale to the Hindus.

It is often said that the Hindus must have been upset at seeing Turkish and Mongol soldiers trampling the floors of their temples in their heavy boots. The question is, which Hindus? For the same temple now entered by mleccha soldiers was open only to a few upper-caste Hindus and its sanctum was in any case barred to the majority of the population consisting of the indigenous mlecchas, and their feelings were immaterial to the caste Hindus who had worshipped at these temples. The trauma was therefore more in the nature of the polluting of the temple rather than the confrontation with another religion.

I have tried to argue that if one is attempting to understand 'Hinduism' in history, then one has to see it as far as possible in its indigenous form. The distinction between the two traditions of Brahmanism and Shramanism are significant. These separate identities were carefully maintained. In the eyes of the former, the latter were obviously inferior and for this one has only to look at texts of Brahmana authorship of the second millennium AD referring to monks and mendicants. Brahmanism also maintained a distinction between itself and other 'Hindu' religious sects such as those associated with the Bhakti and Shakta movements which, although not Shramanic in the strict sense, were nevertheless the inheritors of some of that tradition.

The separateness of the two was forced to narrow, though not to amalgamate, from time to time when historical situations demanded it. A formal closeness was imposed on them by the coming of Islam and the categorization for the first time of all indigenous cults as Hindu, where Hindu carried the connotation of 'the Other'. Islam had a more extended dialogue with the inheritors of the Shramanic tradition perhaps because of the presence of Buddhism in Central Asia but was relatively silent with Brahmanism.

A further crisis in India came with the arrival of latter-day Christianity riding on the powerful wave of colonialism. In the projected superiority of the Semitic religions, it was once again the 'Hindus' who were regarded as 'the Other' and this again included both the Brahmanic and the Shramanic traditions. This time the dialogue was with Brahmanism. Of the social groups most closely associated with power, the upper castes were the genitors of the new middle class and among them, initially, Brahmanas were significant.

Inevitably, the Brahmanical base of what was seen as the new Hinduism was unavoidable. But merged into it were various bits and pieces from upper-caste belief and ritual with one eye on the Christian and Islamic models. Its close links with certain nationalist opinion gave to many of these neo-Hindu movements a political edge which remains recognizable even today. It is this development which was the parent to the present-day Syndicated Hinduism which is being pushed forward as the sole claimant to the inheritance of indigenous Indian religion.

It goes without saying that if Indian society is changing, then its religious expressions must also undergo change. But the direction of this change is perhaps alarming. The emergence of a powerful middle-class with urban moorings and a reach to the rural rich would find it useful to bring into politics a uniform, monolithic Hinduism created to serve its new requirements. Under the guise of a new, reformed Hinduism, an effort would be made to draw a large clientele and to speak with the voice of numbers.

The appeal to the middle class would be obvious. To those lower down in society there would be the attraction of upward mobility through a new religious movement. But the latter, having forsaken some of their ideologies of non-caste religious sects, would have to accept the dharma of the powerful but remain subordinate. A change in this direction would introduce new problems as it has already begun to do. In wishing away the weaknesses of the old, one does not want to bring in the predictable disasters of the new.

Perhaps the major asset of what we call 'Hinduism' of the pre-modern was that it was not a uniform, monolithic religion, but a juxtaposition of flexible religious sects. This flexibility was its strength and its distinguishing feature, allowing the existence even of non-caste, anti-Vedic groups disavowing the injunctions of the Dharmashastras, which nevertheless had to be included within the definition of what has been called 'Hinduism'.

The weakening or disappearance of such dissenting groups within the framework of at least religious expression would be a considerable loss. If Syndicated Hinduism could simultaneously do away with social hierarchies, this might mitigate its lack of flexibility. But the scramble to use it politically merely results in the realignment of castes.

Syndicated Hinduism draws largely on Brahmanical texts, the Gita, and Vedantic thought, accepts some aspects of the Dharmashastras, and attempts to present a modern, reformed religion. It ends up inevitably as a garbled form of Brahmanism with a motley of 'values' drawn from other sources, such as bringing in elements of individual salvation from the Bhakti tradition, and some Puranic rituals. Its contradictions are many. The call to unite under Hinduism as a political identity is anachronistic.

Social and economic inequality was a given fundamental of Brahmanism and whether one approves or disapproves of it, it was an established point of view. To propagate the texts associated with this view and yet insist that it is an egalitarian philosophy is hardly acceptable. Some religions like Islam are, in theory, egalitarian. Others like Buddhism restrict equality to the moral and ethical spheres of life. The major religions after all arose and evolved in societies and in periods when inequality was a fact of life and the social function of these religions was not to change this but to try and ameliorate the reality for those who found it harsh and abrasive.

Further, as a proselytizing religion, Syndicated Hinduism cannot accept a multiplicity of religious manifestations as being equally important: clearly, some selected beliefs, rituals, and practices will have to be regarded as essential and therefore more significant. This is a major departure from the traditional position. Who does the selecting and from what sources and to what purpose also becomes a matter of considerable significance.

Another factor of increasing importance to this Syndicated Hinduism is the 'Hindu' diaspora. 'Hindu' communities settled outside India experience a sense of cultural insecurity since they are minority communities, frequently in a largely Islamic or Christian society as in the Gulf or Europe, North America, or the Caribbean. Their search is often for sects which will support their new enterprise or, better still, a form of Hinduism parallel to Christianity and with an idiom comprehensible to Christians which they can teach their children (preferably, we are told, through Hindu schools and video films). Such communities with their particular requirements and not their inconsequential financial support will also provide the basis for the institutions and the ecclesia of Syndicated Hinduism.

The importance of this 'diaspora' is clearly reflected not only in the social links between those in India and those abroad supporting the new Hinduism, but also in the growing frequency with which the sanghs, parishads, and samajs hold their meetings abroad and seek the support and 'conversion' of the affluent. The aspect of conversion is new and aggressive, both among 'native-born' Indians and whites.

This is not to be confused with the guru-cult in affluent societies, where there is little attempt to convert people to Hinduism, but rather to suggest to them methods of 'self-realization' irrespective of their religious affiliations.

The creation of this Syndicated Hinduism for purposes more political than religious, and mainly supportive of the ambitions of a new social class, has been a long process in the last hundred years or so and is now coming more clearly into focus. Whatever political justification there might have been for this development, as a form of nationalistic assertion under British rule, no longer exists. Social groups in the past have expressed their aspirations in part by creating new religious sects.

The emergence of Syndicated Hinduism is different both in scale and scope and is not restricted to the creation of a new sect but a new religious form seeking to encapsulate all the earlier sects. The sheer scale as well as the motivation call for considerable caution. Syndicated Hinduism claims to be re-establishing the Hinduism of pre-modern times: in fact, it is only establishing itself and in the process distorting the historical and cultural dimensions of the indigenous religions and divesting them of the nuances and varieties which were a major source of their enrichment.

Attempts to insist on its legitimacy increase the distance between it and the indigenous religious articulations of Indian civilization and invest it with the ingredients of a dangerous fundamentalism. With each aggressive stance, based on the false alarm of Hinduism in danger (as when 500 'Hindu' untouchables were converted to Islam at Meenakshipuram in 1981 out of a population of approximately 500 million 'Hindus' at the time), this Syndicated Hinduism forces a particular identity on all those who are now technically called Hindus. But not all would wish to participate in this identity. There is something to be said for attempting to comprehend the real religious expression of Indian civilization before it is crushed beneath the wheels of a new juggernaut.

V

MUSEUMS

15

MUSEUMS IN INDIA PAST AND FUTURE*

The museum as an institution is virtually unique to modern times. It is a gathering and display of information originally about archaeology and history, but also latterly with specialization about the purpose and functioning of the technologies that we use in our current lives. The scope of the museum is therefore gradually spreading across a spectrum of activities. Understanding even the original functions of a museum has undergone much change, a change that needs to be explained if the museum is to play its proper role in our cultures.

PEOPLE WITH LEISURE AND SENSITIVITY to artistic objects have been known to collect these for many centuries. However, placing collections in a museum for public display has a more recent ancestry. In Europe it was more evidently nurtured as part of a search for a European identity that surfaced in the Renaissance and later in the Enlightenment period. Identity was crucial to Europe at that time since Europe was undergoing radical change. The traditional aristocracy was being edged out by a newly emerging moneyed middle class, and colonialism was confronting Europe with cultures very different from its own. People like Hans Sloane and Joseph Banks with large private collections were eager to combine money with knowledge. This provided the nucleus for some of the leading museums in Britain. The money, of course,

*An earlier version of this essay was first published in 2014.

grew with industrialization and was augmented through colonial ventures. Identity was tied into the definition of culture and class. The Renaissance underlined the idea of European culture being rooted in ancient Greek culture, but the latter was unfamiliar to everyone in Europe except the elite. Therefore, when museums emerged, they were contributing to the creation of a European classical culture, as indeed they were to do in exhibiting what were thought of as classical cultures in many parts of the world.

Private collections of art that had become a symbol of status did not always remain with the family. By the nineteenth century they were becoming the nucleus of public museums, some assisted by state funding. This coincided with the European need to assert its superiority among world cultures, an assertion legitimizing colonial and imperial power. Bringing the finest objects from other cultures to European museums was a demonstration of power and of the capturing of other cultures and to a lesser extent, curiosity. Used in comparative studies these objects illustrated what was projected as the hierarchy in the ranking of cultures.

The intention of the museum was to display objects in a classified manner. The general classification was fairly simplistic. It began with separating natural objects from those that were made by humans. Geological samples, plant and animal fossils, and some recent specimens were included in the first category. These were easier to organize using the classifications of Charles Darwin and Carl Linnaeus. The objects made by humans—ranging from tiny coins to huge obelisks—were more difficult to classify, since the intention was not only to identify them locally but also to relate them to a universal history of human evolution. Historical change required explanation so the stages of human life were applied to the history of a society. Primitive beginnings were followed by a period of growth, culminating in a golden age, subsequent to which there was a gradual decline. European culture however remained at the apex.

What were collected in museums from private collections and

some purchase were objects that came to be defined as 'antiquities' from earlier times. These provided a tangible picture of the past. In the period of the Enlightenment, this activity was expanded in two ways. One was the assumption that a museum should exhibit geological and natural history. The museum had to keep up with advances in knowledge. Second, the intention of the museum was to educate the public. The museum was in a sense the companion institution to the university. Some universities had museums, but when these became expensive to maintain there was a separation, although a connection was retained through close collaboration.

Turning to India, the institution of a museum was initially a colonial introduction of the idea. Its establishment lay in colonial views of knowledge about India with a recognizable ideological purpose of giving an identity to the Indian past. The museum did not grow from the individual collector's activities. There had been collectors of special artefacts in the pre-colonial past, such as the collections of Serfoji in Tanjore, the Mughal princes, the bhandaras of Jaina monasteries, and occasional small collections made by the landed aristocracy or wealthy merchants. Old and rare illustrated books in particular were to be found in such collections, before some of them inexplicably got dispersed. But these collections were initially ignored perhaps because access to them was limited. Had the libraries of the Mughal aristocracy been collected there might not have been a tragic dispersal of the books. However, the major museums were from the start state institutions tied into colonial ideas about the Indian past. Even where existing collections were incorporated there was seldom discussion in any detail on who had made the collection and why.

The notion of a museum gradually changed. It ceased to be just a collection of objects—what we today call the vastu sangrahalaya. It began to be seen as an institution reflecting new knowledge about the biography of the environments and cultures. Some were isolated cultures previously unknown. Some when juxtaposed with others began to suggest connections that had not been envisaged earlier. The old wunderkammer or chamber of curiosities gave way to an institution of learning and additionally, aesthetic enjoyment. In India, the ajaib-ghar, the house of curiosities has not quite been converted into an institution of learning in every case.

What the British collected in India to begin with came largely from their own explorations and excavations and from donations. The need to house these objects began with placing them in the Asiatic Society premises in Calcutta, conjoining them to Indology. But the objects outgrew the space. It was then thought to house them in the Indian Museum established in 1814. This was about half a century after the British Museum was founded. The awareness of the museum as essential to both heritage and history was familiar to Europe but less so to India.

Museums encouraged the parallel study of objects that were gradually becoming the counterpart to texts. Information from texts is intangible and abstract. Objects are tangible and three-dimensional. Often the juxtaposition of objects creates or erodes connections. The pattern of their proximity is therefore significant. The larger collections fuelled a study of historical change through objects that came from the same region over a number of centuries. The change could be of material, from clay to stone to metal, or it could be of form. Such collections also enabled a comparative study of the same object from different regions—the most striking example of which was the icon of the Buddha. Thus the Gandhara, Mathura, and Amaravati heads of the Buddha, representing the same person, sculpted in three different regions, are physically quite distinct. Central to this difference are historical styles and the local aesthetic.

Acquiring a collection was doubtless motivated largely by curiosity about the culture and its authors. Housing a collection, however, required classifying it. Classification was dependent on theories both of history and aesthetics which, as we know, change with new knowledge. These drew on the history of the colony as envisaged by colonial scholarship and which had an interface with colonial policy. This was present even in the broader relationship of European to non-European cultures. The merger of colonial interests and intellectual curiosity led to an interest in the ancient histories of other cultures. This led to deciphering hieroglyphs allowing a reading of Egyptian history and the cuneiform script that gave access to ancient West Asia. And parallel to this came James Prinsep's decipherment of the Brahmi script that opened up a world of inscriptions in India. Information on the ancient world was now different from what was contained in ancient Greek and Latin texts. But the European bias remained, and these texts continued to have priority as sources of history.

Historical classification was either by subject or by chronology. Subject matter was influenced to some degree by extending the concept of evolution from natural history to social history. For chronology historical-dynastic labels became the norm. In the process of tracing the evolution of a culture and evaluating it, one of the past cultures was treated as the norm. If Europe chose Greek art, the choice for India was Gupta art. But the choice was arrived at after much argument. Some preferred Gandhara art of the Indo-Bactrian-Greek period since it incorporated the Hellenistic aesthetic, whereas others dismissed this as a hybrid form. The sculpture that came from places more centrally located in British India was described by some as Aryan, adding even more confusion to the use of this label with reference to things Indian.

In classifying objects primacy was given to objects representing religion and the life of the elite. This was more so in India as according to the colonial reading of the past, religion was seen as the single factor that identified various Indians. And the elite were of course the stuff of history in those days. These were thought to be—and still are—appropriate objects for a museum. This unnecessarily narrowed the area of knowledge. For example, some of the most exquisite scientific instruments of earlier times, aesthetically on a par with other objects, such as the superb medieval astrolabes, were not thought to be that important and, therefore, few found a place in the museums of India. Astrolabes are not deities and although they tell us more about the universe than do deities, such objects come low in the hierarchy. Part of the reason was that Indians of past times were not seen as supporting rational and scientific thought despite their impressive contributions to mathematics, medicine, and astronomy. But these were the very subjects that should have been reflected in museums as they demonstrated what historians were speaking of when they defined civilization as a collective process and not a unique event.

The nineteenth century was obsessed with questions such as which culture could be described as the earliest civilization. These are questions that we now consider less relevant. The concept of distinctively separate civilizations, each with its demarcated territory, its single major language and single dominant religion, has now been largely discarded. Today we study civilization as a porous, ongoing process, the making of which was dependent on considerable cross-fertilization with other cultures. Territorial control, the use of language and the practice of religion, constantly change. What is important is to track the change, and to ascertain how much of it has evolved from local factors and what emerges out of interaction with other cultures. No culture is ever an island unto itself. This interdependence needs to be reflected in museums.

Yet, an impressive example of this has been demonstrated in the Ashmolean Museum in Oxford. The museum has a collection of Indian, Chinese, Central Asian, and West Asian objects. So, instead of confining them to four separate galleries it linked the four areas by using a theme, that of the Silk Route. This was the pan-Asian trade route that went from China through Central Asia, drawing in India and reaching the eastern Mediterranean. Its time span was approximately the entire first and early second millennia AD. The museum display demonstrates the interface between four areas and their cultures, highlighting the impact that they had on each other. It gives form to precisely how the new concept of civilization should be defined. This could be done to great effect for the Indian subcontinent, with overland routes, maritime contacts, and migrations to and out of, the subcontinent.

It is sometimes said that museum displays remove objects from their context. Whether it is a sculpture taken out of a temple or a stupa, or calligraphy taken from a mosque or a tombstone, or a miniature painting that was once a book illustration, none of these objects have a context when they are displayed. The context obviously does not have to be physically present but should be made apparent. When taken in isolation, the object becomes a commodity. This often leads to its commercialization. When this happens two new categories of specialists emerge. The private collector becomes an art connoisseur—someone who knows about art and can appreciate and value the object. The other is the antiquarian dealer for whom objects from the past are primarily commodities for purchase and sale.

Commodification puts a price on each object and it becomes an investment as is common now among the wealthy. This introduces the category of private patronage, and in a society moving into the market economy, this has become an effective way of investing high incomes. One of the interesting trends in all such societies is that often the commercial side of dealing with art objects is in the hands of the wives of the wealthy. Does this make it less of a commercial enterprise?

With wealthy individuals now treating antiques as investments, private collections and even private museums will doubtless increase in number and in holdings. Museums dependent on state funding will slowly fall back in bidding for special objects in the art market. Prices are frequently determined by the international market rather than the domestic market which makes it even more expensive for developing economies. Yet as a historian, I do feel that some significant objects should be located in accessible public museums. Perhaps we should consider some of the ways in which other countries cope with this problem. One of the more common is, of course, for the state to give tax benefits for objects that are donated to a particular museum, but held by the donor in his/her lifetime. The problem with private collections is that converting an antique into a commodity seriously curtails its centrality in research.

But enough of the general scene. Let me turn to the Indian Museum whose 200th anniversary was celebrated in 2014. Established in 1814, it had expanded by the late nineteenth century to include objects pertinent to geology, zoology, ethnology, archaeology as well as arts and crafts, for collection and display. The inclusion of all these aspects of human existence, seen as interrelated, was essentially in conformity with nineteenth century philosophy relating to the evolution and interface of life and cultures. But some of what was cutting edge knowledge a century ago is now no longer so.

For example, the then current knowledge of ethnography was reflected in the museum by the contribution of Herbert Risley on racial types. The nineteenth century saw the establishing of what was called 'race science'. It was avidly applied to the classification of various cultures in the subcontinent frequently with a racial label. Risley went around collecting data on cephalic indexes and nasal width. But by the mid-twentieth century, the idea of race had been virtually discarded as having little basis in fact. Given the tenacity with which we still hold on to the idea of race, perhaps a museum could have a small exhibition explaining why race became a category of classification, and why this has now been discarded.

Moving from the natural world to that made by humans had an underlying message. It demonstrated progress from the natural to the primitive to the civilized. Exhibiting the past in a particular way was a method of showing that it had come to be understood by those who studied it. This was a conviction that grew, amongst other things from the idea, perhaps best expressed by the German historian of the time, Leopold von Ranke, that history could reveal the past as it had actually happened. Historicity was to be based on precisely what the sources tell us. Such empiricism has been dismissed as the narcotic of the nineteenth century. Yet, archaeology and the museum can discover and exhibit the realities of the past. Merely laying out the objects bypasses the responsibility that historians and curators have of selecting and analysing the information that they present. The selection is inevitably linked, consciously or subconsciously, to the theory explaining the significance of that which is being presented.

In setting up museums it was additionally intended to state that the colonizing power was giving attention to understanding the alien cultures over which it ruled. The attention tended to be paternalistic and not participatory. Until 1910, the Board of Trustees of the Indian Museum, for example, was overwhelmingly British with a small scatter of Indians. The British representation was in part that of professionals specializing in the knowledge of the sections represented, the rest being employees of the government. These latter tended not to be particularly innovative and seldom took the initiative to change the format. This is a problem that we continue to face in our state institutions linked to education.

Administrators assume that they too are specialists in disciplines. With the pace at which knowledge is advancing today even specialists find it hard to keep up, leave alone administrators. Changes therefore tend not to be made when most required.

The objects displayed in the galleries of the arts section in many museums were generally recognized as symbols of high status being associated with deities and royalty. Among the displays was a section called Industrial Arts. This referred to objects that were either handmade or with a minimal use of machines in contrast to the real industry where objects were made with sophisticated machines. This distinction has not been discussed sufficiently. Sculpture and painting are handmade just as are embroidered textiles.

Was the individual artist all that different from the individual craftsman in past times? Both were anonymous, but for the rare sculptor named in ancient times and the painters associated with the Mughal court. What we call classical art came from guilds of craftsmen, as is attested to by inscriptions at Sanchi and other sources. By way of contrast, one thinks of the names of individual artists that are associated with the finest pieces of Greek classical sculpture. When does the individual artist begin to be recognized and what does this mean for the way in which what we today call 'art' is understood?

The separation of art from craft also encouraged a distinction between popular culture and high culture, between the work of the craftsman intended for relatively routine use and that intended for royalty and special occasions. The craftsman who sculpted the figure of a deity was in fact just another craftsman, similar to the one who wove textiles. But the sanctification of the figure gave it a special status that set it aside from the mundane. This problem had earlier raised a couple of questions, still substantially unanswered. When does art cease to be a craft? Did those who used these objects regard them as functional or as aesthetic objects? Presumably there would have been no problem in using an aesthetic object in a functional way.

The distinction between classical and folk was, of course, made in medieval times. The courtly culture often referred to as marga was differentiated from the folk culture or desi. Was this also an indirect distinction between the artist and the craftsman? The artists who painted birds and animals for Jahangir did so under their own names. They followed the rules of their training but could innovate if they chose to. The craftsmen of this period remained anonymous although they too were technically trained and did innovate.

Associated with this is how medieval times perceived earlier periods. Epic heroes said to belong to the ancient past are sometimes depicted in medieval dress and style in miniature paintings. Are they being seen as people distant in time or is this an attempt to update personalities from the past? We today accept this pictorial updating of ancient narratives, but would shudder if the epic heroes were painted in shirt and trousers. Perhaps it suggests that in medieval times the past was seen as more integral to the present, whereas we are more alienated from the past seeing it as distant and apart.

Yet, style and patronage are complex matters. The Chandela kings of Bundelkhand were patrons of some of the finest sculpture in the medieval temples at Khajuraho. Nevertheless, they were also patrons of the small shrine to their ancestral deity, Maniya Devi in Mahoba. Maniya Devi was aniconic but was in worship and was later converted to the goddess Sharada. Was Maniya Devi too obscure to be sculpted into an icon? Was there some other reason for keeping the original form of the rock, even after its patrons had been associated with temples to Puranic deities? Should lesser and aniconic deities not be accommodated in a museum if only just to make the point that other forms were also part of the cultural pattern?

To return to the idea of the museum in 1814. The existing European museums such as the British Museum, the Ashmolean in Oxford, and the Louvre in Paris, were substantially collections of what were believed to be objects of interest and importance pertaining to the past and creating a European identity. The museum acquired, collected, conserved, and exhibited these objects. The museum also became a centre for advanced research. This required an up-to-date reference library of books and journals, open to public membership. The library of the British Museum in the nineteenth century was more than just a museum library. It was home to a variety of intellectuals who through their research and theories have changed the face of the globe in different ways. To the library would now be added a phototec and a conservation unit. In conservation the controversy over the degree to which the object should be changed in order to conserve it, was solved in Europe by arguing for the minimum. In India, the restoration of objects to their original forms can sometimes have distinctly unhappy results.

Another dimension is introduced when objects are viewed as items of heritage contributing to the identity of the society. This is the point at which history entered the functioning of the museum. It is perhaps worth reminding ourselves that the hegemonic history of India in colonial times, was that of James Mill, *The History of British India*, published from 1817. It was, therefore, contemporary with the establishing of the Indian Museum. Was there a link between the two? It can be argued that the understanding of the Indian past at that time, rooted as it was in colonial interpretations, was in turn reflected both in the histories of the time and in the display of major museums.

As noted earlier, Mill periodized the history of India into Hindu, Muslim, and British, a periodization that still lingers despite its having no basis. Museum displays often follow this idea. Chronology can be maintained without giving objects dynastic labels. Where a dynasty has ruled briefly such as the Shunga, can a sculpture be accurately ascribed to this dynastic period, or would it not be better to give a somewhat broader time bracket? Sometimes the technical form is more helpful in understanding the nature of change. Whereas mural painting is profuse in early centuries of the first millennium AD, it is miniature painting that is more common later in the second millennium AD. What accounts for this radical change? Surely not just the use of paper, however significant this may have been. Changes in court fashions and styles have multiple explanations.

Chronology itself is multifaceted. The past has its own genealogy onto which we impose our chronology. The French historian Fernand Braudel spoke of the three dimensions of time relevant to every historical event. These are, the moment when the event happens, then the broader context of the event, and finally the long duration—the many centuries that mould the landscape of the event. To this has been added the fourth, namely, the point in time when the observer perceives the object in a museum. I am not suggesting that the chronology of each object should have these three time measurements, but only that the consciousness of these may be reflected in statements on chronology.

With some rare exceptions, the display of objects in our museums tend to follow the periodization based on religion and dynasty rather than considering other categories. Yet historical periodization itself has now changed to a considerable degree. A search for new classifications could be a useful cross-disciplinary study between historians and curators.

This is also tied into the labels given to objects. These tend to be minimalistic, giving information on dynasty and, if required, on religious identity. This is perfectly legitimate provided they carry a precise meaning and sufficient information. But such requirements are generally lacking. Where an icon or frieze is taken from the external niche of a façade, this needs to be stated with some explanation of why it was placed where it was initially, preferably with some graphic presentation of its original location. Where a painting was part of an illustrated manuscript, we need to be told what the text was about and why it was commissioned, and by whom, and the incident is being depicted in the painting, in addition to the name of the artist and the date. Even where there are paintings of familiar stories, there is a need to draw attention to special features.

All this means lengthier labels and more work for the curators but without that the purpose of the museum is defeated. It also means that labels have to be constantly updated and corrected. Where the information in a label is controversial, this should at least be mentioned. If all the objects belong to a single dynasty, then various links evoking the period can help provide a context. I am not suggesting that every gallery should be a textbook in itself, but explaining why the gallery is arranged the way it is and justifying the arrangement and what it is attempting to say, would be a necessary addition. And for the visitor it provides accessible ways by which the object can be understood both in isolation and as part of a collection. Fortunately, there are many electronic devices now that can be employed quite easily for this purpose of providing background knowledge.

Curators, art historians, and other scholars may well be familiar with the history and value of the objects on display. For them, the museum as a place that houses, conserves, and exhibits a collection of antiquities and historical artefacts, may be sufficient. But the function of the museum today is far larger in its role as educating citizens. These two aspects are interrelated. If the display does not give access to knowledge it ceases to be of value in educating the public. Thus if a museum claims to project a visual representation of Indian civilization to the public it has to be aware of the more recent discussions on what constitutes civilization. Does the concept still continue to convey what it might have done a century ago?

Educating the public through museums has its own problems. An object exhibited in isolation with just a brief label loses its meaning. What the public sees is partial, limited generally to its aesthetic quality. The German literary critic Walter Benjamin has argued that any object thus exhibited is embedded in a tradition and if one is seeking for the aura of the object it lies in the tradition. Others would argue that the museum liberates the object from its tradition and introduces other facets in its appreciation. But then these facets have to be indicated.

The museum is also the location of what is regarded as heritage. There are problems with defining heritage. It draws from a constellation of past events. What we regard as our heritage today may not be the same as what our ancestors believed was the heritage they were bestowing on coming generations, no matter how far back we go. It might be salutary to remember that for many centuries people did not know of the emperor Ashoka and his concept of dhamma. His is just one among dozens of names in the Puranic king lists. Only the Buddhists remembered him and they were silenced by medieval times. He was rediscovered in the nineteenth century. But today he is viewed as part of our national heritage that continued unbroken for over two millennia. How did this happen and why? We have a diverse and multi-layered heritage, and as with the construction of all national heritage we face the problem of selecting the cultures that we regard as national. The cultures of the dominant communities invariably get pride of place even if the attempt is to present a homogenized packet as a national culture, as is preferred by most that call themselves a ministry of culture. This does not always reflect the sensitivities of a heritage constituted by multiple cultures. The definition of heritage has to become more inclusive.

The Western world has defined its culture in a linear trajectory, but it is now facing the pressure of immigrant communities bringing their own heritage. It will be fascinating to see how their national cultures will be defined a couple of centuries from now when immigrants will be integrated into their societies. It will be equally interesting to see how the immigrants in the diaspora will define their heritage brought from the home country. The constituents of this image will inevitably include the imaginary and this will increase over time.

A museum carries a message. In colonial days it was the message of presenting a past, and incidentally in doing so, also glorifying what colonial scholarship had done for the colony. This effort deserves appreciation, although not by ignoring its motivation. But two centuries later the contours have changed—both in terms of what the museum stands for and what are its functions. The appeal is no longer to colonial authority but to a public being made aware of and seeking to articulate its identity. This it seems to me is a major change in the concept of the museum since the last two hundred years. The ingredients of this identity are complex since they are no longer just the narrow definitions of nineteenth century scholarship. The identity has to reflect a society constituted of many cultures each seeking visibility. It is not only a recognition of our culture but also of the many other cultures of which we are increasingly becoming a part, and to which we are contributing. Such a reflection is not an impossible task. But it needs both sensitivity and an understanding of the interface between cultures.

The future of the museum requires us to think again about the museum as an institution. It is not enough that objects are displayed. We have to think about how this is done and why it is done the way it is. Are there other more effective and pertinent ways? The purpose of the museum has changed as it is bound to with conceptual changes in how we view the past and relate it to our present society, and how we use the past. As with the writing of history the museum also represents mediation between the past and us. And the past is not something out there, it is a part of us. We need to understand the past, not in isolation but in context. I can only repeat the sentiment often repeated, that a museum should make the invisible visible.

16

EARLY FORMS OF PATRONAGE*

This essay describes early forms of patronage that we take for granted and most often do not read beyond the bare facts of who was the patron and who was the recipient and what was the nature of that which was given from the former to the latter and whether there was a reason for giving a gift. Today we look much further even if reading texts of centuries ago and search for a better understanding of those involved, the reasons for the gift and how this activity affected the community.

PATRONAGE IS AN ESSENTIAL ACTIVITY in virtually all societies. It may begin in an informal way and not be very noticeable. But gradually as societies become more complex it becomes more formal and can even surface as an institution. At a basic level the concept assumes an approximate relationship between two entities, two persons, two institutions, where one is the donor, and the other is the recipient. Both these can increase in number. It can be as simple as a relationship within the family where the provider of the wherewithal becomes a kind of donor and the rest are recipients. A very small part of patriarchy can sometimes hint at patronage. The essential feature is that the donor and the recipient are unequal, and this feature is present in all the forms of patronage. Maintaining the inequality is in a perverse way, what allows of status being bestowed on the donor. And yet in a contradictory way it could be the donor that legitimizes the status.

*An earlier version of this essay was first published in 2022.

The definition of patronage is popularly viewed as a restricted one: it involves the gift, or the wealth given by a person of superior status to one of an inferior status to enable the latter to carry out his/her activities. It involves various social categories. Patronage therefore can act as a catalyst or as a means of stabilizing an existing condition.

The item that is exchanged—the donation—can be in kind or in a monetary form or even symbolic. But the distinction between the two is clear. Donations in kind can be any moveable object that has some value; or it can be immovable such as land and property. The monetary donations make the idea more fluid. Moveable objects are generally consumable or are small objects. Immovable objects can be large. Objects are not only valued in currency but also have the possibility of being exchanged, and they may also have a symbolic value which has to be recognized. Money is different as it is a unit to use for exchange, or to finance other things. The exchange can be of tangible items for intangible acquisitions.

An aspect of patronage is the eligibility of the donor since the donor is the pivot of the system. Obviously, the donor has to be wealthy and preferably a person of some status so that the recipient is grateful to him and looks up to him as does the rest of society. This gives the donations social value as well. Caste and class therefore play an important role in defining the donor.

The donation creates a new relationship between the donor and the recipient, but if it is large enough it also creates a new institution. This happened with the establishing of a Buddhist stupa, or a Hindu temple, or a mosque, or a gurdwara, or a church. These became new institutions controlled by the recipients of the donation but often under the supervision of the donor.

Some examples from early history might illustrate what I am stating. Direct examples of man-to-man patronage are given in the Rig Veda in the dana-stuti hymns (hymns in praise of making a gift). A bard would compose a verse or a hymn in praise of his patron who was generally the chief of a clan. The composition would be in praise of the prowess of the chief, of his success in a cattle-raid, or whatever hostility occasioned action against another chief. This was of great importance in a society of agropastoralists where the herding of cattle was economically a necessity, and cattle were the primary source of wealth. The bard who had composed the eulogy on the chief was rewarded by a small share of the wealth—or so the bard claimed. It was also said by some bards that chiefs could be niggardly. However, to maintain status, the bard always claimed to have received much wealth in cattle, horses, gold, chariots, and slave women.

The symbolic relationship had other manifestations. The bard maintained that it was his invocations to the deity that brought successful results, and this was what he was being rewarded for. The eulogy enhanced the status of the chief in the eyes of society. The stuti was the claim to fame of the chief but it also reiterated his right to be the chief. The gift-giving was a transference of wealth. Above all, the bard claimed that he had bestowed immortality on the chief by composing a eulogy on him. How right this was. We today hear of these chiefs and their activities largely through the compositions of the bards. The eulogies by exaggerating the gift were nudging other chiefs to match the imagined gift.

In a society where status was ostensibly conditioned by birth, it was necessary to claim the highest lineage connections. These were provided by the genealogies kept by poets and bards and later by priests, and this also gave them some authority vis-à-vis the patron. The eulogy became the rhetoric of this relationship. The bard since he passed judgement on the lineage status of his patron not only enhanced his own status but came to be regarded as inviolate, thus acquiring his own authority. This in a sense also gave him the right to dissent. In some states in Rajasthan in later times, the bard could announce his disapproval of a royal act and threaten to fast unto death—a dharna. Should he die as a result of the fast, the guilt would be on the ruler, and who knows what calamity he might suffer. It would be a terrible blot on the ruler. The social reference to the bard and to the relationship with the ruler was a complex one and much beyond just that of a donor and recipient.

This then becomes one pattern of patronage. There is a category of person who has an almost independent standing in society and is respected for what he does, who also legitimizes in various ways those who come to power and need such legitimization. This is naturally more prevalent in periods of social uncertainty when upstarts come to power and need legitimation. It often takes the form in early times of a claim to Kshatriya status in the social hierarchy. Curiously, in the period prior to the Guptas, many dynasties were not Kshatriyas and did not bother to acquire this status. But in the post-Gupta period, perhaps with the dominance of Brahmanism, a claim to Kshatriya status is often made, and this then requires evidence, hence the importance of the keeping of genealogies. The tradition was also present in the composition of the prashasti (eulogy) dedicated to royalty and to others that were being honoured.

This activity is the function of the bard who memorizes the genealogies and the lesser priests who keep written records. This is also the process that illustrates the malleability of caste identities. In earlier history, many Rajput castes of uncertain origin claimed the status of Kshatriya or its equivalent. Today the more impoverished Rajput castes sometimes claim the status of an OBC since this enables access to certain social benefits such as education and employment. The relationship of the legitimizer and the legitimized is a continuous one in history although who constitutes which category may well change over time. Identifying this feature can provide worthwhile clues to understanding the social history of different periods.

The other form of patronage which also begins in early times and continues in various forms through history is of course religious ritual and forms of worship. Here the person who endows the ritual is the patron and one who performs it is the recipient, although the latter consists of those who perform it for others—the priests, and those who perform a small ritual by themselves—the usual worshipper.

In earliest times the major religious ritual was that linked to the yajna (sacrifice). In the agropastoral societies that were the context to the Vedas and that time, the yajamana (patron of the sacrificial ritual) was usually the chief of the clan who requested the priests to perform a yajna. He was then the patron and donated the vast amount in wealth required for constructing the huge altars and providing the goods and services required for the ritual that often went on for many days. The recipients were the priests who claimed to be in communication with the gods via the ritual and who prayed for the increasing power of the chief that would also bring about the prosperity of the clan.

The wealth of the Kshatriya was consumed and destroyed in the course of the ritual. Some scholars have argued that this was an attempt by the Brahmanas to keep the Kshatriyas under control when they became too wealthy, by forcing them to expend their surplus wealth on the ritual. What is striking in this donor-donee exchange is that the Brahmana gets the tangible wealth in fees, whereas the Kshatriya gets the intangible wealth of status and celestial blessings. It is an exchange of material wealth for an immaterial abstract idea. This was also a form of exchange that had a historical continuity.

The rise of the Shramana religions—Buddhism, Jainism, Ajivikas—saw new forms of patronage. This was not only in terms of what was donated but also in the donors being multiple and coming from a cross section of society. Buddhism became well established in the period from the Mauryas to the Guptas, a time when Puranic Hinduism was starting to take the forms that came to fruition from the Gupta period onwards. Buddhism has marked its presence through the construction of viharas (monasteries), chaityas (halls of worship), and even more dramatically in the building of stupas that entombed holy relics. These are found in slightly varying forms across the subcontinent, some on flat surfaces such as the east coast of the peninsular or others as cave structures in central India.

The stupa begins as a commemorative tumulus or enshrining a relic taken from a man thought to be holy and revered because of his pursuit of teaching and consequent liberation from karma. The stupa is relatively small in north-west India, grew larger in central India and the peninsula, still larger in Sri Lanka and became of an enormous size in Indonesia. Were the donations gradually increasing at these places thus allowing for larger and more fully decorated structures?

Inscriptions recording the donors to the stupa extended over a cross section of society. Wealth was largely in kind as well as in monetary form. Donations came from royalty but not exclusively, as they also came from the setthi-gahapati families (small-scale landowners and merchants, from artisans, and guilds of craftsmen) and from monks and nuns. Some craftsmen record their donation as the skill with which they carved a section of the sculpture of the stupa and the donation is listed as that from a guild of skilled workers. The donations of monks and nuns would be somewhat smaller simply because they were not allowed to retain personal wealth. The arrangements for these donations may have been through familial sources. Royalty was not heavily involved. In some cases, such as that of the Shungas, they are said to have been hostile to Buddhism.

Clearly these donors and recipients constitute a different segment of society from those of earlier times as also the religions being supported. The nature of exchange involved also differed. The making of dana (gift) was in exchange for punya (acquiring merit) that would assist in liberation, in reaching nirvana. Such gifts could be made for oneself as also for others such as family members. Donors could be from the immediate locality or more distant places. Since many of the donations came from traders, the locations would depend on the reach of the trade. Buddhist monastic institutions were not themselves averse to participating in trading activities which provided additional income. Some of the donatory arrangements were a little complex. Thus, royalty would invest in a guild and the interest of the investment would be given as the donation. It is noticeable that some of the donors were women, and not necessarily from royal families. This was a relatively new feature.

I have elsewhere referred to this as community patronage to differentiate it from donors who tended to be the sole financiers of a religious structure and its rituals. The latter came more frequently when patrons were members of royalty. This is not to imply that the community was not involved in other forms of patronage but to say that these forms of patronage to Buddhist institutions were gathered from a wider body of people in a society than those in some other forms. It is a distinguishing feature of this patronage.

In the post-Gupta period, that is the latter half of the first millennium AD, the physical forms linked to patronage change, both in art and architecture, and with the change in religion. The focus of Buddhism is now limited to eastern India after which it gradually declines in the subcontinent, although it remains the premier religion in Central Asia and China, moving on to Japan and by the maritime route to Southeast Asia. This replacement in the subcontinent comes with the rise of Brahmanism now linked to Puranic Hinduism, the Vedic religion having become by now more marginal in practice. The initial and widespread forms of Puranic Hinduism are mainly Shaivism, Vaishnavism, and the Shakta religion.

The changes are many and noticeable. The old deities Varuna and Mitra were overtaken earlier by Indra and Agni, and these in turn are now overtaken by Shiva and Vishnu. One major change is that the deities are no longer abstract as in the Vedas but are now icons based on anthropomorphic forms. Therefore, they have to be crafted and craftsmen have to be trained to make them.

The craftsmen's guilds become important as the recipients of grants from patrons, either directly or indirectly. The huge sacrificial altars of Vedic times give way to small shrines which from the Gupta period onwards take the form of the major places of worship. They start as a single room and eventually become vast complexes of buildings where the primary icon that is worshipped is housed in the central shrine. The objects of patronage are now the structures, that is temples, and the icons of deities. The forms are very different from the Buddhist as is the ritual of worship but the idea of a permanent place of worship may well have been borrowed from the Shramana religions.

The temple is not only the chief place of worship, but it is also in its precincts that the rituals are formulated and sometimes the texts are written. Later, however, some texts were written in the mathas occupied by Brahmanas. The framing of the religion by reference to the Vedic texts now gives way to other texts, such as the Puranas dedicated to the new deities, as well as a range of commentaries. The popular literature such as the epics are also infused with aspects of this new worship. The texts are no longer regarded as revealed by the deities and are accepted as written by Brahmana authors.

Patronage moves from a wide social spectrum as with the Buddhists, to a narrower and more elite patronage coming largely from royalty and the aristocracy and given to Brahmanas. Large donations are given for the building of temples. Numerous land grants are made to Brahmanas for their well-being and the performance of rituals.

Extensive donations in the form of monetary grants, and property and gifts, were also made to the temple. The larger temple was viewed as an estate that employed vast numbers of people in various capacities. It came to be held that the temple was the private property of the presiding deity of the temple. This in fact meant that there was a body of administrators, Brahmanas, that received the donations and paid out of this for new buildings and repairs of old parts and other expenses. The treasuries of the larger temples were always overflowing. Temple administration was also given rights to collect revenue from local villages according to some grants.

With the increase in the rights and revenues of the Brahmana administration, the process of patronage also became more complicated, and was linked to the administration of the kingdom. The expertise of those running the complex temple administration had to include those who had knowledge of architecture, art, accounting, and revenue. This expertise is not included in the functions of the Brahmanas as given in the Dharmashastras. It is more akin to those of the Buddhist monks who performed similar functions in relation to the monasteries. Brahmanas who were into trade, were also donors to temples as is stated in the Pehoa inscription where Brahmana horse-traders make donations to temples from the profits of their trade.

Inscriptions on temple walls are sometimes legal documents recording the administrative rights and legal functioning of the temple as an institution. When it reaches this point then either the temple through its own resources is so rich that it does not require donations, or, and probably more often, it still receives donations since the richer the temple, the greater the status that it can claim and also bestow on its donors. Such inscriptions when they come from royalty and the officers of the administration of the kingdom, are indications of the political supremacy as also of the religious affiliation of the donor. Furthermore, those who administer the temple also become the legitimizers of political authority, not only in terms of their right to rule but also as conforming to what is required from a legitimate ruler. This is one level at which politics and religion are intertwined.

The administration of the temple as an institution parallels the Buddhist Sangha. It is a property owner; it houses the deity; and it is a source of legitimacy. It is thought of as speaking for the deity when taking decisions on rules of worship and of social behaviour. This leads ruling dynasties to refer to themselves as the feudatories of the deity. The Gangas refer to themselves as the rauta, the feudatories of Jagannath at Puri. Temple ritual imitated the daily routine of the royal household, and the deity was treated as the overlord. Its functioning integrated a hierarchy of services required from various castes. It prohibited the entry of untouchables to its sacred precincts.

The temple was thus a recognized social institution as well. This may be one explanation for why, when Hindu kings in a condition of fiscal crisis, desecrated and robbed the temples of their wealth, as did some kings of Kashmir as reported in the *Rajatarangini*, they are not quoted widely as behaving in a despicable way, perhaps to avoid giving publicity to it. The considerable wealth of temples was doubtless one reason why many were raided. In later times the difference of religion was in some cases an added reason.

The history of the patronage of religious institutions continues unbroken into later times with new forms and structures being added as new religious requirements needed them. The mosque was similar in its needs and functions to the temple as was the Sufi khanqah, the Christian church, the Sikh gurdwara. The patterns of patronage and the relation with the community are broadly parallel. Much of what I have said about the earlier institutions would apply to the later ones, although there would of course be some differences of identity.

I have referred to varying cultural categories that are involved in the relations between the donor and the donee and the result thereof. It can result in a prashasti or eulogy, or a structure associated with worship in particular religious rituals, or the construction and maintenance of such a complex structure that it required additional administrative controls.

We have given much attention to the patron and the donation in our studies of patronage, but less to the transformation of the recipient or to the actual creator of the cultural idiom required of the patronage. The relation between the donor and the donee may be confined to just an act of patronage, but the outcome may become a cultural form, and in some cases may ripple out extensively to accommodate other cultural forms. This happens frequently with changes in the idiom of form. Such changes have aesthetic differences which have to be discussed in terms of adhering to or differing from, the texts such as the *Natyashastra*. But it is the craftsman who is actually creating the form. What needs exploration is the process of persuading the craftsman to create a form other than that prescribed in the texts or currently receiving patronage.

Patronage therefore is a relationship of exchange, but since the two categories involved are unequal it also endorses authority and status. This becomes all the more important with the redefinition of culture as not something that emanates from the elite—as it was earlier defined—but as the pattern of living of an entire society in all its levels of existence. Given this, there is inherent in this inequality the germ of dissent in relation to the outcome of patronage. The dissent is expressed in the clash of identities or in the utilization of the patronage. We need therefore to be aware not only of the nature of the patronage but also what may evolve from it.

VI

EDUCATION

17

THE ACADEMIC PROFESSIONAL*

THE RESPONSIBILITY OF THE ACADEMIC is not restricted to being an intellectual in society. It also involves both the nurturing and the protecting of the free pursuit of ideas and themes of research. Since early times this has run into confrontations with patrons and with those who control the freedom. But the values cultivated in contemporary times should strengthen the functioning of the academic professional in this matter—provided of course that such a person has the courage to defend freedom.

Paradoxically, it is when the functional role of the intellectual becomes more marked that there is the maximum claim on the intellectual's part to being disembedded from society. The emergence of intellectuals as a distinct group is relatively recent although the phenomenon of the academic intellectual has a much older existence. The supposed disembedding of the intellectual is a nineteenth century phenomenon, when the professional handling of new categories of knowledge gained an elevated status with the artisan falling back to the level of the skilled worker. The elevation of status had to do both with the dependence of society on professional-based knowledge as well as the professional himself coming from the middle class which became the inheritor of political power. The cultured aristocrat and the inspired dilettante of earlier times gave way to the professional intellectual.

A more subtle refinement distinguishing an intellectual from a

*An earlier version of this essay was first published in 1978.

professional was the implicit assumption of the ability of the former to focus on more than just the dimensions of his skills and to apprehend the quality of knowledge and its application to society. (In the context of the academic intellectual, with which this essay is concerned, a distinction may be suggested between the scholar who functions more in the nature of the skilled professional and the intellectual who, in addition to being a scholar, can project the application of the results of scholarship to his society.) But this refinement, although sharpening the definition, also narrows its scope. The disparity between being a professional in the limited sense generally unconcerned with the wider application of knowledge, and the intellectual recognizing the need for a larger perspective, is often at the root of the problem concerning the role of the intellectual.

The subaltern role of the intellectual is therefore not altogether surprising in view of his or her wider identity with the group in power since this cannot be completely rootless and classless. Complete autonomy is open only to those who are outside the society or are regarded as eccentrics or are free from the dependence on patronage. The absolute freedom of the intellectual is, to that extent, a myth. It has been fostered by the belief that democratic institutions are implicitly open and liberal, and it is therefore possible for intellectuals to remain as observers above the fray. Political ideologues are often uncomfortable with the questioning which intellectual participation entails and would prefer intellectuals to comment at a distance. This encourages the description of the intellectual as far-removed, isolated, and unconcerned with the problems of his society. The more authoritarian the ideology the greater the emphasis on anti-intellectualism. (It is not entirely coincidental that use of the derisory term 'egghead' for intellectuals and particularly for the academic variety, was most frequently used in the mass media in the United States, during the McCarthy era.)

This attitude is accepted in some intellectual circles as it spares them from having to take carefully considered positions on the controversies of the day. The populist emphasis that intellectual objectivity lies in being at a distance from the problem is unfortunately often accepted by many intellectuals. The argument that intellectuals should not be politically involved, does not mean as frequently understood, that they should avoid analysing political problems. The freedom of the intellectual in the abstract is an ideal and, in actuality, is a relative situation dependent upon the framework of the society, generally epitomized in the state system.

The state comes more clearly into focus as the expression of power in societies moving towards representative forms, industrial technology, and sustained by nationalist ideologies. What is more significant is that in such situations the state takes on a monolithic aspect, which in earlier times had been more diffused. Militant nationalism and populism whether they select race, religion, or caste as their ideological avenue will attempt to use the state as their agent. The intellectual has to decide quite consciously as to how he will relate to the state as participant or supporter or opponent. The role of observer, more often than not, is a euphemism for the first two categories. Alternative systems can only be effective if they are powerful or if there is the feasibility of building an alternative society. The freedom of the intellectual essentially lies in his right to be critical of authority, if need be, to suggest changes without the fear of suffering for his non-conformity.

It is rightly argued that militant nationalism is likely to present the most serious threat to the free and unfettered pursuit of ideas. It becomes necessary therefore to be aware of the dimensions and forms of militant nationalism. The distinction between nationalism and militant nationalism needs constant emphasis. The former expresses itself in the focus on development and the prevention of intervention—whether internal or foreign—of a kind which may be seen as inimical to development. Militant nationalism expresses itself as national chauvinism. It not only appeals to emotion alone but denies attempts at rational explanation. The diffusion of knowledge is seen essentially as a catechism in which questions and answers are pre-ordained and vetted by those in authority.

Militant nationalism inevitably makes an appeal to tradition. But this raises the more fundamental questions of the identification of the former as well as those aspects of the latter to which the appeal is being made; the legitimacy of the shape which is being given to tradition by militant nationalism and the reason for this. These are questions with political implications and are therefore often skirted around. Cultural nationalism, particularly in a colonial context, treats tradition as a holistic and sacred entity. This treatment requires to be explored.

In the construction of intellectual traditions there is a continual interplay between those who opt out of the system for whatever reason, and the attempts of the intellectual establishment to accommodate such dissent to suit its own needs should the dissent become too powerful. In India, the intellectual context has been discussed with little meaningful reference to this interplay. It is assumed that the intellectual tradition has functioned like a sponge, mopping up everything. For example, what is often defined as the Hindu tradition is the syncretic amalgam of nineteenth century social reformers and Indologists who maintained that its growth was a continuous process of the new accreting onto the old. They emphasized continuity, tolerance, powers of absorption and assimilation, since these were relevant to the particular problems of nationalism in nineteenth century India. Yet the most powerful thrust of at least one facet of the Hindu tradition—in Bhakti—is characterized by the discarding of the old, as and where necessary.

It has been argued that sectarian conflict, heterodoxy, and protest are alien to the broader Indian tradition in spite of the many occasions in the past when precisely such forms of dissent have been prevalent. That they are frequently not recognized by modern scholars may be due to the fact that, as in many other similar societies, such activities were often manifest in the garb of religious movements. Sectarian rivalries and conflicts, sometimes of a violent kind, often carry social and political dimensions which scholars have so far tended to ignore—acrimonious debates on theories of knowledge were not devoid of a social context. The detailed organization and administration of individual religious sects and their properties did impinge on political requirements and associations. The containment of dissent either took the form of dissenters opting out into an alternative system such as ascetic groups or monastic orders where the impact of their dissent would depend on the power of the alternative system; or was impounded by social barriers which acted as obstacles to the diffusion of dissent as in a variety of caste taboos reducing the potential of inter-caste association.

There was also, as in many other societies, the system of modifying and absorbing some aspects of dissent which in turn changed certain trends in the intellectual establishment. The latter rarely confesses to radical change in any society and by accepting its unchanging continuity in the Indian past, the dimension of change has been overlooked. There was and continues to be a general hesitation of an analytical exegesis into the Indian intellectual tradition except at the level of interpreting it in a nationalist context. By treating dissent as somehow un-Indian, it is sought to be negated. The few modern scholars who have pointed to the existence of intellectual tensions, conflicts, protests in the past have either been ignored or have been, with few exceptions, dismissed as being politically motivated.

One of the negative effects of nationalism is that it debars critical self-analysis at the national level. Popular descriptions of those that attempt this calls them alienated or disloyal. The exclusiveness and suspicion engendered by exaggerated nationalism has of course been known to take very perverse forms, such as fascism. In the tensions of underdevelopment such forms can become more imminent, and in this situation, the critics of militant nationalism are attacked as distorters and frauds. The attack is never at an intellectual level but is essentially an emotional assault.

Inevitably, it is the social sciences which are the largest victims of this kind of attack. The ideology of militant nationalism, since it lacks an intellectual base, makes no concession to countercultures or dissent. It is by its very nature impervious to modifications or change, or even to analyses. The accommodation of the counterculture in the intellectual establishment was and is a tried method of containing protest and rebellion. What is accommodated has however its own significance and needs to be recognized, as does the point at which the accommodation occurs. That which has acquired power is accommodated and this happens prior to a situation of confrontation bordering on revolt. The attempt of the intellectual establishment is to concentrate and centralize patronage which not only gives it flexibility of manipulation but also more power to soak in dissidence when necessary. The more resilient a system, the greater its ability to discard the redundant, incorporate the new, and adjust to change at the right time.

The state as the agency which works this system has become increasingly perceptible in recent decades. Nationalism and democracy introduce the impersonal system of the representatives of society, where, in theory, the inequities of the earlier system are sought to be overcome. The ideological and 'real-life' constraints on a democratic system need far more attention than they are generally given. In a sense, Max Weber's fears regarding the impact of the 'bureaucratic system' have been borne out.

Without taking the extreme anarchist position of the French nouveaux philosophes and arguing that the state is a Gulag of the forced labour camps, and is everywhere and has to be countered, one has to concede that the presence of the state is overpowering. Not only does Louis Althusser give it the status almost of *the* superstructure but even Antonio Gramsci's concept of hegemony underlines the role of the state. The mushroom growth of studies on fascism and dictatorial systems in the past few decades is an indication of interest in the functions of the state. This is not merely a concern with the politics of the twentieth and twenty-first centuries but the realization that the state is the new patron and can dominate intellectual life.

From the point of view of the acquisition and dissemination of knowledge, the involvement of the state appears almost unavoidable in contemporary times. Any area of research, no matter how remote or esoteric, requires the intermeshing of information from various channels of knowledge and the need for communication between these channels, and at some levels the need for coordination. With increasing specialization, the function of communication and coordination becomes the pivot in the growth of knowledge. Individuals in institutions can coordinate up to a limited point. But in a network of laboratories, computers and the fast flow of data, it is very often the state and corporate offices which can perform this function efficiently.

Backyard discoveries are no longer the backbone of science since even the simplest observation has to undergo complicated application and testing before it can be accepted as an innovation in knowledge. A lifetime of laborious labour can be saved by using sophisticated facilities as has been demonstrated recently in the work on the Harappan script. The gentleman scholar working quietly in his private library is an image of the past since fundamental research today requires a well-equipped library cutting across many disciplines. The possible exception may be a literary composition.

In the sciences, the laboratory is a sine qua non of research. In the social sciences, possibly a brilliant insight based on observation and the inter-connection of ideas may still result in a breakthrough in knowledge; but once again the occasional brilliant insight is no longer enough to sustain a body of knowledge or build an intellectual tradition. The more mundane process of testing such insights and refining the quality of generalization is equally important. The latter cannot be done in isolation and without data.

Part of the problem of the low quality of the general academic level at Indian universities is that the facilities for research are inadequately funded or inappropriately utilized and are the first victims of budget cuts. There is a persistent belief that research rises like Venus from the sea, unaided, out of the shell of the human brain. It does, but not unaided. Who is to provide the laboratories and the libraries? The state, a private endowment, temple funds, or party funds? The crisis of the relationship between the academic intellectual and the state arises both out of the changing political forms whereby the state is assuming more and more power as well as the change in the nature and communication of knowledge.

The academic intellectual has a choice of action. He or she can work towards a change in the application of knowledge by attempting to reorient the technological basis of society. This is often talked about but it frequently remains a catchphrase for the shrewd politician, a slogan for the anarchist, and a mystic dream for the idealist. As an exercise it would be worth taking a specific area and working out the methods and implications of such a change at the empirical level. Such an exercise would either convince the disbelievers or silence the supporters.

Any purposeful action in this direction would require a considered application of modern knowledge in improving the existing technology. The emphasis then is not on the discarding of modern knowledge but on changing the perspective and areas of application. This is very different from the slogans thrown by politicians at intellectuals demanding either a back-to-the-village movement or the claim that advanced modern technology was known to our ancestors. Therefore, it merely has to be revived. This attitude is suited to the anti-intellectualism of militant nationalism and populist politics. The reordering of the application of modern knowledge could be one agency by which the control of the state as patron could be reduced.

Such a reordering is crucially necessary at this stage where the unending repetition of identical institutions calling themselves universities have in some cases almost reached a point of redundancy so far as the furtherance of knowledge is concerned, or indeed even as training grounds for skilled professionals. The reordering of what constitutes a body of knowledge is as apposite as the reordering of the institutions. So much dead wood is carried by so many universities that this in itself constitutes a huge financial waste. The pruning of a body of knowledge is not to be confused with stripping knowledge down to a packet of received information—as so many governmental agencies would like it to be. The purposeful pruning of knowledge requires centres of innovative thought or at least the encouragement of innovative thought, and the ploughing-in of advances in knowledge at every level of the educational system.

Given the constraints of the mechanism of the state, the intellectual can try and assert his role in a more forceful manner. One aspect of this would be an attempt to reduce to a minimum the role of the state as the coordinator of intellectual and academic activity. This would require giving substance to what is now regarded as innovation, although it should be foundational to the functioning of a university; developing the university community as a *community* and not as a hierarchical structure of vice-chancellor et al., faculty, and students; in effect, curtailing the powers of the administrative element to routine function and strengthening the role of the intellectual component in both faculty and students and their interaction; the insistence that the university community and not the hierarchy of authority within the university be the final arbiter of academic problems; guarding university appointments from becoming patronage points for vice-chancellors and ministers; upholding and supporting true autonomy of autonomous institutions even where they are financed by government; ensuring that the University Grants Commission (UGC) does not become subservient to government; working towards a more flexible university system with a variety of institutions as, for example, some research oriented, some privately financed, where the governing is in the hands of the university community and not the patrons; the insistence on more direct communication between academics in various universities; the possibilities of a visiting appointment in a university other than the one to which a regular appointment is held, which would give greater independence to the academic and disallow the university administration from controlling the calculation of salaries and pensions without basing these on the norms and rules that change from time to time; and other means of preventing a monopoly of the state over the work of academic intellectuals.

Even the autonomy of the academic institution is not a sufficient safeguard. Administrative hierarchies in institutions of higher education and research frequently abrogate to themselves the powers of the state and adopt a 'more-government-than-government' attitude. The autonomy of the individual academic has to be sustained and this can be strengthened only by academic colleagues. The assessors of the work of the academic are his or her colleagues—particularly those in the same discipline and area of work—and not the government. The community of academics are the arbiters of his professional work and he is professionally accountable to them.

An assertion of the academics' absolute right to their own decisions in matters intellectual is long overdue. The plea that education has dimensions other than the academic has not resulted in what was being aimed at, namely, a development-based educational system, but in the subservience of the academic to the bureaucrat and the politician. The realization of this subservience was seen more forcefully in the heightened consciousness regarding various 'freedoms' subsequent to the ending of the Emergency in 1977. What were earlier echoes of the curtailment of academic freedom are now being feared given their enforcement. What are described as the routine decisions of the bureaucrats and the politicians on academic matters are now tied to the power factors that have entered the handling of such matters. It is startling to find the minister for education making a policy statement for which he or she is professionally unequipped, that academics are not free to accept invitations to conferences and seminars, or temporary positions from institutions outside India, without a clearance from the government.

The restrictions that were being mooted during the Emergency and during the tenure of other authoritarian regimes were sought to be justified on grounds of 'national interests'. It is assumed that the government alone is the arbiter of national interests and this is an assumption which any free society must question. If 'national interests' in this context are the crucial reason as has been made out, then they must be clearly defined and fully discussed in public. National interests can vary from government to government in time. Recourse to 'national interests' carries its own dangers since the same justification can be given for a variety of bans, prohibitions and restrictions on syllabi, publications, and other academic activities. Ultimately, the choice should rest with the academic as a free citizen to question 'national interests' if he or she so choses, as could any other citizen.

These two aspects, namely, guarding against unauthorized state interference and a conscious attempt to build networks of communication with colleagues, would provide a modicum of independence and perhaps dull the edge of Gramsci's scathing criticism of the function of the intellectual as the 'deputy' of the dominant group. Patronage is not a one-way process. A distinction has to be made between enabling and controlling. It succeeds in controlling if there is a group willing to be subservient. If the nature of modern knowledge is such that it has to be dependent on the patronage of the state, the state in itself and in its methods of functioning is equally dependent on the expertise derived from modern knowledge in various fields, and it would be as well for the patron to be reminded from time to time of its dependence on the client. The use of the terms 'patron' and 'client' is deceptive as it hides the dependence of the state on the intellectual whether it be at the seemingly simple level of the extension of literacy or at the far more complex level of highly specialized expertise, or even for that matter that governments have sometimes to seek legitimacy from intellectuals, whether academic or others.

To abstain from accepting state finance would be a futile exercise in a situation where the only substantial source of finance for academic work is the state and where state finance implicitly furthers its own priorities of demands. But this should not be allowed to corrode the independence of the academic since his status as an intellectual comes from the quality of his work. There are and can be, only a few genuine 'opters-out' these days, those whose independence takes the form of a refusal to be included in the network of jobs and the 'perks' of the system and those whose eccentricities are essential to their being. Such opting out requires either the negation of material comforts or the economic support of institutions which can sustain a parallel system or, ultimately, considerable personal wealth. All the more reason then that those who are using the system should refrain from indulging in the sub-infeudation of patronage which eventually can only lead to the erosion of academic independence.

This dependence of the state on the intellectuals is also what gives the intellectual a freedom of action. The intellectual's response to the state is ultimately a matter of individual choice, social constraints notwithstanding. In periods of crisis, it is often not the social constraints which act as a lever, but the consequences of the choice. The experiences of totalitarianism in the modern era have demonstrated that there is in every situation scope for such a choice. This dependence also permits the intellectuals to mobilize themselves, and if need be, as commentators or critics of political action in more than just a neutral sense.

The pressures of state and society as reflected in hierarchical structures cannot be wished away or legislated away. Such changes are slow in coming and require a reordering of social functioning. But, with even a minimal removal of pressure, the fear of intellectual experimentation and speculation might be reduced as also the dull repetition of clichéd knowledge which is sometimes mistaken for intellectual activity. In this context links with centres of excellence outside India can help diffuse some of the pressures within the country, as, indeed, the reverse has also been the case on occasion. The portmanteau of 'Oriental Studies' was often an adjunct of colonial interests and foreign policy in Europe, the Soviet Union, and United States. The recasting of these studies or their continuation when reclassified in contemporary terms, was largely due to political changes in and among both societies, the erstwhile colonized and the colonizer.

But, admittedly, the lifting of pressures through these means is marginal. As an aspect of growing internationalism, the links among scholars in various countries will continue. This carries the danger of imported creativity and subservience to the affluent, but it also carries—at the level of research—the possibilities of communication through channels other than governmental, and to that extent the strengthening of the independence of the academic intellectual. Beyond a limited point one cannot talk about national research and foreign research but one can refer to the ideological underpinnings of both national and foreign researchers in a particular field.

However, the use of these contacts is circumscribed since they can be discontinued by the state if it so desires. For instance, the demand that academics have to get 'political clearance' from the government before they can leave the country even for the short duration of a specialized conference, does make a mockery of international contacts. Where individual academics have been stopped from doing research in centres outside India because political clearance was denied, as happened to some of us not so long ago, indicates that for those in positions of authority the Emergency has not ended.

Ultimately, whether the intellectual is working towards changing society or diversifying the mechanisms of knowledge, much of his action revolves around his political decisions. Here the pull of social background, the availability of access to ideas, and the race for patronage will come into play. If there is more than just tinkering involved it needs a political perspective—political in the sense not of small-time manoeuvres for local advantages but of an awareness of the given situation and the consciousness of a direction of change. And this often determines the effectiveness of individual choice. A distinction must be made between politics per se and a comprehension of the political implications and uses of knowledge.

An equally important aspect of communication is not only communication among intellectuals but between them and the interested wider audience. The intellectual's concern with the application of his discoveries and research should be to ensure not only that they are not abused but also that the authentic results reach the wider audience. If the intellectual tends his academic garden and is unconcerned with the wider perspectives of his discipline he is described as failing in his social responsibility. If he relates his work to contemporary problems he is described as being 'politically' motivated.

Perhaps the dichotomy can be lessened by suggesting that the academic intellectual often uses two levels of articulation, that of 'pure' research and that of the wider generalization. Both are equally motivated but it is argued that the motivation can be more easily contained by the methodology of the discipline at the former level and some concession to motivation is generally conceded at the latter. It is at the latter level that the application of knowledge has to be carefully watched by academics. The distinction between the two levels is however slippery.

A confusion between the two in part accounts for some of the intellectual shoddiness of much of what is often published in India these days as research. There are academics for whom the profession is merely a job, carrying little interest beyond the wage it earns and a minimum of intellectual concern. Such academic material easily succumbs to political pressures, as for example, through governing bodies of private colleges and to populist opinion, as in the indiscriminate rush to have politicians inaugurate seminars on subjects about which they know nothing. All this tends to confuse the meaning of political motivation.

As academic intellectuals we derive a certain satisfaction from believing that we are detached from politics. Yet, we all reflect a political perception in our intellectual attitudes and it is this perception that we should admit to. In the past, liberalism has softened the political edges of decisions and given them the contours of seemingly pure intellectual actions.

In a liberal ethos the use of state patronage was seen as acceptable, provided it did not impinge on intellectual independence. There was a complacency about guarding against state interference in the more fundamental principles of academic freedom. It was taken for granted that in a liberal regime there is a flexibility in the relations between government and intellectuals which does not require the imposition of rigid restrictions or careful vigilance. With the challenge to liberalism which militant nationalism poses, confrontations may result in sharper dissent, which one hopes will heighten the consciousness of the need for dissent and alternative systems, as also the need among academics to protect the freedom of the academic intellectual. A clash between the emotive and populist articulations of militant nationalism and the search for analytical explanation may provide the lever to intellectual effort in raising it out of its complacency.

18

SEARCHING FOR THE PUBLIC INTELLECTUAL*

SPEAKING ABOUT THE PUBLIC INTELLECTUAL in the India of today is problematic. Some of the spoken and written articulations of intellectuals get eased out of the requirements of current thought. Some intellectuals are jailed and forcibly silenced, others are fearful of the consequences of speaking freely so are hesitant to speak at all. Yet some will have to speak up and speak freely just to keep society alive.

I was thinking the other day that in the current spate of writing memoirs, had Nikhil Chakravartty written his, the TV channels would have exploded. He could not have been silenced. This essay evokes the many like him who contributed to the making of modern India.

Nikhil respected intellectual and academic opinion about public matters. He provided space to those who questioned the nature of the interdependence of society and politics. Today that space has shrunk and the intellectual parameters have narrowed considerably. Those in authority and those influencing public opinion have less respect for the public intellectual now than was so before. Why this is so, is a subject that would have interested Nikhil. It becomes pertinent where there is a concern with the kind of society we want and why we want it.

To begin with one must be clear about the implications of the

---

*An earlier version of this essay was first published in 2015.

presence of public intellectuals. Had there earlier been any doubts about this, these have now been set aside, with the dismissal of the citizen being allowed to express a free opinion on public matters. As a historian I cannot help but instinctively go back in time, and mention a few persons from the European past associated with the kind of thinking that in modern times gave rise to the public intellectual, and some from the Indian tradition who played a similar role. There is a connection between the two, but they are also parallel in many ways. They are both antecedents to what could be the role of public intellectuals in current times, and why there should be a greater visibility of such persons in our society today.

Public intellectuals frequently concern themselves with issues related to human rights and to the functioning of society such that it ensures the primacy of social justice. These issues cover an immense span. I shall choose a couple from among them, those that I think have priority. One is the question of what we regard as authority—whether it be religion, the state or anything else, in accordance with the issue under discussion, and how we assess the choice. The second is how we draw upon knowledge and the use to which it is put. We must expect for instance, that new knowledge opposes existing orthodoxies or well-established authorities. How do we handle the opposition? This hinges on the primacy of reasoned, logical argument, in explaining the world around us as well as its past. In emphasizing the rational I am not expunging imagination as a process of thought, but the distinction should not be ignored.

Such concerns are not recent. They go back to antiquity and were addressed many centuries ago. I shall mention a few people from the past whose thinking laid the foundation for our right in the present to ask questions from those who are shaping our society. In earlier times the questions emerged largely from rational argument and logical thinking, but tempered by recognition of the human condition. Their answers did not foreclose the imagined future of a better society on earth, and did not require us to wait for heaven, or the next birth. Europe claims a tradition of such thinking. And its presence in Indian thought is more often dismissed. But I would contest this dismissal. Societies invariably have to allow the questioning of orthodoxy and authority, at least at challenging moments, or else they rapidly become moribund.

To turn to the European past. The forerunners of the public intellectual indulged in philosophical questioning, but this thinking also penetrated the political sphere and was reflected in suggested social action. Such persons claimed the right to critique authority even if on occasion they had to suffer for it, as did Socrates. The Athenian Greeks objected to his denying the existence of deities and to his criticism of the methods of justice in Athens. For this he was condemned to drink poison. This does not speak well of the ancient Greeks!

However, an important strand of European thinking traces itself back to the Socratic method of the fifth century BC. A statement was subjected to many questions, and was prised apart to observe the interconnections of its component parts. These could then be linked causally in a hypothesis and tested. A proposition counterposed by its opposite could lead to a dialectical form of debate. The Roman orator Cicero, of the first century BC, who exposed the corruption of some Roman governors, claimed the right to question whatever he thought needed to be questioned, and used his legal brilliance to do so.

In the second millennium AD, the Catholic Church wielded power over kings. This power was subsequently questioned. It was one of the issues that stoked European thought in later centuries into the movement known as the Enlightenment. Philosophers, with whose names we are familiar—Locke, Hume, Voltaire, Montesquieu, Diderot, Rousseau, and others—began questioning conventional knowledge and practice. There were disagreements among them and with others, but by and large their questions were conceded because they drew on critical reasoning. This brought them together, apart from their common challenge to the moral authority of the Catholic Church, especially in matters concerning what we would today call civil society. The latter was now seen as constituted of essentially secular institutions, some run by the state. Religious exclusiveness and intolerance were viewed as backward. Progress, it was argued, lay in inclusiveness and the tolerance of differences.

It was not because of wanting to oppose religion per se that the Church was criticized but because of opposition to the hold that formal religion had on the institutions of society—the family, education, governance, and justice. The divine sanction of these institutions was rejected. Thus, the source of authority for governance was said to be a social contract among people. Apart from other things an emphasis on reasoned analysis rather than on quoting faith, made it easier to locate the mainsprings of social functioning, and to suggest changes in society where necessary.

However, the public intellectual, as distinct from philosophers, is said to have emerged as a recognizable category in the nineteenth century, linked to what has been called the Dreyfus Affair. A Jewish captain in the French army, Dreyfus was wrongly imprisoned, charged with leaking secrets to the Germans. Those opposing this action argued that the general staff of the army, in league with the politicians, had unjustly punished Dreyfus. This accusation written by Émile Zola carried the support of a large number of writers, artists, and academicians, all of whom jointly came to be called 'intellectuals'. Eventually an enquiry, divorced from an emotional anti-Semitism, declared Dreyfus innocent and reinstated him. The meaning of 'intellectual' crystallized around the notion that such a person need not be a scholar but had to be someone who had a recognized professional stature, and who sought explanations for public actions from those in authority, even if such explanations required critiquing authority and power.

Such questions come more easily if there is a critical analysis of the intellectual tradition of the society. Basing arguments on accepted modes of reasoning involves verifying and analysing the evidence, even if the historical context changes the mode of questioning. Incidentally, this method is now basic not only to the sciences but also to the social sciences, providing intelligible explanations of social and political institutions and activities. Unfortunately, it is not always appreciated when applied to historical research with conventional views being questioned and the increasing attempt to replace history by an imagined past.

The notion of rational argument over the last two centuries has, however, faced criticism. Its centrality was questioned in the statement that the premium on rationality cannot provide complete explanations, and that all explanations—rational or otherwise—are equally viable. Critiques based on rational thought could be diverse depending on the evidence and the logic inherent in causal explanation. However, although the idiom of critical reasoning may differ in changing historical contexts, critical reasoning itself can and does continue.

It is worth remembering that many of the roots of modern thinking, such as liberal values and democracy, by which we describe ourselves as not being medieval or feudal, go back to these debates among philosophers and others. Nor were the debates confined to Europe since some of these ideas met with confirmation or rejection when they arrived in other parts of the world, initially riding on the back of colonialism.

Let me turn now to the Indian tradition and randomly refer to a few persons that challenged existing ideas and practices and who advocated reasoned and logical explanations for change. We have been so implanted with the theory that our ancestors had no use for rationality as an avenue to knowledge that we tend to ignore our heritage of rational thought.

The Indian philosopher who encouraged questions and explored causality and rational explanations was a close contemporary of Socrates in the fifth century BC, although they lived continents apart and had no links. I am referring to the Buddha. The latter fortunately did not have to drink poison, but his teaching was strongly opposed by early Brahmanical orthodoxy. It was described as delusional and misleading. This was one among many other reasons why Buddhism slowly got edged out of India. It went into neighbouring lands where it flourished, and in some places evolved its own orthodoxy.

One of the most fascinating aspects of the history of ideas is the diverse ways in which societies explain their evolving structures. When asked about the origin of government, the Buddha explained that at the beginning of time there was a pristine utopia where everyone was equal and had equal access to all resources. The first change came when families were demarcated and became the units of society. Subsequent to this came claims to ownership of land as private property. These changes resulted in confusion and conflict. So eventually people came together and elected from among themselves one person—the mahasammat, the great elect—to govern them and provide them with laws that annulled the chaos. It was effectively a social contract. Let me hastily add, tongue in cheek, of course, that neither Jean-Jacques Rousseau nor Friedrich Engels had read the Buddhist texts!

This Buddhist explanation contradicts the many Brahmanical versions. In these the story involves the gods and demons at war, and since the gods were faring badly, they appealed to the great god Prajapati for help. In some versions he appointed his son, Indra, to lead the gods to victory—in which action lie the roots of governance. Appeal to deities and divine sanction is essential and it colours the attitude to authority. The Buddha's notion of the 'great elected one' is in some ways the reverse of the king—who was divinely appointed, concentrating power in himself. The assumptions in the two myths differ.

When religion is referred to in these early texts there is, of course, no mention of Hinduism—a term invented much later. The multiple sects that constituted Indian religion are referred to by their individual names. When speaking generally they tend to get assigned to one of the two streams: Brahmana—associated with Brahmanical belief, or Shramana—representing Buddhist and Jaina teaching. This is the form in which the religions are mentioned for over a thousand years, from the edicts of Ashoka in the third century BC to Al-Biruni's account of India in the eleventh century AD. As noted earlier, Patanjali compared the relationship of the two to that of the snake and the mongoose. Clearly the debates could be virulent, as happens in societies where some believe unquestioningly in what they are told, but others raise questions.

And then there were the Charvakas also called the Lokayatas. They were opposed to most philosophical schools as they adhered to a materialistic explanation of life, making virtually no concession to other ways of thinking. No text of theirs has survived, but references to them keep cropping up, sometimes unexpectedly, in various nooks and crannies of known texts. The Buddha compares the arguments of some of these sects with 'the wriggling of an eel'.

At the turn of the Christian era, when Buddhism had the patronage of royalty, traders, landowners as well as popular support, important Brahmanical texts registered sharp opposition to the Shramanas describing them as heretics, referring to them as nastika—non-believers. From the Brahmanical perspective, the Shramanas, Charvakas, Ajivikas, atheists, materialists, and rationalists, were all one category—nastikas, or in some instances they are labelled as mlecchas. And this because they questioned the existence of deity, and therefore also of the Vedas as divinely revealed; of the rules of caste practices; of the existence of the atman (soul); and their views on karma varied as some rejected the idea altogether. (I am reminded of the followers of Hindutva in our times for whom anyone and everyone who does not support them, are all put into one category and called Marxists! Interestingly, I am told that Muslim religious fundamentalists in India have also starting putting liberal Muslims who oppose the orthodoxy into one category, and are also calling them Marxists.)

The *Manu Dharmashastra* is almost paranoid about the

heretics, calling them atheists and preachers of false doctrines. They are said to be like diseased men and are a source of tamas—the condition of darkness. It was in some ways a time of trouble for the orthodoxy, given that some dominant schools of philosophy were striated with degrees of atheism. But that is what makes it an intellectually exciting time.

Wherever the heretics had a popular following, the attack on them became stronger. The Vishnu Purana, of the early centuries AD, is replete with negative references to a person called mayamoha and his followers. Delusion and deception, as the term mayamoha implies, are characteristic of the group. Mayamoha collects all the evil ones—the asuras and daityas—and converts them to his way of thinking. Some of their practices point to their being Buddhists and Jainas: such as wearing red robes, removing their hair, not observing rituals, and living off alms. Discourse with them is not permitted, since such discourse is declared polluting. A record of such a dialogue would have been fascinating, but only brief references survive.

The Charvakas continued to be part of the landscape even if not always directly visible. Shankaracharya in the ninth century AD refers to their theory of the primacy of matter over spirit. And the Sarvadarshana-sanghraha, a discussion on major philosophical schools put together in the fourteenth century by Madhavacharya, begins with a lengthy discussion on the viability of Charvaka thinking. Although he finally rejects it, he nevertheless discusses it at some length. If the Charvaka thinking had been of no consequence, it could as well have been ignored. This of course, did happen later in the world of nineteenth century colonial scholarship, when some colonial writers argued that rational thought was absent from Indian civilization and was one of the causes of Indian backwardness. This argument although unacceptable to nationalist thinking was not confronted in any significant way by Indian scholars. Those that ask questions are anathema to any kind of autocratic authority. Similarly, those trying to build a single national identity based solely on Hinduism would not have conceded the significance of teachings that contradicted the Brahmanical.

The heretics were dismissed by the orthodox. However, some of their ideas and other similar ideas were explored in philosophical schools of the early centuries AD. At the scholarly level, discussions among learned Brahmanas and Buddhists, gave rise to various impressive philosophical schools. Logic and methods of reasoning were sharpened, as also other methods of thought more sympathetic to idealistic philosophy. The major logicians at this point were interestingly largely Buddhist, such as Nagarjuna, Vasubandhu, Dignaga, and Dharmakirti, some of whom had been born Brahmanas and educated accordingly but preferred to be Buddhists. They teased out the ideas, and especially more so when discussing the nuances of atheism. Views were not uniform and were widely debated, the argument sometimes taking an almost dialectical form.

What would have been of much intellectual significance but which is unfortunately difficult to locate, are conversations between philosophers using critical reasoning with astronomers or mathematicians, even more closely allied to rational thought. Aryabhatta on the basis of mathematical calculation argued that the earth went round the sun. This theory preceded that of Copernicus and of Galileo by a millennium. In Europe the potential of these ideas was feared by Catholic orthodoxy as undermining the Bible and therefore also the control of the Church on society. Galileo had to recant.

In India there was a debate among astronomers on the heliocentric model, but its wider implications seem to have been bypassed, possibly because there was no Catholic Church. But if I may suggest another reason—adopting the heliocentric system would perhaps have upset some astrological calculations. Astrology was one mechanism by which royal power was controlled by religious orthodoxy. Old knowledge therefore continued unshaken in most places. Indian theories of mathematics and astronomy expanded creatively in their own space, but ironically became more influential when taken to Baghdad, the then centre of protoscience.

In India meanwhile, other sects provided an ambience in which similar questions were being raised. Scholars questioned beliefs and practices upheld by religious authorities and by those who governed; or they questioned other orthodoxies, other than the Brahmanical. Some among them were women, such as Andal, Akka Mahadevi, Lalla, and Mira. They flouted caste norms, were listened to attentively by people at large, and were creating their own social codes. But we seldom give enough attention to this aspect of their discourse, focusing as we do largely on religion.

Amir Khusrau was not unknown to the Delhi Sultans. He provides a poetic view of court politics in his *Tughlaqnama* composed in the fourteenth century as a form of traditional history. His study of astronomy, however, underlining a heliocentric universe, distanced him from orthodox Islam, as it implied questioning what were said to be accepted religious truths. And it was his poetry and musical compositions that gave him a status and a following, such that even though he was regarded as a court poet, the sultans and the orthodox thought it better not to antagonize him. His mentor and friend, Nizamuddin Auliya, a Sufi of the Chishti order, kept his distance from the sultans and made a point of asserting the distance.

A few centuries later Ekanath in Maharashtra also questioned the control exercised by formal religion. His versions of the Bhagavata Purana and of the Ramayana defined his Brahmanical scholarship. This did not stop him from questioning the viability of the social order and caste practices.

Not everyone who was teaching a new form of worship was questioning authority, but where they were, this has to be recognized by us. We have hesitated to do this since the form in which social commentary occurs in earlier times is unfamiliar to us. We tend to brush aside the views of such people on matters other than those referring to belief and worship, forgetting that religious belief does make the claim to be all encompassing, and to speak on all aspects of life. Therefore even those who were primarily religious teachers did have views on society and social values. These views are of considerable interest and especially at moments in history when religious sects were incorporating ideas from a wide range of sources.

Turning to modern times, the ideology of nationalism made attempts to reorder society. Nationalism may have opposed colonialism but was not always averse to appropriating theories from colonial scholarship. Social reform movements pertaining to upper-caste Hinduism, such as the Brahmo Samaj, Prarthana Samaj, and Arya Samaj, suggested new forms of Hindu religious organization and the role of caste. We are all familiar with Raja Rammohun Roy and socio-religious reform, but so little is said about his exact contemporary in Tanjore—Serfoji II, a minor Maratha raja. He questioned orthodoxy by focusing on the content of education. His reading of Enlightenment authors convinced him that knowledge was based on processes of reasoning and that these were taught through education. The schools he established were intended for this purpose, as were the books and objects that he collected for the Sarasvati Mahal Library.

Although these movements were not intended to critically question intellectual traditions, they did occasionally scrape the surface. Despite the centrality of caste hierarchies legitimized by religion, the interface between religion and caste was seldom investigated. In the nineteenth century Bal Gangadhar Tilak supported the Aryan foundations of Indian civilization and upper-caste culture, even if, according to him, the Aryans did have to trek all the way from their Arctic homeland to India. But Jyotiba Phule saw the coming of the Aryans as a logical explanation for the oppression of the lower castes. For him the Aryans were Brahmanas that oppressed the indigenous inhabitants who were the Shudras. Tilak extended the accepted view; Phule questioned it to explain existing society. Both readings were historically faulty, but Phule was asking an incisive question.

There were others who were also questioning the legitimacy of caste, and were critical of Brahmanical beliefs. Periyar, or EVR, although not an academic, was known to be as well read, as were his academic colleagues. He was critical of the contradictions in Hindu mythology, which, as a rationalist, he dismissed as fabrications of the Indo-Aryan peoples. He took a strong position in favour of social equality, and more particularly the equality of women.

The people I have mentioned were not public intellectuals in the modern sense. They were among those who questioned the existing reality as a means of attaining an improved society. They were listened to because they were respected in their diverse professions. The point is not the similarity or otherwise of their questions. It is the way in which they reasoned even if the nature of the questions changed in accordance with the issues of the moment. Such questions are not arbitrary. They have to be governed by acknowledged critical reasoning. And people who question, were and are, articulate at moments of significant historical change.

Moments of historical change coincide with the exploration of new ways of ordering society, as has been happening off and on in the Indian past. Now we have more insightful ways of understanding social and economic conditions and how they give a form to society. These connections require exploration. Public intellectuals, playing a discernible role are needed for such explorations: as also, to articulate the traditions of rational thought in our intellectual heritage. This is currently being systematically eroded.

Mainstream anti-colonial Indian nationalism and the emergence of a liberal democracy, aspiring to be secular, made space for the visible presence of the public intellectual. More than a few took on this role especially in the years just after Independence. They were responsible for wide-ranging debates. Later events, be it the Emergency or the genocides of religious communities, heightened our awareness of the need for public intellectuals, if only to speak out and prevent a repetition of such events. We must remind ourselves that Nikhil Chakravartty, Romesh Thapar, George Verghese, and others like them, strongly opposed forms of censorship, and the attempt to silence alternate voices.

Today we have specialists in various professions, but many among them are unconcerned with the world beyond their own specialization. It is sometimes said that they are replacing the public intellectual. But the two are not identical. There are many more academics for instance, than existed before. But it seems that most prefer not to confront authority even if it debars the path of free thought. Is this because they wish to pursue knowledge undisturbed, or because they are ready to discard that knowledge which authority requires them to do?

Much has been written on trying to define the public intellectual. Such a person, it is assumed, should take a position independent of those in power, enabling him or her to question debatable ideas, irrespective of who propagates them. Reasoned critiques are often the essential starting point. The public intellectual has to see himself or herself as a person who is as close to being autonomous as is possible, and more than that, be seen by others as such.

An acknowledged professional status makes it somewhat easier to be autonomous. The public intellectual of today, in addition to being of such a status, has at the same time a concern for what constitute the rights of citizens and particularly on issues of social justice. And further, there is a readiness to raise these matters as public policy.

A justification for the critique is the claim to speak for society and to claim a degree of moral authority. The combination of drawing upon wide professional respect together with a concern for society can sometimes establish the moral authority of a person and ensure public support. This is a conceded qualification and not a tangible one. In the past it was those who had distanced themselves somewhat from society that were believed not to have ulterior motives in the changes they suggested. But this was not always so. Formal affiliation to a political party in our times can inhibit free thinking and prescriptions for action, even if it has the advantage of providing support.

As an attitude of mind, autonomy is more readily expected of the professional specialist or the academic. Such persons, and they are not the only ones, can suggest alternate ways of thinking, even about problems of the larger society. Such thinking emerges from reasoned, logical analyses. Yet academics today are hesitant to defend even the right to make what might be broadly called alternate, if not rational interpretations, however sensitively they may be expressed. This is evident from the ease with which books are banned and pulped, or demands made that they be burned, and syllabuses changed under religious and political pressure, or the intervention of the state. Established publishers are beginning to suffer from a paralysis of the spine. Why do such actions provoke so little reaction among many academics and professionals? The obvious answer, usually given, is that they fear the instigators who are persons with the backing of political authority. Is this the only answer?

Many today comment on the narrowing of the liberal space in the last couple of decades. It was earlier resisted; but now it is upon us again. To question those that represent conventional authority and to demand responsible action, needs to be repeated again and again, especially where it involves a negation of justice. The social media were thought of as a free space and to some extent they were. But people now hesitate to share critical comments on religious activities or on contemporary politics, for fear of action against them. More specifically, when it comes to religious identities and their politics, we witness hate campaigns based on absurd fantasies about specific religions and we no longer question these frontally.

Such questioning means being critical of organizations and institutions that claim a religious intention but use their authority for non-religious purposes. They invoke the rules and regulations of formal religion, sometimes recently invented, in order to legitimize their actions. Their actions may bring murder, rape, and mayhem. Those not associated with such organizations maintain that the values of religion are such that none preach violence. But that is not the issue. Of course, all religions endorse virtuous values. But it is not the values that are under question; it is the beliefs and actions of organizations that act in the name of religion, although not always in conformity with religious values.

We are only too familiar with such organizations that have identified with Hinduism, Islam, and Sikhism and have not hesitated to breed violence and terror. Can the law be brought to bear against those that disrupt the law even if they speak in the name of religion? Although necessary, it is not enough to castigate such actions and rest at that. We have to understand why such actions, supposedly to defend religion, but which are harmful to society, are resorted to and how they can be brought to a close. Do believers identifying with the religion and claiming protection, endorse such actions? And if not, should they not be defending the values of their religion by disassociating themselves from the perpetrators of violence and terror, using their religious identity?

There are many reasons for the decline of the public intellectual. I can only mention some. The most obvious but least conceded are insecurities generated by the neoliberal culture. These have arisen out of the economic boom it was supposed to bring, but which boom has misfired. Jobs have become far more competitive and this adds to existing aggressions and erodes a reliance on human relationships. Almost obscene disparities in wealth further the aggressions. Values are being turned to tinsel with the endorsing of ostentatious display. The ready acceptance of corruption has become normal. Money is the new deity lavishly worshipped among the rich. The rest wait anxiously for the trickle-down. There is a clash between the excitement of having the right to demand equality, but of its being denied because of new versions of caste and money power.

The neoliberal culture and economy cannot be easily changed but its ill-effects can be reduced, provided we are clear that society must be rooted in the rights of the citizen to resources, to welfare and to social justice. This, after all, was the issue at the time of independence when the nation-state was created. I can recall the arguments and debates in the 1960s and 1970s on how to create a society where citizens had equal rights, not just in theory but in actuality. If such discussions are to continue, as they should in a vibrant society, and questions raised, then we have to turn to public intellectuals to bring them to the fore. But beyond that it also needs a public that would regard the asking of such questions as appropriate.

How can we create a public that is aware of what needs to be discussed and why, a public that would respond to questions drawing from critical reasoning? The response does not invariably have to be an affirmation of what is being suggested, but at least alternative ideas can be subjected to discussion and solutions suggested. This assumes for a start, an educated public, and a public that would not only appreciate the role of public intellectuals but also the need for them.

In order to become an educated public, how should we be educating ourselves? The question involves both professionals in various disciplines and many public intellectuals who in part draw their alternative authority from their professional standing. Today there are effectively two sources of educating ourselves. One is the informal indirect visual media as an oral form, and the second is the formal category of educational institutions. The intermediary here is the internet, and like the other two, at present its catchment area does not include the entire society. TV channels, with rare exceptions, imitate each other with panellists playing musical chairs on the channels. Everything but everything is seen in terms of current politics, even where this may be irrelevant. So every discussion is overloaded with representatives of each political party whose propaganda disallows searching debate. Seldom do programmes investigate the reality beyond their statements.

I have begun to wonder whether it is not possible to have an alternate channel on TV, and if this is difficult to finance then even a broadcasting station on radio, one that is not solely concerned with commercial profit? One that encourages exploring alternate ideas and solutions, and goes well beyond the single byte, and draws its inspiration from critical enquiry? How do we finance the voice of those that have more than a momentary interest in society, extending to the next election? And who are thoughtful about its future?

Then there is the other source, that of formal education. This has to be seen at two levels: the content of education and the autonomy of educational institutions. Education is moving out of the hands of educationists and into those of politicians and of political organizations, pretending to be cultural and religious institutions. This makes it crucial to be aware of how politicians today relate to intellectuals—if at all they do so.

Ideally, the essence of learning lies in enabling a person to think in forms that are analytical, logical, and autonomous, not to mention creative. It is only by using the power of reasoning that an educated person can, for instance, be made aware of the fact that knowledge where it takes the form of a technology has a particular context that produces that knowledge and sustains it. It cannot take shape from nothing. Specific technological inventions of the twentieth century can only have been made in that century. They cannot have existed three thousand years earlier without the technical and associated knowledge. Scientific inventions have a long gestation period and historians of science can mark such a period by drawing out the evidence for it. They can observe how the technology and knowledge, that has made the invention possible at a particular point in history, evolved and advanced.

If we are to claim scientific advance in our society then we have to track the role of science in the past, both at the level of knowledge and its application through technology. Instead of claiming the prior existence of twentieth century inventions in ancient India, many thousands of years ago, and which is a thoroughly inappropriate activity, we should be investigating the nature of the knowledge and technology that we actually had, and even more importantly what we did with it. If the Kerala mathematicians discovered calculus in the fifteenth century AD, why was this discovery not used as a method of advancing knowledge?

The first step in education is to provide information of existing knowledge. The next step is to question existing knowledge in order to assess whether there is a need for replacing existing knowledge with new, improved knowledge through the process of learning and research. The educational system today does not even reach the first step in most schools. Some suspect that the acute shortage of schools and the poor condition of those that exist may be deliberate policy, arising from the fear of a citizenry that is not only literate but also educated. Hence the striking neglect of school education in the last half century. We have an absurd situation where there is virtually no preparation even for secondary school, leave alone university, in terms of handling knowledge. Yet, we are rushing to open more universities, IITs, IIMs, and what have you, the focus being on the highest institutions of education, instead of on the schools that should be laying the foundations of an educated citizenry. Inevitably this situation will lead to diluting education to the point of being almost meaningless—in fact to reduce it to the lowest common denominator, what might therefore be called 'LCD education'.

For most young people the methods of thinking that are essential to the nurturing of enquiring minds and those that might resonate with public intellectuals are stymied by the very system of education. One is thankful that there are some who do manage to think independently and creatively despite the system. But they don't add up to the critical mass that we require. Imagine what an energetic, thinking society we would have if the concept of education we adopt were to encourage students to ask questions and be provoked to think independently.

One might ask, what are the issues that could be raised by contemporary public intellectuals? For the underprivileged citizen, in fact the majority of Indians, good governance would require changing the current ways of survival in an anachronistic system clinging to its colonial roots. The unjust distribution of national wealth keeps the poverty line high. Caste and religious priorities still prevail using the same categories as were created by colonial policy. Colonial administration invented majority and minority communities and encouraged the identity politics of religion. These are now treated as permanent categories. They disallow democratic functioning because in a democracy those that make up a majority should change from issue to issue. There are no permanent majorities in a democracy. Reservation in education and employment, if retained on a permanent basis, reiterates these religious and caste identities whatever the marginal benefits may be. The solution actually lies in ordering our society and economy in a different way, such that these colonial identities are set aside and attempts are made at a more equitable distribution of wealth.

The ultimate success of a democracy requires that the society be secular. By this I mean a society that goes beyond the coexistence of all religions; a society whose members have equal social and economic rights as citizens, and can exercise these rights irrespective of their religion; a society that is free from control by religious organizations in the activities related to these rights; a society where there is freedom to belong to any or no religion. Public intellectuals would be involved in explaining where secularization lies and why it is inevitable in a democracy and in defending the secularizing process.

Public intellectuals are not absent in our society, nor are they alien imports. They do have a lineage as I have argued. Historical change requires us to recognize that their role, although not entirely dissimilar to that of earlier intellectuals, nevertheless needs to be extended in our times. Their predecessors added new dimensions to understanding our society. Were they nurtured subconsciously by earlier heterodoxies that explained the human condition through rational and logical argument, and by exercising a secular moral authority over those that controlled society, and were closer to us in time, by negating colonial dominance? Public intellectuals drawing on critical reasoning are the inheritors of this bequest.

I would like to conclude with a long question. It is not that we are bereft of people who think autonomously and can ask relevant questions. But frequently where there should be voices, there is silence. Are we all being co-opted too easily by the comforts of conforming? Are we fearful of the retribution that questioning may and often does bring? Do we need an independent space that would encourage us to think, and to think together?

19

THE PAST OF LANGUAGE*

COMPLICATED RELATIONS TOWARDS ONE ANOTHER are inevitable in complex cultures like those that have taken form in India. These have to be known beyond just their origination. Therefore their history comes into play. Every language has a history and a cultural idiom. The choice of a national language in our times was earlier thought to be determined by its history and by its demography. Today it has to also serve as the medium of communicating up-to-date knowledge which can also be transfused into other languages.

We are faced today with the dilemma of not having a national language—in part because historically this is the first time that we are a single nation-state. Language has always been—the world over—the means of communication within a section of a society, more or less understood by those that form that section. This is not unique to India. The solution does not lie in selecting the language of the demographic majority, nor in going back to that language which is associated with what is taken to be a 'golden age' of the past. The purpose of language is to communicate, both with others and as self-expression. But every language has a history and this surfaces in the discussions on the choice of a national language. Discarding a language means discarding a history and selecting a language means giving its history a status. In most situations many languages vie for this status making for a difficult choice.

Nationalism has fostered many myths: among them the

*An earlier version of this essay was first published in 1965.

frequently accepted one that language is the articulation of the thoughts of a particular race or a particular culture. Yet language did not evolve as the mechanism of expression of either of these two categories and certainly in the twentieth century the distribution of a language does not coincide with the distribution of a particular race or culture. The use of various languages in the post-colonial situation, as for example, English or Spanish in different parts of the world, poses questions. It is true that language is one of the channels through which the content of a culture is expressed; through the use of words (which are its tools) and of concepts (which are its crystallized experiences). But precisely because language communicates experience, it can transcend the boundaries of a particular culture or race.

In periods of physical communication between cultures, the range of experience which a language can articulate is often wider than the actual experience of its culture. There are moments of growth in a language. The vocabulary may remain in closer contact with the narrower culture, but the concepts may have a larger range, leading to the enrichment of the language.

Borrowing is one of the results of contacts between cultures and in language it leads to the introduction of new words and new concepts. The degree of borrowing is often conditioned by the means through which borrowing occurs. The migration of a people or a culture can be an unostentatious way in which words and concepts are borrowed and lent. But conquest is the more dramatic although this has the disadvantage of making the borrowing a very self-conscious process with a variety of political and social undertones. The dominant language is that of the conquerors who become the elite and the language of the conquered becomes the lower language which tends to borrow more from the dominant language more often than vice versa. However, this does rather depend on the conquerors becoming settlers.

Yet in normal circumstances where there is no migration or conquest, the pattern of development in a language is often different.

The spoken language is the more dynamic form of a language (in the social context) than its written form. Consequently, the spoken form can mould and change the written style as it often does. This is a process against which 'purists' and the literati are constantly fighting, the result on occasion being the stultification of a literary style.

At Different Levels

Language is a powerful symbol of solidarity among those who speak the same language: hence its legitimate association with national movements. At this level, language acts as a unifying factor. But language with particular forms can also be the symbol of a sub-group where it is expressive of a primary emotional need of belonging to a small group which 'talks the same language': a need which becomes intensified as social institutions and therefore social associations change. The need for adjusting two varieties of language within the same nation has to be recognized. To impose a uniform language at every level and expect it to function in an unchanging manner is untenable.

The choice between the identity of religion or language was demonstrated in the twentieth century in the history of the subcontinent. In 1947, religious nationalism triggered Partition. In 1970 however, it was a form of linguistic nationalism that split Pakistan into two nations, making religious nationalism subservient to the nationalism of language. The hostility between Bangladesh and India might decline if there was greater sensitivity towards this fact.

Language is the articulation of the experience of a culture. Even within this limited definition it will reflect the growth and attitudes of the culture. Experiences cannot be amputated even if they have been undesirable. They become part of the texture of a culture and are inevitably reflected in the language of that culture.

The above formulations may appear to be self-evident and their spelling out irrelevant to an essay on language, yet it is necessary to do so since one often forgets that they apply as much to Indian languages as anywhere in the world. Languages in India underwent the same general processes of change, development, and stagnation as most languages do elsewhere.

The exact nature of the earliest languages of India are difficult to define. There were the languages of which traces are believed to survive in the Munda-speaking and similar groups. Another linguistic layer probably emerged from the proto-Australoid presence in India and is thought to have provided the base for the Dravidian group of languages. The coming of the Indo-European or Aryan speakers in c. 1500 BC introduced a further distinctive language structure which was to dominate the evolution of languages in the Indo-Gangetic plains. On the northern fringes, in the sub-Himalayan regions, the matrix was Sino-Tibetan. The configuration of language groups tended to broadly follow this geographical pattern almost throughout the course of Indian history, although with some pockets of variation.

Geographical configuration and historical continuity in language groups occurs fairly frequently in India. One of the more remarkable cases is that of the distribution of various Hindi dialects such as Mewari, Khariboli, Kanauji Braj-bhasha, which follow the geographical boundaries of clan societies and later states—the Kuru kingdom, Maurya, northern Panchala kingdom, southern Panchala, and Shurasena, which by the late first millennium BC had their own distinctive differences in dialect. Of these various groups, the two which were to provide the main structure of Indian languages throughout Indian history were the Dravidian and Indo-Aryan. The minor content in terms of vocabulary and concepts came occasionally from these and other languages in the vicinity such as Arabic, Persian, the Central Asian, and finally, the European.

The earliest evidence of a developed language with a possible script is that of Harappa, but the fact of its not having been deciphered does not allow much generalization. The language has clearly to be related to its urban background, which in turn explains the need for a script. If the language was associated with the overseas trade, then a relationship with Elamite is a possibility as has been suggested. But the language may well have been of a largely indigenous growth. (Recent attempts by some enthusiasts to describe it as a kind of proto-Sanskrit stem largely from a desire to provide a Sanskrit and Hindu ethos to all aspects of the Indian past, even pre-history and proto-history!)

Sanskrit

The most important historical language of the Indo-Aryan group was and is Sanskrit. Its oldest form was Vedic Sanskrit which gradually gave way to a variant form from about the first millennium BC. This covers classical Sanskrit and other language systems derived from Sanskrit such as Pali and various regional Prakrits. Somewhat later, a decentralization in sound and form led to the evolution of Apabrahmsha (crooked or broken language). The Sanskrit used in northern India at this time was not a uniform, standardized language, but one which registered regional variations. The mid-centuries AD saw an acceleration in the spread of Sanskrit south of the Vindhyas. The Mauryan imperial system, by bringing almost the entire subcontinent under a single political control in the third century BC, assisted in the migration and settlement of Aryan-speaking peoples in various parts of the subcontinent as is evidenced by the use of Prakrit in the inscriptions of the Mauryan emperor Ashoka scattered across the empire. However, this Prakrit was not uniform and registered differences of dialect in the language of the edicts. Presumably the particular regional dialect was spoken by the lower castes, and of course by women—even of the upper castes.

Sanskrit gradually became the language of higher learning and of administration. Its spread throughout the subcontinent was largely in this form. It became the vehicle of the Brahmanical tradition and essentially the repository of upper-caste life and thought. By extension, it was the language of the court circles and upper castes. The social exclusiveness of Sanskrit was firmly maintained in Brahmanical seminaries and schools which were the main centres of formal education. The Brahmanical control was maintained by the appropriation by Brahmanas of the religious, administrative and educational functions over large areas of Indian life, particularly in the centuries AD.

Prakrit

The more commonly used language with a larger distribution in terms of social groups was Prakrit with its various regional modifications. Those who differed from the Brahmanical tradition used Prakrit, hence the Buddha preached in Magadhi Prakrit. Dramas written in classical Sanskrit used the literary convention where men of high social status used Sanskrit, whereas the women and those deemed to be lesser persons spoke in Prakrit. Clearly Sanskrit had the status of an official language, whereas the use of Prakrit came more readily to those ranked lower in the social scale. The ranking of all categories of women was low and even those of the royal family spoke Prakrit. This makes for an interesting social commentary on attitudes to women in upper caste society.

Inscriptional evidence tends to support this view.* The earliest inscriptions found so far, dating to the third century BC, are in Prakrit. These are the inscriptions of Ashoka clearly intended for the public at large. A few scribbles on potsherds may be a little earlier. That Prakrit was the commonly written language in India is further corroborated by the fact that the inscriptions of Ashoka

*The evidence from inscriptions tends to be more precise than literary evidence from documentary sources, since inscriptions on the basis of epigraphical and palaeographical analysis can be dated.

found in Afghanistan are not in Prakrit but in Greek and Aramaic. These were clearly meant to be read by the large Greek and Persian populations of cities such as Kandahar, who were not using Prakrit.

Elite status

Prakritic forms continued to be used in inscriptions until the early centuries AD. An early Sanskrit inscription is known and is of the second century BC located at Besnagar (near Ujjain), in which a Hinduized Greek declares his adherence to the Vishnu cult. The next important group of Sanskrit inscriptions came interestingly from royalty of Central Asian descent—Scythian, Parthian, and Kushana; the Junagadh inscription of the Shaka satrap Rudradaman, of about AD 150 being a fine composition in classical Sanskrit. The consistent use of Sanskrit by dynasties which were non-Indian in origin would support the contention that Sanskrit was the language of the elite. Significantly, many of the early grammarians and dramatists using Sanskrit came from northern and western India, suggesting that perhaps Sanskrit was patronized to a greater degree in these areas and only gradually came to be accepted in other parts of the subcontinent.

The inscriptions of the Gupta period of approximately the mid-first millennium AD show evidence of the frequent use of classical Sanskrit. In eastern India, there is a gradual transition from Prakrit to Sanskrit during these centuries. In southern India, the mixture of the two continued until the sixth century AD when in the Pallava inscriptions, the tendency to use Sanskrit alone increases. At the same time there were inscriptions in Tamil in South India.

In some parts of Southeast Asia, Sanskrit was superimposed over the existing linguistic systems, where the latter borrowed words from Sanskrit, probably because it came to be used in some royal courts. Again, Sanskrit was essentially a language of the elite.

Regional Growth

The more frequent use of Sanskrit in royal inscriptions, and as a means of intellectual expression from the fifth century AD onwards, did not in any way stultify the development of Prakrit. In fact, from the eighth century, the development of language reflects the overall tendency in the subcontinent of regional growth and loyalties. The regional Prakrits begin to assume distinct identities and gradually take on the characteristics in some areas of what came to be called Apabrahmsha. These encouraged the evolution of the modern regional languages from about the thirteenth century onwards.

South Indian inscriptions of the sixth and subsequent centuries are commonly found in Sanskrit with Tamil taking more and more space over time. Tamil inscriptions were originally written in Brahmi, the script commonly used for all the Indo-Aryan group of languages, though later a Tamil Grantha script was evolved which came to be used in South India. The combination of Sanskrit and Tamil is also reflected in creative literature. But Sanskrit again was used in some places as the language of the court, the Aryanized elite and centres of higher education.

Popular movements such as the Tamil devotional cults used Tamil. A differentiation continued where the more Sanskritized forms of the South Indian languages—Tamil, Telugu, Kannada, and Malayalam—were spoken by the upper castes. Royal grants inscribed in Kannada and Telugu point to the growing importance of these languages before the end of the first millennium AD. The verse composition, *Amuktamalyada*, by Krishna Deva Raya the king of Vijayanagara in the sixteenth century is indicative of the respectability of Telugu. A thirteenth-century inscription provides evidence of a groping movement towards Malayalam.

The growth of regional languages in the northern and western part of the subcontinent emerged from a variety of factors. On the eve of the establishment of the sultanates in 1206 in Delhi and then in the peninsula, regional loyalties were beginning to crystallize into regional cultures, and the languages which were spoken in these areas were deeply intertwined with this development.

The Sultanate Pattern

The Turkish conquest resulted in some social changes both through the upheaval on conquest and through migrations and commercial activities. The caste–class pattern underwent a change and a number of non-Sanskrit speaking people moved up the social scale, taking their language with them. Land grants, so essential a document in a feudal system, came to be recorded both in Sanskrit and the local language. In areas where the Turks were politically powerful, Sanskrit as the language of administration was gradually replaced by Persian. The recording and the recognition of the grant of land was necessary both in court circles and in the records of local administrations.

The Tamil–Sanskrit relationship makes a good comparison. In most matters of largely local interest the regional language was used. For example, the eulogies on memorials to the deeds of heroes, and in connection with sati were in Marathi, Gujarati, etc. Private records, unconnected with official administration, were also in these languages.

In subsequent centuries the extensive use of Persian for official purposes encouraged the use of regional languages in other fields. The Bhakti movement, drawing on an audience of lower castes as well—artisans and cultivators—in its earlier phases, gave a further impetus to the widespread use of local languages. The frequent pilgrimages and fairs in Indian society throughout history have always been a factor of cohesion in local communities, and the association of some aspects of the Bhakti movement with such gatherings (e.g., the cult of Vithoba in Maharashtra) strengthened the relationship between the local community and the language. The popularization of the regional language via the Bhakti movement also resulted in the use of the language for creative literature. The latter began as an offshoot of religious literature but as it became more and more secular and popular, it slowly tended to move further away from Sanskritic forms.

Urdu

With the elite both Hindu and Muslim using Persian in addition to other languages, the interest in Persian increased not just as the language of administration but also as a literary language, with much interest in its literature. One of the most significant developments in the growth of languages during the medieval period was the creation of a new language—Urdu—the camp language, whose structure was mainly of the Indo-Aryan type, but whose vocabulary was largely borrowed from Persian and the regional languages of the area directly under the control of dynasties of Central Asian origin with an admixture of Marathi and Kannada. Dakhni as it was once called grew in the region of Hyderabad and the north-western Deccan and eventually spread over many areas of the subcontinent.

Urdu now became a popular link language in certain areas and its association with urban centres where it was most widely used, gave it its vitality and liberal character which led to its rapid maturity. Not surprisingly, until recent years, most major urban centres anywhere in the subcontinent from Peshawar to Mysore had a large body of Urdu-speaking people. In the Hindi-speaking areas, the relationship between Hindi and Urdu became closely intertwined largely through the use of both and its variants by the socio-religious teachers of the Sufi and Bhakti movements. Urdu has continued to maintain its urban roots, which were strengthened by the adoption of Urdu as the language of the law courts in many parts of northern India. Much of the literature of the social reform movements in the late nineteenth and early twentieth century in the Punjab was in Urdu perhaps because of its urban appeal.

The period of maturity in Marathi was during the seventeenth and eighteenth centuries, when the rise and establishment of Maratha power provided a firm foundation for the language. Urdu spread eastwards through the Sufis and soldiers of fortune, and Bengali was enriched with new words and concepts (as also was Punjabi in a different context). The use of Tamil and Malayalam by Muslims settled in those areas was similar to the situation in Bengal, where the existing regional language was preferred to any other. Both Urdu and Hindi were languages of common usage, but slowly such usage gave rise to a substantial literary turn—as was so with other regional languages.

English

With the declaration of English as the official language in the early nineteenth century, the pattern seemed to repeat itself. The elite gradually became English-educated and there was a gulf between the English-speaking and those who spoke the regional language. The emergent Indian middle-class was bilingual in English and the regional language. Once again, a camp language—Hindustani—began to emerge. Possibly in another hundred years it might have developed into a functional link language, but such a possibility has been terminated by its being officially replaced in present times by a Sanskritized Hindi.

That the Persian and Sanskrit tradition was by now close to static in terms of common usage, seems clear from the fact that the cultural matrix of which English was the communication channel, made little impact on either of these two languages in India. Its impact both direct and indirect was on the regional languages. Indirectly, missionary activity and educational activity led to the translation of new ideas into these languages. The battling of theological concepts and the conflict over new and traditional ideas marked a further phase in their growth. Those who had access to English became bilingual and this was a further source of new experiences which were articulated in translation from one language to another.

The Middle Class and Languages in India

The birth of a completely new social factor on the Indian scene—the middle class—weighed the balance somewhat in favour of using English, partly because it was the language of governance and the language used by the elite, and partly because it was an effective link language. The national movement, particularly its later phase in the twentieth century, righted the balance. In an effort to draw in a mass following, the middle-class-dominated urban national movement had to reach out to the rural masses. This necessitated the use of the regional languages and in turn acted as a revitalizing factor in the growth of the regional languages.

The orthodox religious tradition in India whether Hindu, Buddhist, or Jaina was preserved in Sanskrit, with the latter two also in the associated languages of Pali or Prakrit. The official language during the period from the second to the eighth AD was Sanskrit, strongly associated with learning of all kinds and Puranic Hinduism. The legal literature and administrative literature of the pre-thirteenth century was documented by the Brahmanas and the records carefully preserved: these were all in Sanskrit. It became a symbol of upper-caste status. The heterodox sects such as the Buddhists and the Jainas began by using Prakrit but when the competition from the Hindu sects increased, they adopted Sanskrit. Lower-caste groups when they moved up the social scale, within the confines of Hindu society, they tended to keep to the regional language.

The establishment of the Delhi sultanate and later the Mughal empire introduced important changes. Persian and Turkish became the languages of upper-caste status. But since these were foreign languages, and took a while to come to terms with, it was inevitable that the regional languages and the link language, Urdu, would in effect be more important. Centres of Sanskrit learning continued to flourish but the use of Sanskrit became somewhat marginal and ceremonial. With the introduction of English, Persian was also given the status which Sanskrit now had.

The continuity and evolution of language in India as of now has to be traced through the regional languages and the link languages, and not through Sanskrit alone. Sanskrit served a particular, specialized purpose and as long as it was a living language, it contributed vitality to the Prakrits. But as it slowly stultified it ceased to make any significant contribution to the growth of the regional languages. Arbitrary Sanskritization of the regional languages merely introduces outdated concepts and does not vitalize these languages.

To try and eliminate any concept which is of Persian or English origin, is to try and erase a historical experience and this, whether in human or social psychology, results in warped attitudes. The vitalization must come from the very roots of the actual life of the people born out of the tensions and harmonies within which we live. To inject words into a language is not a difficult process but the same cannot be done with concepts. Concepts cannot even be grafted; they have to grow out of the ethos of a society. To try and provide India with a well-tailored, readymade national language overnight is to attempt not only the impossible but the undesirable. The national language will grow out of the society which we build in the next few decades. If we can make something worthwhile of our nation then we shall in the process also acquire a viable, worthwhile language.

Choosing a national language for India—an ex-colony—inevitably involves a bilingual situation. Formal teaching that widens the contours of the mind has to be in the mother tongue if it is to be effective. This would invariably be the regional language. But there also has to be a language that brings together the many regional languages to unify the nation. A common language is essential as a national language of unification. Here, the adoption of English has many advantages. It has existing roots in Indian education (even if they are declining fast), and where these do not exist, new entrants will be joining at about the same time. English is now the global medium of advanced knowledge and will therefore have to be learnt in any case—as a third language. The burden of three languages will be reduced to two, if English is taught simultaneously with the mother tongue. An English contoured to Indian needs would be advantageous. Therefore, can the solution lie in bilingualism that will ensure reaching out to contemporary knowledge through English, and at the same time be a continuingly meaningful communication with Indian roots through the mother tongue?

We like to think that the history of a language is a simple straightforward history. But we forget that language is the articulation of a culture and reflects the historical changes that all cultures experience. No language is static. All languages change. In the process of change they give rise to new forms of the language—which forms can distance themselves from the original and become new languages. When there is an interface of cultures there are also interfaces among languages. These provide many clues to the history of the cultures from which they emerge.

20

THE SEARCH FOR A SOCIAL ETHIC*

I WROTE THIS ESSAY TOWARDS the end of the twentieth century but it continues to be relevant, with minor modifications, well into the twenty-first. This speaks for a lack of sufficient social change in the essentials of our society. In fact, the visibility of a social ethic has now faded further and has almost become invisible.

During the lifetime of *Seminar*, we noticed the thinning of the social ethic. A major jolt came with the Emergency and attempts were made to bring back the ethic. Nevertheless, its invisibility did not recede as fast as it has done in the recent past. It is striking that what was written decades ago still has relevance—perhaps even more so—in terms of unsolved problems and the unacceptability of the solutions being attempted. Have we in the last few years forsaken the vision of the anti-colonial freedom movement and reconciled ourselves to the backwardness of what pretends to be the carrot of today?

The 1960s saw journals such as *Seminar* and later the *Economic and Political Weekly* assuming a centrality in public discourse. This was not surprising. If one can speak of a paradigm shift in Indian thinking, particularly in the social sciences, it began to be articulated in the 1960s although there were murmurings in the 1950s. The received wisdom of colonial, and to some degree, nationalist, explanations of knowledge began to be questioned and alternative explanations were sought. These grew out of an interface between various disciplines. If the major concern at that time was with growth economics and plans for economic development, the

*An earlier version of this essay was first published in 1999.

questions which this raised were often relevant to new thinking in sociology and history as well.

Characteristic of much of this thinking was the move away from single explanations to considering multiple causes and their diverse effects. Associated with this was the emphasis on priorities in explanation, an emphasis which was to change much of the interpretation relating not only to questions relating to society and economy but also of the past. The plurality of Indian society was being explored and the recognition of this plurality further challenged the explanations which had been accepted in colonial times. Not only was the plurality being explored but new ways of understanding it were under discussion, some influenced by Marxism and some by other alternate systems. Looking back on that period, it seems to me that it was this which *Seminar* was attempting to capture.

Over fifty years ago, the scene is inevitably different. Explorations and analyses have resulted in the surfacing of ideas which have provided insightful dimensions and taken us some distance away from the explanations with which we started our studies after Independence. The fundamental change relates in part to these explanations but much more so to the end purpose to which the new thinking has been directed, and to some degree closer to understanding what we aspire to and what we have or have not achieved. Mutations and alterations are to some extent necessary but the directions they take cannot be arbitrary. They must uphold the social ethic of a secular democracy for this determines what the nation-state represents.

It is possible that my concern with this is in some ways tied into the nurturing which pre-Independence nationalism provided when I was young. We were aware of two things in particular: one was that there was an Indian identity and it was all inclusive, gathering together many peoples, customs, beliefs and forging what we thought was a homogenous Indian society; two, that Independence was to bring the construction of a new society, especially for the young, where the hallmark was to be the removal of Indian poverty and the dismantling of caste. Planting a tree and making a little speech in school on 15 August 1947, I predictably began with '....bliss was it in that dawn to be alive, but to be young was very heaven....' But it is both these issues which we raised then and with which we are still grappling.

The question of identity has now superseded other concerns. There has largely been a reversal of the pre-independence mainstream nationalist view, of the Indian identity being inclusive and gathering in all those who live in India. Nationalism constructs its own identities and one may not today subscribe to these, but the identity which is now being projected and has wide acceptability, especially among the middle class, is a travesty of what was earlier understood as the Indian identity.

If the earlier one was inclusive, the present insistence on religious nationalism and Hindu nationalism in India, presupposes a particular identity which encourages the exclusion of non-Hindu characteristics which in the past have legitimately been included as Indian. The ideologues of this persuasion have neither use nor respect for democratic rights. The methods being used to instil fear among the excluded groups—the Dalits, tribals, Christians and Muslims—are nothing short of fascist inasmuch as they endorse the use of violence—the burning alive of Christian missionaries, the organizing of anti-Muslim riots and the threatening of those Dalits and tribals who seek means of redressing social inequality.

There has been disjuncture in the last several decades and these seem to have accelerated in the last decade. The concept of ethics is not what it proclaims these days. Anti-ethical behaviour is not condemned. Pertinent to the perceptions of an Indian future are the economic interventions of globalization and their involvements, as well as the need to integrate perspectives arising out of the two most significant movements of recent years—those related to changing the quality of life for Dalits and for women. The way in which globalization is changing the economy, both in positive and negative directions, but more so that latter has been widely discussed, but for obvious reasons the way in which a globalizing economy is affecting our social attitudes is ignored. Some would relate the increase in social insecurity of all kinds, and the dominance of money and/or political patronage as the ultimate measure of social effectiveness, to increasing globalization.

We have welcomed the market and the radical change in the economy which this involves, even if half the population continues to be below the poverty line or generally impoverished. The important lacuna is that we have avoided discussion on the ensuing change in social and individual ethics, brought about by globalization: a change which is only too evident in daily life. If money is to be the major criterion of human worth, then will the social ethic of earlier times and situations have to be replaced? By social ethic I mean the totality of the ethics of a society. To treat globalization as entirely a matter of changing the economy is to hoodwink ourselves.

The lack of social ethics shows up in multiple ways. We spend hundreds of crores on detonating a nuclear device—a futile attempt at mega sabre rattling—yet when it comes to a war and human life is involved, we send our soldiers to the firing line largely ill-equipped. This reflects less concern with human life and the contradiction makes the negation even stronger. The well-known technique of deliberately trying to shatter the self-respect of a citizen by accusing him or her of being unpatriotic is also being resorted to. To call a person deshdrohi, is an accusation to which there can be no comeback since it is made in parliament. How do I effectively challenge M. M. Joshi for calling me anti-Indian because of the history textbooks for schools that I write? The targeting of individuals is a pernicious way of both trying to break the individual and give strength to those making the accusation and to underline the fact that a social ethic now has no place in our society.

Two groups which today are demanding participation in power

are the Dalits and women. The marginalization and oppression of both Dalits and women was inherent in the traditional institutions and norms of many aspects of earlier Indian society. The democratic solution of making equality more feasible and opening up opportunities to the marginalized should have taken the form of a programme of radical change: conceding their participation in power and extending facilities to them through initiating compulsory education and professional training, providing healthcare and social welfare.

Such facilities should have been open to all segments of society. Little of this is done, not even now, as a back-up to the policy of reservations. Instead the politically easier way was chosen with the introduction of reservations. With every political pressure the number is enlarged. The concern is not with fundamental human rights and furthering the functioning of democracy. Instead, it has become a question of numbers since it is easier to play politics with numbers. Reservations will continue to be demanded by more and more groups. Yet virtually nothing of significance is done at the essential level to democratize Indian society. This is not negligence but deliberate policy to prevent the real empowerment of marginalized groups. Caste has to be assessed in terms of multiple articulations—tied to economic, political, social and religious factors—which have frequently been changing the rules of play.

The society which was to be constructed after 1947 was based on well-reasoned Enlightenment notions of the state and the nation. The state was to be directed to make the necessary changes and the state would provide for all. And the state did make some fundamental changes: adult franchise, for example, would still have been beset with obstructions but for the intervention of the state. Despite the ballot box being captured or interfered with or defections overthrowing the results of elections, or Dalits being prevented from voting in some constituencies, there are still many in which the process has a meaning and conveys the opinion of the voters.

In our more doubting moments it is salutary to recall that the Emergency was voted out through an election. There is an argument that adult franchise encourages majoritarian politics and this is inimical to democracy. The defence of democracy does not lie, however, in denying adult franchise but in protecting democratic functioning and preventing predetermined majoritarianism. This introduces the centrality of the freedom of expression and of opposition to censorship. It also makes it incumbent upon us to prevent the misuse of liberal democracy in the name of democratic functioning.

However, disillusioned we might be with the state—and now more than before—it is as well to remember that in the 1950s it was viewed as the major agency of change. Some today scoff at Nehru's sentiment that dams are the temples of the twentieth century. Yet at that time the construction of dams by the state had a historical context and was viewed as a mechanism of socio-economic betterment for the less privileged, as was claimed in earlier international projects as well, not only in the building of the Dnieper dam but also in the project of the Tennessee Valley.

The failures have been less of the dams and more in the distribution of the resources that ensued. What actually has happened with this distribution subsequent to the construction of the dams needs to be made public. Which categories of people have been the beneficiaries of big or small dams? Was the water released for irrigation and, if so, was it made available to the small peasant to enhance his production? Have those who have had to undergo the horror of displacement, and sometimes repeatedly, benefitted? The beneficiaries are more frequently government departments and contractors hand-in-glove with politicians, all out to make a fast buck. But who has the courage to name names and expose such connections? The callous manner in which communities are uprooted because of submergence or a Covid pandemic, often without seeing them properly resettled prior to further action, reflects not only an inability to comprehend the human dimensions of a project but also an unconcern with the life and well-being of such communities.

In the case of some small dams the distribution has seen a judicious use of the technological benefits, but such examples are limited. State enterprises when they become too large nullify their own effective functioning. We may well decide not to build any more big dams, a decision of which many of us would approve. But this in itself will not solve the problem of those below the poverty line. The alternative has to be a demonstrated plan in consultation with those most closely affected in order to terminate the condition of poverty.

It is fashionable in some circles today to project the state, the nation, the processes of modernization and secularization as the source of evil. The emphases of the Enlightenment are regarded as a disaster and a preference for the fragmentary surfaces. This seems to be part of the present problem. Our comprehension of India is far better than it was some decades ago, but in the process of teasing out the intricacies of problems and of unravelling the skeins of the argument, we seem to have forgotten why we are doing this or whether there is even a purpose in this exercise. Is it merely to understand the problem better, or are we also concerned with bringing about change? Teasing out and refining the threads of ideas outside a context of reality, can become a privilege of a few, and be distanced from the everyday world. This neither provides alternatives to the state, nor gives direction to the state.

If the state is the repository of power then this power has to include a range of groups some of which have been denied power so far. This will require a radical change in the nature of the state. In changing the representations and concerns of the state a greater consciousness of the role of civil society comes into play, a role which in the past has been neglected. This is not to suggest that there be a switch in the roles of the state and of civil society, but rather that there be a strengthening of the function of civil society so that it can be used to pressure the state into action.

Strengthening civil society also relates to the concerns of those groups who are now being recognized. This will also involve adjustment to changing gender relations and to Dalit groups. Needless to say, such a strengthening of civil society would be resisted by those who have worked out methods of manipulating the legislative processes and would view the new form as problematic for themselves. It will also be resisted by those who have a limited definition of Indian identity.

Strengthening the role of civil society involves the secularization of Indian society. Unfortunately, in India the debate on the process of secularization has tended to confine itself to the issue of religion in public life and is treated solely as a form of anti-communalism. But it involves far more of equal significance which is conveniently set aside, such as the insistence on human rights and social equality, gender justice, and a more equitable distribution of national wealth. These are concerns which have to be demanded and nurtured and do not come automatically.

An emphasis on civil society in itself is not the complete answer, for it is not just an antidote to the state. Priorities within the concerns of civil society and how best to make these effective are essential. Civil society is not necessarily a neutral arena for it is also a site of contestation depending on the directions of the pressures. But to the extent that it can provide a solidarity and create a sense of community which cuts across identities, it becomes an effective agency for change.

The agenda for making the institutions of civil society more effective in the demand for change would cover various areas of routine activity. Existing rights according to the Constitution have to be implemented, and for levels of society which up to now have not received adequate attention. There is already in theory the equality of all before the law but in many situations this is nullified not only by concessions to social status and political clout, but also by not conceding in practice the access of all to the law. Those whom the law admits to its presence and to whom legal assistance is given are the privileged few. Even the registering of an FIR in a police station often requires the backing of the powerful. Would legal advisory groups in neighbourhoods, and a time-limit on the decision of cases in the courts, help make the law more accessible to the underprivileged? These would have to be so structured that they are not merely another stumbling block.

Some investigation into clearing out the blockages inherited from a colonial system of justice and administration require attention. The ethos of a colonial system runs contrary to that of a democratic society. We have to remember that as a colony we were governed by laws that were antithetical to both a democratic and a secular society. We have still to reverse these laws if we are to be a secular democracy as was intended by the anti-colonial national movement. Those currently governing did not experience Indian nationalism and the struggle for freedom and the making of a truly independent nation-state. Some of us were nurtured on the idea and fought for it in our own albeit limited way. The vision of an autonomous nation state unencumbered by religious visions of Islamic and Hindu states, cluttering up the subcontinent, is not what we inherited. This we have to reiterate. Perhaps informal citizens' courts could process the simpler cases and explore out-of-court settlements—a procedure which has historical antecedents, but also carries the danger of social pressure from the privileged. The system itself needs to be made more user-friendly, both for those administering it and for those at the receiving end. There is scope for negotiation in this procedure and the underprivileged have at least a sporting chance of some concessions which could well be absent in the perceptions of a court of law.

However, negotiation as a procedure of public functioning introduces other problems stemming from the present centrality of corruption in public functioning. The rules are set aside and each requirement has to be individually negotiated. This encourages an aggressive attitude since aggression gives an advantageous edge to negotiation. Such aggression is frequently explained away as an assertion of equality, but in effect it also reflects prevalent norms of behaviour.

If social change is to involve, as it should, the quality of life, then the fundamental requirements are obvious: in the relationship of the citizen to the state, the state must guarantee and implement rights and obligations of both the citizen and the state. This means ensuring food, water, and shelter to the citizen, compulsory education up to school leaving standards, the providing of basic health facilities and similar social welfare. Employment would have to be provided to alleviate poverty. At another level the social equality of all citizens is a requisite to ensure social justice, and this in turn assumes the freedom of expression. It has to be conceded that the free citizen is a responsible citizen and there is mutual respect. We are still a long way from all this. We are no longer even thinking seriously about the implementation of these rights. Education is included in the Constitution but rarely effectively implemented, doubtless through fear that it would challenge the status quo. There would have to be thousands more of schools, but if the teachers are from the village or from the neighbourhood and given training, there would be more chances of their remaining on the job. The achievements of Kerala and Himachal Pradesh are a pointer to this requiring an effort of will rather than lavish expenditure.

The emphasis on the village and on the urban neighbourhood providing personnel for medical clinics would also reduce the distance between the person and the institution. Informal organizations need not replace the more advanced institutions but could fill the interstices left by the latter. A sense of participation in the process of acquiring knowledge or healing one's body can be effective in itself.

We cannot rely solely on governments to see us through, although the constant prodding of the government to act in a manner beneficial to the citizen has to remain unabated. Governments are diverse and act in diverse ways. Some are reasonable and try to bring in genuine change, others are atrociously malfunctioning. We still have to work towards insisting that the state be responsible and take positive actions. This pressure is necessary at least to ensure the legislating of change. But there can also be pressure from other directions and this can be better articulated if there are institutions however informal, which are geared to making people aware of their civil and human rights and helping to ensure that these rights are practised. Suffusing all this is the need to replace that which is primary but of which we as a society are now bereft—the ethic that commands human behaviour.

We are currently in a period of disillusionment and uncertainty. It may take a a decade or two to emerge out of this darkness and to heal the current decimation. But hopefully we can still recapture the mood which demands and works towards a more purposeful society, a venture in which *Seminar* can continue to participate as it has been doing, both in articulating demands and in suggesting ways of achieving them. Can we still proclaim loudly and clearly that we do have a commitment to being an ethical society, and that we shall reinstate a society governed by social ethics—a society where men and women do not have to work for a demarcated few who appropriate money and power but where money and power are made to work for the betterment of all men and women in that scoeiety? If one may rephrase a well-known quotation: the choice before us is one of either limiting ourselves to understanding Indian society, or of deciding on the basis of that understanding to move further and change it for the better.

FURTHER READING

Alf Hiltebeitel, *Rethinking the Mahabharata: A Reader's Guide to the Education of the Dharma King*, Chicago: University of Chicago Press, 2001.

B. R. Ambedkar, *The Constitution of India*, 1950.

Bhadriraju Krishnamurti, *The Dravidian* Languages, Cambridge: Cambridge University Press, 1998.

Bipan Chandra, *Communalism in Modern India*, New Delhi: Har-Anand Publications, 2008.

David Reich, *Who We Are and How We Got Here: Ancient DNA and the New Science of the Human Past*, New Delhi: Oxford University Press, 2018.

Franklin C. Southworth, *Linguistic Archaeology of South Asia*, Abingdon: Routledge, 2005.

G. D. Sontheimer and H. Kulke (eds), *Hinduism Reconsidered*, New Delhi: Manohar Publications, 2001.

Iravatham Mahadevan, *Early Tamil Epigraphy from the Earliest Times to the Sixth Century A.D.*, Cambridge, MA: Harvard University Press, 2003.

K.N. Panikkar (ed.), *National and Left Movements in India*, New Delhi: Vikas Publishing House, 1980.

M. M. Deshpande and P. E. Hook (eds), *Aryan and Non-Aryan in India*, Ann Arbor: Karoma Publishers, 1979.

Niraja Gopal Jayal and Pratap Bhanu Mehta (eds), *The Oxford Companion to Politics in India*, New Delhi: Oxford University Press, 2011.

Paula Richman (ed.), *Many Ramayanas: The Diversity of a Narrative Tradition in South Asia*, Berkeley: University of California Press, 1991.

R. Salomon, *Indian Epigraphy: A Guide to the Study of Inscriptions in Sanskrit, Prakrit, and Other Indo-Aryan* Languages, New York: Oxford University Press, 1998.

Rajeev Bhargava, *Politics and Ethics of the Indian Constitution,* New Delhi: Oxford University Press, 2009.

Romila Thapar et al., *Which of Us Are Aryans?*, New Delhi: Aleph Book Company, 2019.

Romila Thapar, *Asoka and the Decline of the Mauryas*, New Delhi: Oxford University Press, 2012.

——, *The Penguin History of Early India: From the Origins to AD 1300*, New Delhi: Penguin Books India, 2003.

——, *The Public Intellectual in India*, New Delhi: Aleph Book Company, 2015.

——, *Voices of Dissent: An Essay*, Kolkata: Seagull Books, 2020.

Sarvepalli Gopal, *Jawaharlal Nehru: A Biography, Volume I–III*, London: Jonathan Cape, 1975–1984.

INDEX